GAY FICTION
SPEAKS

D0731860

BETWEEN MEN ~ BETWEEN WOMEN
LESBIAN AND GAY STUDIES
LILLIAN FADERMAN AND LARRY GROSS, EDITORS

RICHARD CANNING

CONVERSATIONS WITH GAY NOVELISTS

GAY FICTION
SPEAKS

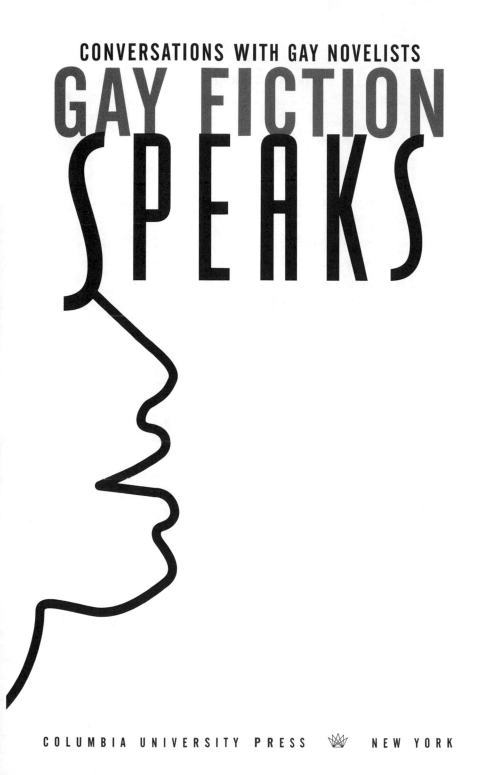

COLUMBIA UNIVERSITY PRESS ❧ NEW YORK

♛

COLUMBIA UNIVERSITY PRESS

Publishers Since 1893

New York   Chichester, West Sussex

Copyright © 2000 Columbia University Press

All rights reserved

Library of Congress Cataloging-in-Publication Data

Canning, Richard.

Gay fiction speaks : conversations with gay novelists / Richard Canning.

p. cm. — (Between men—between women)

Includes bibliographical references.

ISBN 0–231–11694–2 (cloth : acid-free paper) —ISBN 0–231–11695–0 (pbk : acid-free paper)

1. Novelists, American—20th century—Interviews. 2. Homosexuality and literature—United States—History—20th century. 3. American fiction—20th century—History and criticism—Theory, etc. 4. Gay men's writings, American—History and criticism—Theory, etc. 5. Gay men—United States—Interviews. 6. Fiction—Authorship. 7. Gay men in literature.   I. Title.
II. Series.

PS374.H63 C36 2001

813 ' 54099206642—dc21

00–060143

∞

Casebound editions of Columbia University Press books
are printed on permanent and durable acid-free paper.
Printed in the United States of America

Designed by Lisa Hamm

C   10   9   8   7   6   5   4   3   2   1

P   10   9   8   7   6   5   4   3   2   1

BETWEEN MEN ~ BETWEEN WOMEN
Lesbian and Gay Studies

Lillian Faderman and Larry Gross, Editors

Advisory Board of Editors

Between Men ~ Between Women is a forum for current lesbian and gay scholarship in the humanities and social sciences. The series includes both books that rest within specific traditional disciplines and are substantially about gay men, bisexuals, or lesbians and books that are interdisciplinary in ways that reveal new insights into gay, bisexual, or lesbian experience, transform traditional disciplinary methods in consequence of the perspectives that experience provides, or begin to establish lesbian and gay studies as a freestanding inquiry. Established to contribute to an increased understanding of lesbians, bisexuals, and gay men, the series also aims to provide through that understanding a wider comprehension of culture in general.

CONTENTS

FOREWORD

Richard Canning's interviews may help change the way we regard the genre, which is often relegated to a place somewhere between journalism and public relations. In a culture that elevates individualism, formal completeness, and reproducibility, the interview's collaborative, improvisational nature is understandably (but unfortunately) underappreciated. Yet in Richard Canning's hands—or, more literally, through his microphone—the interview is raised to a high art, a kind of conversational jazz, that drove me to read on for hours, caught up in the drama of his dialogues.

Early on, Canning made two interrelated decisions that facilitated his task and won him the trust of authors who are usually rather guarded. First, he avoids personal questions; second, he wants to know about the artistic decisions that inform these writers' works. In short, he takes his interviewees seriously as artists. Such an approach is surprisingly rare, especially with gay writers. At least it's been my experience that interviewers, if they acknowledge that I am gay, are more interested in exploring my personal life than my artistry. The work seems secondary. One of the ways that gay authors have been ghettoized is by people overlooking their achievements as writers and viewing them as merely spokespersons for a social movement. This is understandable since writers like Edmund White, Armistead Maupin, John Rechy, and Larry Kramer have been public figures whose political involvement has sometimes overshadowed their work as writers. Indeed, many of these men come from an era when the most famous "out" gay men were writers—Truman Capote, Tennessee Williams, Gore Vidal, or James Baldwin—whose lives frequently eclipsed the recognition of their artistic achievement. It is not surprising, therefore, that writers in these interviews sometimes seem a bit touchy about how their works are regarded as art, because their books have been so often treated not as fiction but reportage or social polemic, or—worse—as a form of free group therapy.

If I put great stress on Canning's decision to address these men as artists, it is because this is so rare. Few before him have explored such basic questions as point of view, narrative pacing, or fictional structure. Even those who should know better have fallen into the trap of reading these works not as the complexly constructed imaginative art that they are (or aspire to be), but as transparent documentary or as a means to make people feel better about themselves. Bruce Bawer tells us in *A Place at the Table* that "the Gay Writer's novel says: *This is what it means to live as a homosexual man in a mostly heterosexual world that doesn't understand or sympathize*."[1] Because he expects gay writers to present a generalized view of the homosexual condition, Bawer attacks them for presenting lives that are "decidedly untrue of homosexuals in general," as if they were writing sociology.[2] David Leavitt has been no better. He thinks gay writers must present good role models for young readers, as though they were writing textbooks for some high school health class of the future. Leavitt attacks Holleran's *Dancer from the Dance* because its "voyeuristic fixation with beauty that powers the novel . . . compels younger gay men who don't know better to wonder if

---

1. Bruce Bawer, *A Place at the Table: The Gay Individual in American Society* (New York: Simon and Schuster, 1993), 198 (italics in original).
2. Bawer, *A Place at the Table*, 204.

that's all there is to the business of being gay."[3] It never occurs to Leavitt that Holleran is an adult who writes for adults, and that, of course, children who pick up his book—like a friend who, after reading Lawrence at fifteen, came to believe that all English gardeners were going to be as kinkily sexual as in *Lady Chatterley's Lover*—will misunderstand what they read. Of course, in an age saturated by "infomercials" and news entertainment, it is sad to think that most people "don't know any better" than to confuse fiction and its imaginative truth with reportage and its facticity.

Nor are academic readers necessarily better. Robert McRuer, in a turgidly written, jargon-filled tome, will castigate Edmund White's *A Boy's Own Story* for containing only two black characters—as though novels operated as equal-opportunity employers.[4] Gay novelists have been expected to bear an enormous weight of social expectations. Without ever arguing against such pressures in his interviews, but by his very approach, Canning lets his interviewees be artists first—people whose work, if not independent of the culture, obeys not ideological or social imperatives, but the inner logic of form and language.

The best interviews are a form of drama in which character and ideas are simultaneously developed and revealed. I know several of the writers interviewed in this book, and I was delighted to hear their voices come alive for me in these pages: Edmund White, discussing the failure of *Caracole* and slowly turning it into his private success, or Andrew Holleran trying to interview the interviewer to deflect attention from himself. James Purdy's impatience; Ethan Mordden's self-assurance;

---

3. David Leavitt, "Introduction" to David Leavitt and Mark Mitchell, eds., *The Penguin Book of Gay Short Stories* (New York: Viking/Penguin, 1994), xv–xxviii (quotation from xix–xx).
4. Robert McRuer, *The Queer Renaissance: Contemporary American Literature and the Reinvention of Lesbian and Gay Identities* (New York: New York University Press, 1997).

Felice Picano's expansiveness: all are captured here. And I heard voices of writers I wanted to know more about. After reading the interview with Patrick Gale, I had friends from England send the books that have not yet been published here in the United States because he sounded so smart, inviting, and, at the same time, challenging.

Again and again, Canning captures his subjects in characteristic moments that show us something we could never see in their art alone or in criticism about them. Some of the interviews are surprises. Armistead Maupin comes off as a very different person, far more serious and conscious of himself as an artist than I had imagined. Alan Hollinghurst seemed to be far less assured, less certain of direction than the narrators of his novels. It is gratifying for me to witness once again that people, when discussing ideas, nevertheless reveal their character, and that personal revelation is not necessary to give a sense of who is speaking. If these are little pieces of theater, they are Shaw not Ibsen. Sometimes, of course, the conflicts of these writers' literary lives emerge. How could gossip be completely removed from such discussions? But Canning never lets it serve as the center of an interview and, more than likely, it becomes the avenue for a more profound discussion of what it means to be an artist, a *gay* artist, in the English-speaking world.

We must, however, be sure that we don't equate the person who emerges from these interviews as the "real" author. The face presented to us is yet another mask to put aside the authorial voice in their works. Nor should we be fooled into believing that what they say is necessarily true. I caught at least one baldfaced lie. The role of the imagination does not stop at the covers of these men's books. It filters richly into the way they present themselves to us as authors. What Philip Lopate said about Mary McCarthy might well be said about several of these men: that their finest imaginative creation is themselves.

But if we see the interview as another stage on which authors can "perform themselves," we will learn something about how they wish readers to see the relationship between their authorial personae and their narrative personae. I don't mean to place these authors in some never-never land (a creation of an earlier homosexual writer), where they are untouched by the events of the material world. Indeed, more than some authors, their careers have been affected by the cultural attitudes toward homosexuality and its representation. To be sure, before the 1970s there had been "mainstream" gay fiction. James Baldwin's *Giovanni's Room* is one good example; Sanford Friedman's *Totempole* is another. But, in general, fiction that dealt with homosexuality fell into one of three categories: pornography, problem novels, and "high" literature. Gide, Proust, and Thomas Mann could get away with writing about homosexuality because they were Europeans and thus had a certain license to speak of such decadent matters; and also because they were such highly celebrated authors (after all, two won the Nobel Prize for literature) that they were regarded as being beyond prurient interest. But even in the mid-eighties, editors were nervous about using such a term as "gay author" to describe Edmund White, Andrew Holleran, or David Plante, because they were afraid their journals would be sued for libel. An editor kept hounding me about an essay I wrote, asking over and over again how I could justify calling someone a "gay novelist," until I blurted out: "I *know*. I slept with him." She was then either legally satisfied or just too embarrassed to question me further.

Since then, however, there has been a remarkable change. The entity "gay literature" has established itself as a regular feature of the literary landscape—and worthy, as recently in the case of Michael Cunningham's *The Hours*, of prestigious awards. Gay fiction adopted no single strategy for responding to these cultural changes, but no writer could go unaffected by them. Canning's interviews are themselves part of the cultural forces they comment upon. Indeed, part of their importance is how much they run against the tide of scholarly concerns. For unlike other literatures—Southern writing, Jewish writing, African-American writing—which have developed very rich bodies of supporting analytic and evaluative work, gay litera-ture—especially contemporary gay literature—has not been so well served by academics. The major scholars, such as Eve Kosofsky Sedgwick, Judith Butler, Wayne Koestenbaum, and Michael Warner, have mostly concentrated either on canonical works of literature or on nonliterary phenomena (opera, film, politics, philosophy). Alan Hollinghurst's or Andrew Hol-leran's novels have excited far less scholarly attention than *The Rocky Horror Picture Show*. The truly extraordinary cultural phenomenon of the burgeoning of gay literary production has gone relatively unexplored by the very people who are best trained to understand it. One must view these interviews as an important "intervention," to use that fashionable term, in the cultural construction of queerness.

Of all the events that have shaped gay life, none has so dra-matically altered it as the AIDS epidemic. Many of these men were sexually active and actively writing at what Andrew Holleran has called "Ground Zero"—the epidemic's epicenter. All of these writers—to my knowledge—came out sexually (if not in print) before the appearance of AIDS, and they are wit-nesses of, as well as participants in, the changes it has wrought to the way we love now. Their own views of how best to repre-sent the pain, suffering, and death that they have witnessed on a massive scale has changed over the years. Again and again, Canning brings the authors back to this crucial issue—not only because it constitutes the greatest artistic, political, and personal challenge of their lives as gay men, but also because in respond-

ing to it (or by not responding to it), they define themselves as
gay writers. Homophobia may have created the category of
"gay writer" as a way of containing such representations, but
AIDS has been the event that makes such a category salient.
Like Jews who must imaginatively and morally view the exodus
from Egypt as an event that they personally experienced despite
the intervening millennia, the gay man is a person who must
imaginatively and morally view AIDS as something that has
defined him directly. If nothing else, it is this crucial event that
not only justifies the singling out of gay authors as a category
but also demands that they speak.

David Bergman

INTRODUCTION

A year or so ago, while preparing this book, I had the good fortune to see Edward Albee's latest work *The Play About the Baby* at London's Almeida Theatre. In one typically surreal monologue, Albee's character "Woman" talks of her youthful dreams of becoming a journalist, and of a project she undertook toward that end:

> "My assignment was to interview a writer—to try to comprehend the creative mind, as they call it. [*Pause*] Don't try. Don't even give it a thought. There seems to be some sort of cabal going on, on the part of these so-called creative people to keep the process a secret; a deep, dark secret from the rest of the world.
>
> "I mean, really, what's the matter with these people? Do they think we're trying to steal their tricks—would even want to? All I want to do is understand, and, let me tell you, getting through to them, these 'creative' types, isn't easy. I mean even getting through to them. I wrote politely to seven or eight of them: one biographer; two short-story writers; there were a couple of poets; one 'female creator of theater pieces'—and not one of them answered. Silence. Too busy creating, I suppose."

I joined in the audience's laughter at "Woman's" monologue, partly because of its brilliant rendition by Frances de la Tour, but also because of the way Albee made me recon-

sider the objectives of *Gay Fiction Speaks*. Did my status as a
tenured academic, I asked, give me any greater right than
"Woman" to take on the task of "comprehend[ing] the creative
mind"? I felt not. Like her, I'd embarked upon the whole thing
rather naively—as a fan more than anything else. It would have
made little sense to approach these writers from a critical standpoint. In any case, I did not feel inclined to do so. Now that the
interviews were completed, did I feel any better informed as to
how they should be done? Not much—though I did feel I'd
learned quite a lot about how to interview writers of fiction,
specifically. Was I confident my results could help others to
"comprehend the creative mind"? Well, I felt—and feel—that
there's compelling material here. Some of it, certainly, concerns
the creative process; things which writers invariably don't
reflect upon, or at least aren't publicly encouraged to. But I
hope readers find more in them too. On occasion, these writers
reflect on long, distinguished careers. Other moments see them
digress on enthusiasms, literary and otherwise, one never would
have anticipated. There's the odd comment, frankly, that's
nothing more than good gossip—and there's nothing wrong in
that.

   Unlike Albee's "Woman," I should point out, I had nothing
but good fortune in my dealings with the twelve authors featured in this book—*and* with a further twenty-four novelists
(interviews with whom will appear in subsequent volumes). Not
one writer declined to be interviewed, or to collaborate afterwards in the time-consuming exchanges necessary for the shaping and updating of transcribed text. Auden claimed that, for a
writer to stick to literature and make a living, he or she must be
in love with the "drudgery" of the profession. If what he meant
by that was dealing with the kind of endless spin-off requests
and inquiries I made of this dozen, I'm sure he's right. Everyone featured in *Gay Fiction Speaks* responded at every stage

with diligence, speed, insight—and, vitally, considerable wit and humor. I am greatly indebted to all.

Gay Fiction Speaks began with a research award for travel granted by Sheffield University—to which institution I owe many thanks. The proposal, swiftly improvised into being (as such things often are), named the thirty-six gay novelists writing in English whom I felt were the most celebrated, prominent, and promising subjects. I've long enjoyed reading in-depth interviews with writers: in the everyday press, certainly, but, more relevant to this project, the pioneering pieces in the *Paris Review*, and in books such as those of my colleague at Sheffield, Professor John Haffenden, whose collections of interviews with British poets and novelists were an important influence.

I should note that there have already been at least four books of interviews with gay writers. Though these could not help but be full of compelling comment and revelation, the organization and origin of these works were, to me, unsatisfactory. The first, put out by Gay Sunshine Press long ago, featured authors of great talent—many of whom, sadly, could never become part of this project: William Burroughs, Christopher Isherwood, Tennessee Williams. The pieces feel uneven, though, and often of rather "local" interest. Written for a specific issue of a magazine, they read very much as of their time and place. Later, a second Gay Sunshine Press volume appeared, featuring writers of (to me) less interest. The other two precedents are *Talking To* by Peter Burton, a talented British journalist, and *Something Inside* by the American writer Philip Gambone. *Talking To* appeared in the early 1990s—and soon disappeared. The role call was impressively varied but, once again, the pieces—republications from the monthly *Gay Times*—were merely thumbnail sketches or snapshots (some a bit dated) rather than in-depth pieces. Gambone's line of questioning in *Something Inside* was captivatingly led by his own priorities as a fiction writer, but there was, I felt, for all the great moments, a sense of the book being less of an integrated whole than a sum of impressive parts. This I put down to the interviews being commissioned for journals and magazines, and undertaken over a period of years.

I thought about these precedents when drawing up my proposal for funding. I was always clear that I'd insist on interviewing authors in person: at their homes or, when it was more convenient, where I was staying; otherwise (rarely) over lunch or dinner. I was suspicious about interviewing at a distance. The telephone or e-mail may be fine for fact-checking or for the quick soundbite, but I wanted my work not only to come out of a relaxed atmosphere, but to read as if it did. Generally, the sessions ran for between two and four hours; often considerable time was spent—usefully, in my view—"warming up" the conversation.

To some extent, I wanted the peculiar patterns of everyday speech to be retained too, with their moments of friction, contradiction, and tangentiality. Equally, it was vital that my interviewees did not feel "on guard"—potential victims of a journalistic setup, that is, for we live in such times. I knew I wanted the interviews to be presented as transcripts—that is, without substantial embellishment or interpretation from me. Readers could feel they were being given the material from which to draw their own conclusions. I soon realized the interviews would not "close" after the tape was turned off. A further stage would be necessary, where the interviewee and I consulted over the transcript: checking for accuracy and, yes, removing the odd indiscretion, but also adding to and improving (upon reflection) what had come to mind in the moment.

I knew the interviews would need some thematic coherence. The fact that all the interviewees were gay would not be enough. Some discussion of issues concerning sexual politics and the rep-

resentation of gay men in culture would doubtless be interesting.
I thought, though, that these weren't likely to be the only things
my interviewees, as writers, could or would want to talk about.
To some extent, writers are readily tapped by the media for their
views on such matters—in some cases, pretty exhaustively. My
hunch was that my interviewees would have as much in common
as writers as they would as gay men—and that discovering the
links and contrasts in this respect would probably make my venture fresher. Wherever possible, I wanted the direction of conversation to remain open to the interviewee's suggestion, not my
own, so that the interview as published would come to reflect his
enthusiasms, or some of them at least. I determined not to have
an agenda as such, though I did keep in the back of my mind a
brief list of general questions—on writing methods especially—
that I invariably found an opportunity to ask.

I sketched out a travel itinerary for the States that was to be
conducted during October and November of 1997, in the middle
of a semester's sabbatical from Sheffield. Britain and elsewhere I
decided to handle later. The schedule was characterized by an
absurdly optimistic faith in two things: first, the professionalism
and reliability of U.S. airlines (no further comment); second, my
capacity for rereading about two hundred novels in the evenings
and—as it transpired—long nights between interviews. Still, all
went smoothly enough—barring the odd hundred or so major
mishaps en route. If transcribing hundreds of hours of tape and
then editing for sense and conciseness sounds like hell, it is—
though having the good fortune to do much of this work in sunny
Cape Town over the "winter" (their summer) of 1997–98 did help.

Something must be said about the selection of authors. This was
based entirely on merit. I felt—and feel—confident about this,
in the sense that I knew I'd feel more dishonest using any other
criteria. Nevertheless, I've identified six questions in particular

which arose out of my deliberations and which have nagged at me, to greater or lesser extent, since. I've reproduced them here in the hope that they illustrate my intentions in this volume.

The first question: why choose novelists, as opposed to writers generally? My own doctoral research had predominantly concerned gay fiction. I've always been a keen devourer of novels and stories first and foremost. That's a personal disposition. But it's also true, I think, that many—if not most—of the advances in gay literary self-representation since the war have taken place either first or most influentially in fiction. The last half of the twentieth century witnessed the most profound struggles and changes in gay people's sense of their place and role in society. It's not surprising that the novel—the literary form commonly understood as best equipped to deal with relations between the individual and society—should be so privileged.

My second thought was more one of regret than a question. I was struck by the obvious sad truth that so many fine writers of gay fiction had been lost during recent years—many, though not all, to AIDS-related illnesses. A ghost volume of *Gay Fiction Speaks* haunted me, featuring people such as Allen Barnett, Christopher Coe, David Feinberg, Robert Ferro, Michael Grumley, Peter McGehee, Paul Monette, and George Whitmore. William Burroughs, obviously slated for inclusion, died shortly before the project got under way. Two things mitigated my disappointment over these absences: first, clearly, nothing could be done to change this cold fact; and, second, came the consolation that tributes to such writers and their legacies might feature in the interviews I *could* undertake. I'm glad to say that this generally happened.

My third concern was over how many non-American writers to include. It didn't surprise me that most of my chosen number were American, nor do I feel apologetic about that. It's a straightforward tribute, I'd say, to the quality of gay fiction-writing currently emerging from the United States. Still, research for another forthcoming book on contemporary gay fiction and AIDS has led me to much fine international gay fiction. I've come across writers from Australia, Canada, and South Africa whose work I've found interesting and accomplished, but who haven't yet had too much published compared to those on my list. Reluctantly, I crossed these off—for now. I had five or six names from Britain and Ireland whom I strongly felt merited inclusion; interviews with two of these, Alan Hollinghurst and Patrick Gale, are gathered here.

The fourth consideration was the extent to which my list could reflect the ethnic and cultural diversity of gay fictional voices that is today's reality (and thank God for it). This was—and has been—my biggest headache. There are scores of gay fiction writers from ethnic minorities whose work I have loved. Several have died; most others are only now making a name for themselves. Should I set aside the general principle of including only the most-established and prominent writers in order to reflect the still-developing ethnic range of gay writing more fully? I decided not to do this—in the first volume, at least. The structure and size of each interview required a considerable body of published work to discuss. I also determined, for the coherence of the project, to keep with "literary fiction"—a nebulous construct, admittedly, but one that excluded certain popular literary genres, such as the detective novel, romance, and science fiction. Each of these categories describes the output of several possible nonwhite interviewees.

Let me be first to acknowledge, then, that in consequence *Gay Fiction Speaks* represents an almost entirely white tradition (though John Rechy is Mexican-American). Nonetheless, the two planned subsequent volumes of interviews now in process *do* feature a greater variety of ethnic voices. Stick with me.

My fifth worry arose in response to the realization early on that the interviewees were extremely interested in the list of names I'd proposed. They'd frequently ask about people they felt I'd overlooked. You'd probably challenge me similarly if you could. It's therefore worth explaining a couple of further criteria that affected my choice. The first relates to genre. Some prominent gay writers, unsurprisingly, are known for both prose and nonprose work. I judged each case distinctly, but my rule of thumb here related to my keen awareness that, after the fiction-based books were done, a further volume of interviews with gay playwrights and scriptwriters might appear. Though I propose that interviews with dramatist-novelists, say, would range across the genres in which they've written, these pieces would sit better in a volume dedicated to drama and performance texts.

Another thought in this regard concerned the issue of "gayness" itself. Many—if not most—of the writers in *Gay Fiction Speaks* healthily sought to question the very idea of categorizing fiction as "gay." In discussing such reservations, I admit occasionally resorting to fancy intellectual footwork—though it was based on my own views. I understand the awkwardness that the labels *gay fiction* or *gay novelist* instill in writers, who commonly aspire to the universal. Even where they don't, writers nevertheless often resent the "separate shelving" of so-called gay and lesbian titles in bookstores, as this can put their works out of the reach—or minds, anyway—of most readers. Many authors abhor the routine ghettoization of gay-themed work by the mainstream press.

Still, the post-Stonewall phenomenon of "gay fiction" is, for gay male readers and others, a reality—hence the viability of this book. In selecting authors, the matter of "gayness" presented a substantial problem and led to certain contentious exclusions.

I decided against including a number of esteemed, openly gay fiction writers precisely because their relationship to what is commonly considered "gay fiction" remains tangential, notwithstanding the occasional venture into gay themes. It's often argued that the late 1970s—the year 1978 in particular— saw the development in America of a distinct and unapologetic gay fiction tradition. I'm proud to see featured in this book many of the most important contributors to that development: Edmund White, Felice Picano, Armistead Maupin, Andrew Holleran, Ethan Mordden.

Clearly, I could have featured substantially more gay novel- ists who began writing prior to this period than the two I finally decided upon: James Purdy and John Rechy. What led me to include these, however, is pretty simple. The two bodies of work speak volumes. It's obvious that the five novelists just mentioned above are all, to some extent, in the debt of Purdy and Rechy, while the more recently established Gurganus, Cooper, Hollinghurst, Leavitt, and Gale have written not so much in the shadow of these, their predecessors, as in the liter- ary and cultural space created and legitimated by them. This doesn't mean that relations between individuals will be straightforward or harmonious, naturally. (Which relationships ever are?) One last point about Purdy and Rechy: both con- tinue to publish prolifically. Recent works, like earlier ones, sometimes engage directly with gay themes and characters; at other times, they reflect a "queer," indirect, or sardonic take on nongay life.

The last question was actually the first to be answered in planning *Gay Fiction Speaks*. Why only men? Ultimately, as most critics of contemporary gay and lesbian literatures have acknowledged, these literatures spring from different sources, and refer to distinct traditions. Indeed, the differences in literary tradition between male- and female-authored texts are as real as the contrasting origins and emphases of gay male and lesbian experience, social organization, and subcultural life. I'm a great fan and avid reader of works by many gifted lesbian novelists. Their inclusion in this volume, though, would widen its scope to its overall detriment. A "lesbian sister" volume to this book is what's needed— among whose contributors, inevitably, would be Jeanette Winterson.

In May 1998, I attended a reading given by Winterson at the Hay-on-Wye literary festival. At the outset, the redoubtable author sought to forestall questions she found most irritating and commonplace by anticipating them all. Her checklist went: "Yes, I work in the morning. No, I do not write straight onto machine," and so on. Winterson expressed amazement— perhaps tongue-in-cheek?—that anyone would find the answers to such questions compelling: "They're not the first questions I would ask if I had the chance to meet one of my literary heroes," she commented. You could hear mental cogs whirring as people wondered: "What *would* I ask?"; or, for Winterson's many fans, "What *do* I ask?" In my case, I thought of this book: "Well, what *did* I ask? Was it what I'd *want* to ask?" More to the point was this: "Was it what I'd want to have asked if I were reading a book like *Gay Fiction Speaks*?"

As with the experience of watching Albee's *The Play About the Baby*, the moment caused some doubt. Perhaps questions on writing practice, literary traditions, and influences, on the relationship between sexuality, writing, and culture and so on were rather rarified? The enthusiasm toward this book expressed by many friends, colleagues, and acquaintances, however, has restored my confidence in this regard—and made *Gay Fiction Speaks* all the more pleasurable to complete.

This is the place to record the thanks I owe, first of all, to the writers included here, all of whom generously devoted their time and energy to this project. The result is, above all, a tribute to their earnestness, enthusiasm, and kindness.

Of the many others who helped with practical arrangements, I'm especially indebted to David Bergman, Terry Bird and Clark Lemon, Michael Bronski, Ron Caldwell, Nicole Campbell, Harlan Greene, Allen Gurganus, Andrew Holleran, Keith Kahla, Patrick Merla, Felice Picano, and Edmund White. Max Manin and Tarani Chandola offered vital personal support and friendship over a difficult couple of years. Jason Ray was, for some time, prime inspiration for all I did, and remains a loved and close friend. Craig Fraser and James Davidson were both inspiring friends and academic examples at Oxford whose influence can be traced here. At Columbia University Press, a great debt is owed to Ann Miller, a dedicated and formidable editor, her efficient erstwhile assistant, Alex Thorp, and to Roy Thomas, a superb manuscript editor. Sincere apologies to anyone I have omitted.

GAY FICTION
SPEAKS

ONE

JAMES PURDY

J ames Purdy has been a published author for over fifty years, and has been admired by many writers and critics, including Dame Edith Sitwell, John Cowper Powys, Angus Wilson, Gore Vidal, Dorothy Parker, Tennessee Williams, Edward Albee, and younger authors such as Paul Binding and Matthew Stadler. Born in Ohio in 1927, Purdy studied at universities in Chicago, Madrid, and Puebla, Mexico, before starting his first job as a teacher at Lawrence College, Wisconsin. He has subsequently worked in various capacities in the United States, Mexico, and Europe.

Purdy's first published works were *Don't Call Me by My Right Name and Other Stories* (New York: William Frederick, 1956) and the novella *63: Dream Palace* (New York: William Frederick, 1956). His British debut was the collection *63: Dream Palace—A Novella and Nine Stories* (London: Gollancz, 1957). The same year, *Color of Darkness: Eleven Stories and a Novella* (New York: New Directions, 1957), a commercial edition of previously published material, appeared, and Purdy won awards from both the National Institute of Arts and Letters and the Guggenheim Foundation. Dame Edith Sitwell provided an introduction to *Color of Darkness* for its British publication (London: Secker and Warburg, 1961).

Two of Purdy's most popular and celebrated novels followed: *Malcolm* (New York: Farrar, Straus, and Cudahy, 1959; London: Secker and Warburg, 1960), later adapted for the stage by Edward Albee, and *The Nephew* (New York, Farrar, Straus, and

Cudahy, 1960; London: Secker and Warburg, 1961). Next came a collection of ten stories and two plays, *Children Is All* (New York: New Directions, 1962; London: Secker and Warburg, 1963). This was followed by *Cabot Wright Begins* (New York: Farrar, Straus, and Giroux, 1964; London: Secker and Warburg, 1965), and two much acclaimed and more openly gay-themed novels, *Eustace Chisholm and the Works* (New York: Farrar, Straus, and Giroux, 1967; London: Cape, 1968) and *I Am Elijah Thrush* (New York: Doubleday, 1972; London: Cape, 1972).

Two parts of a proposed three-part "continuous novel" appeared around *Elijah Thrush*: *Jeremy's Version: Part One of Sleepers in Moon-Crowned Valleys* (New York: Doubleday, 1970; London: Cape, 1971) and *The House of the Solitary Maggot: Part Two of Sleepers in Moon-Crowned Valleys* (New York: Doubleday, 1974). More critically and commercially successful were Purdy's last two novels of the 1970s, *In a Shallow Grave* (New York: Arbor, 1976), subsequently made into a film in 1988, and *Narrow Rooms* (New York: Arbor, 1978).

In the 1980s, Purdy was equally prolific, writing *Mourners Below* (New York: Viking, 1981), *On Glory's Course* (New York: Viking, 1984), *In the Hollow of His Hand* (London: Weidenfeld and Nicolson, 1986), *The Candles of Your Eyes* (London: Weidenfeld and Nicolson, 1987), a collection of stories, and *Garments the Living Wear* (San Francisco: City Lights, 1989), a novel addressing the AIDS epidemic. More recently, Purdy has published the novels *Out with the Stars* (London: Peter Owen, 1992) and *Gertrude of Stony Island Avenue* (London: Peter Owen, 1997). His story "The White Blackbird" appeared in David Bergman, ed., *Men on Men 6* (New York: Plume, 1996), and "The Anonymous Letters of Passion" was included in Ben Goldstein, ed., *More Like Minds* (London: Gay Men's Press, 1991).

Throughout his career, small press editions of Purdy's

poetry, stories, and drama have also been published, such as *An Oyster Is a Wealthy Beast* (story and poems; Los Angeles: Black Sparrow, 1967), *Mr. Evening: A Story and Nine Poems* (Los Angeles: Black Sparrow, 1968), *On the Rebound: A Story and Nine Poems* (Los Angeles: Black Sparrow, 1970), *The Running Sun* (poems; New York: Paul Waner, 1971), *The Wedding Finger* (play) in *Antaeus* 10 (1973), and *Proud Flesh: Four Short Plays* (Northridge, Calif.: Lord John, 1980).

Purdy has most recently completed a collection of short stories, "Moe's Villa and Other Stories." He lives in an apartment in Brooklyn, New York, where this interview took place on Wednesday, November 5, 1997.

JP   Are you Irish? I looked up your surname and it's a famous Irish one.

RC   Not to my knowledge. There was a prime minister called Canning, who has a statue near our Parliament.

JP   I think it would be terrible to have a statue. Don't you think that would be awful?

RC   Oscar Wilde's about to get one in London.

JP   He's too good for a statue. He's a marvelous writer. I visited his grave at Père-Lachaise, but it had been damaged by vandals.

RC   When were you in Europe?

JP   Four or five years ago. The Dutch brought me over there. Then one day they called from Israel and asked if I wanted to go there. I said: "Yes, but I'm not Jewish." They said: "We know that." So I went. The young ones seemed to like my stories. Then I had to go to Finland and Germany. The U.S. paid for that. I don't know why they chose me. My God, I was a wreck when I got home. You had to take a plane every few hours. When I got to Berlin, I met my German publisher. They were very nice to me. After we had this nice dinner, they said: "We don't earn most of our money from publishing. We have another business. Would you care to visit it?" I said: "Of course." It was a glorious, old-fashioned ice cream parlor where young poets came and read. But I thought maybe it was a house of ill-fame!

RC   This book is concerned only with gay novelists. Some authors have a problem with that.

JP   Well, I have a problem with everything! Today everything has a subject, but when you look at it there's no content. That's true of so many gay novels. It's true of everything written today: it's all subject; no content. If you write like I do, they just don't like it. They say: "Where's the subject?"

RC   By "subject," what do you mean?

JP   Something topical. Those books are just unreadable to me. The plays are the same. They're all just: "This is the way it is." The characters aren't real.

    Most of my books aren't about gay themes. They scolded Rembrandt for doing studies of blacks and old women. Those things he painted of Negroes are the most wonderful things I've ever seen. He really got their souls. But they wanted him to paint people in lovely costumes with beautiful ruffs—like "The Nightwatch." I thought: "That's the problem today; you're supposed to please people."

RC   Can we pursue the matter of race? Today many people feel uneasy about the idea of a white writer adopting a first-person black narrator, as you did with *I Am Elijah Thrush* and William Styron did with *The Confessions of Nat Turner*.

JP   Well, when Angus Wilson and Dame Edith Sitwell came to America, they were under the assumption I was black. Dame Edith read my story "Eventide," which is about black mothers. She thought it so anguished only a black person could have written it. There was a famous black writer—I think it was Langston Hughes—who admired my book. He's said to have said: "James Purdy's the last of the Niggers." I thought that was wonderful. I really feel I am, because I don't write subject but soul, you might say. I write the inside. John Cowper Powys, who also admired me, said: "He writes under the skin," which I like very much. I write about blacks under the skin.

When I was interviewed at the New York Public Library, I told them I liked that sentence of Terence, the Roman writer: "Homo sum"—"I am a human being; I count nothing human foreign to me." But the modern writers are ashamed of their real humanity. You should be dressed nicely or terribly; it's all costume and where you eat. That isn't about your humanity. It's about your style.

RC   In part your novels *are* concerned with social manners, though. Are you saying there's always something beyond that?

JP   Right. I think you finally see that what's under the social manners is a human being—not a very nice one, maybe.

RC   Those who resist the premise that there's such a thing as universal human experience might say that clothes and matters of style aren't the same as skin color. That's not necessarily because they believe in skin color as something essential, but they do think social responses to skin color constitute something more fundamental and politically more pressing than something like clothes.

JP   What they don't always admit is that what's beneath a homosexual and a black is something that's neither homosexual nor black. There's something very archetypal that goes back thousands of years. But we have seized on these other things now as the sole reality.

RC   There are moments in your work where—even metaphorically—this is suggested: that underneath mankind lies some entirely concealed truth. In *Narrow Rooms* there's this line: "Behind this story so far is another story, as behind the girders of an ancient bridge is the skeleton of a child, which superstition says keeps the bridge standing."

JP   I love that! Of course the critics thought that was a disgraceful book and the author was utterly irresponsible and mad. But I got under the boys' homosexuality to something very archetypal and ancient.

RC   Are the "archetypes" which lie beneath race and homosexuality the same or distinct?

JP   I think each archetype's different.

RC   In the quotation I cited, you suggested only that "superstition" felt the child supported the bridge, as one story supports another. I understood in that a sense of equivocation, but now you seem to be claiming the notion of concealed, underlying, archetypal behavior and character as a truth.

JP   I think so. Not to strike an attitude; I've lived with people of different races and was tutored by them.

RC   Is it that familiarity which brings you to these archetypes?

JP   I think I'd have got there anyhow. Maybe I already knew it before I was born. I remember when I was a young boy, my mother didn't have time sometimes to make a dessert. She said: "Go down the lane to Aunt

Lucy and ask if she has something." Aunt Lucy was about a hundred and lived in a shack with another black lady. They loved to talk to me. My mother would say: "You were gone two hours for a cake?" I didn't know enough then about racial prejudice. Those two black women seemed to me perfectly familiar. I found out who they were without knowing I'd found out.

I've found that people like Dame Edith Sitwell, who always said she was a Plantagenet, and myself, so different, were much closer to each other than these critics, who have so many hang-ups—not just emotional, but intellectual. They're so cut off from life. They're absolutely incapable of approaching my books.

RC You've had a range of good responses from very famous writers though.

JP Yes, unusually. But I've got the other kind, of course; the ones who say: "Don't buy a book by him; he's not respectable." But how wonderful it is not to be respectable! That's what's happened to the gay movement— it's become respectable. I always say: "I don't want to belong to these people or have them like me. They can't like me, unless they're converted."

RC Many writers feel strongly alienated from the normalizing tendencies of gay culture today.

JP Well, of course we had to have the gay movement just as we had to have civil rights.

RC Where did it go wrong?

JP I think it became bourgeois. I've had the most vicious reviews from gay people. I think Gore Vidal said of my work that the gays try to say they're just like everyone else only nicer, but in James Purdy's books, it's just the opposite!

RC   Most gay writers I meet feel their work isn't contributing to the glossy world of positive images that comprises mainstream gay culture. Within literary gay fiction, isn't there a certain general resistance to that world?

JP   There are so many books that treat being gay like you were finally able to join such a comfortable club. And: "Of course my daddy's gay!" It's all such a lark. But for most of us, being gay was a very heavy burden. I think it still is. I don't think the world as it's constituted today is ever going to welcome gays and blacks. With civil rights and all, they're still burning churches in the South. Up here in the street, they still treat blacks horribly. Just to say: "We came out now and everything's alright"! It isn't. It's still very tragic to be gay.

RC   Do you think contemporary gay novels, then, have lost their hold on reality?

JP   I think they have a superficial vision, which is alright. I often like books which are superficial. They're charming to read—like Henry Green. He is wonderful. But I don't think they're true. There's this book—I forget which—where the son found out his father was gay. They just had this lark together. That's fantasy! When you think of the suffering most gays have suffered through the centuries: they've been burned at the stake; mistreated by the literary establishment. Really the first treatment of homosexuality in European fiction was Balzac.[1] Even that's rather obscure, but marvelous. Balzac has different names for it. In Boccaccio, a great writer, there isn't a whisper of homosexuality. But in Shakespeare there's a lot. In all his plays there's this homosexuality. And isn't it wonderful he wrote those sonnets?

---

1. Honoré de Balzac (1799–1850): French novelist. Purdy presumably has in mind the novels *Illusions perdues* (1837–1843; translated as *Lost Illusions*) and *Splendeurs et misères des courtisanes* (1839–1847; translated as *A Harlot High and Low*). See interview with Felice Picano.

RC   But where you find homosexuality in literature, isn't there invariably an awkwardness in relating it to the wider culture? Any books which embrace a more or less utopian gay world have to close or confine it from the outside.

JP   I think if you just live with other gays and never go out, you're hardly free, are you?

RC   Some gay men find "ghetto" life attractive.

JP   Well, it's wonderful that they have that. But their enemies are out there. I think in some ways people are more prejudiced today than ever—both against blacks and anybody else who isn't like them. I've been so mistreated by the *New York Times*. The one thing they love is shekels and the golden calf—those are the real gods there. They finally became pro-gay, but I still get terrible reviews there, from the gays themselves!

RC   Many would argue the *Times* isn't really pro-gay.

JP   I agree. That's all just window-dressing. They're antigay; they aren't even connected with it. They don't understand it. But to sell it now they have these black men dressed up—giving you copies of the *New York Times*. I said to one of them: "That newspaper doesn't like you or me." He got very upset. I said: "Go ahead—you have to live."

RC   I know that paper receives a lot of attention here, so has a certain importance. But do you really need to worry about it?

JP   When you're hit with a brick, your body knows it. You can forget it, but you're going to have a wound there. Then they embrace a writer who isn't talented really. His books sell, so they're really taking bread out of your mouth.

RC   To return to Edith Sitwell thinking you were black: her mistake, based on her reading of the textual evidence, would fit the contemporary cultural mood perfectly. Authors are encouraged nowadays to make confessional statements; to verify the experiences they write, as if to say: "This person really did this." The paradox in the case of fiction is that if you paid attention to that, you could never invent anything.

JP   That's merely propaganda, isn't it? The boy I wrote about in *I Am Elijah Thrush* I knew very well. He was unhappy when the book came out. Later, he got so he loved it. But I told him and others that by the time a book's written, they're not really the character so much as it's somebody I've invented. Even if you do a drawing of someone, it's not really them; it's just all, with your poor powers, that you can do.

RC   Is there always a real-life model for your characters?

JP   Usually. Sometimes I've written books and later thought: "That was really based on that person I'd forgotten." But I still think it's a creation. It's not a biography.

RC   How do you feel when critics try to unpick the work—to say, for example, that *Out with the Stars* is about the composer Virgil Thomson?

JP   Well, it's partly true and partly not true. I imagine Shakespeare knew somebody like Falstaff. Maybe he was Falstaff.

RC   Luckily for Shakespeare, when people reflect on that, there isn't much they can do to prove it. It must be in some way beside the point for you.

JP   Yes. One person who is an accompanist with singers thought *Out with the Stars* was a hatchet job of Virgil, which I thought was terrible. I've done hatchet jobs to a degree—with *Cabot Wright Begins*. Of course

I never knew a Cabot Wright. I don't know any rapists. But actually *Cabot Wright Begins* isn't about a rapist; it's about people that try to write about one. It's about writing. I think nearly everybody missed that.

RC   Some critics noted that the conclusion of *Cabot Wright Begins* constitutes a renunciation of writing. Several of your books end with a decision by a would-be writer not to write. *Eustace Chisholm and the Works* is another.

JP   That's true. Those people weren't writers, I guess, because a real writer can't stop.

RC   In such a case, do you only know once you have reached the end of a novel what's going to happen?

JP   Yes. A writer doesn't know much.

RC   Writers respond differently to the question of narrative control over their work, though. Some novelists know where their stories are going.

JP   Well, sometimes I don't. But I don't think an author knows anything. That would be to be God.

RC   One view of writing has it as an aspiration to Divinity.

JP   It's Godlike in the sense that you're creating something out of seemingly nothing.

RC   I'm interested in the process of writing in your case especially because critics have tended not to consider your books in terms of differences in structure and form. They talk of them collectively, whereas there are very different kinds of James Purdy books.

JP   Yes. That's why some people complain that each book's different. But I think they don't read deep enough. Also, the characters change the structure of the book and the prose. *In a Shallow Grave* is being mouthed by a semiliterate soldier. Virgil Thomson, who loved American speech, gave a little party for that book. He said, in his high-pitched voice: "Where did you get this lingo?" He saw that I don't talk like that. But I hear like that.

RC   People have identified the midwestern twang in your books.

JP   Yes. I'm stuck with that. Some people say it's Southern, but Ohio has this semi-Southern quality.

RC   Presumably you don't consciously plan such things.

JP   No. It's memory; how your grandmother used to speak. I was talking to some young writers. I was shocked they didn't know what brickbats or powderkegs were. I said: "You've heard of bricks, haven't you? Brickbats is a blow from a brick. But in its other meaning, it's something you do to hurt other people. It isn't necessarily a brick." The next day on the radio, they used the word. I thought: "My God—I thought everyone knew that word!"

RC   Is contemporary writing in general characterized by a narrow vocabulary?

JP   I think it's like our culture, which has gone downhill, and also our government. It began a little with the Korean War. We didn't understand what we were doing there. Then Vietnam has been a cancer on America. I think that's one reason people take drugs. I used to believe what the government said. Now I don't believe anything they say. What we've done in Guatemala, for instance: the CIA killed two hundred thousand people! We were behind that—maybe secretly. Also in El Salvador. Then we murdered [Salvador] Allende in Chile. We don't have anything to do with Cuba, yet we're in bed with Communist China, which is a horrible country. So you feel helpless; impotent with government. Also, it's now a government of the super-rich. And all the statistics you read in the different newspapers are lies. They say unemployment's very low. That's a total lie. All these young black people quit looking a long time ago. You quit looking when there's nothing there.

RC   This is depressing stuff, but is it new?

JP   It's always been here, but it's gotten worse. I imagine if you lived during the Civil War, that must have been awful, especially if you were Southern.

RC   In several books you have written about the poor in the Depression.

JP   Yes. Now the poor are hidden; they don't exist. In the Depression everybody knew they existed.

RC   A writer might respond: one thing my fiction can do is make them visible.

JP   Well, that's thinking. I never think. The subject finally appears like a phantom and I know that's the story I have to write. If I worried about other things, I'd be a sociological writer. Many writers are; some, like Theodore Dreiser, are great writers. But I'm not that kind of writer. I think, though, if people read my books, they see there's hardly a topic I haven't covered. But they don't think that's true—they think there's something wrong with them. The people that make the books sell say: "Don't read him; you won't get it."

RC   So the question of subject has never preoccupied you?

JP   No. Otherwise I'd probably be very successful. This may sound peculiar, but I wait until I know I can write that book. For a long time I thought I could never write anything in the first person. Now I've written short stories like that—like "Some of These Days," which works because it's in the first person; then *I Am Elijah Thrush* and *In a Shallow Grave*. We forget Melville's *Moby Dick* is in the first person.

RC   Most of your first-person pieces are relatively short.

JP   Yes. The last book, *Gertrude of Stony Island Avenue*, caused me so many problems. She's a woman I'm not too crazy about. But I wanted to write her story. Also, her speech is quite different from mine, so I had trouble with her. But I finally got through it.

RC   Was it slow to write?

JP   Yes. I got really stuck. Then a friend helped me to deal with it. But I felt I couldn't do her justice. I'm not that woman, but I know her. Those young men like the Negro in *I Am Elijah Thrush* I feel quite at home with. I feel I am a N——. So Carey, for instance, I liked. I feel very close to her. But I don't speak like that.

RC   How does "liking" a character matter?

JP   I think you have to love your characters even if you hate them! I don't know that I ever wrote a book about someone I really hated. If you hate someone, I guess you're just not into them. You just know you hate them.

RC   Yet you've produced men who approach the monstrous.

JP   Oh yes—Captain Stadger in *Eustace Chisholm*. I sort of feel sorry for him, because he's crazy. Then, very few people mention my humor, as though I didn't have any. There's a lot of humor in my works.

RC   There's more in some than others, I'd say. Some works seem over-whelmingly bleak. Paul Binding compared *In a Shallow Grave* and *I Am Elijah Thrush*, and found the first tragic, the second comic.[2] Once again, I suppose the question of tone doesn't occur to you when you are writing.

JP   No. It's like being in a battle. You're so into it you don't have any high ideals. You're just doing it. I have all these boxing prints on my walls. I always feel that's what I am—a boxer. I get my brains knocked out every so often.

RC   Does a story ever defeat you?

JP   I had a lot of trouble with *Cabot Wright Begins*—I think because I don't know any rapists. But then I realized the book isn't about a rapist but about people trying to write about that. Of course there are some stories I never finished. But later I find out they have reappeared in another form.

RC   Do you put them in a drawer to come back to?

JP   Yes. I have filing cabinets full of them. The other thing nobody knows about, except in France, the Netherlands, and off-Broadway here, is that I write many plays. They won't do them here. They say midwest-ern speech isn't suitable for Broadway. Then again, the plays aren't gay. That puzzles my gay friends. But I know these stories from my great-grandmother. I like them. I'm queer for stories! It doesn't matter to me what kind of people are in them. If I like their story, I'm going to write it. If gay people don't like it, they can just go hang out in the rain. I'm not going to let them tell me I can't write it.

---

2. Paul Binding, an English novelist and critic, wrote the introduction to British editions of Purdy's *Eustace Chisholm and the Works* (London: GMP, 1985) and *Narrow Rooms* (London: GMP, 1985).

RC   Which writers—of prose or plays—do you feel an affinity for in this respect?

JP   Tennessee Williams came to all my off-Broadway plays and said: "You're a playwright." I said: "Excuse me—do you mean that I'm not a novelist?" He said: "I think you're more of a playwright." I don't believe that. But he saw I was writing plays. But producers don't want them. Still, they're done off-Broadway all the time.

RC   One couldn't say Williams didn't care about the representation of sexuality in his plays. Some would argue he came to care about that too much in the end.

JP   Well, he had drinking problems and was taking pills. He was sick. But I was disappointed in some of his later plays. Who cares about all that sex stuff?

RC   How do you know when an idea should be executed as drama, not prose?

JP   That just takes over. I see it's a play.

RC   Does that happen at the beginning?

JP   Usually. I start writing something and think: "This is a play." They're very different, because all the work has to be done by the actor. A big load's taken off your chest in a way, because in a novel you're talking to someone. You're telling them: "This is the way it happened." Many people can't read plays.

RC   Do you ever have an imaginary reader in mind?

JP   I suppose that flits in and out. But I'm so engrossed in the sweat of getting this out of me. This isn't to make me out as better than other people, but I never care to please the public. I think most writers write to please, asking: "Is this going to go over?" Many people threw up their hands when I wrote *Narrow Rooms*. They thought it meant I didn't ever want readers. Friends said: "You're really going to be burned at the stake for this." I said: "Well, I have to write it. If I wrote *Pollyanna*, they're never going to like it—the people in power."

RC   Presumably you don't choose to write transgressively either.

JP   No. It's like being on a sled. You're going down a hill and no one can stop you.

RC   How do you react to the charge of blasphemy?

JP   Has that been made against me? I must tell you a story about that. I went to Tulsa, Oklahoma, to read at the university. The secretary there said: "There's a call for you from Oral Roberts. He's an evangelist people sort of laugh at. He has a lot of money and runs this sort of school of street evangelists, though it's more well-heeled." I said: "They have the wrong writer, I guess." But they wanted me to go over there. I said: "Excuse me, have you read my books?" They were indignant and said: "Yes." I thought it must be a mistake. I went, and the first book I saw them reading was *I Am Elijah Thrush*. They think those books are like Bunyan's *Pilgrim's Progress* or Spenser's *Faerie Queene*: religious allegory. That's what they saw me doing. I couldn't get over it. But they'd read everything of mine though they were all religious.

RC   Did they want you to confirm it?

JP   No, they didn't press it. They said: "Are you a religious person?" I said: "Yes, in the sense that I believe there are mysteries we will never fathom." I feel very comfortable with people like that, though I know I couldn't go and live with them. But it shows again what one of my publishers said: my work appeals to such a heterogeneous audience that they don't know how to market them.

RC   The spiritualism of your books I can see.

JP   I think *Narrow Rooms* is a religious book. Certainly *In a Shallow Grave* is. I said: "I'm especially interested that you liked *I Am Elijah Thrush*." They said: "That's our favorite." These are young people, all dedicated to religion. As I laughed, they stuffed three hundred dollars into my pocket. I thought: "Religion must pay round here."

      The life of Christ was very interesting. One wonders what was going on. I'm sure it wasn't any ordinary gay thing. But it certainly has that feeling.

RC   Characters in your books come back to it: Jonas, for instance. In that case, you write about a vision of Christ in a sexual context; a "blessed" Christ, as it were. In Britain, a poem by James Kirkup was prosecuted for blasphemy for describing the sexual desire of a Roman soldier for Christ.[3]

JP   Ridiculous! When *63: Dream Palace* was published in England, they had to remove a word.

RC   "Motherfucker"?

JP   Yes. That made Dame Edith furious. She said in her introduction that the word wasn't obscene the way the boy uses it. See, only Negroes understand that—that "motherfucker" can mean something deeply affectionate. White people don't get it.

---

3. James Kirkup's poem "The Love that Dares to Speak its Name" led to the successful prosecution of *Gay News* for blasphemy in 1976. See John Sutherland, *Offensive Literature: Decensorship in Britain, 1960–1982* (London: Junction Books, 1982), 148–54.

RC   Nowadays writers can use any kind of language.

JP   But it's all dead. They've used "fuck." Who wants to use that any-more? They ruined it. I taught a class in writing once. I couldn't stand it. I said to them: "That word is dead. It's used up."

RC   Should fiction be striving to find a language for itself other than the everyday?

JP   That's up to the individual writer.

RC   But if you say "that word is used up," do you mean in normal dis-course or in literary works?

JP   Well, if you're a real writer with your own style, you don't want to use clichés.

RC   How did the word *fuck* become a cliché?

JP   Partly because of the army. When I was in the army, I thought: "If I ever get out of here, I don't ever want to hear that word again." It's like with very effeminate women every other word's "darling" or "dear." I used to hate those words.

RC   There's a lot about the army in your books.

JP   Right. That nearly finished me. But I'm glad I was in it.

RC   Is there ever a time when, in writing about people in the army, you feel you were drawing on your own experience?

JP   I feel all my works are lies, but in the lies are the real truths. But to begin to write what I actually saw would be journalism to me. That doesn't interest me. It has to be put in this furnace that is very hot. Then, when it comes out: that *was* my life in the army; now it's an opal, or an emerald or something.

RC   To pursue the reading of literature through biography: have you been approached by would-be biographers?

JP   Yes. I tell them to get out. I *have* no biography. It's all in the books.

RC   What are you currently writing?

JP   The new book I've written is a collection called "Moe's Villa and Other Stories." But I"m not sure who will publish it.

RC   Will it collect the stories recently published elsewhere?

JP   "The White Blackbird" will be in it, from *Men on Men 6*.

RC   And "The Anonymous Letters of Passion," from the British volume *More Like Minds*?

JP   No. These are stories; those are letters. I love those anonymous letters. Of course they're not actually anonymous. People know I wrote them. I'm still trying to fix one story called "East Street," about two black women and a young black actor.

RC   You've written an impressive body of work. Does writing come easily?

JP   Yes, yet I have terrible problems putting it all into shape. But I can sit here and write all day without any trouble.

RC   Do you write at regular times?

JP   Usually in the morning. You get stuck, you know. It's like driving an old car. It breaks down and you're wondering how to get home. Each day you have a Waterloo. You're defeated. The next day, you find a way to do it.

RC   Do you work every day?

JP   No, but a lot of days. Sometimes I'll wake up in the middle of the night and write something. With the story "Moe's Villa," I didn't know how to end it. But I dreamed it, where my mother told me: "The jewels are candy." I said: "How ridiculous! That's unbelievable." Well, it isn't believable. But you fall under the spell of the story and believe it.

RC   Do solutions often come from dreams?

JP   Yes. I thought the jewels being candy was wrong. Then I kept thinking about it and decided that was it. That's why many critics and readers have trouble with me. I deal with the unconscious. One of my greatest fans was a Jewish girl who was almost gassed under Hitler—Bettina Schwarzchild. She came to America and found "63: Dream Palace." It nearly killed her, because it revived the horror of her life. But then she wrote a beautiful book about it. It was hard for her to write English. She grew up speaking Yiddish, Polish, and German. Each word was hard for her. I loved that.

RC   Do you write longhand?

JP   Often. I type too. It's quicker.

RC   Do you think it makes a difference?

JP   No. Nothing makes any difference, because I'm doing what [French writer Joris Karl] Huysmans said: writing À Rebours—"against the grain."

RC   Do you feel a great kinship with him?

JP   With *Against the Grain* I do. When he got Catholic I had trouble
with that. He isn't a big influence, but I do like the book.

RC   Are there writers associated with the Midwest that you've liked?

JP   Sherwood Anderson.

RC   He wrote that odd, almost gay story, "Hands," in *Winesburg, Ohio.*

JP   I think he was gay. That was one of his troubles. He was great. I
think we were dealing with the same kind of landscape and speech:
Ohio. I don't know that any writer influenced me deeply. I got a little
help from the way Gertrude Stein wrote "Melanctha," about that colored
girl.[4] I liked that kind of speech.

RC   You have spoken of the influence of reading the Bible.

JP   Yes. That helped a lot. I guess that's why the Jews in Israel liked me.
I was made to memorize long sections of the Bible. Sometimes I thought
I was a Jew, because how many young boys are made to read the Bible?
It's terrible. Like the boy who'd never heard of "brickbats" or "pow-
derkeg." Now he's looking up words . . .

RC   Some of your stories feel like rewrites of Herman Melville: *Narrow
Rooms*, for instance, was close to "Billy Budd." Was Melville an influence?

JP   No. But I think he was gay. I just follow my unconscious. If I can
just get it out of me, that's as much as I can do.

---

4. Gertrude Stein, *Three Lives: Stories of the Good Anna, Melanctha, and the Gentle Lena* (New York,
1909).

RC   You have been called a "Calvinist" writer.

JP   I was brought up that way. Paul Binding is a marvelous critic, but he complained that I should have made Malcolm gay. I was disappointed in that, because that boy *did* love that girl sexually. He didn't know any better. Maybe if he'd lived longer, he'd have been gay. But I thought that showed a parochial view of human nature in him: to blame *Malcolm* because it wasn't more gay.

What's also strange about *Malcolm* is that it's about an abused child. They never mention that. They don't see why it's funny, because it's so terrible. Well, it's both. We often laugh at very tragic things. It's a form of hysteria.

RC   Malcolm describes himself at one point as a blank piece of paper. That reminded me of Edgar Allan Poe.

JP   He's a great writer.

RC   How would you feel about being compared to him?

JP   No. Well, "The Cask of Amontillado" is sort of like something I might have written. It's quite a horrible story, isn't it?

RC   I was thinking of *The Narrative of Arthur Gordon Pym*, a very homoerotically charged novel. The eroticism's bound up with racial difference.

JP   Well, Americans—unlike those in most other countries—have this strange relationship with black people. I've complained to some of my black friends because they said jazz was the only contribution America made to music. I said: "But it's not all black! You could never have written that in Africa. You had to be here in America and have your guts pulled out of you!" It's just as much white as black. It's the meeting of the two cultures that made jazz. Without being here, they'd never have written it. They don't like to hear that.

RC   Should they be grateful?

JP   No, they shouldn't. I'm not saying it was good. But that's why it was jazz. If they'd stayed in Africa, there wouldn't be any jazz. It'd be something else.

RC   I wanted to ask for your opinion of Edward Albee's dramatization of *Malcolm*.

JP   That was terrible. Awful. I like Edward Albee, though. I'm glad he did it. It had moments, but I don't know that anyone could put *Malcolm* on the stage. I think it might be a film. It's very cinematic.

RC   Do you watch films?

JP   I used to, but they're so bad now. They're just like everything else in America. America exports Coca-Cola, which can give you sugar diabetes, heart disease, and everything else. Young people drink four or five bottles of it a day. It's worse than drinking coffee.

RC   What do you drink?

JP   Water or lemonade. I'm not blaming anybody. I've learned never to criticize anyone.

RC   Do you go to the theater?

JP   No. I hate to say this, but I don't have the money. I never made any money from publishing.

RC   You've never reviewed, which many writers do for money.

JP   No. I couldn't stand that. I've made what money I have in other ways—none of them critical, but strange. Then people have left me money—not enough to survive on, but it helped.

RC   You taught for a while.

JP   Yes. That was torture. I'm not much interested in other people's writing. I told them I was a terrible judge of other people's writing. I think that's true of most writers: they're fallible. Angus Wilson said that. I said: "My opinion's probably not as good as some housewife's, or some beggar's on the street."

RC   Angus Wilson kept teaching though.

JP   Isn't that terrible? Someone told me he died in poverty.

RC   Yes. His reputation's in limbo, I think, despite the biography of him by Margaret Drabble.

JP   She edits the *Oxford Companion to English Literature*. I wasn't in it. She didn't have me, but she did have all these nonentities like Joyce Carol Oates. She reviewed *I Am Elijah Thrush* unfavorably. She threw up her hands and said she didn't know what it meant.

RC   Have you read a lot of contemporary writers?

JP   I try to. But I usually give up after four or five pages. I see this isn't what I'm interested in. I really haven't cared much for American fiction.

RC   What about foreign literature?

JP   I like the French. Gustave Flaubert's *Madame Bovary*. Lautréamont's *The Songs of Maldoror* is a great book.

RC   Anything more contemporary?

JP   Jean Genet. I like some Sartre. I never liked Camus, though. I
thought he was a fraud.

RC   Didn't Paul Binding suggest an affinity between you and the exis-
tential Genet, as described in Sartre's *Saint Genet* [Paris, 1952]?

JP   Right. And with Federico García Lorca too. I like the Spanish pica-
resque novel. I lived in Spain, went to school in Mexico, and taught
school in Cuba. I loved those Cervantes stories about young boys. And
Lazarillo de Tormes. They don't know who wrote that.

RC   These are books with a strong narrative drive. Is that something that
you find lacking in contemporary fiction?

JP   Yes. A book I've read four times and never got crazy over is James
Joyce's *Ulysses*. I failed each time. I just don't think he was a novelist. I
don't find any of his characters interesting. I liked *Finnegan's Wake* better, because I had an Irishman read it aloud to me. We both laughed a
lot. But that's all words. I don't like Joyce's short stories in *Dubliners*
either. They're very poor.

RC   What about other modernists, like William Faulkner? I mention him
because Stephen Adams described your work as part of a tradition of
American gothic writing.[5]

---

5. In Stephen Adams, *The Homosexual as Hero in Contemporary Fiction* (London: Vision Press, 1980).

JP   I don't even know what that is. I'm not too fond of Faulkner either. There's something so constipated about him—like he had a thistle up his ass. But he wrote some pretty interesting books. *As I Lay Dying* is quite a feat. But a lot of it's like if you ordered spaghetti and they brought you wood shavings and you had to chew and chew.

RC   People have called your early work reminiscent of Flannery O'Connor.

JP   I think she's dreadful. It's all in her head. She's a "head queer"—all that ersatz violence. I find her violence all thought up. I guess she was a disappointed lesbian.

RC   How do you write violence authentically?

JP   I have a terrible time writing violence. In fact, when I finished *Eustace Chisholm and the Works* I had to go to hospital. One morning I just couldn't get out of bed. I couldn't get up.

RC   Three endings of yours in particular led supportive critics to account for their violence by making somewhat humanistic claims for the work: "63: Dream Palace," *Eustace Chisholm*, and *Narrow Rooms*. In each case, your defenders have argued that the criticism that there's something wanton or inappropriate in the violence is wrong because your handling of language conveys the suffering of the author himself, which parallels that of his protagonists. Is that an appropriate defense, to your mind?

JP   Well, I had to go to hospital. Those endings made me sick. But I knew that was the story to be told. One story my grandmother told me was *House of the Solitary Maggot*. When I began to rewrite that, I thought I'd take out the section where he blows the eyes out of the boy, picks them up, and puts them in his mouth. I thought: "I won't have that." Then I dreamed my grandmother told me: "You put that back. I told you that, and you're going to write the story the way I told you." My mother used to scold her, saying: "You shouldn't tell him those things. He's already so strange. He's too young to hear terrible stories."

RC   Were you a strange child?

JP   I think I must have been.

RC   You found your literary voice early on. Did you recollect it coming fully formed?

JP   I think so. When I was a small boy, I used to write these terrible things that my mother said. One was about our landlady. I wrote that these gorillas attacked and destroyed her. My mother found it and said: "My God, that's awful." But she didn't destroy it.

Most of the stories in *Color of Darkness* were written in my twenties, but no one would publish them. They said they were terrible. The magazine that especially loathed me was the *New Yorker*. They published one of my stories, but changed it all so it didn't have any meaning. The changes were so inappropriate. The fiction editor there hated me. But the *New Yorker* don't want anything about being human. They want it all to be fashion, wit, and chic. But their chic is cliché. It has to go with the ads for Hotel Pierre, Courvoisier, and Italian chocolates. The ads are what's important, not the stories. I never send stories anymore.

RC   You mentioned revising one book. Is there a substantial process of revision?

JP   Often. I rewrite a lot. *Gertrude of Stony Island Avenue* took a lot of revision. I got stuck in the mud with it. It was originally four hundred pages. A friend of mine helped me cut it down. That woman talking like that—it couldn't go on too long. The reader just couldn't take it.

RC   Do you often ask for the input of friends?

JP   Well, they do help. I used to have these young men come and read. That would help.

RC   Because you could hear what was superfluous?

JP   Right. I had "Moe's Villa" read to me. People liked that.
    Gertrude of Stony Island Avenue isn't getting reviewed in England. The big publishers don't like me. They dropped me. Especially Jonathan Cape. They were terrible to me. They turned down *House of the Solitary Maggot*. They said it wasn't good enough. It was my best book in some ways. It's my most ambitious.

RC   In the middle of your career, you wrote two of three projected "epic" novels concerning family dynasties—*Jeremy's Version* and *House of the Solitary Maggot*. Why?

JP   Whatever comes to me I go with.

RC   Why did you bracket the two books together?

JP   Doubleday felt the books should be a trilogy, but then there was the failure of *House of the Solitary Maggot*, which the *New York Times* didn't review. That was unheard of, because I was considered a major writer. The third volume in a way was *Mourners Below*. But it was packaged separately.

RC   Which books have been most successful commercially?

JP   I think *Malcolm* and *The Nephew*. But I never had publishers that really pushed me.

RC   Do you support your books through public appearances?

JP   I used to do it. It nearly killed me. I'm not at ease in big groups. They say I read very well, though.

RC   You don't seem reluctant to be interviewed.

JP   With you, yes, but most people who come haven't read the books, so I'm not sure what to talk about. They come here and I can tell they don't really like the book.

RC   Other writers have speculated over the difficult task of having mainstream culture accept books with openly gay content. Do you think that's been part of the problem for you? Your works have got more explicit. Readers of, say, *Malcolm* and *The Nephew* can get away without thinking too much about homosexuality.

JP   Well, *Gertrude of Stony Island Avenue* is more like *Malcolm*. It mentions sex but doesn't go into it.

RC   Some writers feel there is a difficulty finding a readership for explicit books.

JP   But the people appraising work change like the seasons. The big literary publications in America are all anti-writing. There's no first-rate literary publishing in America. When I first came here, the slick women's magazines were all publishing my stories. Now they don't publish stories.

RC   You talk of the lack of cultural seriousness in America. But is it better anywhere else?

JP   I wonder. Certainly Russia never showed any interest in me. The French spend a lot of time writing about me. But they're bourgeois too. But not as bad as America. The Germans have published nearly everything I've written. One day the police appeared in all the bookstores there and scized *Narrow Rooms*. The publisher was horrified. The book was put on trial. They told me not to go there—I'd be arrested. The book was read aloud—every word. The publisher was very upset because the judge, a woman, looked very cross. She sat there, looking meaner and meaner as the book was read, which must have taken all day. At the end she said: "It's outrageous to bring a book of imagination and put it in court; to take the court's time with a book written by a brilliant writer." A women's group had brought the case, saying *Narrow Rooms* was indecent. But she let it go.

RC   It's curious how liberation movements become puritanical.

JP   They are. The gays attack me all the time. They say no one speaks that way—the way of my language. Well, not in the bars, maybe, but people do speak the way of my books. Those people just haven't traveled.

RC   Does it matter if they don't speak that way now anyway? Sometimes you're writing about the past, after all.

JP   Mostly. "Moe's Villa" is nearly a hundred years old. It takes place between the World Wars. I'm a historical writer. But people don't like the imagination, do they? They want everything topical.

RC   *Garments the Living Wear* was topical.

JP   I thought so. Quentin Crisp liked that. He likes my books and comes to my plays, though he's so deaf I don't know if he hears anything. He's brilliant—very bright.

RC   *Garments the Living Wear* tackled AIDS, which was an unfolding story at the time.

JP   Yes. Although it was before AIDS, people think "Some of These Days" is about it, because the doctor tells the young man he has a sickness that has no cure. But I'll never write about AIDS again, I don't think. It's not my subject really. It's too topical.

RC   Did that one come to you as the book's subject in the same way as the others—through people you knew?

JP   Yes. Each character was modeled on a real person. I lost people—not always close friends. But over fifty people that I was talking with. Some of them I didn't even think were gay, but they must have been.
    AIDS is too topical right now. It's a cliché for me. Then the gays annoy me. They say: "When did you come out?" I say: "I was born out." I'm too hopeless to be categorized.

RC   I've read you described as a "visionary writer," which is a sort of category.

JP   Well, it's true in a way, because I'm not a conscious writer.

RC   In English there haven't been too many self-proclaimed visionaries.

JP   There was William Blake.

RC   And Emily Brontë.

JP   Yes—she had that. A writer I admire is [Irish novelist and playwright] George Moore. I fell under his spell when I was a young man of about fifteen. I read *Esther Waters*. I think he's much better than James Joyce. His *Héloise and Abelard* is a wonderful novel about those two great lovers. Moore's prose is so interesting. He thought *Ulysses* was shit. Nobody reads *Ulysses*. It's unreadable. I never found even a page that I liked. I really tried.

RC   You mentioned earlier the archetypal position of marginal figures in our culture. Joyce did at least think about archetypes.

JP   Well, I don't think his book has anything to do with myth or the unconscious. I think it was very conscious. In a way Homer's *Odyssey* isn't archetypal either. It's a marvelous narrative and the people are just what they are. Odysseus isn't someone else; he's Odysseus.

RC   Do you read the classics a lot?

JP   Yes. One of my favorite books is Xenophon's *Anabasis Kyrou* [*The Anabasis*]. When I took beginning Greek we read a little of it. I don't read in Greek now, but I'm glad I had beginning Greek. I had more Latin and finally ended up reading Virgil. I like the *Eclogues* more than the *Aeneid* which I think is a mess. But I'm not competent to say that because I don't read Latin very well. They don't even teach Latin anymore.

RC   This is a leap, but I wanted to ask what effect, if any, you felt living in Brooklyn had had on your writing?

JP   Well, people think anyone that lives in Brooklyn is low class. I say: "I *am* low class." No wonder they called me a N— because I'm not respectable. Edward Albee came here one day. He was shocked at this room.

RC   Why? It's lovely.

JP   Well, you've never been to his place. He bought a building. It must have been a factory. The ceilings must be forty feet high. He gives these parties, but in order to get up to where he lives you get in an elevator.

They pull a rope up, which always scares me. I always wonder if it's going to fall.

RC   To return to the question of visionary writers, do you think anyone writing today shares that status?

JP   Madame Blavatsky![6]

RC   Everybody was circumspect about embracing her—even at the time. People claimed William Burroughs was a visionary.

JP   I read *Naked Lunch*. I thought it was just drugs, which isn't visionary. I loved Thomas de Quincey's *Confessions of an Opium Eater*, though. What I love is the writing. I don't care anything about his opium.

I have something I'm embarrassed to tell you. I don't work on it, but they say I'm psychic. This young man who helps me—my director, off-Broadway, John Uecker—will ask me what I get about a person. I just tell him whatever comes into my mouth and it turns out to be true.

John has no education, either—that's why he can direct my plays. I said: "If you were educated you couldn't direct my plays, because you'd make me change them." He directed my last play, *Forment*, which is about these young religious boys who think they're imitating somebody. Some people got up and left in the intermission.

RC   Have your plays been published?

JP   There are limited American editions and also Dutch editions of them—and of my poems too.

RC   Have you tried to publish the poems in America?

---

6. Famous theosophist from the Ukraine who moved to the United States in 1873.

JP   Yes. They said they were drivel. Do you know who loved them though? She called one day and I thought: "Maybe I've gone mad." She said: "James, this is Gloria." Gloria Vanderbilt! "I've just read your poems." Then she started reading them to me. She said: "I'm mad about them. Why weren't they published in America?" I said: "Well, one publisher said: 'These are just like *Mother Goose.*'" She said: "*Mother Goose* is one of the greatest books ever written." I never heard from her after that.

RC   I've never heard your work compared to nursery rhymes before. Paul Binding compared you to Jacobean playwrights.

JP   Yes—John Webster and so on. Well, I do have a relationship with them. *Narrow Rooms* is Jacobean.

RC   Do you read Jacobean theater?

JP   All the time. Thomas Middleton's *Women Beware Women* is brilliant. And John Webster's *The Duchess of Malfi*, though I'm not so crazy about that. But it's the language; they just let go.

RC   They approximate biblical language, so it's unsurprising you like them.

JP   Yes. It's marvelous. I met the film director Derek Jarman, who did Christopher Marlowe's *Edward II*, which is quite good. He was going to film *Narrow Rooms*. If he had, it wouldn't have been the same book. He's the one who said to me: "James, Edith Sitwell's the last person on earth I'd have thought would have liked your work." I said: "Well, I went back and read a lot of her work—like *Gold Coast Customs*. Her childhood was terrible, with her mother being sent to prison; her brother was gay and carried on with men. She was treated terribly. So she'd been mistreated as I was." Also, I like aristocrats because they don't have this silly middle-class prudery.

RC   Was Jarman's the only approach that has been made to you regarding film adaptations?

JP   No. *In a Shallow Grave* was made into a film. It wasn't very good. It's beautifully done, but they were scared of the homosexuality. Still, I don't think the book's about that. There's a kind of loneliness that's like death, then someone comes along and touches you. That isn't homosexual. That brings you to life. That's what *In a Shallow Grave* is about: a young boy that brings you to life. If you want to call it homosexual, go ahead.

RC   Wasn't *Cabot Wright Begins* optioned for film?

JP   Yes. That was the only money I ever earned. I had about twenty dollars in the bank—then I had this check for $75,000! They looked at me at the bank; then they looked at the check and said: "You can't draw any of this money for two weeks."
      They never made the film. It couldn't have been made. They thought the book was about the rapist. But it's a book about how awful America is.

RC   Have you ever been tempted to leave America?

JP   Well, I have several times, but I came back as I wasn't hearing my English. My tongue used to get so tired speaking Spanish. It just made me ill. I thought: "I never want to speak this anymore."

RC   Do you think of Brooklyn as a kind of exile—from Manhattan, at least?

JP   Yes. No one speaks English here.

RC   I want to talk a little about your most recent work, *Gertrude of Stony Island Avenue*. Something that struck me was how in that book, and then ultimately throughout your work, same-sex relationships—sexual and nonsexual—prove deeper, more viable, and more significant than relationships between members of the opposite sex.

JP Yes. Someone said *Gertrude of Stony Island Avenue* was a lesbian novel. But women do love one another. They're not lesbians in the book, but they kiss one another and weep with one another—which men aren't allowed to do in our culture. Some cultures allow that. The Poles kiss one another on the cheek.

RC Your portrayals of marriage seem universally lacerating. Marriage is both unavoidable and tormenting.

JP Yes, but you'd be sicker if you weren't married. Marriage must be terrible. You get so sick of living alone, but at the same time, take the woman who lived here. She was so happy with her husband. Then he died, and she just looks terrible now.

RC What do you think of gay marriage?

JP I loved what Quentin Crisp said at a public meeting. There was a young man who looked about twelve—I suppose he was about twenty. He said: "Mr. Crisp, what do you think is the future of gay marriages?" He said: "They have no future." This man fell back as if he'd been shot!

RC Are gay men wrong to want it?

JP I don't see anything wrong with it. They're trying to imitate the heterosexuals, aren't they? Marriage is entirely to have children. Sometimes gays adopt them; they allow that, which I think is rather queer. I'd think the child would be uncomfortable. When you go to school, they'd say: "Who are your mother and father?" And you'd say: "Two men." I'm sure some of them are wonderful parents, but it still isn't quite right because our culture is heterosexual. Even if you're going to be gay, I think you need both sexes to grow up. You need a woman to tell you what she knows and a man to tell you what he knows.

When I first went to Chicago, I had no money—as usual. I drifted into this awful rooming house. They had an old black woman that cleaned every day. I'd talk to her; I was probably getting material. Her name was "Stel"—from Estella. She belonged to the African-American Missionary Church. One day I knew she wanted to say something serious to me. She said: "I noticed you were talking to those ladies who live upstairs. I wonder if that's wise." I said: "What do you mean? I just talked to them." She said: "Well, I wouldn't want anybody that I cared for talking to them. That's my opinion." I said: "What's wrong with them?" She said: "They's besions." I said: "What?" She said: "Oh, Mr. Born Yesterday—don't know what besians is! Besians is ladies that has carnal knowledge of one another!" Besions was N— talk for lesbians. I don't even think she was right. Those women lived together but were probably straight.

RC You said earlier there was a need for gay liberation, yet you imply that much of what has resulted from liberationist politics hasn't done you any favors.

JP Well, I'm such a hermit, I'm only connected with the imagination. There's nothing out there for me. They made a lot of gay novelists into successes. Some gays they worship on bended knee. But they don't like my work.

RC Things are changing. A lot of writers mention your work. Maybe your time is still to come.

JP Yes—when it's too late.

RC Is that horrifying?

JP   No. I'm used to everything. I gave up ambition a long time ago. I just write and don't worry about it. My poems, I think, one day will be recognized. Nobody ever dared write such poems. They're like a child would write, and that's considered terrible.

RC   With best wishes for posterity, thanks very much for your time.

JOHN RECHY
TWO

John Rechy's first and most famous novel, *City of Night*, was published to great acclaim from James Baldwin, Christopher Isherwood, and many others nearly forty years ago. Born in El Paso, Texas, in 1934 to Mexican immigrants, Rechy studied for a B.A. degree at Texas Western College. He continued his studies in New York before going to Germany with the U.S. army.

Rechy's writing career began with "Mardi Gras," originally a letter written to a friend, but published as a story in *Evergreen Review* no. 6 (n.d.). This formed part of *City of Night* (New York: Grove Press, 1963), a semiautobiographical fiction concerning hustlers, transvestites, and other street life, set largely in New York. Four years later, Rechy transferred his novelistic attentions to Los Angeles, where it has largely rested since. His celebrated *Numbers* (New York: Grove Press, 1967) documented the serial sexual conquests of its troubled gay narrator "Johnny Rio" in L.A.'s Griffith Park. Three further novels followed: *This Day's Death* (New York: Grove Press, 1969), concerning sexual entrapment in Griffith Park; the gothic *The Vampires* (New York: Grove Press, 1971); and *The Fourth Angel* (London: W. H. Allen, 1972; New York: Richard Seaver/Viking, 1973), which features a collection of disaffected L.A. youth.

However, it was the nonfictional *The Sexual Outlaw: A Documentary* (New York: Grove Press, 1977), a return to the world of public sex of Rechy's first two novels, which next caught the attention of many gay readers. *Rushes* (New York: Grove Press, 1979), a controversial fictional exploration of the gay S&M subculture, was followed by *Bodies and Souls* (New York: Carroll and Graf, 1983), a return to the teenage world of *The Fourth Angel*.

The 1980s saw Rechy move away from predominantly gay subject matter. The thriller *Marilyn's Daughter* (New York: Carroll and Graf, 1988) examined the nature of celebrity, using the example of Monroe. *The Miraculous Day of Amalia Gómez* (New York: Little, Brown, 1991) considered the life of a poor Mexican-American woman in Los Angeles. *Our Lady of Babylon* (New York: Arcade, 1996) deployed elements of fantasy to review Rechy's background, career, and reputation.

The Coming of the Night (New York: Grove Press, 1999), Rechy's most recent novel, has marked a return to the themes of *City of Night* and *Numbers*. It concentrates on a 24-hour period in 1981 as the HIV virus first reaches L.A.'s gay sexual subculture. While writing this, Rechy continued working on "Autobiography: A Novel," a sequel to *City of Night*. An excerpt from "Autobiography" ("Love in the Backrooms") was published in George Stambolian, ed., *Men on Men 4* (New York: Plume, 1992).

Rechy has adapted *Rushes* for the stage, and written two other plays, *Tigers Wild* and *Momma as She Became—But Not as She Was*. He has also adapted *City of Night* for film. Rechy was awarded the Publishing Triangle's Lifetime Achievement Award and the PEN-Hemingway USA West's Lifetime Achievement Award in 1997. His home is in Los Angeles, where this interview took place on Friday, November 21, 1997.

RC   You've often spoken of the relationship between fiction and autobiography, and of fiction as a way through to autobiography. Obviously such topics are relevant to your earlier works: *City of Night*, *Numbers*, and *The Sexual Outlaw* play on and between these genres. Recent novels, though—especially your last, *Our Lady of Babylon*—contain a lot more invention, transposition, and self-conscious fantasy. Nevertheless that fantasy, I still felt, was deployed as context for concerns which remained autobiographical.

JR   That's very astute. I wish others who'd read *Our Lady of Babylon* and purported to write about it had been quite so astute. In point of fact, it's not really a deviation from my work; nor was *Marilyn's Daughter*. I'm always dealing with self-creation—the imagination and the transformation of imagination into reality, which is, of course, the whole concept of art. In Marilyn Monroe's case, this involved the literal change of an ordinary young girl into a sexual goddess, and also my own fascination not only with the transforming of my work into form but also of my body into form.

RC   What led you to the highly allusive, intertextual handling of such themes in *Our Lady of Babylon*?

JR   The primary influence was the passage I quote from the Book of Revelation about Our Lady of Babylon, and my fascination with who that illusive figure could be: the woman who was branded the mother of all transgressions; mother of all sinners. I think society's hatred of homosexual men is really an extended hatred by the heterosexual male of the female, so I found that very relevant and it comes into play in the book. My view about why homosexuality's so detested is that the powerful group in society—heterosexual males—considers it an abdication of their maleness; therefore, a betrayal of their machismo. They equate homosexuality in their wayward equations with choosing to be the weak female. Yet of course the female controls them by her passion and power. So my fascination with women like Our Lady of Babylon is that they've been blamed for enormous catastrophes because of their sensuality. Sensuality's a subject I write about all the time.

RC To some readers, your recent books simply suggested a moving away from your earlier preoccupations—specifically, with male homosexuality—in favor of considering the social position of women.

JR Yes. Of course it's nonsense because there's a connection. But as early as *City of Night* I was already dealing with form, appearance, and the idea of converting oneself into the figure of what one appears to be. I dealt with that idea constantly in my earliest books. The narrator of *City of Night* is a very sensitive young man who converts himself into a pose. So are all my other characters, such as Marilyn Monroe who fascinates me. So I'm developing themes I've dealt with all along.

I consider *Our Lady of Babylon* possibly my best book. I think I've been evolving towards it. I've always been very attentive towards literary form. The misconception occurred early on that I was an accidental writer; that I hadn't actually written these books, even—all kinds of nonsense. Because the subject was sexual, the form and structure of the books wasn't viewed.

RC There was that odd review of *City of Night* which suggested "John Rechy" didn't exist.[1] You rework that in *Our Lady of Babylon*.

JR Yes. I have a passage in *Our Lady of Babylon* in which Our Lady's in a salon—supposedly with Racine. I placed Alfred Chester there, the critic in question, and Richard Gilman, who was another. They're both there questioning the identity of a writer Our Lady knows very intimately.

RC You've repeatedly said that formal questions are neglected in accounts of your work. There's such a distinctive form to *Our Lady of*

---

1. Alfred Chester, "Fruit Salad," *New York Review of Books* 1.2 (1963): 6–7.

Babylon, however, that, though we can speak of continuities with the earlier works, at the same time there seems to be a formal break in your embrace of an entirely fantastic world. What led you to that?

JR   Well, *Our Lady of Babylon*'s actually very realistic. I've yet to encounter anyone who understands what I do at the end of it; what makes it—to me—an astonishing literary creation. At the end, a new interpretation of the book's form is revealed, which is that it may be that Our Lady of Babylon is really a very wounded woman, living in Los Angeles in some kind of tenement. She lives next door to an outrageous psychic, who's out to exploit her but actually takes compassion and listens to all her stories—stories which then find a parallel in the very tragic, realistic life of a woman from a great family. She's like a Patty Hearst figure who gets abused by men, is forced to kill her own child, moves into drugs, becomes a prostitute, and therefore sinks into this grandeur of imagination. Finally she sets out to become *all* violated women. Then I wanted to add an additional twist, which is that at the end I reverse it all and have her now—through this experience—having achieved what she was only pretending to be.

It was very carefully prepared. Every myth in the book corresponds to something that might have happened to this woman. Her lover may have committed suicide; that becomes Adam's suicide. Her tyrannical father sent her out; that becomes God expelling Our Lady. She's had various lovers, some of whom have abused her, and one of whom did love her—the man who pimped for her. The novel within the novel reasserts certain themes of the book, which may after all exist in the present day, as a satire on this great family, this American dynasty.

RC   When writing *Our Lady of Babylon*, you must have been aware of the danger that its blasphemy and shock value could blind readers to these other elements. Were you conscious of writing only for the most discriminating readership?

JR   I always have. I can tell you truthfully that when I wrote *City of Night*, I was convinced it would be critically hailed and sell very little. The reverse occurred—which astonished me.

I find very distressing the kind of censorship that came and squelched *Our Lady of Babylon*. The publisher ran scared. With my next book, *The Coming of the Night*, I'm convinced people will say I've run away from this new direction. In fact, I've done nothing of the kind, though at the same time it returns to the subject I left with *City of Night*. This will also be the first time I deal with AIDS, though I don't mention it.

RC   Why not?

JR   The book takes place on one day in 1981; AIDS wasn't even named at the time. I imagine a day in summer in Los Angeles when AIDS entered the city. I gather all the characters in a single sexual encounter. It's based on something I saw, and couldn't bear to write about all these years. The interim wasn't the time for this book to be written. It's only now that there seems to be something more hopeful with AIDS—though, then again, a greater danger of the replication of the whole thing, too—that I feel it's right.

RC   Wasn't your other work-in-progress, "Autobiography: A Novel," going to reach into the time of AIDS?

JR   Yes, but that will deal completely with its arrival, then move through to the present. *The Coming of the Night* concerns simply one day. It was a memory that haunted me of something I actually saw in 1981. It was so powerful that I haven't been able to shed it. In West Hollywood Park one very hot Santana night, a very beautiful young man pressed himself against a toolshed, pulled off his clothes, and allowed everybody to fuck him. It was right when people were asking: "Have you heard? No, it's impossible."

I wanted to convey the franticness that had been reached in gay men's lives, where we were now in danger of surrendering everything to our sexuality and entering a new time of danger, where that same confusion of realms may occur. It's about the question of where abundant sex is rich and where it devours us. I don't mean only in illness, but when psychically it destroys us.

RC   Taking your works together, you've very carefully documented both contexts in which sex seems to you liberating, and those in which it seems the opposite.

JR   Yes. I think the line's clear. I think confusions occur presently because of a lot of loud-mouthed people who I wish would shut up. Abundant sexuality—which is what I've always propounded and continue to—is one thing. But then there's pushing that to a point where everything else is throttled and sex is no longer sex, but dips into a self-hatred which then takes over entirely. That's what I saw coming and wrote about in *Rushes*. That's when I stopped writing about the homosexual world. I thought we'd reached a dead end—not because of AIDS, which nobody foresaw, but because I thought we were now destroying ourselves and confusing sensation with violence and humiliation.

RC   Presumably this was not a message people wanted to hear then.

JR   That's right. Likewise I remember when *The Sexual Outlaw* came out. People thought it was very romantic; everybody bought it. Then there was an incredible wave against it, when people reached the point where I very intelligently discussed S&M and my opposition to it. I don't think the people who once admired me on incorrect grounds have ever recovered from the discovery that I'd feel that way about S&M—and from my own participation in it, which is important.

RC You spoke of sexual drives spilling over into self-hatred. Is this behind your dismissal of S&M?

JR Yes. In fact, I say the most honest manifestation of what's happening to us occurs in S&M. It's the most honest, yet most destructive form of relationship. [Gay porn director] Fred Halstead and I were friends some years back. We'd seem to be diametrically opposed philosophically, but we got along very well. He agreed with me about S&M, but said: "I *like* that sense of humiliation." My point was that humiliation *is* there in gay lives; that it's the most destructive thing on our horizon and the main thing that keeps us from freeing ourselves, as long as we ritualize it and turn it into another lifestyle and don't question it. I'd never suggest banning it or anything of the sort. I'd fight against anyone who wanted to do that, or close bars or anything. But people should just question it.

RC Why does gay sexual culture tend toward extremes? On the one hand there's extreme sexual libertarianism. On the other, there's monogamy, self-censorship, the fight for gay marriage. Then there's the debate over the middle ground.

JR Which is a terrible one. For one thing, that nonsense about monogamy doesn't take into consideration what we are and how difficult it is in the gay world. I can see a new development where we'd have gay spinsters whom we'd ostracize for not having found a partner. I hate the word *lover*, by the way. But the question of dealing in extremities makes me want to speak of that nonsense that divides our history at an event called Stonewall. What an absolute abomination that is—the way of thinking that makes a line and says: "Before this, all was repressed; after this, all was liberated." It's wrong on both counts. It distorts history and becomes very harmful.

RC In literary terms, it suggests a disservice to a range of gay writers published before the 1970s.

JR   Yes. It is a disservice because the literature hasn't really changed. It's crass stupidity, yet people go along with it: the "Stonewall Parade"; the terms "before Stonewall" and "after Stonewall." Stonewall was one event. But equally disastrous is the fact that the line indicates that, after it, everything became liberated, whereas in reality we were faced with sexual excess and AIDS. How could we say our horizons had been cleansed?

RC   Clearly, "Stonewall" and the distinction it led to is a myth. The question must be: "Why is it so prevalent?"

JR   I'll give you one reason. You're going to think I'm being flippant, but I'm not—truly. The fucking thing occurred in New York! A lot of those New York homosexuals were there. A myth's made when some-body's there to record it. There were several people there to do that. It happened in New York; there were a lot of people about then, so it became the nonsense it is. Meanwhile we had the Black Cat riots here in Los Angeles. I'd been in several demonstrations and parades on Holly-wood Boulevard and the raid on the Slave Auctions and the trials that happened out of that.

RC   Some books seem to suggest New York invented "gay."

JR   There's a dreadful book out now, Charles Kaiser's *The Gay Metropolis*, that says just that. It's very much like the clutch that New York has in determining literary things. The New York establishment has had to deal with me, but it hasn't done so correctly. This is one rea-son I'm so glad just to have received the PEN-Hemingway West Coast award.

RC   The idea of gay literature emerging in the seventies ignores your own early work. But are there other writers you feel have been similarly neglected?

JR   Well, I don't want this to seem self-serving, but in effect it will be. When I look at literature that's considered "pre-Stonewall," I find so much defiance and honest-to-God pride because there were real dangers then. The dangers were jail, arrest, persecution. Nevertheless, you have a book like Christopher Isherwood's *A Single Man*, which is beautifully accepting and full of pride. Then you have the brazenness of Gore Vidal's *Myra Breckinridge*—my God! And I have mixed feelings about Mr. Vidal. We've had conflicts, and for good reason. But that doesn't detract from the fact that *Myra Breckinridge* is a work of absolute revolution in its questioning of genders, in its gender transformations back and forth, and in its mockery of attitudes. It's much more revolutionary than anything I could mention that's recently been published.

RC   These two examples, and many gay novels predating Stonewall, generally didn't consider themes of sexuality and sexual identity narrowly, or even as the main focus of interest. Have there been more recent works of comparable breadth?

JR   None! Let me say this without qualifier or hesitation: I'm always astonished at some of the attitudes of the people who criticize pre-Stonewall culture. They're based on ideas I propounded back in 1977 in *The Sexual Outlaw*. I was on a conference panel where some of the things I'd expressed in that book came out. It really is silly when you think of some of the things that present themselves as so brave and daring. If you go back to *The Sexual Outlaw*, you'll know what an enormous effect it has had—nowadays, always without attribution.

RC   Since your novels were always about blurring the boundary between the real and the imaginary, between fiction and autobiography, why was *The Sexual Outlaw* classified as nonfiction?

JR   I didn't really care whether it was or not. I think that the line between fiction and nonfiction's blurred. I don't see any rigid separation.

RC   You've spoken of the importance of the authenticity of that book, though.

JR   Yes, but *The Sexual Outlaw*'s also a composite. That's why I very carefully called it a "documentary." A documentary isn't just a camera sat down; a documentary's a composite too. That book, again, is very carefully structured. I was doing something new in form, which wasn't seen.

RC   You speak of its structure and form in terms of an analogy with film. Has film been an influence generally in the structuring of your work?

JR   Yes. Both film and comic strips were great influences—on a lot of the large images especially. I used to love movie serials such as *Terry and the Pirates*. I loved comic books like *Batman and Robin* too. I always saw myself as Batman; never Robin. They were both great visual influences. My writing's mostly very visual; almost filmic.

RC   There's the scale of your books too. They have the ambitious canvas of cinema. People talked of Christopher Isherwood being influenced by film, but he isn't—not in this sense, anyway.

JR   No. Christopher's being influenced by film would've been because he wrote so many screenplays—very good ones. I knew Chris and got along with him. One of my friends here's another Englishman, Gavin Lambert, who dealt with all sorts of wonderful things in his novels such as *The Slide Area*. He's terrific.

I'm not nostalgic about past times. I just very much resent attitudes that were created in the past now being arrogated as only from the present. Some of these fuckers don't even know what it was like to walk into a goddamn bar where you could get busted for walking in. Most gay people think history begins the last time they had sex with somebody.

I've pointed out that our history's very long, but the record of it's very short. The gay culture I know is very often unconcerned about that. I know it's terribly unpopular to think this, but there are reasons for it being so. The reasons lie in our oppression. As long as we don't deal with those, the thing extends.

RC   This suggests that "gay culture," if there is such a thing, hasn't come very far. To look at it from the outside, for example, one measure of the maturity of a community might be the extent to which it can take criticism. Gay culture often can't. Positive images, for example, still have a hold on gay creativity.

JR   Yes—that nonsense of positive images and of the artist as role model! We have to be cheerleaders. Then there's the posturing around the idea that everything's liberated now. We've just had our Holocaust, yet that, apparently, doesn't lie in anything we did. Promiscuity's not to blame; it isn't the reason for AIDS. AIDS is just an illness, and out of it we've seen a lot of courage. But now I think there's a lot of recklessness appearing in people's attitudes, and a forgetting of the courage that emerged out of AIDS.

If I sound a bit saddened about the whole thing, it's because of things which haven't happened, especially because we're saying they have. The evidence is overwhelming that they haven't. The danger is that in insisting they have, we'll simply perpetuate the same disasters. Also, look at what's happening to our art and literature. It's getting smaller and more narrow. We now have a genre called "gay litera-ture."

RC   Which is more numerous, though.

JR   Yes, but very little real art's emerging from that subject anymore— and I read a lot.

RC The context of fiction seems a good one to test out your ideas. In fiction, one might expect the dissident voice to appear.

JR Yes—not only the dissident voice, but the dissident artistic voice; the intelligent voice. But you have writers now who delight in squabbling with each other about who had more sex. Really silly things. So I find the literature's shrinking.

RC Notwithstanding these reservations, are there fiction writers—gay or not—whose new work you seek out? When does a book come out and you say: "I have to read that"?

JR I get sent every gay book that appears. The demands now are for a gay writer to write about gay subjects. We're not even penetrating the state of literature. I'm delighted when I learn my books are taught in literature courses—which several are. A whole course is going to be done on my literature at Irvington University. My *Miraculous Day of Amalia Gómez* I'm going to Harvard to lecture on. I think something's happened that didn't happen before: gay freedom has allowed us now to ghettoize and see only each other; so we preserve all our attitudes—which are all the same attitudes.

RC Some gay writers I speak to suggest they resist ghettoization in their work, and that they write about archetypal and/or nongay themes: the state of the family, for example.

JR Yes. I was writing about the need for that in *The Sexual Outlaw*. I don't like to talk about individual writers; it always seems as if one's in competition. But I can say that in general the reaction against David Leavitt and his work has been very symptomatic of the problems we face. I think he too was seen to be deviating from the expected. I'm not saying I admired him any more than any other writer, but because he was deviating by putting things in a greater context—whether he was achieving it or not, attempting to create literature—I think you now have him being pushed away most dramatically. It becomes rote that a dismissal of such a writer has to occur.

RC   I wanted to ask you about writing practice. How do you approach writing?

JR   I've gone through the whole evolution of it. I began writing in long-hand; then moved to a Royal typewriter my father had bought me. Then I moved to a rented Underwood, which is still here, on which *City of Night* was written. I couldn't part with it, so I bought it. Then I bought an IBM Selectric; now I use a computer. However, I still print out all the drafts and rework everything in pencil. I don't think I've ever written anything, including my articles, that hasn't gone through at least twelve complete drafts. The finished one begins at around the sixth draft; then begins the honing for language, sense, structure.

RC   How much do you have before the first draft?

JR   Well, I've used many different techniques. For example, *City of Night* began as a letter, which is well known. It was written entirely out of sequence. It almost killed me trying to bring it all together, in fact. *Numbers*, on the other hand, was written in three months. I had the sexual experiences in Griffith Park and, with the same urgency to give meaning to those adventures, I wrote *Numbers*.

RC   You've vividly described yourself at the steering wheel, dictating parts of that book to your mother, who sat in the passenger seat with notepad and pen. Are you going to insist that image is true?

JR   Yes! How can I convince you it's true? I know. When we were children, my mother's firstborn was called Valesqua. She died before I was born. She became a saint-figure in our Mexican-Catholic upbringing. When we didn't want to doubt anything somebody said, we'd say: "In the name of my dead sister Valesqua." What followed then was never questioned. We used that as children, but I'm going to borrow it now to say that, in the name of my dead sister Valesqua, *Numbers* was begun on the console of my Mustang. I looked up and saw Los Angeles, all shrouded. My mother was with me. She hadn't stayed with me in Los Angeles; I was in a motel. The pad was a legal pad; she held it and I wrote.

Numbers was as near as possible to autobiography. How can you recapture experience? Now, if you asked me whether *City of Night* was entirely autobiographical, I'd say: "Of course not." It's what is remembered.

RC   Do you mean to say that as soon as you describe experience, you're lying? That language is lying, in effect?

JR   Of course it is. There was something really wonderful about where I got the PEN-Hemingway Lifetime Achievement award. It was at the Biltmore Hotel, downtown. Many years earlier, when I was hustling in Pershing Square, a gentleman tried to get me into that same hotel. We were accosted by the detective and I was sent out. Many years later in the same hotel, I received a Lifetime Achievement award for my writing. That feels appropriate.

RC   I wanted to ask about your coinages: your use of the term "youngman," for instance. Did you start doing that by chance?

JR   In point of fact not. It always astonishes me that that particular combination's credited to me. My goodness, I borrowed it from John Dos Passos. It just seemed good. The odd capitalization I used, though I developed it into a theory of my own, comes from A. A. Milne's *Winnie the Pooh*. Nobody's ever asked me about that before. But you can find "youngman" and other combined words in Dos Passos. That wasn't imitation. It was being influenced by something very good.

RC In your recent books, how much of a project's clear from the start? Is the shape and size of a book clear, for instance?

JR Increasingly so. This new book *The Coming of the Night* was shaped in my mind. *Our Lady of Babylon* was too. They usually become grander though. I sometimes think I'm going to write a short novel; by the end, it's become much bigger. Like *Bodies and Souls*, another of my best books. I began calling it *Bodies*. It was about people who cherished formations of the body. Then it became *Bodies and Souls* and just grew. I think *Rushes* is my perfect novel. It takes place in a leather bar, ends up in an S&M orgy, and is constructed just like a mass. *Rushes* is perfect in terms of structure, theme, language, and narrative all coming together.

RC *Numbers* is the book that has received most attention from critics.

JR *Numbers* isn't bad, though it's very flawed. I'm the best critic of my work. I wouldn't change a word of *City of Night*, but I wouldn't write it like that again. God, what I thought was so realistic is so romantic and so young! *Numbers* is flawed—though I love it—simply because it doesn't have the thrust of horror which I wanted throughout. There's a sag in the middle. After it, I wrote a horrifying book—*This Day's Death*—which I've asked to be left out of print. It'll never be published again until I lose control of it. It's terrible. Then I wrote *The Vampires*, which augurs *The Coming of the Night*; then *The Fourth Angel*, a very wonderful book about my mother's death, where I change myself into a child. Then came *The Sexual Outlaw*, which is very good, though some of the essays by their very nature have become a bit dated. But the form of it's superb. If you look at my work, you'll see I've adapted style to content. Call it arrogance, but fuck it, I *am* at a point where I can be arrogant for Christ's sake: I'd compare my sentences to those of any other writer—gay, bisexual, Chicano, female, whatever.

RC Who would you want them to be compared to?

JR   The best. Anybody where somebody'd say: "This is the best we have."

RC   In your case, who's the best?

JR   I don't really want to say that. I veer away from that hierarchy.

RC   It's just that in *Our Lady of Babylon* and in *Marilyn's Daughter*, there is so much literary cross-referencing.

JR   Well, Nabokov, very much. Henry James. They're both dead, so I'm safe. But I've found it very troublesome to mention modern writers. Emily Brontë—I loved the melodrama and the toughness that lies under her so-called romanticism. There's a parallel between the theme of my *Marilyn's Daughter* and Brontë"s *Wuthering Heights*: in both, a very frail young woman has enormous power. I also admire Marcel Proust very much and James Joyce. I finished a lecture on Joyce last night.

There are some contemporary writers I think are terrific; first-rate. But I really don't like to evaluate them here.

RC   I want to return to the various stages in the creation of your works. What does a first draft typically look like? Is it a rather unformed outpouring of ideas, in need of much shaping, given how many revisions you said you typically make?

JR   Yes. *The Coming of the Night* I've actually finished, for instance. But I haven't had chance to do the crafting. It's all very loose, but I've put everything down. Now my mind's ordering much more as I go. The books start finding their form much more clearly. Then I have much more time to craft; to sculpt.

RC   Is the experience of writing things down as first draft typically much quicker than the subsequent crafting?

JR   Well, I've used different approaches. *City of Night* was written chapter by chapter. I wouldn't let a chapter go until it was finished. That was stupid and drove me crazy. *Numbers* was written from an outline. First I knew what I was going to write; then there was this anarchy of memories. When we reached El Paso in the Mustang, I had the opening of the book, as I said. I didn't have it refined, but I did have the opening pages. Then I outlined: in this chapter, Johnny Rio did such-and-such, giving order where there had been none. The reason *This Day's Death* became so bad was that it was dealing in a trial I was involved in. I'd been arrested myself and I couldn't shape it. But a book that ended up relatively short, like *The Vampires*, was originally two thousand pages long.

RC   Do you have all the drafts of your books?

JR   Yes, except for the original manuscripts of *City of Night*, which were all destroyed. But I have the galleys on which I rewrote that book.

RC   Why did you destroy the manuscripts?

JR   Romantic stupidity.

RC   That sounds like regret.

JR   Oh, absolute regret—good Lord.

RC   Is it financial regret in part?

JR   Financial regret, yes, though what's really now considered the acquistion at Boston where my papers are are the galley proofs on which *City of Night* was virtually rewritten in pencil. Now I keep all my manuscripts. I could show you boxes of pages of *Our Lady of Babylon*.

RC   Is the process of revising your work, then, usually more a matter of cutting down material than adding to it?

JR   Of course. I wish I could show you some pages from an early draft. Sometimes you'll find in twenty pages that maybe one phrase will remain. This is one thing that delights me so much about getting the PEN prize: I'm a terrific writer, and it hasn't been acknowledged.

RC   Fiction's invariably considered and discussed more widely in terms of content than technique and craft. In your case, the kinds of things you wrote about and the frankness with which you wrote about them both contributed to a certain notoriety which led people way from thinking of you in literary terms.

JR   Yes. It'd be sheer ignorance to deny that.

RC   Don't you feel you contributed to it to some extent? That sweaty, topless photograph of you on the cover of some of the books, for example. You were having fun.

JR   Of course. Also, my enormous narcissism comes into play. There was a certain amount of exhibitionism in that; my delight in my body and in bodybuilding. All those things come into play and all of them alienate. I know that. On the other hand, that's part of the creation; it is what I am now. When a book's formed, then it becomes an art form. So now I'm saying: "Yes, all these other things are there; now look at this— look at craft."

RC   Do you think the humor in the books has been acknowledged? When you spoke of your narcissism, it occurred to me that where critics were preoccupied with that, they took it far too seriously. Surely it was meant to be amusing.

JR   Well, I think I'm hilarious, so of course it is. Something I put in the books that's missed is that they're not only about myself, my body-building and posturing. They're also about the posture being crushed, whether in reality or within the books themselves. So the humor in that's enormous, and the awareness of the posturing is very much there.

RC   *Our Lady of Babylon* is funny, too—maybe because this great abstraction, this move away from something immediately true to something fantastic and untrue; this diffuse approach—not withstanding what you've said about it also being realistic—to your own experiences and to your own literary reputation: all this makes the humor that much more obvious.

JR   But the humor's always been there. The sections on the queens in *City of Night* are hilarious. In *Numbers* Johnny Rio does some things that are very serious but absolutely hilarious.

RC   In that book I'd mention the "double standoff" scene, where neither sexual partner will feminize himself by making the first move.

JR   Yes. And the playing at cowboys with their cocks, for example, which to me's parody. I've played at that myself, yet I find it really hilarious.

   Now about *Our Lady of Babylon* being realistic: look, that's only on a certain level, because obviously it's also an enormous fantasy—those two women sitting there having tea; the beautiful character Emily Guildo, the peacock.

   But the humor's always there. I have characters in *The Coming of the Night* that I love, and that make me laugh, particularly in their poses, because I share their knowledge of posturing. It's an art form, and a good one.

RC   Its physicality makes it a difficult thing to capture in language, I suppose. In a sense, body language is the opposite of written or spoken language; after all, it involves a decision not to render oneself through language but something else.

JR   Yes, but one can convey it. The language itself can be very narcissistic and humorous. In one passage in *Our Lady of Babylon* I have God exhorting the angels, and directing them in a certain entertainment. I give to God verbatim a little lecture I give my students. It's about how to highlight this and that. Then I give him some of the same gestures I've been told I use. That amuses me very much.

Something I appreciated very much happened some years back when I was teaching at UCLA. I was still on the streets. At about three o'clock in the morning on Santa Monica Boulevard—which was thriving then—I was standing without a shirt, with an oiled body, obviously ready for a certain person. A young gentleman drove by in a car, lowered his window and said: "Good evening, Professor Rechy, are you out for an evening stroll?" I loved that. It called into account the duality of the situation, and its humor: the fact that I was both teaching at UCLA and standing on the street. This young artist came along and brought the two together.

RC   He caught you staging yourself in another context, and, in effect, gave you permission.

JR   Exactly. It was thrilling; a terrific moment. I'd have given him a prize for that. In my writing I try very much to bring the sort of energy there was in that moment.

RC   Do you miss that sort of self-staging on the street? Are there other contexts now—university lecturing, perhaps—which offer similar opportunities?

JR   Well, I'm still very good at posturing when I'm not a writer. I'm a very good actor. I adhere to my philosophy of living, which is that one should live as the star of one's life.

RC   You've always experimented with voice and person. I'm interested in how you'd characterize writing in the first person as opposed to the third person.

JR   It just happens. I don't really know how. I just start and the voice's there. Sometimes I get confused about it. For example, there are times when I think *Numbers* is told in the first person. For a moment when we were talking about it, I thought *Marilyn's Daughter* was told in the first person, but it isn't.

RC   Throughout your career, you've oscillated between voices. But you're saying you don't think of that as significant?

JR   I really don't. One could say: the closer you are to the thing, the more likely you are to use someone like you. But that's not so, because though the material in *Our Lady of Babylon* is very close to me, I use a fabrication.

RC   *Our Lady of Babylon* involves a sort of merge. There's a first-person narration, but for extended narrative sections, it gives way to the third person.

JR   Exactly. I'm glad you saw that so clearly. I wanted the voice to disappear.

RC   In earlier works, though, you've more of a split. A new reader of your first two novels might say: "There's a clear split or movement here." What's the shift from the first-person voice of *City of Night* to the third-person one in *Numbers* about?

JR I really don't know. It's like explaining the fact that "youngman" came from Dos Passos, and knowing I'll strip some kind of mythical quality from the book. I can tell you that the first person of *City of Night* probably came out of the fact that I started it as a letter, then simply continued in the same voice. Why did I choose Johnny Rio in *Numbers?* I used to use that name on the street myself. It was very wonderful because after *Numbers* came out, I returned to the park as Johnny Rio— in Boston, in fact. A gentleman said somebody'd written a book about me, not knowing I was the author. That sort of thing pleases me very much. As a writer, I've then become my own character.

I was still cruising after *The Sexual Outlaw* came out. Somebody would take me home and I'd see a copy of the book. Later I'd tell a friend of mine, who'd say: "How could you possibly keep from saying you wrote the book?" But the whole thing would've been destroyed. It was and continues to be a private pleasure of mine. I don't like to play writer.

RC What do you mean by that exactly?

JR Well, when I'm talking like this to you, I want to be thought of strictly as a writer. But I don't like to play writer in the sense that writers assume a role born of what they think a writer is; what they carry with them. I like to shed that when I go out.

For example, because this apartment doesn't look like it belongs to the person I was pretending to be on the street, if anybody came over here from the street context, I'd say: "I'm keeping this place for somebody," because I'd clash with the surroundings. That's also the source of my fascination with Marilyn Monroe. I think she undid herself because she forgot she was always Norma Jean.

RC This move between extreme or oppositional roles is figured in the earlier books as something to do with the need to escape: to escape background, identity, family.

JR   Yes. But it's really escape from death. In *Numbers* I modeled a man who at the end of the book becomes death. He stalks Johnny Rio, who tries to push him away.

RC   So if one were to say your theme is death; that your work's about death . . .

JR   That would be right. That, and transformation: the transformation from what one is to what one becomes or appears to be.

RC   This brings us neatly to film. Have filmmakers taken an interest in your work?

JR   Yes, and I've influenced several of them. There is a thrilling script of *City of Night* that I wrote myself that's completely accurate to the original. Everybody who reads it loves it.

RC   But nobody proposes to make it?

JR   Well, for one thing, it'd be very expensive, unlike the small movies we're allowed today. This would have to have an epic scope.

RC   There are problems with the graphicness of the sexual material, presumably?

JR   Sure. It's very sensual and sexual. And I'd kill whoever played the lead.

RC   Do you mind if it never gets made?

JR   I'd love it to be made, only because my companion's a brilliant director; eventually he'd make it, and that would bring us even closer together. That I'd like to see.

RC   I wanted to ask why "Autobiography: A Novel" has taken so long. Parts of it were published some years ago: "Love in the Backrooms" featured in *Men on Men 4*, for instance. Have you been writing it alongside or between other projects?

JR   It's been happening simultaneously with other things. "Autobiography" will be the book that brings everything together. A CD-Rom's being made on it—an equivalent to the book in CD-Rom form, where you can move into certain areas and reinterpret them visually. That's why this person went to Boston University—to get all my photographs. "Autobiography" has taken me a very long time. It'll be my *Remembrance of Things Past*. It moves from the thirties to the present. It will be very long—it already is. There are different versions of it, because it keeps changing. I may never finish it, but if not, I'll let my life be it instead.

RC   Do you have any idea when it will feel right to close it?

JR   I think once I've moved from *The Coming of the Night*, I'm going to move into "Autobiography" and concentrate on finishing it.

RC   Apart from "Autobiography," have you invariably worked on a single project for a fixed period of time before moving on?

JR   No, several books have come between others. For example, *The Miraculous Day of Amalia Gómez* I had no intention of writing. I was sunbathing in Griffith Park and saw two clouds intersecting. I thought: "My God—those look like a cross. What would a Mexican woman from my background think of that? She'd think it was a miracle." I stopped *Our Lady of Babylon*, which was already in a thousand-page draft, to write *The Miraculous Day of Amalia Gómez*. I stopped something else to write *Marilyn's Daughter*. I've stopped several books when another one takes over. I probably stopped "Autobiography" to write *The Coming of the Night*.

RC Are there ideas that don't work: abandoned projects, in other words?

JR Sure. I know Christopher Isherwood put out a book called *Exhumations*. I'd put out a book called *Extractions*, featuring what I've taken out of books and ideas for books. I think a book about the books and stories one has never written would be fascinating.

RC I was thinking specifically of a project you might have tried to execute; then, at a certain stage, realized wasn't what you thought it was, or lacked, for the time being, a suitable form.

JR Well, they develop. For example, *Bodies and Souls* was originally just about people who specialized in constructing their bodies; then it moved far beyond that. It became entirely other than what I'd intended. I never abandon anything though. I wish I had: with *This Day's Death*, I wish I'd done what I knew I should when I saw I was going out of control. But I couldn't bring it back. I should just not have written it. But if I start a book, I'll finish it. I've started stories that I don't finish, though. But a book's a major commitment and too big to let go of.

RC It seems as if ideas come easily to you; there are always enough of them.

JR There are always too many! There are so many I'll never write.

RC Have you never suffered from writer's block?

JR I don't believe there's such a thing. I think it's a fancy name. I mean, "grass-mowing block"; "plant-watering block": these are things we don't want to do. But you give it a fancy name. None of the writers in my workshop had better tell me they're suffering from writer's block. Just write—and keep writing. But don't be fancy by calling that writer's block. It's nothing but laziness. If you don't want to write, you don't write.

RC   How much writing are you capable of in a day?

JR   When I'm really into a book, I can write from the time I get up without stopping—after I've worked out, that is. Working out's an ordering device. I work out with weights for two hours, four days a week. I've written fifty pages in one sitting.

RC   Some writers prefer to start in the early morning, before their heads fill with other things. It's interesting that you like to work out first.

JR   I do it early morning on the mornings I don't work out. But my energy's higher when I've worked out; and working out's become a part of my life. Once I've worked out, I'm very energized and ready to write.

RC   You spoke of not being interested in the idea of the retiring, disengaged writer. But there's always something solitary about writing itself, isn't there?

JR   Of course. I don't mind the withdrawal. In fact, I'm as close to reclusive as one can get and still go out as much as I do. The older I get, the more selective I am about things. I cherish my home life. Michael and I've been looking for a house together. The reason we haven't lived together until now is because of my need for privacy. When we do find a house, it'll have separate quarters. It worries me that he's so much younger than I am. He might be sacrificing some of his own contacts. Anyhow, we live a very good life.

RC   I wanted to ask about your creative writing teaching. Some writers involved in teaching are privately skeptical about how much can be taught.

JR The majority. But I could show you at least twenty novels either dedicated to me or acknowledging me—books that I've nursed from the very beginning.

RC So you do believe creative writing can be taught?

JR I don't think you can teach it exactly. But if you find talent you can certainly encourage it; make it much better by bringing consciousness to it: the same consciousness I bring to my own writing; a consciousness of technique.

RC But you didn't need that nurturing yourself.

JR No, truthfully I didn't. But so what? Maybe I'd have written twenty books if I'd had that.

RC The finding of the letter which led to *City of Night* suggests the accidental finding within yourself of John Rechy, the writer. Was that how it began—accidentally?

JR No, that isn't true because I'd already been writing. I'd just never conceived of writing about the world I was living in.

RC Had you always thought you'd be a writer?

JR No. I was an actor when I was a little kid. Then I painted and drew. I started my first novel, which was about Marie Antoinette, when I was about eight. Then I wrote an exposé of high school. At eighteen, I wrote a novel, *Pablo*, which I've never wanted to publish. I wrote some articles, too, under a nom de plume—Jack Chance—before I wrote *City of Night*. There was always a writer in me, and an artist.

RC Have you ever written drama or poetry?

JR   When I was a kid. It was in rhyming pentameter at a time when all that was out. I did parodies of *Paradise Lost*.

RC   It seems that narrative's what really grips you.

JR   Yes. I have to admit I don't understand poetry. I read some and like it, but I don't understand what the form's attempting to do, and form's so important to me.

RC   Do you reread the writers you revere for pleasure?

JR   Yes. I read a lot, but prefer to reread now. I get virtually every gay book that's published in this country. I feel a duty at least to sample it. A lot is terrible; appalling. Jesus Christ. So after that I like to read Proust a lot.

RC   When we were speaking of overlooked figures that predate Stonewall, we didn't mention James Purdy.

JR   Yes. Again, there's the imagination, lucidity, and humor of his work—especially in *Malcolm* and *69: Dream Palace*. They're fantastical but also very tough. What's the one about the rapist? *Cabot Wright Begins*. The imagination of that book—and terrific writing! I think I've read every one of his books, except for this last one, *Gertrude of Stony Island*, which originally only came out in England. He's been thrust away by everyone—including gay writers, who don't even know about him.

   I was invited to a literary thing PEN was doing in New York on "the literary gay hero." They'd asked Mr. Purdy. It was really wonderful, because they mentioned that they were going to get him. I said yes when I knew he was going to be on. To my delight, he also said he'd appear if they could get me. This was perfection! At the last moment I couldn't go. I had to have three knee operations, but—again, the posturing—I pretended it was because they hadn't given me adequate accommodations. They substituted a dreadful writer, so I rue that. And Mr. Purdy didn't show up either.

RC   Like you, he feels very much that he's written things people just don't want to hear.

JR   Don't want to hear, don't understand either, and don't see the art of. I'm very lucky in this sense: I've had commercial success. *City of Night* was a huge bestseller and continues to sell. So do *Numbers* and *The Sexual Outlaw*. *Marilyn's Daughter* did well, as did *The Miraculous Day of Amalia Gómez*. What's really sad is when you're underrated and also undersold.

RC   Still, any lineage of postwar gay writers would feature you—if, perhaps, for reasons you're less than happy with.

JR   More important is when people put out lists of *all* writers. You might think who the hell cares. But I'm in *Webster's* and the *Oxford Companion Guide to English Literature*. That's one thing I don't think we're aiming for anymore: to be acknowledged in the general requirements of reading. I'm in the *Columbia Encyclopedia of Literature*. Actually I'm more often left out of gay and Chicano anthologies than I am out of so-called mainstream books.

RC   Do you think the one identification causes problems for the other?

JR   No. I think it's because I don't toe the line. I've been very celebrative of the gay world, but also very critical of it. The same's true on the Chicano frontier. I've never totally fitted. I've never seen myself totally fitting in anything. I suppose that's conveyed in the books.

RC   What is left to do, other than to keep trying to educate a readership by writing more?

JR Writing terrifically, so I leave ample evidence that I was right.

RC To make a mark, then? To say: "I was here"?

JR More than a mark. A big splash! I don't like small goals.

RC The PEN Award stresses your regionalism, which I find interesting. One can't imagine your works coming from anywhere other than Los Angeles.

JR Yes. It's also Los Angeles being very brave: giving this award first to Billy Wilder, then to Neil Simon, Betty Friedan, and me. I like that.

RC You convey the feel of Los Angeles very distinctively to non-natives. Have you ever written with a particular reader in mind?

JR Never.

RC Would that amount to self-censorship?

JR Very much so. That's one thing I dislike very much about the genre of "gay novel" and publishers who advertise in gay magazines only. I know gay writers who feel a review in *The Advocate* is their goal.

RC I wasn't thinking only of marketing. Do you ever have a sense of the reader of what you're writing?

JR No.

RC Do you show the finished work to trusted friends?

JR I read it to Michael now. I read *City of Night* to my mother.

RC This I find astonishing—all of it?

JR   Selected passages I translated into Spanish for her. None of the sexual parts. Michael now even reads drafts. He's often been very instrumental. I trust him; he has impeccable critical sense.

RC   But you've effectively waited a long time for that sort of critical relationship. To some extent you must have learned to live without it.

JR   Yes—to write by myself. I do trust myself finally, because I know what I'm about. Not too many writers know that.

RC   Do you have a good relationship with editors and publishers?

JR   With some; some not. Don Allen was a legendary editor—terrific. Ken Carroll too. But then they try to screw you: as with one of my best books, *Bodies and Souls*. Then there's somebody like Richard Seamer, who published *Our Lady of Babylon*. The son of a bitch ran scared! He reduced the advertising; turned down the number of copies. Then he told me I'd been blacklisted by the *New York Times* and that I must write letters of protest. Christ, that kind of lack of courage!

Our Lady of Babylon hasn't gone into paperback. I don't hesitate to say it's a great literary creation and is going to be discovered as such. I'll see to it. But that fucking publisher saw that too. He's a legendary figure in publishing; he knew what the book was. But then a juggernaut occurred. The sex scene between Jesus and Judas became a thorn—not with him. But once it was clear to him that the bookdealers weren't going to carry this book, he just ran away from it—and lied about it. He knew by the advance orders that they weren't going to carry it, so he cut down the first printing to something miniscule; the least any book of mine's ever been issued at. Then he just issued it with no advertising.

RC   Norman Mailer wrote about a sexualized Christ in *The Gospel According to His Son* and publishers made it a selling point. Do you think it's the gay element?

JR   Yes. I'm still controversial in the oddest way. I can identify why but can't understand why it should be: the kind of arrogance I've expressed; the kind of thinking that I won't deviate from something just because it's not popular. It took me over thirty years to get the *New York Review of Books* to publish an apology for the *City of Night* review they ran. I pursued Gore Vidal for praising that review in his book of essays, *United States*.[2] I reminded him that he's been the object of this kind of derision too. He wrote me back, telling me how much he admired my work, and that he'd just fallen under the spell of this reviewer, and that he was never going to write again for the *New York Review of Books*. The son of a bitch writes for the *New York Review of Books* every other issue!

RC   These concerns can become very distracting from the real purpose: to write. Is there ever a point where you just want to give up public disputes?

JR   Never. I have enough energy for all of it, believe me. I'll never leave it.

Criticism is fine; assault—which I've been the object of, from the very beginning—is cruelty. Fucking Alfred Chester in that review: ". . . despite the adorable photograph on the rear of the dust jacket, I can hardly believe there is a real John Rechy."[3] Chester created real problems for me. The rumor was out that there was no John Rechy; that it was fabrication. I've struggled through those things. Every time the artistry is in my books, then I have to battle for it. I had the previous editor of the *New York Times* on the telephone after I wrote her a scorching letter. I've been told that's why I've been blacklisted—fuck it! In fact, I tell my student writers to protest. There's too much mistreatment of writers.

---

2. Gore Vidal, "Every Eckermann His Own Man," in his *United States: Essays, 1952–1992* (New York: Random House, 1993), 3–9 (see page 8).
3. Chester, "Fruit Salad," 6.

RC   What if somebody simply reads a book in a way you haven't antici-pated? There are writers who in that case say simply: "This is my book; it goes into the wider world; people think of it what they will." Some writers are even stoical when the response isn't what they imagined.

JR   That's fine for them. It isn't for me. I can't stop it. I'll write letters when people get things right, too, and thank them—always.

RC   I asked James Purdy whether he'd accept the term *visionary*. It sounds rather elevated, but would you consider it being applied to you? I think what one means by it is simply that one has something that has to be translated in literature that . . .

JR   That hasn't been seen or told before—or told that way before, yes. Then my answer for myself would be yes.

RC   On that note, thanks very much for your time.

THREE
EDMUND WHITE

dmund White has been much praised by fellow writers and figures in the literary establishment since his first novel, *Forgetting Elena*, first caught the attention of Vladimir Nabokov nearly thirty years ago. To many gay readers, White remained better known until the early 1980s as the author of an innovative book of gay travel writing—*States of Desire*—and coauthor of *The Joy of Gay Sex*. This changed with the breakthrough success—both in the United States and Great Britain—of the first of White's semiautobiographical fictions, *A Boy's Own Story*, in 1982. Born in 1940 in Cincinnati, Ohio, and raised there and in Chicago, White majored in Chinese at the University of Michigan. He moved to New York on graduating, working for Time-Life Books from 1962 to 1970. White then lived in Rome for a year, before returning to New York and briefly working for *Saturday Review* and *Horizon*.

White was writing prose and plays from an early age. His first published novel, *Forgetting Elena* (New York: Random House, 1973), was an elaborately written work of fantasy set on an imaginary island. Though critically well-received, the book sold sparingly. In 1977, White raised his profile among gay readers by coauthoring *The Joy of Gay Sex* (New York: Crown, 1977) with Dr. Charles Silverstein. A second novel, the equally baroque *Nocturnes for the King of Naples* (New York: St. Martin's, 1978), received much attention and praise. *Nocturnes* self-consciously invoked the school of religious devotional literature, though it could equally, if implicitly, be read as the narrator-beloved's homage to his older, second-person lover.

The widely acclaimed and best-selling travel book, *States of Desire: Travels in Gay America* (New York: Dutton, 1980), followed. Between 1979 and 1981, White formed part of the "Violet Quill," a reading group of six New York gay authors which included Andrew Holleran and Felice Picano. Manuscripts of various unpublished works from this period and earlier—including the novel "Woman Reading Pascal" (sometimes entitled "Like People in History," and referred to below)—are now held at the Beinecke Library, Yale University.

White's breakthrough fictional work was the semiautobiographical or "autofictional" novel *A Boy's Own Story* (New York: Dutton, 1982), in which his prose style displayed a new lucidity, and gay themes appeared explicitly for the first time. This was followed by White's fourth published novel, the less well-received and commercially unsuccessful *Caracole* (New York: Dutton, 1985), a highly wrought, imaginative telling of the maturation and sexual and social initiation of a heterosexual adolescent.

White next published the sequel to *A Boy's Own Story*, the similarly acclaimed *The Beautiful Room Is Empty* (New York: Knopf, 1988; London: Chatto and Windus, 1988). This dealt with the gay protagonist's growing acceptance of his sexuality, culminating with his witnessing 1969's Stonewall riots. The same year, White wrote three stories on the AIDS epidemic—"Palace Days," "An Oracle," and "Running on Empty"—for a collection coauthored with Adam Mars-Jones, *The Darker Proof: Stories from a Crisis* (New York: New American Library, 1988; London: Faber and Faber, 1988).

Having himself been diagnosed HIV-positive, White remarkably took on the monumental research task of the first, and authorized, biography of *Genet* (New York: Knopf, 1993;

London: Chatto and Windus, 1993). This won both the National Book Critics Circle Award and the Lambda Literary Award. The following year, a collection of White's essays appeared as *The Burning Library: Writings on Art, Politics, and Sexuality, 1969–93*, ed. David Bergman, (New York: Knopf, 1994; London: Chatto and Windus, 1994).

White's small book of reminiscences about life in Paris with his lover Hubert Sorin, who had recently died, was first published in Britain as *Sketches from Memory* (London: Chatto and Windus, 1995), then in the United States as *Our Paris: Sketches from Memory* (New York: Knopf, 1996). The volume was coauthored with Sorin in the form of line drawings which accompanied White's stories. The year 1995 also saw the publication of a collection of stories, *Skinned Alive* (London: Chatto and Windus, 1995; New York: Knopf, 1995), including those from *The Darker Proof.*

The Farewell Symphony (London: Chatto and Windus, 1997; New York: Knopf, 1997) marked White's completion of the "autofictional" trilogy he began with *A Boy's Own Story* and *The Beautiful Room Is Empty*. *The Farewell Symphony* dealt in fictional form with the sexual hedonism of New York in the late seventies, and the loss of many of White's acquaintances to AIDS during the 1980s.

White has recently published a small biography of *Proust* (New York/London: Viking, 1999) and completed a novel, *The Married Man* (New York: Knopf, 2000; London: Chatto and Windus, 2000). He lives in the Chelsea area of New York City and teaches at Princeton University, having previously taught at Yale, Columbia, Johns Hopkins, New York, and Brown universities. Among other positions, White was executive director of the New York Institute for the Humanities between 1981 and 1983. In 1983, White received a Guggenheim Fellowship and the Award for Literature from the National Academy of Arts and

Letters. In the same year, White moved to Paris, where he spent most of his time until 1998, when he returned to New York. In 1993 he was made a Chevalier de l'Ordre des Arts et Lettres. He has also been a judge for Britain's Booker Prize.

This interview took place on Saturday, April 25, 1998, in Princeton, New Jersey.

RC   In *The Farewell Symphony* you describe Paris as a "middle-aged town," "ideal for someone of a certain age." You've just decided to move back to New York.

EW   Well, Chelsea, where we're going to buy a flat, isn't at all a young person's place. Everyone seems to be thirty.

I never said I wanted to live in a middle-aged city. I was just characterizing Paris. I didn't find it especially congenial for that reason. If anything, it's slightly strange to live in a city like Paris that doesn't have any youth culture. I find England, America, and even Germany, where there's a very strong youth culture, somewhat more interesting. Also, I think in England and Germany there's a working-class culture, which there isn't in America or in France—though some black culture you could say is working-class. In any event, the fact that there are all these different cultures in America makes it very vital. In France, it still hasn't gone beyond a certain saturation point. French culture tends to be very strong. Minority groups are forced to some extent to assimilate: whether you're American, Vietnamese, or from the Ivory Coast, you have to behave in a certain way in order to pass in the ordinary daily functions.

RC   You've been teaching at Princeton recently. What do you think the experience of coming back here permanently will be like? Things must have moved on.

EW   Yes. It'll be like discovering an entirely new city. All the people are different; all the behavior is different. Everything seems different. I left

New York when it was still a fairly poor city. Now it's terribly rich. Most of the time I lived in New York, you could still be a middle- or lower-middle-class person and live there. There were always apartments available. Now it seems there's nothing available. The middle class have been squeezed out. Also, gay culture—especially in places like Chelsea—is utterly triumphant and completely visible. But it seems very much a body culture; not at all a bookish culture.

RC   Gay literature now has a peculiar relationship to this gay subculture—one in which, AIDS notwithstanding, many problems seem solved. Gay life can seem perfectly straightforward in Chelsea. Key political questions from the past seem to have receded, even where they haven't necessarily been solved.

EW   I think only in certain big cities, and then only in certain regions. To me the Christian Right still seems strong. One out of every four Americans still counts him- or herself as a member of the Christian Right. I find most Europeans always underestimate the importance of religion here. Or else they'll be told about it and take it on board, then they'll forget about it. They don't realize it affects absolutely everything in America. All you have to do is flip through your fifty channels on TV. Three of them will be from the Christian Right.

RC   One point about the contemporary gay subculture that struck some writers as anomalous was the sense you've described of gay self-discovery in the past being intimately related to reading and discovering like-minded figures through fiction. To the extent that popular culture and society at large have moved on, that may not be such an elementary or necessary move now.

EW   Obviously if you're growing up in Chelsea it won't be. But if you're growing up in Evanston, Illinois, I still think you probably won't find very many films or TV programs that speak to you more than once a year—and then somewhat superficially. I think people will still need to read David Leavitt's *Family Dancing*, or my *A Boy's Own Story*, or lots of other coming-out novels. Maybe I'm vaunting my own product more than necessary, but on an impressionistic basis, an awful lot of teenagers still come up to me at readings and say: "I read your book three years ago and came out." Where else do they turn?

RC   Well, Hollywood seems prepared to have a go: *The Object of My Affection*, presumably, will play in the Midwest.

EW   Sure. But that's new. And I think most things that are made into so-called gay movies are mainly about straight people. Take *In and Out*: 99 percent of the people in it are straight. Maybe two of the characters are gay, although the main one doesn't seem too sure about that. But it's basically this whole community's response to this "problem": the sudden outing of one of their members who himself doesn't realize he's gay.

RC   You don't make it sound very progressive.

EW   Well, probably only three percent of the population is gay. If you contrast the problem of gay literature with the problem of black literature, the truth is that once white readers got past the minor barrier of color, they found themselves entire and intact in the black novel. That is, there are mothers and fathers, children and divorce, adultery and breast cancer, and all that stuff: church, sin, drinking, and wife-beating. There's a whole array of subjects they're interested in. It's all there, which isn't so in gay literature, unless it's about straight people, which is the case of *Family Dancing* or *The Object of My Affection* or Armistead Maupin's writing. If you look at the stuff that's been most popular and been made into adaptations for TV or cinema, there's always quite a large cast of straight characters. The gay character tends to be someone who forces straight people to reconsider, or who calls into question some of their assumptions.

RC   But in a "softly, softly" way. These are narratives for bourgeois liberalism.

EW I suppose. There are people who would disagree with us. For instance, the late Gene Siskel, a leading film critic in America who had a weekly television program, wanted me to be on when *In and Out* came out. He thought it was the most subversive film ever made. He said he and his wife came out of the movie saying they didn't want to be straight anymore. They felt the only attractive characters were the two gay men, and that the straight people looked so foolish and hidebound. That's something you and I would never even think of, because it would never occur to us that straight people would think it was cooler to be gay.

RC But what is meant by "being gay" in this context? It sounds like a set of material packages; a lifestyle.

EW Yes. It certainly doesn't mean having sex with a man.

RC In Paris you wrote overwhelmingly about New York and other places. Is the sense of having a contrast to your working environment important?

EW Well, now I'm writing a novel about Paris. In a way it's the next thing to write about. It's based on my relationship with Hubert, and of course that took place in both France and America.[1] But it began and ended in Paris. I always felt very much like an American in Paris, just as I feel something like a Europeanized American in America.

RC Does this book amount to an expansion of the autobiographical trilogy?

EW No. It's called *The Married Man*, and is written in the third person. I've only written about seventy-five pages, but once I started writing in

---

1. Hubert Sorin was White's partner for much of his time in Paris, and coauthor of the nonfiction *Our Paris: Sketches from Memory*. Sorin died in 1994.

the third person, I felt that the character Austin, who was ostensibly based on me, began to drift away from me and become somebody quite different. The fictional Austin is a lot less ambitious than I am. He's a freelance writer of articles, mainly about home decoration and furniture, and an expert in eighteenth-century furniture. His life revolves around a whole world of decorators and antique dealers in Paris. That's why he's there. The Hubert character "Julien" is fairly close to Hubert, although he is starting to drift too. I realize in writing this that Hubert himself was always very mysterious to me. Since the point of view is from the Austin character, it's OK that this Julien should be mysterious, because probably love is always based on finding the other person mysterious.

RC On the move to the third person: you had been trying this out in the short stories of *Skinned Alive*.

EW Yes, especially in "Palace Days," in which there's a character who was sort of based on me, but also on a friend of mine who organized gay travel events. He was a promoter of gay tourism, which AIDS brought to a screeching halt. In real life the guy would organize ships to the Caribbean and up and down the Nile. It was a continual orgy. He always talked about coming to Paris. Every month he'd call me and say: "I'm on my way." But he never came. I took that guy and enjoyed imagining him leading my life.

By the same token, when I wrote "Running on Empty," I'd been to Texas with my mother shortly before she died, and had had a lot of contact with my Texan cousins. Shortly after that, a friend of mine who was a translator from French, Matt Ward, was very ill. So I imagined what it'd be like if he'd made that trip to Texas instead of me. I was in perfectly good health, but he wasn't. Plus I knew from our friendship what his own background was like. Apparently his parents felt a lot of class resentment. He'd risen above their station through his academic prowess; now they were all saying his life had been a terrible mistake because he had the virus. So it was a story about a little virus being allowed to win the argument he'd been having with his rather bigoted parents. Again, I knew enough about Texas and had strong enough feelings about my own Texan relatives. Matt, in fact, was not from Texas but Colorado. But I was able to project his life onto mine. That kind of hybridization is something I very much enjoyed doing.

RC   Is this essentially something new for you?

EW   I think it is. When you write in the third person, you're not establishing a character through his voice, as you do in the first person. The first-person narrator is just this eye that travels over things, and if you come to know the parameters of his personality, it's partly because you learn where this eye goes. You see what he sees, and see what he's interested in looking at. If he looks at sex and cute boys a lot, then you realize he's got that on the brain. If he's looking at nature a lot, you realize he's interested in natural beauty. If he's always looking at the slightly foolish things people do, you realize he has a satirical eye. I think the "I" character in my trilogy has all three of those: an interest in the beauty of the world around us, an interest in sex, and an interest in social comedy. But you only learn that indirectly; through what he looks at. When you deal with a third-person figure, he's more of a character, in which you try to build him up through small strokes into an actual portrait of somebody. So it helps if you hybridize yourself with somebody else; that permits you to be more objective.

RC   It's a much more difficult thing to do. With the first person, you can use consciousness to describe experience cumulatively, and the way it impacts on somebody's sense of him- or herself. With the third person, you must either lean on free indirect discourse a lot, which can get clumsy, or the person has to act the process out in some way. So it's more visual.

EW   It is. And in tune with what you're saying, I'm writing very short chapters—of five or ten pages each. I have a lot more dialogue; therefore it's more scenic, in the sense of setting up scenes. The first-person technique I was mentioning works well over the long haul—if you have a long book like *The Farewell Symphony*. But in a short story it doesn't work at all, especially if the narrator has a peculiar or idiosyncratic point of view. You don't have enough space to discover it. So it's good to write about this third person, whose point of view may be the one you're constantly assimilating, but you still have the opportunity of drawing the camera back and looking at him as an object, too; as a character: summarizing his history; giving a quick sketch of his quirks, mannerisms, and so on, because you can be external from a third-person character in a way you never can from the first person.

RC Do the shorter chapters mean you're experiencing some greater degree of formal control?

EW Yes. I was engaged to write *The Farewell Symphony* by the fact that I'd written the earlier two volumes. At one point I was thinking of writing four books. I abandoned the idea of a tetralogy because I'd waited so long to do *The Farewell Symphony* that by the time I got 'round to it, I thought a third volume that ended with everybody romping around and having a great time would be intolerable to read in this post-AIDS period, just as a fourth volume which would be nothing but everybody dying would be equally intolerable. So it was partly a strategy for keeping the reader interested that made me want to write a very long, single volume that would cut back and forth from the pre-AIDS to the post-AIDS period.

The funny thing is, the actual negative reaction that the book prompted in America in certain quarters was scandal at its sexual excessiveness. That never occurred to me. Just before it went to press I said to Michael:[2] "I have terrible misgivings about this book, because formally it's such a mess. It's too long; it covers too long a period. It seems to me

---

2. Michael Carroll, writer and White's current partner.

out of control." Nobody ever objected to that in the reviews I read. So I thought: "Maybe I did solve it." Certainly I was rewriting it right up to the very last moment: trying to restructure it, simplify it. Originally I had a present tense, in which the narrator is meditating on things, that was also moving forward in time. I had a past tense moving forward in time more or less chronologically with a present tense moving forward in time. And in fact, that's more realistic, because it suggests the person is taking a year or two to write this book.

Chateaubriand was my model. In *Mémoires d'outre-tombe*, he wrote chapters very slowly. It must have taken him ten years to write that book. When he writes about having starved to death as an émigré during the [French] Revolution in London—where he'd have to suck the sheets to get the starch out of them, he was so hungry—he's writing it as the ambassador to London from France. Later, when he's living in Germany, again he's writing as the ambassador. So there's this weird parallelism. But my editor Jonathan Burnham convinced me it was too complicated; it was expecting too much of the readers, and they just wouldn't get it. He felt it would lend a lot more formal clarity if I pretended it was all being recalled in one day.

RC   One possible objection, perhaps only because of the fact that you'd flagged the period it was about, is the sense that ultimately the book doesn't say much about the experience of AIDS.

EW   I didn't want to talk about Hubert in *The Farewell Symphony*. I do talk about him in *The Married Man*. I was sincere about not wanting to get into all that yet. It was partly a formal decision, based on a subjective feeling. That book from the very beginning says: "Will I have the courage to talk about it?"; then the narrator doesn't. I think that's fair enough. There's a little bit about "Brice's" death, and a few readers were kind enough to say that they found that really scorching writing, really powerful, even though it was so minimal, compared to the rest of the book. I think sometimes very skimpy material, when strategically placed, can have a lot of weight.

That was one of the things I learned from *Moby Dick*, which actually only has enough plot to make a short story. Yet it's this great long book. Why? Because Melville was interspersing it with all these other disquisitions on other topics like ropes, boats, tackle, whaling, a lot of technical stuff. It's as though he wanted to let out this extremely powerful narrative material and didn't want to corrupt it by expanding it. He wanted it to remain very nugatory. But he wanted to lend it dignity and weight by placing it in a big book in which there's an enormous amount of delay before he gets to the next installment of the plot. That book always fascinated me, and I wondered how to do that myself. That was one of the echoes in my mind when I was planning that book.

The other book—you're going to think this is name-dropping, but it is one of my favorite books—is a book I think about a lot: *The Tale of Genji*.[3] It's a thousand-page book, which is thousands of variations on the same theme: namely, Genji and his gallant adventures. He's courting all these different ladies; going to their houses, and it's always the same ritual. It's oftentimes some lady who lives in an obscure place; her father was once a great noble, but has died. She's fallen into obscurity and lives in a twilight world where nobody ever sees her. Then Genji hears about her, exchanges letters with her, is impressed by her beautiful calligraphy, and makes a midnight sortie. He calls on her, has sex with her, then there's a great exchange of letters back and forth; then she remains in his heart the rest of his life in an abstract way: abstract in the sense that he doesn't continue oftentimes seeing her, although he imagines building a great palace and bringing together all these different ladies who have meant something to him at some time or another. It's sort of what J. Paul Getty did!

Again, that was a book that I thought gained tremendously by being a compendium of variations on the same theme. You felt there was a

3. *The Tale of Genji*: Shikibu Murasaki (978–c. 1031) was a Lady of the Japanese court and wrote *Genji Monogatari*, or *The Tale of Genji*, the world's earliest long novel.

very poetic and therefore narrow sense of reality. There are only certain occasions that seem properly poetic to Lady Murasaki and that she wanted to keep coming back to. I felt very much that way in *The Farewell Symphony*—about going out cruising, picking up somebody. Of course there aren't that many encounters in my book. There are maybe twenty, not five hundred, as there are in the *Genji*, but it still has somewhat that effect.

RC   There are several gay novels you could think of in the same way: Renaud Camus's *Tricks* especially.

EW   Yes. One of the things I admired in Renaud's book was the idea that not all the affairs were fabulous: some of the guys looked terrible; in some of the scenes he couldn't get it up. In other words, it's a record of what really happens in sex, not just what happens in some pornographic fantasy. That's why I think *Tricks* is so good; it's very realistic. When he wrote the book, he was young and very attractive himself. But he doesn't present himself that way; as a stud. He really presents himself as a fallible human being who has all of these strange encounters. Some of them work; some don't. I think that's true of my book, too. Some people think I'm too harsh on the narrator of *The Farewell Symphony*; that I take the piss out of him too much. I don't know. It is my tendency to do that.

RC   In terms of your novels, *The Married Man* is the first experiment with the third person since *Caracole*.

EW   *Caracole* was a disaster.

RC   You know it wasn't. How do you mean—in terms of ledger sheets?

EW   No—but that way surely it was. It was the worst-selling of all my books. But I think it was also a book that profoundly confused people. It has six major characters and shifts in a very pell-mell way from one point of view to the other. With this book I'm really going to stick solidly to one point of view. That will give it a lot more unity. The other thing about *Caracole* is it took place in some kind of never-never land. Depending on your taste, you either find it an amusing hybridization of Europe and America, the past and the present, Italy and France—or you find it absolutely maddening and can't identify with it.

It's like the whole question of people's tolerance for fantasy in fiction. Those who like it love it—and most people hate it. *Caracole* was my homage to one of the great failed books of all time: Nabokov's *Ada*, which has Terra and Anti-Terra. Nabokov was trying to imagine what it'd be like if there had never been the Russian Revolution, and if America and Russia had been the same country, Amerussia, and you blend their cultures together. It was a hybridization, too, and a kind of alternative version to history as we know it. I was trying to do something similar. I have said of *Caracole* that, if you were taking a course in world literature, went to sleep the night before the exam and had eaten too much Stilton and had a bad dream, then this is what would come out. It seemed to me at one and the same time this sort of compendium of European literature, with a heavy emphasis on figures like Stendhal and Proust, plus a hybridization of straight and gay America and Europe.

Plus, I was very interested in the idea of a subject people who were superior to their rulers. I was thinking of Parisians under the Nazis, or the Venetians under the Austrians, or the Chinese under the Mongols. At one point Louis Malle wanted to make *Caracole* into a movie. Over this long lunch, he was telling me about his childhood, and I said: "That's your movie!" That was *Au Revoir Les Infants*, which I think is his best work. So I convinced him not to make *Caracole* into a movie.

I think this new book will only superficially resemble *Caracole*, because it's very grounded in reality: in a very particular historical moment—the late eighties in Paris; and in the whole expatriate scene; and with AIDS, before the new treatments. Do you think there's a glut in AIDS literature, to the point that there's tremendous resistance now on the part of readers?

RC I think it's long been a problem for publishers. They don't like marketing stories about AIDS, which certainly suggests some resistance.

EW One of my fears in writing this book is that it's yet another book that'll deal with AIDS. I don't know whether the commercial curse on AIDS books is so great I'll have trouble selling it.

I'm not somebody who has ever been terribly interested in writing about the ups and downs of the illness. That, it seems to me, has been done so much. I wonder how many people it speaks to, if they haven't had the experience. For instance, if you read a story about a woman who had breast cancer, I think it could move you very deeply, but I'm not sure you'd want to follow every point of her treatment. Obviously the first gay writers who were considering AIDS wanted to be as close to it as possible. Now that seems to me probably not a good thing.

RC So what hasn't been done—the documentation of the inner life?

EW That's right. Plus, Hubert was somebody who was never totally incompetent. He was always a very competent man, who fortunately never had any kind of dementia, so until the very end he was able to handle his own case perfectly. The fact that I was an American and he was a Frenchman meant he could understand the French system of filling out those millions of forms and getting reimbursements and so on much better than I could. So I never got into it with him very much. I didn't even go that often with him to the hospital. I was working to earn a living for both of us. In France they're quite good about sending you taxis or ambulances, even when you're in perfectly fine health. They take you in charge, so I didn't really go through every detail.

Obviously when somebody dies and you love them, you always feel guilty. One of the things I feel guilty about is that I didn't do more to help Hubert. On the other hand—I didn't, so it'll be perfectly truthful to leave out all the treatment stuff. There were only for me high points and low points. There were moments where he was hospitalized. Then I went every day several times. Then there were times when he was out and in bed. I'd feed and take care of him. Otherwise we traveled an awful lot. We had quite a nice life. His brother would always say: "Our family is grateful to you"—which I found so crazy. What he meant was: "We'd never have had the money to have shown him such a good time, and he needed to compress a whole life into five years."

RC   Some reviews of *The Farewell Symphony* were concerned with the extent to which the book felt so close to lived experience that it was closer to autobiography than to fiction or the hybrid "autofiction." What's your perspective on *The Married Man*, in acknowledging that the "Austin" figure is drifting away from you? Does the kind of book that's written matter to you?

EW   It does. But I'm always thinking more about readers. If there's one kind of criticism that makes sense to me, it's reader-response theory. It's about the only one I ever think about when I'm writing. When I read other kinds of criticism—postmodernist or whatever—I think: "Oh, that's true; that's interesting; why not?" But it never seems to reflect anything that would go on in my mind when I'm actually writing. Whereas what does go on in my mind at a theoretical level—to the degree that I ever think about theory—is a constant concern about how this is going to affect the reader. Then of course you say: "Which reader?" There's that whole question of the ideal reader.

I feel the writer is always modeling a kind of reader as a sort of averaging out of the people he knows and the people he wants to address. In other words, it isn't just a mathematical average of all the people he's ever met, because I think that would lower the tone in a way. You'd be writing down to people you'd happen to have met, many of whom don't like literature or don't even read. But you make a compendium of all the various people who have written you letters, of the reviews you've read that are intelligent, whether negative or positive. You're constantly responding to that.

So one of the things that enters into my considerations when I'm planning a book is that I don't really want to write about a well-known writer who, though not rich, was sufficiently at ease financially that he was able to do what he wanted and travel around as he wanted—because how many people would ever be able to identify with that? Just as the boy in *A Boy's Own Story* I made a little less precocious than I was, both sexually and intellectually. I dumbed him down in the interests of making him easy for people to identify with. Even so, especially in England, people are always complaining in reviews that my characters all lead this glamorous life, and that they're seen as inaccessible. The character I've chosen in "Austin" is sort of lazy; not terribly ambitious—like one of those expatriates who really was a misfit in his own country and has gone abroad partly for that reason—which I find is the usual expatriate—and who doesn't have that much money. Their struggle is partly a financial one to survive.

RC   The way you describe the importance of the reader's reaction to a given situation made me think of the dramatist's conception of character and audience. There's this triangle, with you, the author, and the two figures you have in mind. The hybrid figure of the reader you're describing is essentially a character; then there's your other "staged" character. You're looking at the relationship between these two, rather as a dramatist must; that is, you think of fiction in a dramatic way.

EW   That's very interesting. I think you're absolutely right. But if that's the case, I think a novel like *The Farewell Symphony* is like an extended dramatic monologue, because it isn't really built up in scenes very much. They're often half-scenes, quarter-scenes; not terribly developed. I think people who really start with drama as their template when they're writing fiction—where that's all they've ever thought about fiction—have a lot of dialogue, and scenes of about the same length. They tend to have rather complex scenes in which they try to sweep up all the leaves of everyday life and get them into one big scene. They also tend to believe in things I don't—like turning points in life, or recognition scenes, or denouements.

RC   Isn't there an uncanny relationship between the short story and the play? [American writer] Jim Grimsley said he found the ideas that used to occur to him as short stories he now uses in plays. Tennessee Williams literally worked out of one form into the other. And these turning points and so on you mention do resemble the "epiphanies" of shorter fiction like Joyce's. The nearest your work comes to that is in a story like "An Oracle."

EW   Yes. You've put your finger on something which is true in a complex way in my work. I did start off mainly as a playwright. I was very interested in theater for years and years. I wrote fifteen plays—all but two unproduced. It's certainly something I worried and thought about constantly. When I came back to fiction, it was certainly with a lot of frustrated and failed training. But one of the things that interested me was how fiction was different from theater. It seemed to me that theater was based on a number of lies—like the lie that action always reveals character.

RC   People like Fitzgerald relied on that.

EW   Sure they did. But I don't think it's accurate. Both Hemingway and Fitzgerald would have thought that if, in a moment of great challenge, you turned out to be a physical coward, that says something definitive about you. But I'd say: "Wait a minute, if you've never been faced with somebody crazed and with a gun in his hand before, it's hardly likely you'll have a reasoned position to take there." You'll probably just squeal like a ninny and run away, because you've never thought about the situation before. Anyway, is physical courage in the face of a madman with a gun a very healthy or realistic response? And who wants to prove you're this macho superman who can face a bullet and die bravely, when you could go on living another fifty years if you just were cowardly for a moment?

RC Now I hear the voice of George Eliot the moralist. You're looking at fiction in terms of ethics.

EW Only moralistic in this sense: I oftentimes say to my students: "It's perfectly all right to write an all-dialogue novel. But do you really think the most interesting exchanges between people or the most interesting moments in your own mental life have been based on speech?" Do people actually say the truth when they talk, or are they as Elizabeth Bowen believed they were—either deceiving themselves or deceiving other people? It's a very cynical position, but one you could defend. I also feel there are certain other dangerous ideas: that there's a unitary character; that we have a character that's revealed through how we behave in something like a crisis; that childhood is the template for our later behavior; that sexuality is even more important than childhood, and so on. These are ideas I haven't elaborated explicitly, but when I was writing the Genet book, I was very against this totalizing view of the self. I didn't want to find the clue to his personality. I wanted to show him as somebody who probably transformed himself more than almost anybody I can think of. Genet goes from being this cunning peasant boy in the Morvan, to being a juvenile delinquent, to being a thief, to being a great writer, to ending up as somebody with broad humanitarian concerns for other groups of people, like the Black Panthers and the Palestinians. Obviously there's a continuity in his life, but to get from point A to point Z seemed to me very hard to do if you only looked at A. You couldn't have predicted Z from A; you could only move the way Wittgenstein talks about overlapping definitions as a way of looking at the word *game*. Wittgenstein says if you take that word, any one definition might suit meaning A, or any other might suit meaning Z, but there are all these other meanings in between, and there's no single one that would include all of those meanings. You have to see them as a series of overlapping circles.

I think in the same way the self can be a series of overlapping circles. The boy in *A Boy's Own Story* obviously has some of the same preoccupations as the grown man at the end of *The Farewell Symphony*—but not that many. You can see a continuity. It's not like there is a radical rupture from one book to another, or from one chapter to another, but there's not a predictable trajectory.

RC   When you spoke of the objection to dialogue as deceitful, somebody like Ronald Firbank sprang to mind. He is somebody who seized on precisely what you described as the dramatic possibilities of dialogue; yet he refuses this will-to-truth you spoke against and produces something absurd.

EW   Yes, but his dialogue is very unusual. He, Ivy Compton-Burnett, and an American writer called W. M. Spackman are the only three writers I can think of who write unrealistic dialogue. When other writers get to writing dialogue, no matter how experimental or unrealistic they might present themselves as being elsewhere, it's always coffee-cup realism.

Nabokov recommended that a writer not use any dialogue in the first thirty or forty pages of a novel. He thought it very important that the writer impose his own tone of voice and point of view before handing it over to all these characters, who necessarily would talk in a realistic—that is, banal—way. I think Firbank, because he wrote in this terribly arch, mannered way, treated almost every line as poetry. It's no accident that people like John Ashbery are fascinated by Firbank, and that other poets have turned to him—or that conscious, artistic writers like Alan Hollinghurst have turned to him too. Although I don't see Hollinghurst as a development out of Firbank, it's no accident that he's fascinated by him.

RC   I wanted to return to *Caracole* and your use of the word "disaster." You described it as concerning history. Yet elsewhere you've objected to the Tolstoyan idea of the novelist as chronicler of history. You came up with an opposite understanding of the novelist: as an archivist of gossip, say. Instead of describing *Caracole* in terms of history, then, can't we take it as a kind of absurd or fantastic retake on a trope which is common to all your early novels: the presumption or assumption of innocence or blankness in an individual at the very moment he is inducted into some climate of experience or adulthood.

EW Yes. That's true of all my books.

RC You're remembered in the most celebrated books for this direct and personal account of experience. *Caracole* feels like another writing self, wreaking a kind of vengeance on that material. It's a fascinating book— and one that will last. *Caracole* is the book for which the time isn't right. You've spoken candidly of the ways in which your other books found their moment—which isn't to diminish them, but to contextualize their success. There's the same potential for *Caracole*, too, so I'm intrigued by your use of the word "disaster."

EW Well, I hope I'm wrong. I remember being very wounded by the reception among publishers of a book that never got published, called "Like People in History" or "Woman Reading Pascal." At that time, my psychotherapist Charles Silverstein said: "Well, you mustn't really like it that much yourself, or you wouldn't be suffering that much. I think when you finish a book in the future, you need to ask yourself before it goes out, before anybody else looks at it, whether you're satisfied with it; whether you think it's actually good; whether it's the best you can do. If it is, then fuck it. That's all you can do."

I remember thinking about that when I finished *Caracole*. I thought: "This is a book I've labored on long and lovingly. Every detail seems to me burnished or high-finished. Maybe there'll be people who'll dislike the whole conception—and there were plenty—but I think that, within its terms, it is one that is realized." Its terms are very peculiar, and mostly invented by me. It's not like they were preestablished. I remember in Germany, people hated it. They thought it was like Thomas

Mann; "Weltkulturliteratur," or something. There was something repellent for them about that. They wanted something like David Leavitt: short, minimalist, modern, and contemporary.

RC   Something more transparently written would also be easier to translate.

EW   That's right, whereas with *Caracole*, somebody said it was the most European of all American novels.

RC   Was it not also the work that took the most energy and time? It reads as it if must have done.

EW   Definitely. I found a kind of release in writing it, too, because when you write a first-person autobiographical narrative, you're obliged to be the first person, not really the other people. In other words, you're writing about your own experience, and if you can get in touch with your own feelings; if you can recall them well enough, that's what you're feeling, and it's a pretty simple, one-track story. If you're writing a novel like *Caracole*, you have the possibility of dramatizing your inner conflicts and distributing them over six characters, so in a way you're all of them. That must be the kind of pleasure that real novelists like Dickens had, where he'd whip up characters—or Balzac, who would enter into states of hallucination and not even remember he was writing. He'd take dictation from the people. There was something of that. I really felt that I was Matilda; I was Angelica. I wasn't confined to one person, since there was no first-person point of view.

RC   In *The Farewell Symphony*, you revisit the critical burying of *Caracole* in fictional form; the figure who objects to it, however, is heavily disguised—as a man.

EW   You're talking about Susan Sontag? That's right.

RC So you retell that story in fictional form. Yet *The Farewell Symphony* also risks causing the same offence that the modeling of people in *Caracole* caused to some you knew. Some of the people in it are dead, but there are less disguised portraits of living people—one of whom, Alfred Corn, got to review it and didn't like the portrayal of himself. So there's a peculiar parallel between *Caracole* and *The Farewell Symphony*.

EW Definitely. I was very content that *The Farewell Symphony* came out in England first. It seemed to me that there it got a laboratory-pure reading, in the sense that even though some people liked it, some hated it, and there was a whole gamut of opinion, nevertheless nobody was too concerned about it as a roman à clef. My own feeling is that a real roman à clef is one you don't even enjoy unless you know who the originals are, because the characters tend not to be very well-rendered on the page, whereas I pride myself on having created characters who might interest the reader even if he or she never suspected there was an original. Plus I think a real roman à clef tends to rely upon famous originals, whereas the people I wrote about were people who had some local celebrity, maybe, but who aren't really internationally famous.

RC You got that negative review by Alfred Corn.

EW Yes. I never read it. I don't tend to read bad reviews. But he had given a bad review to my stories in *The Nation*, and I'd been irritated with him. I said to Alfred: "We're old friends. Usually friends don't review each other, but if they do, it's usually because they want to give a good review to each other. Your negative review is the only bad review *Skinned Alive* got in America. It seems odd to me that it should have come from a friend." He wrote back a perfectly hateful letter all about how I was the one who'd had a glorious career, and how he'd had to suffer and been neglected by everybody. So then I said: "Don't worry about it. I don't care. Now it gives me the freedom to say anything I want to in my new book."

I was a little shocked that *The Nation* asked the same person to review me again. Apparently in the review, he actually reveals he knows me, and that he's a character in the book. That seems so peculiar to me, the whole thing, particularly as I'd recently given a large piece to *The Nation*, which was the speech I had given on "AIDS and Literature" at the Key West Literary Seminar.[4] That was just before Alfred's review came out.

Then, of course, the Larry Kramer response was of a different sort—again, though, from a friend. Who needs enemies with friends like that?

RC   That received a lot of coverage. In the case of Kramer's attack, you turned on him. It's the first time you've turned on strongly hostile reaction like that. It felt uncharacteristic of you.

EW   It is. But it was also the lowest blow. Alan Hollinghurst and Adam Mars-Jones gave negative reviews to *A Boy's Own Story*. I've read those reviews, but they didn't bother me, and I actually sought them out as friends, because they were perfectly defensible positions. They expressed them well and had lots of reasons. Also, they didn't know me when they reviewed the book. They had no axe to grind, one way or another. With Larry, I think he's a pathetically bad writer, so I just found it ludicrous that he'd even be given a forum to deliver himself of an opinion about my writing.

RC   You've commented elsewhere on the possibility of being guilty to some extent of perpetuating a cult of the gay novelist as public figure, which is interesting. It put me in mind of the objection in Gore Vidal's *Screening History* to the very idea of the novelist as public figure in a cinematic age.

EW   Maybe in minority groups writers have a certain celebrity. Toni Morrison is really a huge figure in the black community. She teaches

---

4. White is speaking of "Journals of the Plague Years," in *The Nation*, May 12, 1997, 13–18.

here and I know her. I went to a very moving party given for her the
other day. It was all black people, except for me and a couple of others.
They were all saying the kinds of things gay people are always saying at
their literary reunions: "Who'd ever have thought that some day a black
woman—of all things—would be on the cover of *Newsweek*, or would
win the Nobel Prize?"

RC   The gay people say: "Who would ever have thought *he* would
achieve such-and-such . . ."

EW   Well, that's true. There's more resentment, maybe, within the
gay community. Maybe there is in the black community, too, for all
we know.

RC   When you said it was surprising that Kramer should have found a
forum for his ideas, they're ideas deeply removed from literature or aesthetics. I was wondering whether this cult of the figure of the author
might point to some more general movement in culture towards reifying
experience as the fount of creativity: in the current dominance of the
memoir form, for instance.

EW   There's a peculiar American variety of that, which is that the
celebrity is celebrated for being celebrated.

RC   In terms of literature, we're in an awkward climate, in that aesthetic
criteria seem very unimportant—in gay contexts and elsewhere. I was
thinking of the way the author as public figure is invited onto a talk
show to attest to the "truth" of the fictional account he or she gave in a
novel. By contrast, the imagination is distrusted.

EW   That's right. People just become vexed when you tell them: "This
isn't a hundred percent my life." People will review, as Larry Kramer
did, a book as though it were exactly true.

What's interesting is that this has shifted. When *A Boy's Own Story* came out, nobody dared to ask: "Is this really your life, or is this a novel?" They respected the word on the cover: "novel." There was a whole convention in that period—which had always existed, I suppose—that if somebody called it a novel, it was a novel. People would always say: "Your hero says such-and-such." But by the time *The Farewell Symphony* came out, things had shifted so much people would now say: "You got fucked a lot, didn't you?"

There's a technical aspect to the talk show we should mention, which is that even if the interviewer is an intelligent person who reads fiction for its imaginative pleasures, it's almost impossible to talk about the art of fiction in the format of television. Last night, quite an excellent gay poet, Frank Bedard, came up to me. Instead of saying, "Your short story or novel I loved," he said: "Your interview with Terry Gross, in which you talked about Hubert's death, was the most moving thing I have ever heard." He said: "That was the best talk show I've ever heard." It was interesting to me that a talk show now is almost an aesthetic form in itself. A woman said to me: "I heard you on Terry Gross, and I was sobbing, because my father was dying and I was taking care of him at the same time that you were talking about the trials and tribulations of taking care of your lover. I went out and bought your book. I've never had time to read it, but I did buy it." That's very characteristic.

RC   Now something connected to this sense of the writer as public figure. You introduced the question of *A Boy's Own Story* and its fictionality. That book is perplexing because of the ease with which it was accepted by a wide readership. Robert Glück's article touches on this question: how can the presentation of such a dysfunctional state of affairs easily come to embody anything universal?[5]

---

5. Robert Glück, "*A Boy's Own Story*," *Review of Contemporary Fiction* 13.3 (Fall 1996): "Edmund White, Samuel R. Delany," 56–60.

EW Yes. My own feeling is that there was an empty ecological niche at that time. People were looking for a "coming-out" novel. Now it's such a cliché that an editor would yawn if you presented him with another "coming-out" novel.

RC The odd thing, given its content, is that *A Boy's Own Story* becomes one of a group of books referred to with pride in terms of an emerging tradition of portraying homosexuality normatively.

EW But I think a lot of people haven't really read it.

RC It's a shameful book: the book is, among other things, deeply concerned with shame.
EW Sure it is—which is probably what's universal about it. The universal thing about being gay is that you're ashamed of it. In other words, we live in a shame culture; one that uses shame and guilt as one of its main policing devices.

I think gays are made to feel guilty not just about being homosexual but about being sexual. It's the fact we insist on our sexuality that's already the disgusting point for most people. They have abnegated their sexuality in the interests of career, marriage, dinner, or gardening. So many adults have entombed their sexuality in these enormous, corpulent bodies—especially in America—that they just don't have sex. I really think that's the dirty little secret of heterosexual marriage: that there's nothing going on. Gays are resented and detested partly because they're always presenting their sexuality and staking themselves on that.

RC The marketing of *A Boy's Own Story*, too, contributed to its reception. You have to wait till the end of the next volume for the "I" figure to be on the threshold of self-acceptance, and in a position where beauty itself may finally be in reach, as well as political liberation. That casts an interesting shadow over *A Boy's Own Story*'s appearance—including the notorious cover photo.

EW Sure. Because who did that look like? It doesn't look like the hero, who describes himself as funny-looking. Mind you, I gave cover approval for that. I was very excited about it, though it cost us a fortune because the boy who was pictured sued and won a million dollars. It's an interesting story, because so many gay men will oftentimes come up and say: "I've always been in love with that person. Could you tell me who he is? Can I meet him? Could you give me his address?" I say: "I don't think you want his address because he's a horrible pig. Even though you've been mooning over him for twenty years, it turns out you were on the wrong track."

The truth is he was a boy walking down the beach in Cape Canaveral about the time of a launch. A photographer came up to him and said: "May I take your picture?" "Yes." "Would you sign this release saying you're over eighteen?" "Yes." "Will you accept this check for three hundred dollars?" "Yes." "Do you realize I do book covers, and you might end up on one?" "Yes." "Do you understand I don't necessarily know which book it might be?" "Yes."

So far, so good. The book came out. Dutton wasn't a rich publisher, but when it went into paperback, that publisher was, at that point, part of a greater company that was rich. So, about four years after the book came out, the boy's father, a rich real estate developer in Coral Gables, Florida, decided to take it to court, saying the boy had been fourteen, not eighteen—though he looks quite old in the picture—and that his life had been destroyed, although we found out that only three or four copies of the book had been sold in his area. It was settled out of court for a huge sum—I think a million dollars.

I was living in Europe at the time. My poor editor, Bill Whitehead, had to go down and testify. It was one of the last things he did; he was so ill he died soon after. The idea he'd have to waste his last month or two in this idiotic trial with this greedy pig seemed to me so stupid. In any event, I felt as if we all had more energy—if I'd been in the States, and we'd all been courageous and idealistic—the real battle to be fought would have been to say: "Why should being considered gay ruin your life?" That's what he was claiming.

RC   Your books are often caught up in the tortuous relationship between art and life—particularly as understood by the law.

EW   Yes. It's true that there are about a hundred and sixty minor changes in *The Farewell Symphony* in the American version from the English version. They were all legal. One of the reasons the changes were made was they didn't want me to imply anyone was gay. You can be taken to court for saying somebody's gay, even if they are—unless you have absolute proof of it—or better, consent from them.

RC   One incident you took out had caused a big reaction in British reviews: where you drunkenly fuck someone, knowing you're HIV-positive.

EW   I think I was cowardly. Americans are so puritanical—little did I realize to what degree. I thought: "I just can't face going on the road for three weeks having to defend that"—not that I do defend it, even in the book; nor would I. But I felt bad later, because a number of people said to me: "Oh, I'd read the English version and I did that once. I felt you were the only person who ever had the courage to talk for all of us who are positive and have had unsafe sex knowingly without telling our partners." It's one of the dirty little secrets of gay life, and no one has ever addressed it, admitted to it, or done anything about it. Anyway, I lost my nerve too.

RC   I wanted to talk about the unpublished novel you mentioned earlier: "Like People in History" or "Woman Reading Pascal." It would've come between *Forgetting Elena* and *Nocturnes for the King of Naples*. You've now deposited versions of it along with all your papers at the

Beinecke Library at Yale. I know you've long felt that, of all your unpublished work, this is the novel you wouldn't mind being published after your death.

It wasn't what I expected at all. Looking back over your own accounts of your career, a seamlessness is suggested, because it's quite easy for you to talk about the first two books in relation to one another—as to some extent similar literary experiments. But effectively in the middle, there is this very different book: written in the third person; at the "Isherwood" end of your writing style, as opposed to the Nabokovian strain that predominates in the two novels published around it.

EW Yes, it was very realistic. David Bergman, my literary executor, went up to read it and was very enthusiastic. Then Richard Howard begged him not to publish it until he was dead too. So David thought that made sense, although I think my portrait of Richard is flattering in "Like People in History." Also, it's mostly a portrait of me; the "Dan" character seems to me much more me than Richard. I haven't read it in fifteen years.

RC It's interesting stylistically.

EW Well, if you'd ever read the original *The Beautiful Room Is Empty*, it was very simple in its writing and very realistic too. I think the one off in this regard was *Forgetting Elena*. When "Like People in History" went around twenty-two publishers and was rejected by everybody, it was probably the single most painful moment in my life. If it was painful before to have all my novels rejected, at least when I finally had one accepted—*Forgetting Elena*—I thought then I was on Easy Street. The idea that I was back to ground zero—that the next one couldn't get published either—made me wild with desperation. So I think *Nocturnes* was a return not to the style of *Forgetting Elena* exactly, but at least to the level of experimentation. It avoided gay sub-

ject matter in the form I found was most obnoxious to people, which
was middle-class gay life. *Nocturnes* is a very dreamy, poetic book, in
which homosexuality is confused with longing for the father or God.
It's a sort of devotional book—one that certainly wouldn't disturb a
nice middle-class heterosexual man or woman. They wouldn't say:
"Oh, too many cocks and balls in this!" Nor would they say: "This is
too close for comfort," because it's not close to anybody, except in
some poetic way.

RC   Another exceptional element in "Like People in History" is that it's
very funny. Humor has come to be central to your books, but isn't so
much in the first two. Why do you think it emerged in this spare, more
social, accessible style?

EW   I think "social" is the key. My humor has always been social comedy
of an almost Jane Austen-like sort. I like gentle satire about the self and
others. A lot of it comes out of the personality of Marilyn Schaefer [lit-
erary agent and close friend], somebody who has influenced me as much
as anyone. She is the "Maria" in all my books, and plays a very prominent role in "Like People in History." She constantly saw us all in a
humorous light. She was always taking the piss out of herself and everybody in her circle and had this gently satiric view.

One of her favorite books is *Cranford* by Mrs. Gaskell. We'd read
that and giggle; that whole way of treating a little, closed world as
slightly absurd, which is also affectionate. That was a note she
sounded for me. She'd find books and give them to me to read and
find humor in. I think I was so under her spell that she shaped my sensibility quite a bit.

RC   You've divided the books that have appeared into two types: the fan-
tastic/experimental tradition versus the more realist tradition. On a
basic level, the realist tradition won through after *Caracole*. *The Farewell
Symphony*, I thought, however, was interesting in the extent to which

this other, fantastic tradition reemerges. As the third part of the trilogy, it felt as if the book was pushing stylistically quite hard away from the first two; also, in terms of its moralism. Among other things, *The Farewell Symphony* is deeply engaged with morals. Is that an appealing description to you?

EW   It definitely is. For one thing, once you get older and more conscious in your own life, you become more reflective. So if there's an evolution in the style of the books, it's partly reflecting the evolution of the man I'm writing about. It seems to me that once you're in your thirties and forties, and have to deal with questions such as how you treat lovers, how you deal with AIDS, even the opposing claims of love and friendship—all these things are aspects of a life that's entirely chosen.

Descartes said everyone should leave his or her country and move to some other country because by doing so, you invent a life that's entirely chosen; you haven't inherited any part of it. Being an expatriate means having an entirely voluntary life. It means replacing family with friends. All your associations are ones you've actively chosen. I think in a life you've chosen, the life of the expatriate, you are morally accountable for every part of it in a way that's even more vivid to you than it would have been otherwise.

RC   You've written about the way recognizing you are gay means having to make a near-infinite number of choices about how to construct yourself and your life, which sounds similar. So it would seem obvious that the moralist tradition would be a big one within gay literature—but I'm not sure it is.

EW   I don't think it is. I always feel that what a lot of gay writers want to do is normalize—even trivialize—the experience. It would be like treating AIDS from the Monty Python point of view if you were English. There'd be something disgusting about it. I feel that AIDS is a rupture in meaning; a hemorrhage, an outrage—something that no matter how hard you try, you can hardly describe how it took everyone by surprise and reversed all their values. It was a scandal. To try to domesticate it and make it humorous, and to show that Mother Camp is once more up to all this . . .

RC   This is the same controversial position you adopted in the essay "Esthetics and Loss."[6] I thought you'd since modified your views on literature and AIDS.

EW   Well, I have, only in the sense that I think humor of an absurdist sort is suitable now. I was too broad in that essay. But the basic feeling behind it I still embrace: the idea that you shouldn't be on cozy terms with your own experience—ever. The idea of some gay man referring to some phenomenon of his immediate world and saying: "Well, he was a typical Chelsea kind of guy." What is that going to mean to anybody in England?

One of the benefits of living internationally is you realize how these odd references to things don't carry very far; just as, if you're American but speaking French all the time, you learn to cut out all the parentheses, ironies, and all the whirligig of meanings, because you're just struggling to get the primary meaning through. In the same way, I think that begins to influence your own effort to communicate in fiction too. For me, living abroad and in another language has simplified my English quite a bit. It's made me use fewer of those inside references that are strictly culture-bound.

RC   What's the relationship between reading and writing for you?

---

6. "Esthetics and Loss" was first published in *Artforum* (January 1987); reprinted in John Preston, ed., *Personal Dispatches: Writers Confront AIDS* (New York: St. Martin's, 1989), 145–52, and in White's *The Burning Library: Writings on Art, Politics, and Sexuality, 1969–93*, 211–17.

EW   One of the writers I keep coming back to is Colette. I feel she's one of the most underrated writers, though I suppose that's because her books don't amount to much unless you read them all as chapters of one novel. If you do that, your fascination with this persona she's creating— with "Colette"—can sustain you, sort of the way Jean Rhys does, book by book. But she's a more interesting writer than Jean Rhys.

Colette has the largest vocabulary in French, because she's always describing the natural world with enormous precision. She also has a marvelous feel for the sensuality of male bodies—and female bodies— and an awareness of all the cross-grained complexity of every erotic occasion. She renders that beautifully. She seems to be this graceful raconteur; but buried in the midst of all that stylish attitudinizing is a very precise—almost Elizabeth Bishop-precise—view of the body, of sex, of other sensuous moments: the appeal of furs, cars, cats, of food. She's great on food.

RC   Is fiction your first love and duty in reading?

EW   Well, I read Colette when I feel like I am getting dry. It feels to me like I'm filling up the cisterns. I often get ideas about books from books. For instance, one of my favorite writers is a Uruguayan called Juan Carlos Onetti. Nobody has ever heard of him, but he's actually one of the greatest writers of all time. He's very well known in France, where all of his books are published by Gallimard. In English, it's catch-as-catch-can.

Onetti came before the Latin American boom writers. He doesn't write in magic realism at all. It's kind of "film noir" writing, but tends to be very beautiful and philosophical. In a novel called *Bodysnatcher*, he has this incredible situation of a woman, about thirty-nine, who was madly in love with this guy and married him. He dies, and he has a sixteen-year-old brother whom she takes up with. She's really mad; half-mad with grief. I thought: now there's something I could write. I could make a whole novel out of that one incident in this book.

Oftentimes I'll start vibrating to a situation I find in a novel that appeals to me—as a fantasy, perhaps. Or in real life, sometimes, situations will strike me. For instance, in America there was this big case concerning a woman in her thirties who fell in love with this twelve-year-old boy. I'm dying to do something with it. Matthew Stadler has been researching the story for an article. I want him to collaborate with me in doing a film script. We proposed it to Gus Van Sant, but he felt he'd covered that kind of material in *To Die For*.

RC   Are you going to pursue it?

EW   As a film-script idea, yes. Or it could eventually end up as a book or short story for me.

I think I have a kind of pedophilia I've gratefully always held in check; not ever acted on—or not since I myself was a boy. You see it even in the first chapter of *A Boy's Own Story*—this thrill at the pubescent body. Luckily I don't do anything about that. But I certainly would enjoy writing about it. It would be a thrilling fantasy. Anyway, the *Romeo and Juliet* aspect to their love story appeals to me a lot.

RC   Tell me finally about the little book you've written on Proust.

EW   It is kicking off a whole series of short, hundred-page biographies Viking Penguin are doing in the States. Proust actually had a very uneventful life, so it's strange that almost all of the books about him are as long as his own. Mainly he was in bed writing, and suffering terribly from asthma. That's not made up.

What I do is concentrate on the gay aspect of Proust, which nobody has really done very much. One excellent book called *Proust and the Art of Love* does go into it.[7] Proust is a man who told André Gide he never

---

7. J. E. Rivers, *Proust and the Art of Love: The Aesthetics of Sexuality in the Life, Times, and Art of Marcel Proust* (New York: Columbia University Press, 1980).

had sex with a woman. It's so obvious that a lot of the female characters—especially the primary one, Albertine—are based on men, or on several men, in fact. There are all these weird strategies Proust gets himself into because of the transposition. There's what I call "literary lesbianism"—in other words, if you're writing about a heterosexual man you're in love with, and that man cheats on you, his gay lover, by having an affair with a woman, then you have to present him as a lesbian. I find this literary lesbianism completely wide of the mark as far as any realistic description of lesbianism, but it's Proust's way of talking about heterosexuality.

RC   Did you come to feel a greater sense of affinity with Proust, compared to Genet?

EW   Definitely. Proust is one of the great companions as a narrator. You love being in his company. He has a way of normalizing, generalizing, and universalizing everything, whereas, as Gaetan Picon wrote in a brilliant essay on Genet in 1947, he was the only great writer who wasn't universal. When you read Genet, you're aware what a nut he is. He's doing everything to make his experience seem unrepresentative. Even though he was inspired directly by reading Proust, nevertheless Genet came up with something extremely different. In this very prickly way Genet has, he was always insisting on his difference, and that he was elusive and not understandable. Proust, however, universalizes: if he was actually half-Jewish, in the book he was entirely Catholic; if in real life he fought with his parents all the time, in the book he has a pious respect for his parents. If he was gay in real life, he's virtually the only person who is a hundred percent straight in the book. After he died, a lot of books congratulated Proust for his bravery in dealing with this terrible gay subject matter!

One of the things I found was that I felt it was precisely at the points where he had to disguise his sexuality that Proust was at his most creative. I know that sounds as if I'm saying people should all go back into the closet. I think it's too late for that, and that there's been a different kind of energy released by people coming out of the closet. But in his case, it's undeniable that the creative part—the part that wasn't just mimetic but actually imaginative—was about working up all these disguises. It's just like those men my age who are gay. In the fifties, we all had to hide the fact we were gay, so we were endlessly inventing girlfriends, or transposing in the midst of a conversation. If you wanted to talk about going out with Richard, you'd have to say: "I have this girlfriend, Rickie." You'd have to make it a name close enough to the real one, or else you'd forget it the next time people asked: "How's Rickie?"

RC   You've anticipated a good closing question: whether gay liberation might have been bad for gay culture. Is gay culture, in the broadest sense, exhausted? Is there a chance that the material's no longer there; it's been mapped; the disguise's no longer necessary; the subterfuge, the invention doesn't need to be there?

EW   Well, I think even sociologically there are a lot of worlds to be described. Take Lee Williams's *After Nirvana*: that's a world that hasn't been described yet, that I know of.[8] There'll always be that—these hybrid things: gay and Mexican; lesbian and French-Canadian. There'll be all those books to write. In general, though, I think you're right. It *is* exhausting itself, though it seems to me there are some things that will still be interesting to describe—among them, negative pictures of gay life.

RC   Pedophilia remains less mapped.

EW   Yes. One of the great gay novels of the last thirty years is Terry Andrews's *The Story of Harold* [1974]. Nobody knows it. That's an out-

---

8. Lee Williams's *After Nirvana* (New York, 1997) is a novel describing the world of drugged-out street kids in Oregon.

rageous book on that subject—very scary, scandalous, and beautiful. A real transgressive book.

RC   And formally very inventive.

EW   Yes, because of the playing off of the passages from the children's book, and the relationship of the little boy with the masochist. It's all intertwined. Andrews shows there are links between these areas—some of them so transgressive; some, perfectly normal and even considered gooily sweet—like an older man taking an interest in a sad little boy in a big brother way. The fact that that can be linked to these other areas of horror is fascinating.

RC   On that note, thanks very much for your time.

FOUR

ANDREW HOLLERAN

"Andrew Holleran" is still best known for his first published novel, 1978's *Dancer from the Dance*. Born in 1944, Holleran studied at Harvard, went to Germany with the U.S. Army, and began to study law. He abandoned this in order to attend the creative writing course at the University of Iowa. In 1971, Holleran's first story, "The Holy Family," appeared in the *New Yorker*. In the same year, Holleran moved to New York, where he contributed regularly to the gay literary magazine *Christopher Street* and was a member of the "Violet Quill" group of gay writers from 1979 to 1981, alongside Felice Picano and Edmund White.

In 1978, *Dancer from the Dance* (New York: Morrow, 1978) was published. An evocative, poignant study of the culture of sexual hedonism in New York in the seventies, and equally of the gay generation which came before it, *Dancer from the Dance* was immediately acclaimed and has had continued commercial success. It was followed five years later by *Nights in Aruba* (New York: Morrow, 1983) and, after a protracted interlude, by Holleran's most recent novel, *The Beauty of Men* (New York: Morrow, 1996), which addresses questions of aging, ageism, and mortality in gay culture in the context of AIDS. Between these works, a selection of Holleran's essays on AIDS for *Christopher Street* magazine appeared as *Ground Zero* (New York: Morrow, 1988).

Throughout the 1980s and 1990s, Holleran's stories appeared in many places, such as George Stambolian, ed., *Men on Men*

(New York: Plume, 1986) and *Men on Men 3* (New York: Plume, 1990); Edmund White, ed., *Faber Book of Gay Short Fiction* (London: Faber and Faber, 1991); Peter Burton, ed., *Mammoth Book of Gay Short Stories* (London: Robinson, 1997); and David Bergman, ed., *The Violet Quill Reader* (New York: St. Martin's, 1994) and *Men on Men 7* (New York: Plume, 1998). His essays have been published in such places as John Preston, ed., *Hometowns* (New York: Dutton, 1991), and Clifford Chase, ed., *Queer 13* (New York: Morrow, 1998).

Andrew Holleran's most recent publication is a collection of short stories—most of them new—entitled *In September, the Light Changes* (New York: Hyperion, 1999). Holleran lives in northern Florida, where this interview took place on Friday, November 14, 1997.

RC You're currently working on a collection of short stories. Could you gloss the move from novels to stories?

AH I started out writing short stories. I spent ten years sending them to magazines. The first thing I ever published—and what kept me going—was when the *New Yorker* accepted a story of mine, "The Holy Family," in 1971. I was in the army. When I got the acceptance I was so overjoyed, because it's terrible when you want to be a writer and you're not published. It's like being a cabinet maker, but you have no cabinet to show. People ask you what you do, and you say you're a writer—it's humiliating. So I was grateful to have that story taken. But I never had another story accepted by them after that.

When I went to the Iowa Writers' Workshop in 1965, the whole dream was to get stories published in magazines. You'd send your stories out and wait for months to get rejection slips. It was awful. I gave up on short stories and wrote novels. When I finally got published, it was with a novel, *Dancer from the Dance*. But now I have the opportunity to do short stories—my editor said I could—it's been a lot of fun.

I've been looking at these old stories, which are so sad because they were before I was out, before I even knew I was gay. They were about lonely young women in cities, about family dramas. I found them in my trunk and in the closet this summer. I saw first how hard I'd been trying all those years; second, how hopeless it all was. It was so far from being *about* anything. I had no subject matter; I wasn't writing about what I should've been writing about. In that sense it's been a lot of fun finally to be writing stories I know are going to be published.

It's also been instructive because I've learned what everybody says about stories: it's a very difficult form. Also, you're let off the hook a novel puts you on, which is that a novel has to be about something significant, or has to be a certain size, or has to have a certain amount of material or time in it. Edmund White said something perceptive about AIDS writing early on: he thought the way to deal with it was possibly with the short story, because you were in and out quickly and didn't have to have an ending the conventional way. He was right.

RC   Do any of the old stories feature in this collection?

AH   Yes. I thought this a great opportunity to collect the older stories that'd already been published and put them together in a volume. It wouldn't be much work either. But for some strange reason—I guess it's a reflection on the quality of my stories; that some of them seem to me not good enough now, or I don't want to include them as much as I did before—I'm writing as many new ones as I can before the deadline. We'll have this big pool to select from. I don't want to publish many stories in this book, but I do want them all to be the best ones I have.

RC   Are there stories you've excluded already?

AH   I haven't made the final selection, but there are some where I'm already thinking "no."

RC   "Sleeping Soldiers" was reprinted quite recently.

AH   Yes. I worked on that story for so many years and finally published it in the *Violet Quill Reader*. But I'm not satisfied with its ending. I think I'm going to change a little of that. That's the other fun thing about doing this: you can improve your stories—or think you can.

   "Sleeping Soldiers" I'll probably include. There's a real old one that was just republished in the *Mammoth Book of Gay Short Stories* called "Someone is Crying in the Château de Berne." That was the first thing I published after *Dancer from the Dance*—in *Christopher Street*.

RC   What of "Key West," from the *Faber Book of Gay Short Fiction*?

AH   That one I'll have to improve a little, because I've spun off another story from it. I can't overlap.

RC   Two others come to mind: "Lights in the Valley" from *Men on Men 3* and "Friends at Evening" from the first *Men on Men*.

AH   Thank you for asking about "Friends at Evening"! I love that one, but I'm dubious about it too now. Because the one I think can't go in is one I also liked at the time: "Lights in the Valley." I think that's too like *The Beauty of Men*. I'll tell you something funny about "Lights in the Valley," though. It never was a story; it was part of a novel I was working on that never worked. The editor before my current one read it for me and said "no."

RC   Did you finish it?

AH   Yes—with many other novels sitting in my room. This is the mistake I made when I first started out in Iowa City. Everybody knew you got short stories published in a magazine, but if you really wanted to be a writer, you had to publish a novel. That's a snobbery that still exists: that novels are adult; short stories are somehow amateurish or junior league—so unjustified.

So I had a story—"Friends at Evening"—I liked a lot. One mistake I made in Iowa, and that I later made with "Friends at Evening," was that I'd get a story that worked and think: "I'll make this into a novel. I'll just expand it. The material's good; it's a great story." Wrong! If a story works, it should be a story, most often. So I took these characters from "Friends at Evening" and had them go round New York for a much longer time, mostly in dialogue. "Lights in the Valley" was when one character leaves New York to go home. "Lights in the Valley" was a chunk out of that failed novel. It still reads that way to me. It's not quite a story. Maybe I'm being too critical. But I was thinking I might not include it.

RC   I am fascinated both formed part of another book, since one way of thinking of them is as precursors to *The Beauty of Men*.

AH   You're right. Mr. Lark is in "Friends at Evening." He's already this kind of "sad sack" character—eccentric. Then in "Lights in the Valley," Mr. Lark goes to visit the character named Ned. I wrote another short story with Mr. Lark, which was in the *European Gay Review*, called "Pornography and Funerals." He's in his little apartment at the welfare hotel and Ned comes to visit. I love that little story and may include it.

RC   Who are your influences in the short story form?

AH   The stories I admire are: Flannery O'Connor's—the *A Good Man Is Hard to Find* collection; Colette; Chekhov. I love Henry James's tales, and I admire Somerset Maugham, who's underrated. I'm leaving out lots of other great stories: Sherwood Anderson; Frank O'Connor. One of my favorite short stories of all time is "The Mad Lomasneys." It's Neddie Ned and the girl who's so stubborn. It's got the greatest dialogue in the world and the characters are wonderful. I've read that story a dozen times. There are lots of admirable story writers. Carson McCullers is another.

RC   When you have reservations about a story, what's missing?

AH   Good question—because I've been working on some of these stories for fifteen years; "Sleeping Soldiers" is one example. What are the qualities a story must have? My editor and I agree on this. I said to him: "What do you admire in a story?" He said: "I want to be somewhere at the end that I wasn't in the beginning." The danger of the story is that it's such an elastic form, a casual form. Even some of Chekhov's great stories seem like nothings, little slices of life. But they happen to be wonderful.

It's used too much as a lazy form in American writing, I think. You can throw anything into it, or you can cut off any piece of material and call it a short story. It's just not true. I want stories to have a shape, a tension, a meaning. I want something going on underneath it all—something unexplained by the things you think you've done right. It should have something more—the emotional quality.

I have this insane feeling that while I like very much the two stories that will close the collection, there should be some central story in the middle of a collection that should be the heart of the book; that should provide a kind of tenderness that will be the place you get to, then get beyond. I'm distressed by the feeling that I haven't written *the* story. It's so easy to write and avoid the matter of what you should be writing— like what I said of my stories years ago: always avoiding the *thing*. So I don't know if I'll write that story or not. What's difficult is there are so many ways to write a story. I can choose any subject in any form. That's very bad in a sense because it's just too huge; then you miss the real thing that must be in the book.

RC   I'm always surprised at the ease with which anthologists excerpt from novels, particularly gay ones. Writers are clearly happy to submit these excerpts as a story. Somehow I feel cheated as a reader.

AH   I do too. It's ignoring the form.

RC You've recently been returning to old projects and reworking them. Is it true in general that, when a book is finished, you feel it doesn't leave you? Some writers hand their child on to the world, so to speak. If people misinterpret it, they just stand stoical—publicly, at least.

AH I tend to have very few obsessions, I think. Larry Kramer's former agent Peggy Ramsay said something wonderful: "Only write about your obsessions. Don't waste your time with other stuff. Find out what those are and keep writing about them." I think that's true. I have very few characters and very few obsessions, and I could keep returning to them. I could write on and on about Mr. Lark—unfortunately.

This is a question I have to answer in this collection. Part of me would love to have a group of interconnected short stories, in which Mr. Lark appears in four of them—sometimes as the protagonist, sometimes as a minor character. That Balzacian thing of the "human comedy"—I love that. But part of me thinks: "That's cheating; it's lazy. You've got to create new characters for every story."

So I do stick with the same stuff. In that sense, I don't really let books go. I'm a little obsessive. I'd probably like to write *The Beauty of Men* over again—told from an "I" narrator this time, with Mr. Lark as a minor character seen driving by in a car. I'd tell other stories from the boat ramp. A favorite book years ago was Lawrence Durrell's *The Alexandria Quartet* which simply did that. You could do almost every book that way.

RC I originally meant something slightly different.

AH Do you mean when a book comes out, and people in the public sphere start commenting on it and interpreting it—can you be indifferent to that? Yes—absolutely! You accept the rules of the game when you're a writer. Once the thing's out there, anybody can say anything they want. Every writer will go through the experience of reading a review that seems to have missed the point, or to have been wrong-headed, or to have taken an irony literally.

I had an essay in *Ground Zero* that was misread so badly. It was about writing and AIDS. One line many reviewers picked up on was that AIDS writing will be judged by its effect on the people struggling with it. They took this to mean I was abdicating all criteria for judging AIDS literature, which I wasn't advising or suggesting was right. I was saying that in real life what's going to happen is that people will be leery about judging the stuff aesthetically. I think that's what happened. So that was misinterpreted. I don't mind in a sense. You just do your best with the book. Once it's out there, you've done all you can do. In a sense even interviews like this are pointless, because you cannot append to every copy of a book an explanatory addendum that says: "My idea in writing this book was . . ."

RC   There's also the "rock and a hard place" argument: the idea that a writer must protect himself from his books' successes as well as their failures. People critiquing you may be hurtful—but people praising you may be oppressive.

AH   I agree. I had a wonderful teacher in college, Robert Fitzgerald, whose family was the one Flannery O'Connor lived with for a while. He was a poet and translator, a brilliant guy. I remember him one day in the office, pacing up and down. He must've been talking about his own writing career, saying: "When they praise me, I just say: 'Damn it! Damn it!' " The trouble with a mass culture, with a democracy with a culture of mediocrity, is that people are praised too early on for too little. They're let off at such a low level. You can succeed with such shit and get nice reviews. Better the reverse, I think. You'd get better stuff out of people by holding them to higher standards. Praise is imprisoning, I agree.

RC   This pertains only if someone isn't crushed totally by criticism, however.

AH   As I was speaking I was thinking exactly that. The conventional complaint in the theater is that critics are trying to destroy the actors and playwrights. People say: "Don't they *love* the theater? How *could* they say these things about our production?" So you can argue it on both sides.

Lyle Leveridge was talking recently about how Tennessee Williams was undone by success. He said it happened too early; Williams wasn't prepared. Oddly enough, I'd thought Williams had struggled quite a bit before he had his successes. He had a disaster—*Battle of Angels*—before *The Glass Menagerie* and *A Streetcar Named Desire*. But he always said in his *Memoirs* and interviews that success was a catastrophe.

This culture hasn't found a way to treat its artists properly in that sense. Think of poor Tony Kushner getting called the descendant of Tennessee Williams! That must be strangulating. Maybe it isn't for him. But they're so desperate for quality stuff in our culture that when something comes along, they can't help it. They're so thrilled. But you could suffocate people that way.

RC   You've spoken about work that never appeared, that took so much time and never quite pleased you. You're in a unique position, looking back over your work, which to you is of much greater volume than to readers. There are quite large spaces between the published works, in fact.

AH   Yes. Because I didn't publish for a long time and was down here in Florida, I think other writers I knew in New York thought I was producing mountains of manuscripts that were all brilliant. The truth is I was producing mountains of manuscripts that were *not* brilliant. A lot of the stories offstage and in the trunks are dreadful. The novel my editor rejected didn't work—the one I wrote before *The Beauty of Men*. If I were the Count of Monte Cristo; if I had this cave filled with brilliant books I was just not going to publish until I was ready, that would be very nice. But it isn't true.

Writing's hard. It's rare that things really work. I'd love to be prolific; to be Dickens, Shakespeare, or James—anybody who produced enormous quantities. I do think a sign of creative acumen is being prolific. I think if you're being prolific, that means you're writing about what you should be writing about. You're writing at the time you should be writing. You've found a form that's fertile, a subject matter that's rich. Whenever a friend says he's writing something that's just going on and on and he can't bring it to an end, I say: "That's a wonderful sign— you've hit a gusher!"

That's a problem with gay writing in particular: the material is rather limited and thin—or could be. Though let's face it, if you have an individual vision and voice and something to say, it doesn't matter if you're gay or straight. You just do it. That person will find something more in gay life to be written about. On the other hand, on your down days, you say: "Gee, everything I had to say about this subject I've already said."

RC   What of posterity? Joyce reached a certain point in writing *Stephen Hero*, felt it wasn't working, and tried to burn it. Somebody was there to pull it out of the flames and it was later published.

AH   But why should that book have been published? Wasn't that the necessary failure he had to go through? The perfect analogy is Proust's *Jean Santeuil*. Have you read it? It's in the third person and has vaguely the same scenes as in *Remembrance of Things Past*. It's dead on the page. I've always wanted to find out from a biography where Proust made that switch. I think people can trace it; that it was somewhere in "Contre Sainte-Beuve" he got it.

RC   It's Damascene, isn't it? You want to know the exact spot and time.

AH   I really do. Where did he switch to the "I" narrator, and why did that suddenly unlock all that book and make it a masterpiece, whereas the previous version was dead in the water?

RC   Would you throw something into the flames?

AH   I'm just a hoarder. It's a problem. I'm getting to the point where I'd like to take it all to the landfill. There's no point keeping it except for sentimental reasons; to look back and say: "Gee, I was there when I wrote that terrible story."

RC   What do you say to the archivists?

AH   My favorite line about that is Santayana's: "The twentieth-century will expire like the Alexandrian age: exhausted at the doors of its libraries." I think the hoarding culture's necrophiliac and sick in a way. There's something unhealthy about making art a religion in which the sacred texts are guarded in the temple. The Joycean stuff's just insane— and the Proustian stuff now, about which version of this scene is the one Proust wanted. Writing becomes a Torah in which there's commentary.
    On the other hand I'm being silly. If there are people who want to do that as a profession, and find something illuminating in it, and that's their joy and work, then of course they can do that. But don't you think the living art's always the one people aren't treating in that way? The living art we're going through right now is probably film. Maybe it's sit-coms even.

RC   If you look at gay literature, most of the academic interest is still with nineteenth-century figures. Nobody wants to talk about the con-temporary.

AH   Is that a necessary thing, because time has to pass before you can see clearly and objectively? Do you include Proust and Joyce in that?

RC   I was thinking just of gay writers.

AH   You mean they'll talk about Edward Carpenter and Walt Whitman? I'm saying it's worse than that. The Beinecke Library at Yale wants the papers of the Violet Quill club. On the one hand I'm thrilled. It's quite an honor. On the other, I think: "This is just nuts! *Why?*"

I can't go on with this subject because it's academic interest that makes writers thrive. There's a symbiotic relationship right now. We should be very grateful that David Bergman cared enough about the Violet Quill club to put together a *Reader*. On the other hand, I think to myself: "Isn't this too much attention?"

RC What about the status of the author and his work and legacy? I'm imagining a world in which a reader engaged with someone's books, while accepting that an author should have control over what's released. An oeuvre might exist purely in accordance with what an author thought and wanted. We seem far from that culture now, but isn't there something appealing about it?

AH That the writer can stage-manage his own work and image and what he leaves behind; that he's the director? That's what Henry James did— he burned his papers. Horrifying to archivists—but the other part of you thinks: "Good for you, Henry."

My thinking is that a hundred years from now very few of these books will be read. There's so much accumulation as time goes on. Only the best stuff's going to be around. There's no space for all the rest. So I'm saying to myself it's almost irrelevant whose papers are saved. Just a few books are going to amuse, entertain, and interest people in a hundred years. We don't know which ones they are. I'm saying something philistine, and probably incorrect and illogical, but there's something in me that finds the hoarding culture crazy in every sense, not just literature: in painting, in objects.

RC There's hoarding; then there's hierarchy: trying to filter, to determine which books last. This is the opposite of hoarding, really; it's about throwing things out. Critics think they're doing it, but readers do it by themselves, too—by preferring some books over others.

AH That's what I think's the vox populi—the readers. But I'm saying we can't know what they'll value in a hundred years.

RC Does it matter?

AH No. I used to think it was the reason I wrote: that the only reason anyone would be a writer was to give permanence to something so hideously transient. More and more I've come to this idea that you're *dead*. What could be more absurd than caring about your reputation afterwards? There's nothing better than trying to please an audience right now. It doesn't mean you have to pander or lower your standards. I'm saying a good cure for "masterpiece-itis"—for writing for eternity, which is an absurd way to create art—is to try to entertain, engage, and amuse the people who read you right now.

RC Something of a distinction between fiction and drama occurs to me here. Maybe this in part explains that awful devastation of James the moment his play failed.

AH Do you think James wanted that popular success while he was alive?

RC Yes, the immediacy of it.

AH I agree! Daphne Merkin ended a review of [the 1997 film version of] *Wings of the Dove* saying just that: that James would love the mass audience of film.

RC And despite all the monument-building that was involved in collecting and revising his fictional work . . .

AH Which was so undercut by the fact it sold nothing! He was terribly upset by that. James wanted success and pleasure. His career, like Melville's, was so strange. Melville started out with popular success:

Typee and *Omoo*. He just went more and more artistic and ended up writing what we value as masterpieces now, but which his time did not. James started out with *Daisy Miller*, a popular hit. He ends up with *The Golden Bowl*, which now we revere over *Daisy Miller*. So I'm undercutting my whole argument here. I'm saying the things that didn't succeed at the time are things we value a hundred years later.

RC   It's not so much a contradiction as an observation on what compels authors to write. One could infer something about the writing of drama from that. For James, the failure of his dramas seems a kind of primal scene of failure against which subsequent fictions reacted.

AH   You mean the subsequent fiction was the result of the plays' failure? I thought people just said he improved his sense of structure. But they were about something more? Of course—how could they not have been! He was back in his house; he was out of the world again. It hadn't worked; he was just with his books. So he put all of himself into those novels. Maybe they got richer because of it, or more esoteric.

RC   Let's return to Tennessee Williams.

AH   Williams wrote all his plays as short stories originally. I don't think we can draw anything from that. We can simply say his short stories were like a treatment someone writes before writing a screenplay. Williams published his short stories, but I don't know how much he cared about them.

RC   There are people who say they're wonderful.

AH   I like some of the stories very much: "Desire and the Black Masseur" and "Three Players of a Summer Game," which became *Cat on a Hot Tin Roof*. But I think Williams must have known his greatness lay in the plays.

RC   Were you ever drawn to writing plays?

AH   I have three full-length plays in my bedroom. They're awful! They're fluent, finished, the right number of pages—and they're just about nothing. But I'd love to write a play, and I'm going to keep trying. I adore plays, theater, and dialogue. Something happens in the theater that happens nowhere else, as has been said—even now, when so much has been removed from playwriting by other media.

RC   I want to move to a question about first- and third-person narration in your fiction. There often seems to be tension between first- and third-person modes. When you write in the first person, there are elements of traditional third-person narration, and the reverse. In fact, you almost come up with a new kind of voice: the fourth person. Your first-person narratives are full of "we," more than "I."

AH   That's very funny. I'm just doing that in a story I like. While I was going over it, I started changing the "I" to "we." I said: "Why am I doing this?" It was for a practical reason, because the "I" narrator wasn't a character, and I didn't want him to be important to the story. But I wanted to have the "I" narrator start it off by seeing the characters the story's about. Then I thought: "No, it's in a town where everybody saw these characters; I want the 'we.' "

Would you say Flaubert's *Madame Bovary* is a first- or third-person novel? It's third person, but the "I" narrator starts it off with that wonderful scene in the school. I *love* that. Do you know how much Proust does that too? You're never offended by it. It starts out as an "I"-narrator novel, but most of *Swann's Way* is in third person. It's delicious. You never say: "Gee, how could the "I" narrator know what Swann was feeling when he went looking for Odette that night in the boulevard?" You never ask! Why not? Because we accept Proust's voice, and that he's going to tell us a story.

I don't generally use "I" narrators who are characters. I like the "I" narrator to be a ghost. The guy in *Dancer*'s virtually a ghost. He's just someone who witnesses. I love Colette's stories. She said somewhere the real drama of her stories wasn't their content but that she was witnessing them all. In other words, the French public had come to accept this character "Colette" as this witness; this tale-teller. I love that quality, and like to have narrators like that, who aren't really characters, or who may be the author. But if I had to think this through technically I couldn't do it. It's something you do physically, by a sense of touch when you go through.

Last year I wrote a piece about aging called "Wrinkle Room" for the *New York Times Sunday Magazine*. I got into a lot of trouble. People felt I'd been too harsh; I'd painted too extreme a portrait of gay aging. Larry Kramer called me up and said friends of his were complaining. He said: "The trouble is, you and I tend to write 'I' as if we mean 'everybody'; like a stand-in for the gay community." I've always tried scrupulously to avoid that. No one would ever in his right mind say he's writing for the gay community. It's ludicrous.

RC   Kramer might.

AH   Well, we all do it every now and then, because every writer thinks "my" experience is representative of larger things everyone's going through. So maybe I did that inadvertently. Objectively you'd never presume to write for anybody but your own limited self. But you always hope your thing is everybody else's.

RC   When you start a project, is the question of first- or third-person voice perplexing?

AH   It drives me crazy! That's *such* a hard question. I'm going back and forth now with these stories. It's the hardest thing of all. Maybe that's because of what you said: I mix them too much; I don't keep them clear in my head. I do find it difficult, because there are things you can do with an "I" narrator that you can't with a third, and things you can only do with a third. I'm so greedy. I hate to have to give up anything when I do any piece of writing. If I'm writing a piece and think when turning it into "I" that I'm leaving out some quality I could get in the third person, I immediately feel depressed. I think: "God, you haven't found the form. You're not doing this right." You should never write a piece feeling you left something out because you couldn't do it that way. You should write a piece the only way it should have been written.

I had a writing teacher named Peter Taylor, a very successful American short-story writer. He said one day that he wrote every story five different ways. I thought: "My God, that's conscientious." I understand, though, why he did it—because there's a terrible choice between viewpoints. I never thought I'd write a book in the present tense. I always thought it was affected—too modern in the wrong way. But I ended up writing *The Beauty of Men* in the present. It drove me crazy. I kept saying to my editor: "I think I should rewrite this totally differently: with an 'I' narrator and a conventional structure. I could get more lyricism, beauty, and feeling." He said: "No, that'd be exactly the way *not* to write this book." I think he was probably right.

But I was very torn all the time by the possibility that by writing *The Beauty of Men* in the third person, I was missing so many wonderful set pieces I could have done with an "I" narrator looking back at this period at the boat ramp; making it more forlorn, romantic, lost. There was tons of stuff I couldn't do because I was writing in the present tense. That's the bitch of writing. You sacrifice; you make choices. I don't like to make choices in life, and I don't like to in writing. I hate to give up anything.

RC   From what we were saying about short stories, it sounds as if questions of form preoccupied you from the outset. Have you ever been surprised by an idea starting in one form, then dictating a different one?

AH   I know that's happened to a lot of writers. I don't think it's ever happened to me—except after *Nights in Aruba*, in which I don't think I did get a handle on what was fictional and what was autobiographical. I wish I'd taken George Stambolian's course on autobiographical writing. I've often wondered if I should have written that novel as nonfiction. I started writing the opinion columns for *Christopher Street*. I thought: "This is going to be a good exercise. You'll be able to find out by writing nonfiction essays what material should be nonfiction and what shouldn't be. I'll get all the nonfiction out of my system that way."

By the time I wrote *The Beauty of Men*, I think I'd gotten it out of my system. I said: "By God, there are things I can get off my chest in *The Beauty of Men* through the guise of fiction that I couldn't have said in an essay." Mr. Lark has many thoughts I couldn't have argued for rationally; many opinions I could never have defended. The wonderful thing about a character is that people *are* crazy; they do have illogical thoughts. So it was a great relief to have that form at that point. Now I ask myself not so much what form something should take as that central question: "Is this fiction or nonfiction?"

RC   Haven't you published something as both?

AH   Yes—"Memories of Heidelberg," which appeared in *Boys Like Us*. Patrick Merla asked us to tell how we came out. How I came out in real life is very close to what I wrote in *Nights in Aruba*, so there's a perfect example.

RC   But the material's not exactly the same.

AH   No. I used more in the nonfiction piece because I was just concentrating on that topic, whereas in the novel it's one scene of many. I remember when writing *Nights in Aruba* thinking: "God, I'm not getting anywhere near Germany and how I felt about it." Louis Auchincloss talks about a writer's "capital"—the idea that we all have a certain amount of stuff to draw on. I think you must get your stuff out, if you're going to use it at all. Sometimes you can, because of the form. But in *Nights in Aruba*, I don't think I was able to deal with Germany nearly as much as I wanted to. Again, that's when a bell goes off in your mind, saying: "Is this the right place to use this stuff? Is this the right form for this memory, this material?"

RC I was thinking of another piece, "Ties." Didn't that appear in a non-fiction context, then in the fiction anthology *First Love, Last Love* in a different form?

AH Yes. Sometimes those *Christopher Street* essays would be taken as short stories and sometimes as nonfiction. That reflects the problem we were talking about. How could I write something as an essay that's taken as a story? Because you use the "I" narrator and the piece involves memory and has a point or emotional climax. Robert Ferro used to say the story should already be there before you write it. Sometimes a story is already there.

RC You mean narratively?

AH Yes. One story in this collection is written virtually as it happened. Of course I've added things and rearranged the sequence a little. But a lot of it is as it happened. I think as a writer you develop a kind of antenna. Every now and then you stumble on something that's your stuff. You could say that's a failure of imagination. But I don't think it's bad. This only applies to autobiographical writers, I guess. I've often chastised myself for not being more imaginative. But I think you're one or the other as a writer, though there's every blend of the two in between.

RC There are fiction writers who feel nothing need be invented; that stories are just there. Then there are people who will criticize a lack of invention in autobiographical work.

AH That's what's happening in writing now. The imagination is suspect in a way it never was in the nineteenth century. I can't write a novel about a black girl who is eleven, for example. I'd be called to the bar: "How dare you?" We seem to have the feeling you can only write what you authentically know. The imagination somehow doesn't give you the privilege of doing this anymore, whereas in previous eras the imagination was allowed to do that.

RC   I agree we're in a confessional era; one in which there's a need for authors to authenticate the experiences in their work. It makes you wonder: "Why bother with fiction?"

AH   Yes. Why write fiction at all? I think it's science. Science has eroded religion, and it's eroding art. We want facts—reality; information; real stories. It's happened with television, with reality shows following the cops around. Why make it up? It's happened a lot in the culture. You want the real story. You don't want anything secondhand or made up, whereas the making up used to be the whole form, the whole art. *Everybody* wants to know: did it really happen? I was asked many times on my tour with *The Beauty of Men* if the book was autobiographical.

RC   Isn't that horrifying?

AH   It is. It makes you think: "Why didn't I write it as nonfiction?" But what's in *The Beauty of Men* was what was left after I'd written all those nonfiction essays: Mr. Lark's mind; his feelings. Why didn't I write that as nonfiction? Because fiction gives you freedom.

RC   That's a response directed at yourself. But there's another possible one: "Why does my readership require me to stand in direct relation to the book's experiences?"

AH   Yes, there's that mentality that says: "I want what's really happening in Buckingham Palace; I don't want to see them as images. I want the real story about Frank Sinatra." That's just the lust of the moment. I think it comes from science.

RC I wondered if it's to do with the camera. People believe, wrongly, that cameras tell the truth. We've had a century of cameras.

AH That's interesting, because the camera in the hands of the advertising industry and magazines is an enormous lie-teller. But a century of cameras has done it, you think—given people the illusion they are seeing the real thing? So there's nothing that happens which is unseen, so you don't believe in the unseen; you don't give it any respect; you always demand to penetrate it and have it exposed? Therefore my novel is just a screen; a camouflage.

But of course there's still a great role for fantasy. Most bestsellers are pure fantasy books. People will pick up a Tom Clancy or a Danielle Steel—or a soap opera. They get into it just as you get into a bathtub. They want that warm feeling.

RC Genre fiction has a license literary fiction doesn't.

AH You mean literary fiction has become synonymous with realistic fiction?

RC Not exactly. But I wanted to ask a related question after your comments on science. If science is prevalent, what role remains for the aesthetic reader or writer? Must he "live" in the nineteenth century? Is that why Alan Hollinghurst speaks overwhelmingly of nineteenth-century models for his fiction?

AH Take *The Swimming-Pool Library*. I believe Alan Hollinghurst made up that narrator. I don't necessarily believe he knew an old man who had a diary. Yet I read the book and accepted it, so there was suspension of disbelief there.

RC   But you've said elsewhere that you were compelled by the question of where *The Swimming-Pool Library* came from. It's so perfectly executed, yet seemingly invented. You had the same gut instinct: "What's the kernel or truth of this?"

AH   You're right. I was asking for the real version. That's why I was so curious about *The Folding Star*. I thought I'd find out more about where the first book came from. But I didn't. Hollinghurst simply created another mechanism, so that when he had the little autobiographical section in *The Folding Star* where Edward goes back to England, you feel: "Am I tapping into autobiographical fiction here? Am I now seeing his real life? Was that superior to the rest of the book?" That book raises that question right there—in that little center filling that seems autobiographical—yet we've no way of knowing whether he made that up as well as everything else.

   The joke I told on the book tour which always got a laugh was that the stuff you make up people think happened, and the stuff you write exactly as it happened, people think you made up. That's true.

RC   Are you a fan of Hollinghurst's?

AH   Absolutely. I said earlier that it's very funny that writers are reluctant to name their contemporaries as models. It's just an ego thing, I think. I'm going to illustrate that right now!

   Edmund White said something very nice in a blurb for *The Beauty of Men*: that I was a writer where he was actually curious to see what came next. I feel that about several writers. That's the real compliment you pay them. I feel that about Ed's books and about Hollinghurst's stuff. I'm not going to go on. Then you start leaving people out and get into trouble.

RC   I was interested in the more general question of what you read when, and how reading related to writing. Do you have to stop reading when you write?

AH   I do. The one people say they shouldn't give young writers is Henry James. But James was so distinct, so mannered, I was never threatened by it. The writing that did get me was Scott Moncrieff's translation of Proust: that gorgeous prose, supposedly outdated and inaccurate now. But I still think it's the most stately, beautiful prose. I don't know how much is Proust and how much Scott Moncrieff, but it's gorgeous. That bothers me. It's very hard to read Proust and not get into the rhythm of those sentences, with the triple adjectives and the way they end. So I wouldn't read Proust while I was writing.

RC   Have you detected its influence directly in your work?

AH   Sure. *Nights in Aruba* starts with a man in bed remembering. That was so obvious, I thought.

RC   There's a fantastically baroque closing sentence to that book, which has the cadence of Proust.

AH   Yes. Those sentences demonstrate the terrible influence of that wonderful book. Proust's a problem for all writers. As Edmund White said, Proust exploded the form. It's a nice way of putting it. It's such an immense book, and contains every kind of writing there is. How do you get around it? How do you do anything Proust didn't do? How do you do anything better or different? The joke is you start out writing wanting to be better than Proust, and end up settling for anything you can get. You have to ignore Proust and say: "I'll write my little thing anyway."

RC   Do you read nonfiction?

AH   Yes. I love histories and biographies. I'm like the typical American reading public in terms of reading trends. Biographies are the novels of our times in a strange way; I'm one of those people who loves them. I'll read just about any biography. I want to read the biography of Philip Larkin right now, and a biography of Chekhov. I haven't done that yet. I want to read Pepys's diaries. Maybe I love writers' biographies most.

RC   They're a curious contradiction. Often writers haven't done very much other than write.

AH   But here's the perfect test case: everybody thought the J. R. Acker-ley biography by Peter Parker would have to be bad because Ackerley had written so brilliantly about his own life, and he'd just been an editor and not really done anything. But I *adored* that biography. It was fasci-nating; he was fascinating. Maybe superficially he led a colorless exis-tence, but in fact he was incredibly interesting. You're right, though—there are writers whose lives aren't very eventful. That's the joke about writing: writers sit home alone in rooms. It's the people who go into commodities trading or soya bean futures that have interesting exis-tences, traveling and meeting people around the world.

Writing's the most monkish existence. Too many young writers want to be writers without having done anything with their lives. That was my problem with those early short stories. I see it in young gay writ-ers now. They're so eager to be published. I think: "You're too involved already with the world of reviews and book tours." I want to say: "Leave all that. Go and do something totally unrelated for ten years that you may hate. Who knows, it may end up being your material."

RC   Edmund White made a fictional assault on the idea of biography in the story "His Biographer." How would you react to being the subject of a biography?

AH   There'd be absolutely nothing! Would I be horrified by it as an intrusion, you mean? I think anyone would. I'm always a little guilty about using people in fiction. It's a terrible invasion of privacy. That was confirmed for me once—when Robert Ferro used me in *Second Son*. He created a character who lived in Florida that he corresponded with. I forget his name, and it wasn't really me. But for a moment I thought it was. I experienced being on the receiving end of that, and it's not pleasant. It's like journalists who want to write about things without ever being the subject of journalistic speculation. So I'm always at pains not to violate anybody's privacy. Yet all the best characters come from life.

RC   Are they nonreaders, then?

AH   Hopefully, yes; that's the best situation.

RC   We don't live in a culture that respects privacy—the idea, say, of insisting a photographer should ask permission before taking a picture. Ethically you could make a case for that.

AH   Yes. Ethically the New Guinea tribespeople are right: the photograph *does* steal your soul. Don't you think that's what Princess Di was all about—the way her death was treated? Finally people saw the moral quality. There was a wish to hold the photographers ethically responsible for having literally hounded her to death, whether they caused the accident or not.

RC   Still, contracts are sealed for the movie—just as the movie's now being shot of Versace's death.

AH   Is it? Delicious!

RC   Now you're implicated.

AH   Exactly. I can't wait to see it. We're all implicated. We're all on both sides of the line. Yet that's too easy. You and I wouldn't do certain things others wouldn't think twice about doing. You can mitigate it all by respecting people.

138 ANDREW HOLLERAN

But this is also part of the question of why autobiography's prevalent now. Why confession? Why is fiction considered just a screen for another, more real and honest story?

RC Do you think autobiographical fiction is truly revelatory? Does it have the same spirit of inquiry as a wholly invented novel?

AH Are you saying the paradox is that the invented stuff may get at more truth? Absolutely.

RC Wilde knew that already. All his aphorisms suggest it. Dorian Gray is compelled by the artifice of Sibyl Vane as she acts because he can imagine it as true. When he meets her, he's forced to engage with reality, which is repellent and unilluminating.

AH That's in Proust, too. Marcel goes to the theater and becomes disillusioned with Berma.
   I always feel a little sense of failure if people ask how autobiographical my book is. My dream is to create a book in which the characters have such an independent, believable existence, are so compelling, or stand for something, that that's all that's discussed. The author isn't even talked about. That's the only achievement you can work for. Those things are going to last.

RC A curious contemporary example is John Berendt using the category of "true crime" to relate a true story—in which, nevertheless, he invented names and sought to erase the narrator's presence.

AH Yes. I wrote a review of *Midnight in the Garden of Good and Evil* for *Christopher Street*. I said the only thing missing in the book was him, and what a richer book it'd have been if we'd been able to know his response to it all. Plus, at one point the Williams character says: "I give two parties a year: one for Savannah society; one for gay Savannah: which one do you want to go to?" I think the narrator of the book finesses the question. Berendt wrote me a nice note, saying: "I realized that was an issue, and tried writing it another way"—with the narrator as a character, I guess—"and it just didn't work." That's quite possible, because I like my narrators to be ghostly presences, not characters too.

RC I want to ask for your response to comments by the novelist Harlan Greene, who has spoken persuasively of how the realities of closetry are given short shrift in gay literature today. He felt behind talk of a "liberated" gay fiction after Stonewall lay an erroneous assumption that some seismic social shift had taken place. For him gay fiction had forgotten about the enduring prevalence of unhappiness, uncertainty, and lack of openness in many gay lives. Moreover, the circumstances of closetry somehow seem passé in gay fiction; in real life, they're still very often determining and significant.

AH I agree with that completely. One reason I wrote *The Beauty of Men* was as rebellion against this idea that everything was so glossy now: *Out* magazine—its Absolut vodka ads and gay cruises. Everyone was corporate now; gay life had left all its problems behind. But next to the ad for the cruise, you'd have that wonderful ad with the boy in the bathroom, face down, next to the toilet. The copy read: "Problems with self-esteem, depression, anxiety, loneliness? Gay Pride Institute—call such-and-such." I thought: "These are the two poles of gay life. Somewhere in between is where we're all living; we've a foot in both camps."

Then there are all the ads for viatical settlements, in which the men are totally buffed, muscular clones. The copy is: "Have you decided to sell your life insurance yet?" I'm thinking: "American culture, commercial culture, airbrushing culture, magazine culture—it's surreal, and so shameless." It's that general thing of a commercial advertising agency culture airbrushing existence and presenting it in its most positive light that irritates me. The reality is that I go to the boat ramp; Mr. Lark goes to the boat ramp, and you're living in environments with families you're not out to, and it's painful to try to mesh these two worlds. It's not easy being gay, though it's getting easier.

RC When you were writing *The Beauty of Men*, did it occur to you that these experiences were new territory for gay fiction?

AH I didn't. My editor said that. I was nervous about the book, thinking it was just a terrible down. But he said: "No one's writing about this stuff." He kept insisting we should go ahead.

That's the worst thing about writing. During those years when I was trying to write a novel, I was making outline after outline of what I thought was a good idea, and none of them went anywhere. In the meantime, I was writing these little segments that turned into the chapters of *The Beauty of Men*. They were for my own release and relief. I'd come home and just type them up because that's what I'd felt and thought. It came out of reality; that's what I was really thinking, feeling, and living. It wasn't any of the stuff I thought would make an appropriate novel.

RC The subject matter's a great new opportunity for fiction. Nobody else will get there in media or film. They're too constricted by the considerations of the mass market.

AH I agree. That's always the function of fiction. What is that word in Russian—"samizdat"? Where they'd smuggle the manuscripts around, the unofficial stuff? That's the only function for fiction. It's to say what everybody else has left out; what's not said in news, journalism, ads, the movies; what people aren't saying in conversation because it's not proper. There are many reasons to write: to please people, to make people laugh, to remember something pleasant, to tell a story that means something to you, to make up, to fantasize. But part of it's definitely to say what's not being said anywhere else.

RC   Was there a time when you thought you'd do something other than write?

AH   Yes. I struggled against it, as most bourgeois sons do. I thought I had to go to law school, so I went. I thought I'd work for the State Department. And I waited tables. But I think once you start waiting, you're not really trying to do another kind of career. You're putting all your eggs in the basket of writing. It's a terrible chance you take with the arts. You either succeed or not, whereas if you go to work for a corporation, no matter how high you rise, you'll always have a function for the corporation. But the arts are really a make or break kind of thing.

RC   Some writers keep jobs down.

AH   Yes. I always admired the idea of Wallace Stevens being an insurance executive *and* a great poet. It subverted the whole idea that you had to be this lunatic bohemian.

RC   But you couldn't do it yourself?

AH   Many times I've looked at my past life and said: "You've wasted so much time waiting for a good idea and not writing that you could have been a brain surgeon in your free time." I love Chekhov because he was a doctor too.

RC   Since you mentioned Stevens, we'll stray into poetry. Yeats is everywhere in your work.

AH   Yeats keeps astonishing me. We had a terrible time with the title *The Beauty of Men*. I wanted to call it *The Boat Ramp*. The Brits said no. They said: "We don't think it's very marketable." I thought *The Boat Ramp* was the most honest title. It didn't tip it in any way and wasn't literary. The funny thing was that just three weeks ago in New York I went to dinner with my editor and some others. Casually I mentioned that the original title was *The Boat Ramp*. My friend's boyfriend started laughing and didn't stop for three minutes. I guess he thought it was ludicrous. So I felt a little better then. I thought maybe we'd done the right thing.

We started searching through books of poetry for a title. That's where you often get such beautiful titles—in the Bible or in poetry. We were like crack addicts. I'd call up my editor after I'd found a line from a poet. There was one from Wordsworth: "Those the Candles Light." I thought "God, that's beautiful." My editor and I would say: "That's it!" and hang up. Ten minutes later the whole thing would deflate. We'd call each other back and say: "That's not it; we have to keep going." We were going to call it *The Warmth of the Sun*, *Those the Candles Light*, *The Moment He Appears*—I love that last title. Everyone liked it initially. But as we discussed it we thought it didn't indicate enough. It was too arbitrary.

I think Larry Kramer says he's the one that thought of *The Beauty of Men*. It fits according to the Peggy Ramsay theory of what you're obsessed by: the beauty of men. Anyway, in looking through Yeats, I found another epigraph in the poem "Long Silence." It was so perfect, it was uncanny: only in age and decrepitude do we see truth; in youth we're just careless. That's the message of *The Beauty of Men*.

Yeats astonishes me. I don't want to say this unequivocally, because I'm not that well-versed in poetry, but part of me thinks Yeats was the last real great poet. Even Auden, whom I admire enormously, is somehow not as big. I think Yeats wrote the last really great poems. I know people will scream at this.

RC   Is he the last poet in English where you can comfortably use the label "romantic"?

AH   Maybe that's all it is. I'm a romantic, so for me Yeats is the last great poet. It would never have occurred to me to say it that way. It's rare that I come across a modern poem I adore. I think the state of poetry is tragic. Poetry's the heart of it all, and regarding everything we were saying about the loss of the imagination: talk about poetry and you really get to the nub of stuff.

RC   Have you written verse?

AH   I have tons of poetry back in the bedroom. But because I never learned the rhythmical, metrical techniques of poetry, I've never put my poems forward. I don't consider free verse, blank verse, conversational poetry, end-stop poetry as poetry. Yet that's what's produced now. Auden's still poetry, I think.

RC   He's immune to the influence of Whitman.

AH   Yes. Whitman to me is a source of a mix of pride and shame. As an American particularly, I'm very proud of Whitman. He caught something about American life that couldn't have been caught any other way. He's our really American great poet. On the other hand, I am ashamed of Whitman, because the work's so formless and dumb in many ways.

RC   Now, a leap: could you recollect the book tour you did with Larry Kramer in 1978? The idea of promoting gay books was very new then.

AH   My first tour—what a dream that was! Nowadays it's so commonplace that gay writers tour almost automatically. Back then it was something my editor and agent had to really push them to agree to. At times I was on the same plane as Larry. The odd thing about it was that Larry's book was vilified and stirred up a lot of anger in the gay press. Mine didn't, yet I thought mine was critical, too. *Dancer* was accused of romanticizing Fire Island circuit life. I thought I hadn't romanticized it at all—though I guess I had in a way, because part of me did love it. But it was also a very critical book. So I was let off the hook; Larry took all the brickbats.

RC   Much critical discussion of *Dancer from the Dance* still concerns the question of romanticization versus criticism, and the relevance to that of the technical matter of the ordering of the material within those opening and closing letters.

AH   To me that was the only novel I've ever written with a clear conscience, which was fun. I wasn't burdened with having to write a novel with *Dancer* because I was writing a parody of one. The letters were the real thing; the novel was just this manuscript.

That's one thing that appealed to me about Charles Ludlam and the Ridiculous Theatrical Company. I wrote an essay on him called "Tragic Drag." I said the real theater was dying uptown. Nobody could write after Williams. But Ludlam was writing like crazy, making fun of theater. It was as if we couldn't do these things straight anymore. So *Dancer* was the only novel I wrote with a clear conscience and had fun with, because I wasn't writing a novel. The minute I had to write a novel—*Nights in Aruba*—I became constipated and pseudo-Proustian. In *The Beauty of Men*, I got out of that by using the present tense. It's almost a monologue; there's nothing more to it.

RC   I want to ask you specifically about your use of the word "parody" in relation to *Dancer*. Critical comment has ignored its playful spirit, I think. Perhaps that's due to the historical accident of AIDS, which meant the elegiac elements of the book took on more significance subsequently.

AH   The book came out of camp. The way I wrote *Dancer* was by corresponding with gay friends in New York that winter when I was in Florida. They'd write these hilarious campy letters. When I was going around to bars in those days, there used to be bar giveaways with Miss Ruby's column about this and that, dishing the bartenders. I adored this humor and language. It was so wild and crazy. It was like Ludlam on stage. I thought: "Why couldn't I try to write in that kind of language?" That's how the letters started, and that led me into the book.

I like to write in two ways. I like humorous writing and elegiac. One thing that bothered me about *The Beauty of Men* was this question: can you write both in the same book? How do you separate them? In *Dancer*, they were separated nicely because the letters were campy, then the pseudo-novel adopted a kind of romantic, elegiac tone.

RC   You also distinguished between voices very clearly in *Dancer from the Dance*.

AH   Yes. I got Malone and Sutherland, which bifurcated me, so I was able to go full throttle on both. When you can't bifurcate, sometimes you try and blend the two and each kills the other.

One interesting review of *The Beauty of Men* was in *The James White Review*. It said about one paragraph: "It would be funny if it weren't so sad." Then the reviewer describes another scene and ends the paragraph with: "It would be sad if it weren't so funny." That was the other thing about that novel. I was always mystified by why some lines which I thought were so funny were muffled and weren't funny lines—I guess because the context was overwhelmingly tragic. To me, there's a lot of funny in that book too. When I read chapters of it on tour in New York, people laughed. But in other cities, when I read the same chapter, it was dead silence. *Dancer* was taken to be more elegiac than humorous.

RC   The letters in it also suggest this campy quality was to some extent something you saw passing from gay subculture.

AH   Yes. I do.

RC   Yet in *The Beauty of Men*, the Lark character feels a kind of resentment for the end of clone culture. "Clones Go Home," one sign reads. That culture's being replaced by a new, young camp, and the Lark character seems disturbed by the young generation's reclaiming of camp. Is that a different camp?

AH   What you're saying is historically correct. My generation was preceded by generations that used camp in ways my generation didn't. I
think camp, frankly, got diluted and less extreme as generations went on.
That's a loss. I suppose it's like the Jews worrying they're going to lose
Yiddish.

I always felt I'd been preceded by really fabulous queens I'd never
met, could only hear about, and loved hearing about. When Lark sees
his generation being superseded, I don't think he thinks in terms of losing clones or losing camp, but there's definitely the sense that we're losing another generation. And I hated the generation that replaced mine. I
had to live in the Village when punk and New Wave came in. I thought:
"What is it about these people? There's nothing attractive or clever or
fun about this. It's all so nasty, negative, unhappy, and so shitty!" I was
wrong, of course. A lot of creativity came out of that generation too.
But at the time I couldn't see it. I thought I was being shoved aside.

RC   That's the brutal truth of cultural re-creation, isn't it? Every generation shoves the previous one aside; it's entirely meant as a disinheri-
tance, and it is tragic.

AH   It is. It's Oedipal—killing our parents. They have to die before we
take full stage.

RC   Every individual will experience both phenomena.

AH   They will. Of course, we don't want to think it has to be that way.
Ideally, one uses from the past and respects one's elders. I never dissed
my elders. I romanticized them in a way. But when I saw "Clones Go
Home" I certainly felt these people were saying: "Get the fuck out
now!" But that was part of the spirit of punk. You can't hold it against
anybody. The larger truth is that every generation has its moment in the
sun.

RC   People often say in fashion that everything that's invented gets rein-
vented. You'll just have to wait for it to come back.

AH   Felice Picano and I were the benefit of a little of that. Here we
were—these strange, hoary figures from the past who had, for some reason, managed to survive. We were curiosities. What did we think now?
Who were we? We were given a smidgeon of attention and respect for
that. But you're right. The egotism of any generation is: "It's us now."
But how would new art be created if it weren't that way?

RC   Some gay writers today still write about what life was like in the seventies. In your work, do you think the desire to reflect more immediate
experience will remain paramount?

AH   Absolutely. There's a character in *The Beauty of Men*—Sutcliffe—
who's accused by someone else of not realizing the seventies are over.
He's sitting home waiting for the phone to ring. That's obviously not
what one does. One moves on.

Felice and I have discussed whether the seventies were really special,
or whether it was just that we were young then. Felice thinks they were
really special. He can give evidence that convinces me there *was* a creativity that was unique and fresh. But of course you could say that about
any decade. I've always said I'm sure that right now there's a bunch of
twenty-six-, twenty-seven-year-olds having a kind of life we know
nothing about; one that's just as fabulous as it was for us in 1978. I think
that's true. But I think Felice is right that there are historical factors that
make certain moments stand out and produce certain things: the Belle
Epoque or the Roaring Twenties.

But I don't think you can draw only on the past. On the other hand,
part of the problem I've had with this book of short stories is that I've
got this whole envelope of material of people I didn't use in *Dancer* or
The Beauty of Men, people I want to write about and describe. I don't

know how to do it—whether to write a special book of characters from the seventies I found fascinating, or to put them in this book of stories and try to give plots to them. So I haven't abandoned the seventies because I still have too many memories of people and things I think are interesting. It's not that I've closed that box completely and won't use it. On the other hand, you've got to go on and write about what's happening to you now.

I said to my editor at one point I was thinking of doing the short stories chronologically—having an arc, a pattern, that you'd get out of a novel. He said: "Don't tie yourself to that. The pleasure of a book of short stories is that it's a grab bag; you're bouncing around from different stuff to different stuff." That freed me to relax a bit. But now I'm putting them together, I'm going back to that. I *do* want an arc. I think I have one without trying for one: one in which a guy starts out at twenty-two and ends up at fifty-four a different person. I wonder if that will be revealed in the collection as it finally stands.

That's one of the great, interesting subjects I only realized recently. If you hang around long enough, everybody is inherently interesting, because they've gone through illusions, disillusions, sets of beliefs. You can't help but be an interesting person if you've lived, because you've formed an arc, and that's the form of a novel often. Proust's so wonderful because of that. He starts out as the kid in bed waiting for the kiss and ends up as the adult going to the party who steps on the uneven paving stone and realizes that his book is the involuntary memory, the summoning up of all he's just described to you. He's a very different person at the end. He's seen through so many illusions.

RC   So the stories project for you is kin to Proust's aim: to tie up the figure at the end with the figure at the beginning.

AH   Exactly. Psychologists have said that's a characteristic of age: you're trying to bring some kind of order to your life.

RC Another leap: you've mentioned your editor several times, and I know you've stayed with the same publishing house until now. It's such a rarity to have a strong relationship with either nowadays.

AH Yes. I'd love to have been loyal and stayed with one publishing house for my whole career. I did have a three-book contract with Morrow, which I just finished with *The Beauty of Men*, and I had one editor for all of my books until this last one—a woman named Pat Golbitz, who took *Dancer* and did *Nights in Aruba* and *Ground Zero*. The last was a suggestion of [book editor] Michael Denneny's, so I was grateful to him for that. She retired and I got Will Schwalbe and wrote *The Beauty of Men* with him. He's since left Morrow, and my next book will be with a new house.

RC What's the importance of a good editor?

AH I'd love to say I can do all my problem-solving by myself and know exactly what the manuscript needs. But you just can't—although Proust could. He did it without an editor.

RC If you had a good contract and no editor that you felt this necessary relationship with, would you go in search of one?

AH That's a good question. I think you'd survive any way you could. Part of your vanity would be: "I can do it by myself; I don't need anybody." But if you don't have an editor, you certainly need a good reader. You'd find two or three friends to do that for you. I don't see how anyone could be so hermetically sealed or confident. Of course, the great geniuses are. Did Proust show *Remembrance* to anybody before sending it out? Imagine taking on a project that long, that insanely ambitious, and never getting any check as to whether what you're doing made sense! He was *so* confident, and so intelligent in what he believed about art. He was writing his manifesto.

RC   One doesn't have to feel compromised for needing editing.

AH   Well, one does, doesn't one?

RC   Thanks very much for your time.

FIVE
ARMISTEAD MAUPIN

A rmistead Maupin is best known for the highly successful *Tales of the City* novel series, which was published between 1978 and 1989. Born in 1944, Maupin grew up in Raleigh, North Carolina, and graduated in English from the University of North Carolina. After dropping out of law school, Maupin joined the Navy where he served as a lieutenant for three years. He then became a reporter for the *Charleston News and Courier*, moving after a year to San Francisco to work for the Associated Press. He came out as gay in 1976 at the age of thirty.

Two years later, the *San Francisco Chronicle* began serializing his fictional columns on that city's life, "Tales of the City." In 1978 the first volume appeared in book form, as *Tales of the City* (New York: Harper and Row, 1978). Its five sequels followed at approximately two-year intervals: *More Tales of the City* (New York: Harper and Row, 1980); *Further Tales of the City* (New York: Harper and Row, 1982); *Babycakes* (New York: Harper and Row, 1984); *Significant Others* (New York: Harper and Row, 1987); and *Sure of You* (New York: Harper and Row, 1989). Volumes four to six saw a notable darkening of tone as Maupin introduced San Francisco's early encounters with the AIDS epidemic. *Sure of You*, which closed the series, was the only volume not to be serialized in a newspaper.

Maupin's only novel to date since finishing the *Tales* series was *Maybe the Moon* (New York: HarperCollins, 1992), set in Hollywood. A short story, "Suddenly Home," appeared in

Edmund White, ed., *Faber Book of Gay Short Fiction* (London: Faber and Faber, 1991).

In the 1990s, Maupin has been heavily involved in assisting the scriptwriter of two television miniseries made from *Tales of the City* and *More Tales*. His latest book is *The Night Listener* (New York: HarperCollins, 2000). Maupin lives in San Francisco, where this interview took place on Saturday, November 22, 1997.

RC Could you start by talking a little about writing method and its relation to the form of your books? Your case seems so distinctive, given that you originally seemed to fall into a particular method and form, through writing *Tales of the City* for the *San Francisco Chronicle*. Since then, you've had a greater freedom over both. What has been the impact of that?

AM In the beginning, when I was writing for the newspaper, I had to extract eight hundred words a day from myself, whether I wanted to or not, which is a wonderful way to get past the ordinary fears of a beginning writer. As the series wore on, I felt more and more constricted by that form. I began mentally to compose in such a way that I could compile daily episodes to form a chapter in the novel that would ultimately result from the serial.

I've found that I have become more and more perfectionist as my career has progressed, to the extent that now I sometimes take as long as a week to write a single page. I wish I could return to the urgency and the free-form nature of those early days. But I know what a good paragraph looks like now, and I don't tend to proceed until I have composed one. Every writing manual on the planet tells you to let it all spill out and then go ahead and polish it on the second draft. But I've never been able to do that. What I do is spend about four hours a morning, writing and making myself happy with each sentence before

I proceed. I've tried creating artificial deadlines for myself but it never works.

The novel that I am working on at the moment—*The Night Listener*—is three years late. I have a few good excuses, though: a miniseries that never seemed to get off the ground, for one. But for the most part, I work very slowly, and not with a great deal of joy. I've found that it's best for me to work in the mornings. I can tumble out of bed and certain things will tumble out of my subconscious at the same time. I like the feeling of sitting before my word processor as the coffee's kicking in. By the same token, I sometimes do it very late at night before I go to bed, when I'm stoned to the tits and in a more playful mood about writing.

I think play is the key to it all. I'm not tremendously gifted at keeping it playful, but I try to be. My friend David Hockney is such an inspiration because he approaches his work in such a way that makes him seem like an eight-year-old boy getting to play with finger paints for the first time. I think that's the way writing should be. That sense of joy and immediacy is evident when the reader comes across it.

RC   Does the idea of writing as working to deadlines impede you?

AM   Absolutely. The trick is to carry the baggage of your craft along with you, and fool yourself into believing it's still play.

RC   Is there such a thing as anxiety over your past successes?

AM   Well, I'm not the usual case study. My first work wasn't immediately universally beloved. I was still considered very much a local writer— even a pulp writer—at the time that the Violet Quill was holding its meetings in New York. With all due respect to those gentlemen, I am very proud of the fact that I was dealing with gay, lesbian, bisexual, and transgender subject matter four or five years before they even began to assemble.

But my recognition factor in the world of literature was very low. Looking back, I wouldn't have had it any other way, because my success seems to have grown from the appeal of my work to my readers. I've discovered that word-of-mouth remains my best advertiser. So I'm not really worried that my early success was some sort of fluke. I've always been a storyteller, and I'm getting better at it all the time because I'm gradually finding my way to higher levels of storytelling. I'm also learning to dig deeper into my own pain in the process of writing.

RC   One way of thinking of developments in your craft is to think of the move to the first person in *Maybe the Moon*.

AM   Yes. I'm as much an actor as I am a writer. My partner Terry used to fall into hysterics when he would walk into my office and find me gesturing madly at the computer screen. I think writers who are capable of creating vivid characters are capable of imagining the acting process.

RC   This is going to allow a comparison with Dickens, which often happens to you.

AM   Well, they are all accepted with no objection whatsoever! I was struck by it this summer, when I was standing guard over the miniseries of *More Tales of the City*. I was acutely conscious of the way I wanted a particular scene to form. I already knew what emphasis should be placed on which word, and the tone of voice with which a line should be delivered. I had been through that process myself in the writing of the original stories. I did a fair amount of children's theater and "little theater"-acting as a child and teenager. That instinct seems to have found its way into my writing.

I also pride myself on being a very empathetic person. To some degree, that's a virtue. In other ways, it's a Southern affliction, because I was trained to be a good little boy, someone who is tuned in to other people's feelings. I'm aware of that when I write, when I observe the people I'm writing about. My last novel, *Maybe the Moon*, was about a thirty-one-inch actress living in Hollywood, who was inspired by a friend of mine who wore the rubber suit in *E.T.* While she wasn't alive, I felt that she was hovering over my shoulder in the writing of the book. I had no difficulty impersonating her.

RC   Some writers are preoccupied with what is possible in first- and third-person narratives.

AM   I have been. *Tales of the City* made a lot more sense in the third person because I was writing about at least a dozen different major characters. At the same time, it was third person with limited point of view, so it forced the reader to inhabit each of the characters, to feel their personal pain, but also allowed them to look at the overall picture from outside, and to some subtle degree feel the presence of the author. I try not to intrude too much when I am writing in third person because I think the joy of it is not to hear this voice going "Me-Me-Me" all the time. On the other hand, I was so exhilarated by the process of writing in first person in *Maybe the Moon* that I am doing it again in the much more autobiographical novel that currently lies mouldering on my desk.

RC   Your projects never seem to finish. The miniseries must have kept the *Tales* in your frame of thinking. Have you relished having a close input into it?

AM   Absolutely. I am a very rare bird in that regard. Most writers are banished from a set. Terry very shrewdly contracted to have my name placed above the title in both of the miniseries, so it becomes harder and harder to get rid of me.

RC   Nevertheless, deciding to close the *Tales* you described as being like escaping out of a gold-plated cage. That suggested a need to leave the project behind. Subsequently, you must have felt that your days have been colonized all over again by these characters.

AM I do. But the great thrill of *Tales of the City* has been that it has been a sort of slowly opening flower. I don't think it's reached it's fullest potential yet after twenty-one years. We are just working now on the rough cut of the second miniseries. I expect its audience to become larger and larger as more people discover the story. I am not sorry that I ended the story where I did, because I think it has a very graceful shape. The six novels comprise one huge epic novel, as opposed to being a series of sausages cranked out by someone who knows a good thing when he sees it.

Also, I truly believe that the televised form of the story is the best one yet, because I am able to bring the wisdom of middle age to a story I wrote when I was a callow youth. When I first imagined Anna Madrigal, she was an extremely exotic creature to me. In the first place, she was a transsexual at a time when they were scarcely visible. In the second place, she was fifty-six years old, which was beyond the pale, as far as I was concerned. Now that I am just three years younger than her, I am able to create scenes that explain that character more vividly than ever before. I have worked with Nicholas Wright, the screenwriter, in that process. In some cases, we have created scenes on the spot while we were filming, because I could see further potential avenues of exploration.

RC It's fascinating that you think of this version as a new take upon the work, and want to be involved in it, when you compare it to the common view of writers: that they'll allow their project over to people in film, but they often don't expect the result to be successful, faithful, or appropriate. Sometimes they think simply in terms of money—or the chance of a new readership for the fiction.

AM In the beginning, I was resigned to the notion that it might be trash. All I could say to console myself was: "Well, at least it will draw more people to the books, and they will be the form of record." And I'll be able to bitch about the way they bastardized my work, the way every other writer on the planet does. But I found to my amazement that Channel Four in Britain wanted a completely reverential treatment. Sometimes I would have to fight for change, because I would look at something in my own work and think: "That's less than my best effort." Channel Four would say: "No, that's a beloved passage. We can't let that one go."

Yesterday I received the rough cuts of episodes two and three of the second miniseries. Along with them came a note saying that episode three was running a bit long and perhaps we needed to cut a particular monologue that Michael delivers on board the ship in Mexico. I was never so relieved, because I'd always felt that the scene was way too talky, self-indulgent, and self-pitying. I wrote it when I just discovered that my boyfriend at the time was having an affair with someone else. I poured all my pain out on to the page. It made a lot of sense to me at the time. In the context of that story, it's just one queeny wail too many. So I was delighted to be able to lose it.

RC You are so upfront in talking about Channel Four. Even in Britain, where it is fashionable to be iconoclastic, people like to criticize what has been for gay men and lesbians the most incredible gift.

AM And for every writer. Only Channel Four declares itself the champion of the writer. Peter Ansorge, the executive for Channel Four who championed *Tales*, told me from the outset that they wanted me to be in control. They wanted to honor my work, and felt that was the most prestigious thing Channel Four could do. That concept is completely unheard of in Hollywood. Every time I see a great film, there comes the Channel Four credit at the end of it: *My Beautiful Laundrette*, *Four Weddings and a Funeral*, *Beautiful Thing*, Derek Jarman's work. They are the single greatest creative entity in the world. I can say that without any compunction whatsoever.

RC In England people often only criticize.

AM   I know. That's just an English thing. I constantly arrive in England full of praise for one English institution or another, and find half the people I talk to are ready to shoot it down. You have a very rich array of choices there. You can choose from ten great newspapers in one city, and there are still movie companies that make movies about the way people actually live. I am afraid that's slipping more and more. As Britain and Hollywood get more and more cross-pollenated, there's a tendency for British filmmakers to go American. On the other hand, some people hold on to their principles. My friend Stephen Frears went to Hollywood, found it a despicable place, and went back home to make good little movies again.

RC   The thing about iconoclasm is that it's a dangerous freedom to indulge in sometimes, in the sense that something like Channel Four is not necessarily that secure.

AM   No. It may already be leaving its golden age, I don't know. I hope not.

RC   You've spoken publicly about the problems with PBS and the first series of the *Tales*.

AM   The sad thing about the PBS situation is that their retreat from *Tales of the City* simply proved true the most frequently heard argument against government-funded television, which is that any entity that receives government money is bound to be subject to government control. In the United States, that government control comes from places like Georgia and Oklahoma, where the state legislators can destroy the local public television station on the spot. That's what they tried to do when *Tales of the City* appeared on the air. Rather than presenting a united front and standing up against these legislators, saying: "We are going to take the side of freedom of expression, and the side of the public," PBS took the easy way out and talked about their great children's programs. They bragged about a purple dinosaur, and turned their back on a show that had won them a Peabody award.

RC   To return to the *Tales of the City* books, when you spoke about the coherence of the complete project, I thought of E. F. Benson"s *Mapp and Lucia* books, which I know you are a fan of. At what point in the series did you know when it would close?

AM   I really didn't know until I had arrived at the sixth book. But I could feel it happening. So I went with it and trusted my instincts every stage of the game. When AIDS came along midway through the series, I was bound and determined not to stop then, because I didn't want to seem as if I was retreating from the epidemic. I certainly wasn't in my own life, and I didn't want to in my work. But it did pose a rather thorny problem, because I was writing what was basically a comedic story. I was the first to take it personally when Edmund White issued a proclamation that humor should never in any way be used in dealing with the epidemic.

RC   He has since retracted that.

AM   As he should have. It was one of the few really silly things he's ever said. Greater writers than I have proved him wrong. Tony Kushner springs immediately to mind.

RC   In prose though, there is a very small number of books which have dared to use comedy—and even fewer where there hasn't been an HIV-positive author standing behind the comedy, somehow legitimating it.

AM   You mean whether it's impertinent on my part to be funny about AIDS, when I myself am not antibody-positive?

RC   There is something of that in the cultural mood.

AM   It does lie in the cultural mood. It simply posed one more hurdle for me. I have heard that criticism about everything I have ever written about. When I first wrote about a women's music festival in *Significant Others*, there were gay men who told me that this was really going to piss off the women. It did *not* piss off the women; it simply opened my audience even wider. I found that there were as many lesbians standing in line at book signings as there were gay men.

I think the job of the writer is to be empathetic with others—to impersonate others if necessary. Dickens never had that fear. Any writer who really wants to test the limits does not avoid writing about an experience that's different from his own.

RC   We are in a weird cultural moment. Many writers come to know what you've just said through what drew them to writing in the first place: breaking the boundaries of the self, and of experience, and so on. Readers and critics seem more influenced by this cultural move toward authenticity, which leads ultimately to the balkanization of experience.

AM   There is nothing that makes me crazier. I read a review in the *New York Times* a couple of days ago about Allan Gurganus's novel *Plays Well with Others*: a very stupid review, in which Robert Plunket accused him of jumping on the AIDS bandwagon because his last novel wasn't ostensibly a gay novel. That's just total bullshit. Allan Gurganus was out of the closet in the early seventies and writing some of the best gay-themed short stories ever written.

I am afraid as gay people that we contribute to this in a big way when we insist on calling novels "gay novels" or identifying writers as "gay writers," and conclude from that that there's a limitation on the audience and the subject matter. I am very proud of the fact that I have been out of the closet as long as I have. When I die, that will probably be the thing I am most proud of. But I do not want that fact to limit my audience or my subject matter. If there's anyone out there who tells me that it must, then they can go fuck themselves. I find it very restricting to be told that there are only certain things that I am allowed to write about.

RC   It's an assault on creativity.

AM   A complete assault on creativity. I resent it when my books are restricted to the gay/lesbian section in bookstores. I want them in both places—in the gay/lesbian section and in literature, because I am writing for everyone. The gay literary world is now beginning to subdivide into even smaller groups. Now there are AIDS writers and AIDS novels, and we're doing "gay people of color" novels. All of those things should exist, but they don't need to exist with little boxes around them.

RC   It's somehow captured in that phrase, "As a something-or-other . . ." —one of the biggest lies of our time: "As a gay man . . . ," and so on.

AM   Well, I'm guilty of that one, because in the old days that was the quickest shorthand for being out in a public interview. You just put it out there and said: "Here I am." But the truth is I was making those statements as an intelligent, thinking person. It gets to the point more quickly if you identify your homosexuality. I was always in a double bind, because I wanted to be treated as any other writer working in the world, but I detested the people around me who always avoided any discussion of their homosexuality in relation to their work. I still detest them. So the trick is to be completely honest about yourself, and insist on your right to be part of the mainstream.

I think the moral for writers is to tell your darkest secrets, and you'll find out they're shared by a lot of other people. My sister told me a story about her mother-in-law, who used to wear a bag over her head when she saw her gynecologist. The idea was that if she did not see him, she would not be compromised. I got fixated on this bag. Was it the same bag every time? I used it in *Maybe the Moon* and read it out at public meetings, where it always got a big laugh. When I got to Raleigh, North

Carolina, my hometown, I realized at the last minute that my sister and her mother-in-law were in the audience. I took a deep breath and went ahead. Afterwards I asked my sister how it had gone. She said her mother-in-law had just leaned over and said: "See, somebody else does that too!" My theory about fiction is that we read it to see if somebody else does it too.

RC   As you've touched already on the idea that gay literature is something of a canard and maybe unhelpful, what's your reaction to the sense that a sort of gay canon is beginning to form—one in which the "gay-themedness" of a work is a preoccupation. Sometimes the "ghettoness" of a book almost seems an imprimatur of quality. Even in the seventies, one could argue that books that were written in New York described gay experience in a narrow way.

AM   You mean the Fire Island school of gay writing?

RC   We are still reading books about Fire Island in the seventies.

AM   You may be reading them. I'm not!

RC   We're still witnessing them. Is this a wrong step that has just continued?

AM   I think there are no wrong steps. Writers have to write about their own experience. If they find an audience for that, that's great.

RC   But for you, it doesn't appeal, clearly: the idea of, say, a gay social book of manners, for instance.

AM   Frankly, most novels that are just about gay people, and that burrow deep into the rituals of ghetto life, make me feel very claustrophobic. They always have and they always will. I don't think that has to do with any form of self-loathing: quite the opposite. It has to do with a vision of myself that sees me in the world at large. People who dig into any sub-culture—a small town in Missouri, the Castro or Pakistani life in London—are a little bit afraid of functioning totally in the world. That's a natural instinct, because we all feel safer when we are surrounded only by our own kind. But there are lot more rewards when we are being challenged by the existence of others. That's why I've always put het-erosexuals in my books. I want to ask myself questions about me from that viewpoint. That's why I realized that my thirty-one-inch female friend would be a perfect challenge for me when I was writing a novel.

RC One response might concern realism: the argument that people *do* live in ghettoes. At the margins of the *Tales*, there are such people.

AM There are, and their experience is completely valid. The writers who write about their ghetto life are completely valid as well. I just don't hap-pen to be one of them, and for the most part I don't relate to their work.

RC What if they termed their own work realistic? Some people have argued that the worldview of the *Tales* is to some extent fantastic—an imaginary utopia.

AM Well, if you'd like me to tick off the names of my ten best friends, I think you'd see that this is simply the way we live.

RC I wouldn't be asking for that kind of validity. It's absurd to measure books by questions of authenticity and experience.

AM Yes, and the number of fags to be found in them. I thought that *Maybe the Moon* was perhaps the queerest thing I had ever written, because it really dealt with sexual identity and racial identity and the nature of outsiderness, in a way that I had never really tackled before. Yet it was not eligible for a Lambda Book Award because it didn't have a gay or lesbian hero at its immediate center. You begin to ask yourself: "What is a gay or lesbian novel? How well served are we by creating these definitions?"

RC What is your own relationship with the San Franciscan gay ghetto? Presumably there's a high recognition factor when you go there.

AM Sometimes I go there, but one of the hazards of going into the Castro now is that there is a daily tour group called "Cruising." It is run by a lovely old woman who shows people the gay sights. She stops me if she sees me. I get quite a kick out of it, though I think the tour group thinks I am planted there. Once I walked into a juice bar in the Castro that had names of famous gay people on a fresco around the wall. My name was there, between Oscar Wilde and Martina Navratilova. I was so thrilled. I loitered around, waiting to be recognized. But the clerk didn't have a clue who I was, of course. Finally I ordered a ginger carrot juice. She handed me a chit which said "Joan of Arc." That was the name of the order. I sat down, and a woman who had also ordered something sat next to me. Five minutes later, the clerk called out "Armistead Maupin." The woman jumped up and claimed her drink. I enjoyed it all in silence.

RC In *Maybe the Moon*, you had much more scope to consider identity in terms of explicit sexual experience than you would have had in the serialized *Tales*. In one interview, you spoke about the need to describe sex in order to construct Cadence's characterization. That's a contrast with what was possible in the *Tales*.

AM Yes, and I was criticized for it by the reviewer in the *Times*. This woman reviewer knew that I was gay, and said that Cadence was nothing but a gay man in disguise, and that she knew far more about S&M than you would expect from a woman who is thirty-one inches tall. Now what does that say about the reviewer and her vision of other human beings?

And what does it say about the dilemma of writers who choose to be openly gay, and to write about other people?

We pay a price for our openness, because there's an assumption made about the prejudices and agendas we bring to bear upon our work. No one makes that assumption about white straight male writers, but they make it about a fag that chooses to be a fag and write about people other than himself. Even fags are guilty of that compartmentalizing.

RC Regarding the *Tales*, I wondered if the limitations on writing about sex conditioned by newspaper publication felt limited at the time, given what you went on to do in *Maybe the Moon*?

AM I think it was the best thing that could have happened at the time, because it forced me to write stories that weren't just about getting laid. I was compelled to dig into the other humorous aspects of gay life and to make the stories as universal as possible. I've never been sorry that I had those constrictions because in some ways it opened up possibilities for me, it didn't narrow them down. It made me be more inventive about where the humor arose. The great example of that in modern popular culture is the television show *Ellen*, which was bland and uninteresting as any show can be before Ellen's character came out. Afterwards, there was a plethora of material that opened up: rich, new material that really had nothing to do with what dykes do in bed; more to do with the way the culture works.

Having said that, I am delighted that I have arrived at the point in my career when I can write a novel, as I am doing at the moment, that speaks clearly in my own voice and allows me to address all sorts of sexual concerns. But I am not one of those writers who sees gay writing as one perfectly crafted fuck scene after another, because that is only one aspect of being a fag.

RC Another inadvertent consequence is the relative ease with which the *Tales* could be filmed, PBS notwithstanding.

AM Wait till you see what we've got coming up. We've got dicks in *More Tales*!

RC The first series had the gay kiss.

AM That's what I mean about the slowly opening flower. I have felt as if I have been riding a wave of popular culture for the last twenty-one years, and I am allowed to do just a little bit more every year. That's a very exhilarating feeling. Whereas the subject matter of the *Tales* is sometimes described as nostalgia, because it's about twenty-one years ago, the form of its presentation is completely modern, because people are doing things that have never been seen on film before in a way that is accessible to the entire culture.

RC Thinking of the current moment in cinema, reviving the seventies and their liberated sexuality—*Boogie Nights*, in particular—do you think you were a trigger for this?

AM Would it sound immodest if I described myself as the cannon, not the trigger? I *know* we were the first, because the initial response to *Tales of the City*, when it was first announced, was a wrinkling of the nose from people who still looked at the seventies in a disparaging way. The prevailing attitude about the seventies, five years ago, was that it was a time when nothing happened, a time of enormous bad taste and inactivity. That's easy to believe if you are white, straight, and male.

RC It's the view of Russell Rand in *Sure of You*.

AM Yes. If you were a fag or a woman in the nineteen-seventies, you knew that plenty happened. It's only recently that we have been permitted to acknowledge that was the time when gay people first stood on their feet and proclaimed themselves people to the rest of the world. So in the past four years I've seen the culture move from the spot where we had to scavenge in garage sales to find the costumes to the point where, for the last series, we could simply buy some of the clothes off the rack at Urban Outfitters.

You'd be hard-pressed to find another show or film that paid such reverence to the seventies before *Tales of the City*. It's now escalated to such a nauseatingly trendy thing that we are downplaying the seventies aspects of *More Tales* in press releases.

Some of the first reviews of the *Tales of the City* miniseries in San Francisco said it's rather sad to look back on the time before AIDS and realize that all that irresponsible activity was going to lead to the epidemic. There was a very moralistic view of the time, which we simply stared down. The attitude of the show was: "Fuck you—it was a time of great joy and self-discovery, and we will not have a revisionist view of what we did then because of what happened later."

RC You have spoken of the way in which you now have a more mature take on the earlier books, but there is this other "afterness," AIDS, that those books never anticipated. I guess you've just answered the question of how the films are going to deal with that. The answer is: by ignoring it.

AM Absolutely. By remaining utterly faithful to the moment as it was described at the time it was written. I don't regret anything I did in the seventies, and most of the people I know who are antibody-positive, and even the ones who have died, never expressed regret over the lives they led.

RC In literature particularly, there's a spate of books addressing the same period. Some of them apparently aim at nostalgia; others are more ambivalent. Some are celebratory. There's Allan Gurganus's *Plays Well with Others*; Brad Gooch's *The Golden Age of Promiscuity*, which stopped after introducing Patient Zero. The cultural moment, up to and just before the revelation of this "afterness" is one a lot of people have latched onto.

AM Absolutely. Because you can draw all sorts of pat moral conclusions from it.

RC You're suspicious of these narratives?

AM I'm very suspicious. I want to know the point of view of the author. Inevitably the author betrays his point of view in the telling of such a tale, because it's not that neat.

Patient Zero was essentially an invention of Randy Shilts. I remember the day he told me that he had discovered the man. He was so thrilled, because it gave him a chapter that he could excerpt in the mainstream press. He invented a Typhoid Mary for AIDS. That's all the public needed to see—fags as irresponsible people. I still resent Randy for that.

RC The Gurganus book is doubly peculiar. As author, he says: this is the first post-AIDS book, one which takes into account the new medical circumstances and is prepared to describe this period; to allow closure, to close it.

AM I'm not sure I can manage closure yet. But I do know we have moved into another era. My own partner Terry Anderson thought he was going to die for ten years. When protease inhibitors came along, he realized that he wasn't going to die right away. That effected all sorts of changes in our lives, chief of which was that he decided he wanted to live across the valley. We are still very much in each other's lives, and are each other's chief support. But he discovered there was a lot of living he had yet to do, and he wanted to do it under different circumstances. I think we had constructed a life for ourselves that revolved around his imminent death. To some degree, he saw me as participating in that belief. He needed a chance to find who he was after all those years, and he has lots of friends who feel the same way, who are having to completely examine the premise of their own lives because they no longer believe that they are going to die. That means that a new era has dawned. It doesn't mean that the epidemic is over. It means that mentally and emotionally, people are behaving in a different way, so I think Gurganus is right to a certain degree.

RC   It's a great moment in some people's lives. It's also a great possibility in narrative.

AM   I for one am grateful for any new feeling about this epidemic. I think we all felt a degree of exhaustion. Even the creative response to it was beginning to grow dimmer.

RC   Though, in large part, that response was heavily deferred. With the exception of your books and a handful of others appearing in the mid-eighties, the big wave of AIDS literature came around 1990 and later.

AM   That's true. I'll never forget when David Leavitt announced that he had discovered this marvelous new subject matter—in 1987. It's surprising to see how late some writers came to the subject. I've always been very glad that I didn't kill off Michael Tolliver. For a number of years after I had stopped writing the series, people would come to me and say: "Well, I'm sorry you quit the series, but I am glad in a way because Michael would be dead by now." I would always say to them : "No, he is not dead. He tested positive at the same time Terry did, and Terry's still here." So what I have in *Tales of the City* is a gay man who is HIV-positive and is never seen to die.

RC   What was so brilliant about that ending is that you foreshadowed the chance of that ending, by representing a mood that was totally credible, in which many friends of Michael have died.

AM   Some are living; some are dead—and you are in the midst of it. That's what living with AIDS meant from the very beginning: turning to the moment. That's why so many gay men discovered Eastern spirituality in the course of the AIDS epidemic, because many people were truly living that life: tackling each day as it came, and considering that to be life, and to be grateful for that day.

While we are on the subject of foreshadowing, I noticed yesterday watching the rushes of *More Tales*, how eerie it is to see Michael Tolliver on the verge of death in 1977, and how the response to it was so similar to the response heard later on, in novels that specifically dealt with AIDS. Michael was threatened by Guillain-Barré, but he was pulling his extended family closer to him; he was proclaiming himself proudly gay to his parents; he was finding his own as a man because of a mortal illness. All of that happened five years later when AIDS struck. As a consequence, I hope it doesn't feel secondhand, when it actually appears on the screen, because we have seen it done so many times now.

RC You've spoken about the extent to which intuition took hold in relation to the characterizations and plots in the *Tales*. You spoke of having a plot sketch in which a certain amount was up for grabs. I guess characters would progressively show or suggest ways to you of having the *Tales* develop.

AM "Outline" is rather a strong word! I had a general idea of my destination when I set out to write the later *Tales*.

RC On the specific question of Michael's nondeath, for instance, where did the determining moment occur? Absolutely at the last moment, or in that case was there a longer-term strategy?

AM Well, I had spent years watching movies in which the fag always dies at the end. I was determined not to contribute to that canon. I made it pretty clear that Michael might die pretty soon; he was making arrangements for his funeral with his parents. But I felt that I could say more about a man who was still living with the epidemic than I could say through his death. Other writers had done that beautifully. I had the example of Paul Monette. Frankly, in the late eighties, I began to think fiction was pretty useless to a writer who wanted to write about the gay experience, because nonfiction was so extraordinarily eloquent. What I could do through fiction was let people know that the sense of hope for the future *did* exist for some people with AIDS. Not hope for the future, but belief in the present.

RC   In a review of *Maybe the Moon*, Adam Mars-Jones talked about the *Tales* somewhat. He suggested that a part of the project was democracy and interchangeability at the level of experience and hazard. He said that AIDS had undermined the equivalence of experience that the series needed.

AM   That it increased the stakes so high for gay people? That's an interesting remark. I don't think it is true. I think that's a rather myopic view of our situation. There were women dying of breast cancer at the same time that men were dying of AIDS. There were people being hit by trucks.

There's no question that AIDS was a disaster of enormous proportions, especially as it struck a group of people who were still bearing the brunt of society's criticism. But to assume that we are the only people on the planet with problems is to let the drama queen in you take over too much, I think.

RC   The sense of it was, I think, that, given your proclaimed universalism, there was a structural problem for the books at this critical historical moment. Suddenly everything seemed overwhelmingly in jeopardy for one of your constituent groups.

AM   That it was hard to keep the democracy going? Yes, it was hard. To a certain degree, I meant for Michael's dilemma to be the great heart-wrenching core of *Tales of the City*. I was happy to tip it in the direction of gay people whenever I could.

I have a gay agenda.I always laugh when gay people fight the Christian Right over that term. Of course we have an agenda: to change the mind of the world, and we are doing that. Which is precisely why Jerry Falwell and company are so upset. We should admit to it. I can be more subversive about it in the context of *Tales of the City*, because I am creating the illusion of equality. But of course I come with my own baggage. I have my own prescription for the way the world should work.

RC   One consequence is that it becomes a more gay-themed work, and a darker work.

AM   Yes it does. It becomes more gay-themed, it becomes darker; and I am carrying with me an audience that isn't expecting it, but can't put the books down.

RC   This suggests that the writing became more difficult.

AM   It was a challenge. But the series has changed with every book. That's why it doesn't bother me that we're having to film each book as a different miniseries, because the flavor of every book is different.

I'm delighted that I've been able to bring my audience along with me every inch of the way. The people who found *Tales of the City* so friendly and accessible I hope will be buying my next novel, which will show many aspects of life they've never seen before. All of this suggests that I'm doing a bit of fancy dancing to keep people interested and involved, and I have to confess that I am. I care what the reader thinks. I care whether they are still listening. I care whether they find my characters attractive or not. But I also try to tell them the truth as I see it. Maybe that's why it takes me so damn long to write the things.

RC   Isn't there also a tension? You've spoken of waiting for readership responses when certain episodes of the *Tales* appeared in the newspaper—Jon's death, for instance. Nevertheless, the structure imposed by serialization allows you a lot of leeway. You can be selective about what you show, for instance. The hospitalization . . .

AM . . . happens offstage, yes.

RC You can avoid all that. Again, was this something you were always conscious of, or something the *Tales* suggested to you?

AM I knew that if I followed someone's wasting and deterioration through AIDS in the course of a novel, it would completely destroy the balance. I wouldn't be able to do it. I resolved to tell it in such a way that I could be truthful in the episodes that did deal with AIDS, but also allow the other characters to breath and exist. Let's face it, that's the way the world works. Anyone who's ever had a friend die of AIDS knows that they have to leave the hospital, and buy groceries and cook dinner that night, and pick up the laundry next morning.

RC In the first book, you had already sacrificed Norman—maybe an easier character to sacrifice. But even within that book, Mary Ann carries on.

AM Yes, she's rather ruthless.

RC So you'd already solved the problem in a peculiar way.

AM Certainly people had died in *Tales of the City* before.

RC You'd sacrificed Beauchamp Day, too.

AM Yes, but he wasn't loveable—to put it mildly.

RC Nor was Norman.

AM   No, those were clearly villains. That's why the death of Jon rattled people so much, because up to that point they thought only the bad guys had to die. I was allowed to make a very loud point about the nature of AIDS: that our brightest, and finest, and loveliest people were dying. That was the hard part about it. People who were sexually comfortable with themselves and therefore more adventurous were the ones we were losing—people who had stood up and said: "I am a fag, and I am proud of it, and I don't care, and I love my life, and I am not ashamed of sleeping around." Those were the people who were dying and who were already my heroes.

RC   By contrast, Norman and Beauchamp were villains. In both characterizations, there is deceit and exploitation—the opposite of those qualities the *Tales* seem to uphold: openness, honesty, truthfulness. At the same time, when people refer to the *Tales*'s worldview in terms of inclusiveness, it occurred to me, thinking of those two figures who die, that maybe there's a cautionary note to be struck. There are still limits to what can be included. Norman's pedophilic sexuality, for instance, is beyond the pale of this series—and Barbary Lane.

AM   Yes.

RC   Beauchamp, then, not for his bisexuality, but for his dishonesty.

AM   Yes. Beauchamp was modeled after a number of stylish closet cases I met when I first moved to the city, who had a wife and a membership in the Pacific Union club, and a prosperous career, and enjoyed all the fruits of gay life in San Francisco. I thought that was contemptible, because he was robbing his wife of her own pleasure, and because on some level I realized I might have been heading there myself. I remember making the very conscious decision in my mid-twenties that I would not marry any of the young women in Raleigh that people expected me to. I knew I would make her life hell. I couldn't imagine people that would do such a thing. There are people who say to me: "On the one hand, you claim to be compassionate and to accept all the world, and on the other hand, you are not very nice about closet cases." Maybe that's an inconsistency. But I don't care, because that kind of gay self-loathing has been a larger obstacle to us than the misunderstanding of the heterosexual dictatorship.

RC   Careerism is what it's largely about, too.

AM   Yes. We would be very impatient and contemptuous of a Jew who said: "Of course I had to change my name. I had a job at an important company." But we don't apply that standard to homosexuals. We have trained a lot of straight liberals to think the same way in the process. That has been very damaging over the years. It's the reason that this rather simple fact of life has been so slow in seeping into the culture.

RC   It means your work ends up being quite an assault upon cherished national values in America: the cobbling together of materialist impulses and religious ones. The fictional worlds you describe are worlds in which, when people are held at their best anyway, they improvise and place things like personal loyalty above career.

AM   To that degree, *Tales of the City* has always been very political. It has dealt with the closet from the very beginning. Those Fire Island novels of the late seventies had no consciousness in that regard at all. It was just about getting laid, and wearing the best clothes, and going to the right discos. It was all about materialism and the emptiness of it all. The concern of *Tales* has always been the pursuit of an honest, matter-of-fact life as a homosexual.

RC   Not just gay sexuality, and not just materialism, but also careerism and alleged family values—they are all brought in. In other gay fiction we could think of, the context of the family was often missing. Maybe that's changed now. There seem to be more and more novels describing gay sexuality in the context of the family.

AM That began to happen in East Coast novels in the late eighties. I'm lucky. I had this marvelous place—San Francisco—to transform me, so when I was coming out of the closet in the early seventies, I was also making a lot of other decisions about my life and my perceptions. I was throwing off an enormous degree of racism as well, something I had been very carefully tutored in from an early age.

I was also in a broader sense examining my spiritual destiny. All of those things came to bear in *Tales of the City*. I wasn't just writing about coming out. I was also lucky because I was recording my own feelings as they occurred, on a daily basis. When Anita Bryant launched her campaign, I read about it in the *Chronicle* the day it happened. The next day I was able to respond to it in a letter from Michael's mother, in the same newspaper. So I was able to make observations on a very immediate level. I'm not sure I'd be able to do that if I were sitting down today to write the great novel of twenty years ago. I wouldn't remember what my feelings were.

RC I'm interested in the regional element. There have been helpful developments in gay literature recently toward a more regional picture, as against the late seventies, where one could have inferred that to be gay, you had to be in New York. There's a danger of New York, with its great publishing arena, consolidating itself as some vital formative context for gay men.

AM New York is as provincial a place as anywhere else—and as chauvinistic. We're guilty of that here as well. There's a chauvinism that permeates San Francisco that's quite extraordinary. For many years I suffered from that worldview of things. New York's belief that it's the center of the world kept me invisible, until the sheer numbers of my books demanded that I be noticed.

RC For an English reader, that's surprising.

AM I used Britain to crack New York. I made a conscious decision in 1982 to promote my work in Great Britain. I made trips over there to encourage my British publisher. I knew on some level that what I was writing was more firmly rooted in the British tradition than in the American. *Tales of the City* is basically a British village novel set in San Francisco. There's also a very honorable tradition of comic novels there that manage to touch on some very serious issues.

RC Who do you have in mind?

AM The early Evelyn Waugh novels were a huge inspiration to me.

RC What about P. G. Wodehouse?

AM To a certain degree. Wodehouse is a bit too much like eating a box of chocolates in one sitting. But I admire the craft of his work. Barbara Pym was a terrific inspiration. And of course the initial inspiration for writing serially was not Dickens but Jan Struther, who created a character so vivid to the British public that people actually wrote Mrs. Miniver letters and ignored Jan Struther.

RC I wanted to ask about readability. Some of the names we've mentioned have been criticized for the accessibility of their prose.

AM Yes, the ultimate crime!

RC People often think Pym and Isherwood, another name you often mention, cannot be serious.

AM I know. Isherwood's my hero in that regard, because he's such a graceful prose writer, and yet he's so unpretentious about it. He cares about his clarity. As a consequence, he's pleasant company for long periods of time. That should be the goal of a writer, I think.

RC   Why is it not a central goal to other writers?

AM   Because the critical and academic establishment has decided that dense, difficult, ponderous prose is serious prose, and that prose that flows like music is not serious.

RC   Does this have something to do with modernism?

AM   Yes, it has everything to do with modernism. As a consequence, I feel no relationship with modernism whatsoever. I feel much more kin to nineteenth-century authors than twentieth-century ones, except those who have remained firmly rooted in the duties of storytelling.

I can't turn off that machinery; that's what I do. For many years I worried that I would never make it, because I didn't find myself listed as someone to "Bear in Mind" in the *New York Times*. Now I really don't care, because I get all the strokes I could possibly want from my readership. After a certain number of years, you begin to realize that your work is probably going to stick around for a while, because you find that new generations of readers are getting hooked on the story, the way people were when it first appeared in the newspaper. That's very heartening, because it tells you that it's not about the hipness of the story. It's about the issues of the human heart that arise in the course of the story. In fact, *Tales of the City* is anything but hip at this point. It's very rapidly moving into the territory of quaint. Any day now we will start issuing ceramic miniatures of 28, Barbary Lane!

RC   Speaking of spin-offs, I am wearing my *Midnight in the Garden of Good and Evil* T-shirt.

AM   Does it have a picture of a closeted actor on it?

RC   I was so astonished when I heard about the film. Thinking about Berendt's book is interesting in terms of what you have said about sexuality. It appears as true crime, with its claims to authenticity; yet some characters appear under fictional names, and the journalist figure—Berendt himself—is written out heavily. At a stylistic level, fine; that's a choice. If the sexuality is irrelevant to the story, fine; but in the film . . .

AM   . . . he's now been completely heterosexualized. What we've watched is the same process that occurred with the Berlin stories. The Isherwood figure in those is an all-seeing homosexual who never describes his own life. The same is true of *Midnight in the Garden of Good and Evil*. John Berendt has said under duress that he is gay, but that is never made evident in the novel. That's the one thing about the book that I find off-putting. We are never told how he has such access to all these different people. As a consequence, when the time comes around for the conversion to film, the homosexual disappears completely. Of course, Isherwood himself complained that the same thing happened with the Berlin stories.

RC   We touched on the book by accident, but it's an interesting case to bring in. In terms of prose style, I can imagine you'd be engaged by it. And it's good storytelling.

AM   Oh, I think it's one of the most beautiful pieces of writing I have ever seen. It's a brilliant book, and I am flabbergasted that it has been embraced by as many people as it has. I never dreamed that something that well-written, that subtle, clever, and unsensational would be so thoroughly adored. It makes me think better of the American public because it has had such success.

RC   It's a world you knew well; Savannah is very near South Carolina.

AM   Yes. It struck a special chord with me because I spent several years in Charleston, which is just another version of Savannah. There's all that mildewy decadence just below the surface in both cities.

RC   There are lots of reasons to resist the notion of a gay literary canon. But given the chance to enthuse about an overlooked contemporary book with gay themes, what would you choose?

AM   I think *Landscape: Memory* by Matthew Stadler is one of the most unrecognized gay masterpieces of the last ten years. It made me ache with envy for the entire time I was reading it. It's a remarkable work of art.

I love the work of Stephen McCauley, and have loved it for many years. I am a great fan of Patrick Gale. I wish that his novel *The Facts of Life* had had an American publisher. He's somehow seen as too British for American publishers—a preposterous brand to give him, because he writes about the human heart in a way that's very appealing. I loved the notion of a big sprawling novel that made me cry and gave me a hard-on within the course of a few paragraphs.

RC   Do you think creative writing can be taught?

AM   A friend of mine named Anne Lamott has written a wonderful book called *Bird by Bird*, in which she handed me some very valuable advice that was of use to me years after I had become established as a writer. There were two major points. One was: shitty first drafts—meaning they all are. So forgive yourself. Write them, and go beyond them. The other was: short assignments. Don't sit down at the beginning of the day, and say: "I am writing a short story; I am writing a novel. I have this huge task ahead of me." Tell yourself you're writing about the moment the character walks in the door, takes off his hat, sits down at the table, says a few words. Give yourself permission to do that, get it right, then keep writing.

Writing a novel is like driving at night in the fog. You can only see as far as the headlights, but that's as far as you need to see. That kind of advice is useful, but I don't think anyone can tell you how to write. That has to spin out of you like a web comes out of a spider. It has to be in you.

RC   You spoke about the slowness and care with which you write. It still means, presumably, that things are subject to revision after revision.

AM   Absolutely, though most of the revisions occur in the course of writing. I will write the same paragraph ten times in one day, and then decide that's the paragraph. It's polished the way I want that stone to look. But that's not to say that paragraph won't find its way into another section of the novel, or disappear altogether before I finally submit the manuscript.

RC   When you finish a project, you don't have this vast editing experience some have—of throwing three-quarters of a manuscript away?

AM   No, because I don't put down anything that I don't absolutely love, and I hear rhythms when I am writing. There is a music to me. Sometimes I will know that a sentence will need a two-syllable word in a particular place to make it work. I won't even know what the word is, or whether I need a word, but I know I need it for the rhythm.

RC   To return to readability, briefly: the paradox, then, is that readable prose is prose with tons of effort put into it.

AM   Absolutely. The reason it takes so long is I want it to make people feel as if they are running through the woods, and they don't have to worry about tripping over a log. That why it takes so long. It has to be a seamless stream of thought.

I write to be read aloud. The more I have toured, the more I have become aware of that, because if I stumble in the course of reading, I know that the reader will while he's sitting there alone. Those rhythms are very important to me.

RC   You've spoken of how with the earlier *Tales* there was substantial reshaping involved to turn them into novels. What was that reshaping?

AM   Some of the storylines were dead ends. I would paint myself into a corner—to mix my metaphors—time and time again. I had to make sure all that was cleaned up for the novels, so I reduced all of the characters to index cards that would indicate a particular chapter. I'd put them on the floor of the living room and rearrange them to find ways to make the weave work.

RC   Presumably that occurred in the first couple of books particularly. After that, you must have established a weave in your head.

AM   Yes. I learned how to do it. I knew that a hundred and twenty episodes would be the length of the novel, so I would contract for six months' work of the newspaper serial and then stop. After the first two years, I thought I was going to have a nervous breakdown. I told the editors I could write eight hundred words a day, no matter what, and I did that for them. But it nearly killed me. It was much easier if I knew that I would be done after six months. There was light at the end of the tunnel.

RC   You started as a journalist. As the *Tales* turn out, and in *Maybe the Moon*, all of these industries of communication—the press, film, broadcasting—in the end seem antithetical to the values of honesty and truthfulness you revere. Mary Ann gets seduced by fame, and her goodness is sacrificed. I don't know if that's putting it too strongly.

AM   Maybe a little—though most people do feel that way about her.

RC   It felt to me as if there were a kind of either/or statement at the end of the *Tales*, perhaps for the first time. Brian and Mary Ann display opposite sensibilities.

AM   My goal was at least to make her point of view understandable. I do think she sacrificed her principles in a big way, but I didn't want to make it completely black and white.

RC   But she was sent to the East Coast.

AM   Yes, which is the equivalent of going to hell in *Tales of the City*. One of the reasons I was so close to Christopher Isherwood was that we shared those feelings about the East.

RC   He was constantly asked to justify why he was here.

AM   Yes, and why Auden ended up in New York, and they split. The answer is: Chris was an honest man.

RC   Brian gets the reward of a partner, prospectively at least, at the end of the *Tales*.

AM   Oh, he just gets a roll in the hay. The whole point of that is he's just back where he started.

RC   But bearing in mind the example of Mary Ann, the treatment of the film industry in *Maybe the Moon*, and what we've spoken of about gay opinion-making and journalism, is it fair to say that, now you're established as a fiction writer, you can dissociate yourself from these intermediary media?

AM   I use them for my greater end. There's no question that Mary Ann is me. That's why I defend her a little. So is Michael, and DeDe, and Brian.

RC   All except Anna Madrigal, you once said.

AM   Though I am feeling like her more and more these days. I wrote speeches for her in the miniseries that came directly from my own pain. But what Mary Ann and Cadence Roth have in common is this overweening ambition and this fascination with fame and its trappings. I drew on my own instincts about that. So I made Mary Ann into a kind of cautionary tale for myself. It was a way of telling myself what not to do. But at the same time I was doing it. At the very moment Mary Ann was deserting San Francisco and her friends, I was deserting *Tales of the City*. There's a total parallel there.

RC   There's the career side to Mary Ann. There's also her ever more deeply inflected puritanism.
      That part is not a projection of you, surely. Only the career part is the part you were thinking of in terms of your own literary career.

AM   It's just easy to draw the parallel. She's going national. She's going to New York to expand her fame on some level.

RC   You called it a cautionary tale, but aren't her puritanical instincts part of that?

AM   No, that's gone from me. I don't have to worry about that anymore.

RC   That sounds like a good note to finish on. Thanks so much for your time.

FELICE PICANO

F elice Picano has been a prolific author in many genres, and on both gay and nongay themes for the last twenty-five years. He is probably best known to gay readers for the best-selling thriller *The Lure*, for two volumes of memoirs—*Ambidextrous* and *Men Who Loved Me*—and most of all for his epic novel on postwar American gay life, *Like People in History*, the title of which Picano borrowed from an unpublished novel by his friend Edmund White. Born in 1944, Picano grew up in Queens, New York, where he also studied. After a year of travel, Picano returned to New York in 1967, taking various jobs and writing in his spare time.

Picano's first three published novels—*Smart as the Devil* (New York: Arbor, 1975), *Eyes* (New York: Arbor, 1976), and *The Mesmerist* (New York: Delacorte, 1977)—were popular, best-selling thrillers with little gay content. Picano established a gay publishing house, the SeaHorse Press, in 1977, for which he edited *A True Likeness: An Anthology of Lesbian and Gay Writing Today* (New York: SeaHorse, 1980). His fourth novel was the acclaimed gay thriller *The Lure* (New York: Delacorte, 1979). It was followed by a novella, *An Asian Minor: The True Story of Ganymede* (New York: SeaHorse, 1981), and the novel *Late in the Season* (New York: Delacorte, 1981). Between 1979 and 1981, Picano belonged to the "Violet Quill," an informal discussion group of six gay writers that included Andrew Holleran and Edmund White.

Picano next worked with two small publishing houses under

the collective imprint Gay Presses of New York, through which his collection *Slashed to Ribbons in Defense of Love and Other Stories* appeared (New York: GPNY, 1983). *House of Cards* (New York: Delacorte, 1984) saw Picano returning to nongay fiction. Two volumes of memoirs were next: *Ambidextrous: The Secret Lives of Children* (New York: GPNY, 1985) and *Men Who Loved Me: A Memoir in the Form of a Novel* (New York: New American Library, 1989). *To the Seventh Power* (New York: Morrow, 1989), Picano's last work of the 1980s, was another mainstream bestseller.

In 1992, Picano coauthored *The New Joy of Gay Sex* with Dr. Charles Silverstein (New York: HarperCollins, 1992). David Bergman, ed., *The Violet Quill Reader* (New York: St. Martin's, 1994) featured excerpts from Picano's journals of 1978–1982, and an unpublished story, "The Symmetry!"

In the 1990s, Picano continued to be characteristically prolific. *Like People in History* (New York: Viking, 1995), his celebrated fictional account of gay life in postwar America, was followed by three further novels: *Dryland's End* (New York: Richard Kasak, 1995), a science fiction work; the historical *Looking Glass Lives* (Boston: Alyson, 1998); and *The Book of Lies* (London: Little, Brown, 1998; Boston: Alyson, 1999), a witty fictionalization and satire on the "Violet Quill" group and gay academia. A third set of memoirs, *A House on the Ocean, A House at the Bay* (Boston: Faber and Faber, 1997), also appeared. Picano's short story "The Geology of Southern California at Black's Beach" was included in 1998's *Men on Men 7* (New York: Plume, 1998), edited by David Bergman.

Picano's poetry has appeared in two collections, *The Deformity Lover and Other Poems* (New York: SeaHorse, 1978) and *Window Elegies* (Tuscaloosa, Ala.: Close Grip, 1986). He has also written for the stage, in 1986 adapting *An Asian Minor* for an off-Broadway run as *Immortal!* A second play, *One O'clock Jump,* was produced the same year, during which Picano adapted *Eyes* for film with director Frank Perry.

Picano is currently working on a new novel. A collection of previously published short stories, *True Stories*, recently appeared (Boston: Alyson, 2000). He lives in Los Angeles, where this interview took place on Thursday, November 20, 1997.

RC You began writing predominantly third-person narration; now it's mostly first-person. *Slashed to Ribbons* seems to mark the shift. Could you comment on it?

FP Yes. Both 1998 novels—*The Book of Lies* in Britain, *Looking Glass Lives* in the U.S.—are written in the first person. But the book I'm beginning now comes back to the Flaubertian narrative; that third-person, objective, postmodernist style. That's pretty much how all of us from my era learned to write. Modernism was dead; you wanted to drive a nail in it to say so.

The first four or five novels I wrote from a very strict third-person point of view, except I started screwing around with it as early as my second, *Eyes*. I was having a lot of trouble with the heart of Flaubert. Of course he has no heart, whereas Henry James and Turgenev, who use that same style, do. They get around this problem in various ways. I kept trying to figure out how to do that. *Eyes* is told from the point of view of two people, but it's unequal. The male protagonist voice I use involves an almost camera-on-the-shoulder technique. The voice of the female protagonist, however, becomes first-person as you get deeper into it. The narrative strategy was to make her appear more and more desperate and hysterical. I wanted the reader to get closer to understanding what she was going through and why.

In the end, it all comes down to how much you can expose through one method rather than the other. In *The Lure* and *Late in the Season*, I reestablished the third-person in a contemporary manner I call "camera-on-the-shoulder." It *is* a camera—with two lenses, one of which sees only what the narrator sees. The other looks into his mind. So in fact we aren't dealing with Flaubertian technique; cinema got in the way and forced us to reconstruct our literature.

You're right to point out the experimentation in the *Slashed to Ribbons* collection, but the real turnaround happened with *Ambidextrous*. I said: "I will not do another conventional narrative." The problem wasn't so much point of view. It was the texture of the prose. I felt increasingly constrained by what could be done with prose in third-person narrative. There wasn't enough "play" to it. Incidentally, I was amazed the other day when I started writing in the third person again. What I thought would be a very tight, limited voice is actually very rich now. I was surprised to find I'd cut through the constraints I felt were there in the early eighties.

The main problem in narrative is time, actually. In the earlier novels, time's a closed construct, whereas in all my memoirs, I open time up, so as to say there's no such thing. I'll be writing from the point of view of an eleven-year-old; suddenly I jump to a thirty-five-year-old, then back again. *Ambidextrous* is an anti-Proust memoir. Whereas Proust really wants everything to stay in fixed time, absolute time, I'm saying: "I'm not quite sure what the past is. The fact I can recall it so intensely at times suggests it's quite a different type of material to what we've been told." If you can relive things so intensely, who's to say what's happening when?

RC You've used the first person not only in the memoirs but also in invented fictions like *Like People in History*.

FP Yes. What I learned through writing the first two memoirs—*Ambidextrous* and *Men Who Loved Me*—freed me up to do other stuff. When I was writing *A House on the Ocean*, there are two sections in which I consciously sail into the present tense, which wasn't easy. The copy editor kept saying: "You can't *do* this!" I said: "By God, I *am* doing it. I'm aware of what I'm doing here!" I specifically did that knowing people would be startled, and that the moment of surprise would give way to the seductiveness of something occurring in the present. When I segued back into the past tense, people wouldn't even notice. That was specifically done to make something vivid, but also to destroy the reader's sense of comfort in reading about the past.

Recently I wrote an essay called "My Problem with Time." It opens with me having seen on my television three years ago some films taken at Coney Island amusement park around the turn of the century. There were all of these young men doing athletic antics with the camera. Among them was one particularly good-looking guy who was adored by his group of friends. They were all touching him and so on. I realized I was haunted by the fact that by the time I was born, these men were my grandfather's age. By the time I was sexually active, most of them were dead. So how could I have this lustful attachment to someone who's been dead most of my life?

So, especially with the invention of the moving camera and computers, time has become an absolutely fluid medium in which it's difficult for us to assess who we are at any given point. That's something I want to show in my books. In *The Book of Lies*, that's crucial when the character goes back and deals with a personality who's long dead. In *Looking Glass Lives*, too, I deal with people who were dead many years before the narrator was born. I wanted to bring time out as a real problem for us.

RC How did you come across the distinctive structure of *Like People in History*? It has been called an "epic novel."

FP I was a little behind that, actually.

RC If so, it's a new epic—a fragmented, episodic one. What's the relationship between this fragmented structure and the book's content—its attempt to cover such a vast range of human experience?

FP   For that we have to go back to the story's source. A month after I'd completed *The Lure*, I'd already put down the basic story for *Like People in History*. It came from the summer of 1978 and was about two cousins living openly gay but different lives in different places. At that time, they'd have been in their thirties. It would've been the fourth of seven fictional sections in the entire book. But evidently I didn't know what to do with it. For many years I had no idea, though I kept going back in my mind to the idea. Finally, a year before I sat down to write it, I had the framework for it—AIDS—and the ending. The book had been open-ended until then. Suddenly it had closure.

Something I'd noticed, going around the country doing readings, is that we'd not only lost the bulk of my generation of American gay men; we'd also lost the history. I saw these bright, young people who'd grown up in what was essentially a gay world. They had no idea how they'd gotten there. There was interest. But not many people like to read history books. So I thought if I did the book right, I could kill several birds with a single stone. I could make this a history book and also a story about the various lives gay men led in the past and how different these were—not only from now, but from each other. I started fooling around with which stories I'd tell. That was pretty easy. A hundred percent of the book is true. About 45 percent actually happened to me; the rest happened to the real people I name over two pages in the book. Those are people who'd told me their stories. So essentially every anecdote, scene, joke, play of words, piece of language, drag name in that book was told to me or was part of the gay world I lived in.

I wrote *Like People in History* to give those people a voice. I came out of this quite unique blend of people, and I'd like to convey who we were as a group to another generation. The best way to do that was to use their words. I had a vast amount of unassimilable material from these incredible characters who'd never been written about. Andrew Holleran and Edmund White knew a few of them, but everybody else who knew them was gone.

Even in my memoirs, I'm a less interesting character than the people around me. I just don't interest myself or other people that much. On the other hand, I'd known all these wacky, extreme, remarkable characters who should be included somewhere in our literature. Once I knew which of their stories I wanted to tell, I sat for a year, looking for some manner of getting at it.

RC   When did you know it was going to be fragmented?

FP   Early on. The only thing that related the stories was the relationship between the two cousins and the third character, the lover, when he walks in. So I knew it'd have to be fragmented in time, place, and background. That was okay with me, because that size of writing—between twenty-five and thirty thousand words—is my favorite. James called it "the blessed novelle." You can read it in a sitting, yet you can fit tons of stuff into it—unlike that bastard form, the short story, which is very difficult to work with in the best of circumstances. It took me a year of not worrying about it, and not thinking about it while I was writing other things. Then I came up with the birthday party. I sat down, saying: "Let's see where this goes." Where it went was the shape of the book.

RC   Ethan Mordden's *How Long Has This Been Going On?*, Michael Cunningham's *Flesh and Blood*, and Patrick Gale's *The Facts of Life*, all novels of similar scope and ambition, were published in the same year. Why do you think that happened?

FP   I think a couple of us said: "My God—we're still alive. We'd better do something about this." When we looked back, the story—the size of which we weren't quite sure of—got larger and larger. My idea behind shaping it as an epic was to be as pushy as possible—to say: "OK, *you* may not call it an epic, but . . . " Everybody complained about the comparison to things like the *Aeneid*, saying: "This isn't Virgil; this is no epic!" But an epic is the story of a group of people over a number of years. I looked it up, in fact. I really wanted to present the book that way: stick people in the eye with it and say: "We may be outrageous faggots, but we have our epic story. This is my telling of it." Living on the cusp of the sixties and seventies, we were uniquely placed to see the creation of something that hadn't existed before, and beforehand and afterwards.

RC   The epic novel had already been used to describe dynasties—*family* narratives, running over generations. To describe gay culture in those terms is daring.

FP   Yes. I specifically emphasized that by making Roger and Alistair cousins.

When I was on public radio and television and on reading tours for *The New Joy of Gay Sex*, someone would always call in to say: "Where did you people come from? Why don't you go back there?" I kept saying: "If you really don't want to deal with homosexuals, you're going to have to stop having children who are homosexual. It's your doing. *We're* not going around having homosexual children. You're the cause. Stop having homosexual children!" They'd say: "How the hell do we do that?" "Stop having sex—period." [*Laughs*] In *Like People in History* I wanted to rubbish the idea of what family is. These gay kids come out of great middle-class, happy families—I *did* want to push that in people's faces. It pleases me a lot that a younger generation of heterosexuals buys this book, reads and understands it. I don't know how many older heterosexuals do.

RC   That triggers a question about readership. Have you ever imagined an ideal reader?

FP   I had an ideal reader—a living one; my friend and partner, Bob Lowe. He read my books up to *Dryland's End*. He never read *A House on the Ocean* or *Like People in History*, which were being written either as he was ill and dying or afterwards.

Do I think of a readership in Edmund White's terms: a sixty-year-old straight woman?[1] No. When I'm writing gay novels, I write to people like you. You're a fairly ideal reader. I wouldn't know what a sixty-year-old straight woman thinks of—and I am getting there, age-wise. I haven't a clue what Edmund was thinking of when he said that.

RC   From what you're saying, the gay content of some books suggests a gay readership. Yet you're happy at any crossover success.

FP   Yes, especially with *Like People in History*, which is written in a fake gay English. It's not an English anybody's ever spoken, except me and my group in the seventies. The German translation took a year instead of six months, because it's written in what I call "gayspeak." You picked up on it instantly, I'm sure. Younger American and British Gen-X'ers had no trouble getting into the book either. I'd think a sixty-year-old woman living in the suburbs might have trouble. It's about the way we use language; where one boyfriend says: "See you downstairs in Szechwan Sewer"—just the idea of calling a restaurant that; automatically making fun of things. We do that; I don't remember my parents doing it.

RC   You don't think that esprit—camp, even—has always been used by gay men when presenting themselves to mainstream culture?

FP   What we call camp in the mainstream—Paul Rudnick's sort of camp—isn't real camp. It's an interim form designed by gays with the

---

1. This is a paraphrase of Edmund White's comment that in his early novels he had written for "an older European heterosexual woman, an ideal reader who helped me to screen out in-jokes and preaching to the converted." White, "The Personal Is Political," in *The Burning Library: Writings on Art, Politics, and Sexuality, 1969–93*, ed. David Bergman (New York: Knopf, 1994; London: Chatto and Windus, 1994), 372.

consent of some smart and hip straight people to allow people to play the role of insider when they're actually not.

RC The idea of false camp sounds like a contradiction.

FP It *is* false camp. It's designed. Some people are very handy with it—sitcom writers and playwrights. Novelists aren't particularly good at it. The way real gay people talk isn't camp. I think camp's an interim form where gay and straight life are supposed to come together honestly and meaningfully. That's basically impossible.

RC Couldn't you argue that heterosexual readers of *Like People in History*, given what you've said about its style of writing, are doing the very thing you say is impossible?

FP No. I assume if they get past page ten, they either know gay people or are willing to accept this is the way gay people talk. It's interesting that in *The Farewell Symphony* Edmund White for the first time bridges that gap. For many years I saw him writing "an explanation of." Now he doesn't seem at all concerned with explaining anything—as I'm not, from *The Lure* on.

RC Does "explanation" necessarily imply betrayal?

FP Betrayal? I'm not sure. But it's saying: "Like me; give me your approval." I'm not interested in anyone's approval. From the very beginning as a writer, I wanted to shock and make as much mischief as possible.

RC Couldn't "explaining" a subculture be less about seeking approval than about responding to interest? Ethnic subcultures must be explained to those outside.

FP   No question. But there's a big difference between explaining and presenting. I present my subculture—or sections of it—but explain nothing. What's to be explained? You're either getting it or not. Even writers whose work I don't necessarily approve of for other reasons I think are wonderfully bold when they present material without explaining it. I give an immense amount of credit for that. Some of the most popular gay authors present and don't explain. Armistead Maupin presents his 1975 San Francisco life just the way I remember it, without a word of explanation; not asking for anybody's approval. It's universally accepted. Some of mine have been among the most popular gay books. I never explained a word.

RC   Does "explanation" suggest the exploration of motive? In other words, is there a consequence for characterization in your refusal to explain? Justifying motives is an obvious thing to want to do in some contexts.

FP   I think this relates to a personality flaw on my part: I'm very bad at social lying. According to friends of mine, that was a distinct personality flaw. I didn't know how to lie socially; it offended me. That got me into trouble with close friends like Robert Ferro and Michael Grumley constantly. For six months at a time we weren't talking. I'd failed to lie socially in a situation where they insisted I had to. There's nothing I can do about it. But I do recognize it's a character flaw, and we all bring those to our writing.

RC   Does the camp element in a successful play like Tony Kushner's *Angels in America* involve explanation along the lines you've described?

FP   I saw *Angels* two days after it opened on Broadway, not knowing much about it. I was immediately deeply offended because it revolved around one gay man abandoning another because of AIDS. I'd spent the last five years watching gay people doing heroic feats to stay together with other gay people. We've seen gay men and lesbians acting with the most astonishing heroism and dignity compared to straight people under the same circumstances. Whatever else I might have thought about queers before that, AIDS sure changed my mind: watching an AIDS tragedy unfold scene-by-scene, with a straight family and a gay family undergoing it. So to see these gay people on stage acting in the way I thought straight people acted really bothered me. It was untrue on so many levels: a misrepresentation; a libel. I wonder if Kushner at some point didn't say to himself: "In order to make this work on the largest possible scale, I've got to show a weak and betrayal-oriented gay couple. Straight audiences won't accept anything else." Anyway, I despised that aspect of the play. It disturbed me so deeply.

Also, I'd dined with Roy Cohn twice—not of my own volition. He couldn't have been more contrary to the representation of that character on stage. Cohn came to dinner at a house I was visiting at the Pines in around 1976. We were having a high old time among some rich old queens. My partner Bob was very handsome; I was young and quite famous. They were very interested in us. We were having a lot of fun when suddenly there was a knock on the door. Our host vanished, came back ten minutes later, but didn't sit at the head of the table. Instead, this person who I instantly knew was Roy Cohn sat there. He ate our host's meal and kept putting his fork into my dish because I was next to him. He knew everybody at the table except me and Bob. They were all his clients. I watched him make mischief around the table. But he did none of it in the over-the-top, pushy, extreme manner Kushner showed. Cohn did it in this quiet, cold, snake-like manner. At another dinner party his behavior was exactly the same. At that point I asked my host: "Is this his personality?" He said: "That's Roy. He never hides anything."

Aside from those two things, I had no trouble with *Angels*. I thought the plays well-constructed. They moved in an emotionally honest manner. The story of the young Mormon was well done, and I enjoyed the attempt at a heroic dimension for the sick gay character left on his own.

My general feeling is that I'm very happy for anybody gay who makes it by doing something that's not harmful to gay life.

RC   There's surely a tendency in storytelling for things to need to be imperfect; to go wrong, in order to come right. Couldn't that be in tension with a requirement not to write something "harmful to gay life"? If the desire for a positive or healthy representation of gay characters is taken too far, what's left of interest to describe?

FP   These ideas have come up with Larry Kramer's *Faggots*—a deeply untrue book, I believe; motivated by hatred, internalized homophobia, and a sense of alienation from the group in which Kramer found himself, and by his being rejected by a lover. Some people still say: "Yet this book stands for, represents various elements." I'll not gainsay that. They're probably right. But couldn't it have been done another way? Was it necessary for Kramer to be so astoundingly negative? He presents a picture of that group which I know was a distortion because I was in the middle of it.

RC   Some people who were there applaud it.

FP   Yes. Michael Denneny thinks it's a brilliant satire.[2] I never knew what Michael was thinking at any given moment. Maybe he also felt excluded, alienated, and isolated from that scene.

RC   Can you comment on the general tension I've described between the desire to represent gayness positively and the ways in which narrative requires something—mistakes, flaws—to work through?

---

2. Michael Denneny, formerly an editor at St. Martin's Press, is now at Crown Books.

FP   I don't think the two are necessarily mutually exclusive. *Like People in History* has a real hero—somebody who begins and ends a hero. Very few reviewers have talked about the love story between the narrator and Matthew, which fails initially. They're brought together again to make another attempt. The second time it works beautifully—and on a completely unexpected level. The one straight woman reviewer who mentioned that in the *New York Times* found it boring. Yet I don't know any other book where this has been presented: a grown-up, mature, worked-out gay relationship over a period of years. Is it ten years ahead of its time? Twenty? I'd like to say to people: "Recognize this is part of our lives; we're capable of this."

RC   Stories describing the satisfactions of gay life are hard to find. Isn't it probable things are changing in that respect?

FP   As of yet I don't have any indication of that. A lot of it has to do with what Stendhal called the description of the world: "mirrors on the highway." What you actually see is fragmentary because these are spaced-out mirrors. With *Like People in History*, I got such mixed reactions to the character of Alistair. People have told me he's one of the most fabulous characters they've ever read; he can't possibly be real. He's as close to real as I could make him. I could've thrown something and hit five people like him at one point—not exactly so, but close enough—people who constructed their personalities at the age of eleven and worked at it tirelessly. Then a lot of people said: "What a really wicked person. Why write about him?" I said: "Number one, there'd be no book without him; number two, there'd be no Roger without him. He constructs Roger as his counterpart. Very early on, Alistair figures out Roger is a large force in his life. He's not quite sure what to do with him, but he'd better not ignore him. So he pulls Roger in whenever he can. At some points he leans on Roger very heavily. Roger becomes the fabulous gay person: strong; able to do things Alistair could never do because he doesn't have any ethics.

RC   Other gay novels have similarly contrasted two gay men—one embodying reflectiveness, reserve, ethical possibility; the other, immediacy, engagement, aesthetics.

FP   *Dancer from the Dance* is a famous example. I think it's part of a specifically American literary tradition: James Fenimore Cooper's *The Deerslayer* and his Indian counterpart; Mark Twain's Nigger Jim and *Huckleberry Finn*; Herman Melville's Queequeg and Ishmael in *Moby Dick*. I was aware of this tradition when writing *Like People in History*.

    Michael Bronski reviewed *Like People in History* and kept trying to figure out what everyone's politics were—even when they were eight years old; long before gay liberation. Every once in a while I'll pull out that review and howl. Brilliant as he is, Michael really failed to get what I was doing with those characters and their presentation of themselves. We read a book in psychology class in college called *The Presentation of Self in Everyday Life*, from which I learned that people present themselves in a constructed manner: at work; among their family; sometimes to themselves. That's infused everything I've written in the first person: the belief that people play with their personalities. It's something gay people especially did, and, probably to a lesser extent, still do. The people I knew when I was first coming out were astonishingly closeted and false. They'd engaged an entire repertoire; they had different personalities. I think everybody in society does, but gay people do it a little more. We're more willing to play with character and personality. That's the key—not their politics!

RC   Couldn't this idea of self-staging run contrary to the nature of autobiographical fiction, though, which often aspires to the "truthful" confession? To put it another way, does it matter in what Edmund White called "autofiction" which strain dominates: the fictional or autobiographical?

FP   Autobiographical fiction's been there from the very beginning in Western society—from early Greek novels. What I remember of

Thomas Nashe's *The Unfortunate Traveller*, which I first read in college, suggests this sixteenth-century book could really have happened to someone. With Defoe, there's no question this stuff happened to him. It may not have happened on an island somewhere with *Robinson Crusoe*; he was never a woman like *Moll Flanders*. But he's really telling us what life is like in eighteenth-century London. We can reconstruct society from that in a way I don't think we could from anybody else but Pepys, maybe.

RC   Defoe was forced to package the things he'd invented and pass them off as true autobiography. There was no such thing as fiction—the idea of it was illegitimate.

FP   It was considered illegitimate in England because of the Reformation. Cromwell and his group stopped the theater completely. From a very basic understanding of Christianity as a belief system, Cromwell said: "If you dress up, make yourself up and get up on stage and say you're someone else, you're lying!"

RC   But today fiction is possible.

FP   To a large extent what happened in the seventeenth and eighteenth centuries provides a continuous line to us. Our literature goes back to Defoe; maybe back to Nashe. Even gay stuff adheres to the questions that arose then. The strategies we utilize are merely fashion.

I'm working on a collection now called *True Stories* or *Tales from Life*. It consists of five or six shorter pieces—incidents that actually happened to me, presented as fiction—and maybe a dozen other essays, articles, and travel pieces. By putting them all together in one book, I'm saying there's no difference anymore. I don't think there was to begin with. I think Anthony Trollope, sitting there writing about Barsetshire, knew exactly who he was writing about. He'd been in those homes; he'd been listening in the vestry when Cardinal So-and-So did such-and-such to Cardinal So-and-so.

RC   What about Charles Dickens, who spoke of the importance of fantasy—of presences dictating themselves to you? You've also spoken of characters appearing before you when you're writing.

FP   Yes, but where do they come from? It must be the subconscious.

RC   Dickens lived in a pre-Freudian age, so even if that were true, he wouldn't necessarily have conceived of it that way.

FP   This brings us back to the function of the artist. That was defined for me early on. I accepted it, saying: "If I'm going to bother to do this at all, no matter what rewards eventually come, I have to adhere to what I think an artist is." That was set up for me when I was ten by a cover of *Life* magazine. It was a special edition about Picasso, the artist of the century. He was drawing a perfect Picasso sketch on a piece of glass using a flashlight. I said: "This is what an artist does. An artist does *it*, whatever *it* is, automatically; without being able to control it, beyond a certain amount of digital and mental control. He cannot *help* doing it." In the interview inside, Picasso said: "I'm a medium between some force that wishes to express itself through me, and what's left—whether it be a piece of sculpture, a painting, or a sketch. I'm not being humble; I think I'm skillful and technically adept. But I'm the medium this has chosen to use."

The interesting thing about this is watching artists fail. Everybody begins in a group of young artists—fifty of you or so. After twenty years, there are one or two of you left. It seems a fact of life that for every artist that makes it, twenty people have fallen in front of a truck. It may be they never figured out that this thing has to happen; that you have to re-create yourself constantly as a medium for some other force.

RC   I wanted to ask how conscious and how controlling you were of the shifts between the different genres you write in. The idea of a medium still leaves unanswered the extent of personal control over form.

FP   I've worked in all kinds of forms: poetry, essays, screenplays, plays. That's based on two things. First, from the beginning I had enormous amounts of energy. I didn't notice it at first. When you're young, everybody has a lot of energy. By the time I was in my mid-forties, I still had a lot of energy, but a lot of people had wound down. I have less in my mid-fifties, but I'm still way ahead of the game. Having that much nervous energy and time to spare gives me an advantage. I can *do* more. From 1975 to 1985, I was using large amounts of psychedelic drugs every weekend, partying very heavily three days a week, having as much sex as could humanly be had by anybody—and writing at least a book a year, as well as running a publishing company.

Second, to go back to Picasso: he said an artist should work in every medium. Why not? It's a matter of technique; of learning the form. I had no deep pretense of understanding what happens in playwriting. But I've written plays people react to on a constant basis. I feel I have more control over prose fiction, but my drama works also.

RC   What leads you to decide on a particular form for an idea?

FP   Generally the subject itself, though I have had ideas that have gone into three different media, looking for a final form, and have still not worked.

RC   *An Asian Minor* was in two forms.

FP   Yes: prose—a novella—and a stage play. I don't see why we should limit ourselves. I was an art major at a city university, a very hoity-toity place then, around the end of abstract expressionism. I was a talented draftsman, colorist, and sculptor, and wanted to be an artist. Increasingly, it became clear that art as it was being practiced by everybody around me was at its end. I was damned if I was going to do these splotches of color. So I rebelled. I was taking literature as a minor and being heavily encouraged to go into writing and publishing. It took a while, though. I could've gone in either direction. The one thing I learned from my entire experience of art in the sixties was not to close myself down—and not to believe teachers. However much you admire and respect them, don't pay any attention to teachers, who are only commenting on the past. It's up to you to perform the future. You don't know what that is until you've actually done it.

Most teachers can't look into the future because they're beholden to something already constructed. Some aren't. Eric Auerbach wrote a brilliant book—*Mimesis*—all about the past, yet it also told me a lot about what my potential as an author was. Another book by Wayne Booth—*The Rhetoric of Fiction*—opened up the world and looked to the future; it didn't eliminate it. I learned a lot from both.

RC   Have you ever written about your time studying art?

FP   Never. Maybe I'll get 'round to it at some point. I'd forgotten about it until recently. I've left a lot of gaps. But the art period never led to anything. It was a path not taken.

RC   Could you talk a little about writers who influenced you?

FP   Yes. My literary forebears are pretty specific. When I was first writing and wanted to solve a problem, I'd go back to these four authors time and time again—either to see how they'd done something or how they'd failed. One was Balzac, who said that if you're living in a specific time and place, you should write about it, which I believe. Readers should know what people were wearing, what the furniture looked like when you were writing. Very few contemporary novelists give that. Balzac also believed if you set up a historical framework accurately—not overdoing it—at worst, people will read you for history. Balzac did it so accurately, and his work's so vivid, even though he's overwrought. He also takes on astoundingly stupid themes and makes a lot of them work.

Also, he had this sense of the importance of sexuality; the way people are moved by it—sometimes without even knowing why. I remember reading his *Splendeurs et misères des courtisanes*—how it opens with Lucien de Rubempré![3] A character I use talks about Lucien appearing at the opera—this astonishingly beautiful man everybody wants. At the end of the opera he ends up getting into a carriage with another man and having sex with him. I couldn't believe it was happening. Balzac operates at a level of sophistication I admire instantly. You can't escape him if you read him when you're young.

Number two is Henry James, who I fought desperately against reading. I read *Portrait of a Lady* for the first time this year.

RC   You've previously talked of the terrible legacy of James though.

FP   Yes—terrible! Who would know but somebody who had read everything by James? His own work is fine. His effect on other writing has been 90 percent disastrous. James inherited this idea from Flaubert and Turgenev of what a literary artist has to be. Luckily, James didn't live it or write it. He wrote prolifically and covered a lot of areas, so we can see the play of his mind over a variety of surfaces, to use a Jamesian term. He wasn't afraid of being brilliant, which Flaubert was. But because James seems to have been taken up in the thirties and forties as the writer's writer, a lot of people would read one James story or novel, then build their entire writing career based on that, which is the error.

RC   The question of James's legacy is tricky: which one do you mean? The influence of which stage of his work?

---

3. Honoré de Balzac, *Splendeurs et misères des courtisanes* (1839–1847; translated as *A Harlot High and Low*).

FP   It's not only the stage. It's the particular story someone reads. Did he read "The Jolly Corner," not *The Bostonians*? If you read one but not the other, you're seriously screwed as an artist.

RC   What of the legacy of elaborateness in the late novels?

FP   I've read all the late books and enjoyed them immensely. I hung onto the pages of *The Wings of the Dove* to the last sentence. But if I ever write like that, push me in front of a bus! I want to write much more clearly, even though I understand James earned the right to write that way. He did; others have not.

RC   Do you object to highly mannered prose in contemporary fiction?

FP   Well, only when it's unclear. I do a lot reading in contemporary fiction. Take Martin Amis. I've attempted to read *London Fields* fifteen times. I can get fifty pages in. I have the same problem with Dale Peck. I cannot doubt the perfection of the sentences, the beauty of the paragraphs, the marvelousness of each page. But I'm asleep on page forty. There's a cavalier disregard for the reader in a writer saying: "I'm more important than you. I can do whatever I want. You have to sit here and read it, by God—otherwise you're not trendy or fashionable." I don't think there's a meeting on equal grounds between writer and reader.

Jonathan Swift did the same. He just happened to be a lot better at it. As a result we got *Gulliver's Travels*. But he had nothing but contempt for his readers. He wanted to keep himself entertained, so while we get *Gulliver's Travels*, we also get just the contempt—in something like "The Tale of the Tub," which is unreadable.

RC   Do you consciously rein in experimentation with language and form?

FP   Not really. I seem to experiment in different ways, formally and the-matically. Take *A House on the Ocean*, which was literally a folio of four unwritten books. People have said: "This is so beautiful." To me it's still this incredible hodgepodge of different things. It's like somebody dropped the teapot and put it together backwards. But writers especially like that book and the way it's put together. What that means is I wasn't afraid to experiment, given all that mess. Ultimately, I think you have to hold the reader's attention. You make a pact with the reader early on. Because of its subject matter, *The Book of Lies* plays more with language than most of my books.

RC   Who are the other two influences?

FP   Thomas Mann I read early on: first *Buddenbrooks*, then the short sto-ries, then *Felix Krull, the Confidence Man*, which was hysterical, then pretty much everything else. Even where there were long, dull patches, there'd be these moments of astonishing imagination and lucidity. In *The Book of Lies* one character talks about *Joseph and His Brothers*, that long book which, more than any other novel of Mann's, has these incredible moments where something happens and you're just astounded. You think: "How did he get *there?*" There's a scene in Egypt where Joseph goes to fetch his first masters, a brother and sister who are vaguely related to the Pharaoh. Joseph goes into the temple and watches this ceremony to Seti in which everybody is singing, chanting, and hopping on one foot. *Hop-ping on one foot!* I felt: "Boy, am I in a strange place!" I don't doubt it hap-pened. Mann connected in there and got to some truth intuitively.

I've gone back to Mann again and again to see how things are done. The fourth influence is Tolstoy, who's also capable of amazing things. One reason I never wrote an AIDS novel was because of his *The Death of Ivan Illych*. Why bother writing a book about dying when he did it perfectly?

RC   Do you find AIDS literature flawed?

FP   Almost totally. A couple of stories in Allen Barnett's *The Body and Its Dangers* I like. But even they're not equal to a moment I had with him two years after the publication of that at the Outwrite conference. Allen got up and said: "I'm supposed to be discussing narrative ventures in contemporary fiction. All I can think about is the two weeks I spent at my eye doctor's trying to be able to see." He went on for fifteen minutes. Our mouths fell open. The reality of the experience was so much more intense than even what he had gotten at in *The Body and Its Dangers*.

    I have vivid memories of four people dying of AIDS while I was in the room. I don't know how to present that in literature. I don't know whether I should, frankly. It was a remarkably bad series of luck for me to experience it. Why force it on anybody else?

RC   Publishers suggest readers are wary of AIDS.

FP   If that's true, it's realistic. It's not that I don't think the material can be handled. It can, in context; not quite obliquely, but not exactly head-on.

RC   Is that what you were aiming for in *Like People in History*?

FP   Yes. Edmund White did it in *The Farewell Symphony*. I've done it again in *The Book of Lies*. Probably I'll deal with it again in some form. But the only person who can make it his story is somebody who went through the whole thing, then died of it. How the hell does he come back and tell us? Every death experience appears different. I don't think anybody did death as well as Tolstoy. Instead it gets sentimental and bullshitty.

RC   A number of books and films have recently appeared dealing with the great, sexually explosive years of the New York gay subculture before AIDS. What's the appeal of that moment?

FP   There are time periods in which certain things happen. The seventies was one. Right now, straight America is beginning to get into it with movies like *The Ice Storm* and *Boogie Nights*. I don't think the world was ever sexually that free. Anywhere in the world you went—except deepest Africa or South America—there was this incredible sense of sexual freedom. It changed a lot of other things, too: the way people dressed; the way they moved, talked, related, had relationships. Until AIDS came along, it looked like that would be so forever, frankly. Gay culture happened to reach its first peak at that time.

I think it'll be back again. One reason why I'm telling it is to do so unapologetically; to say: "I see nothing wrong with it." We were experimenting. We didn't know what the hell we were doing. We knew we didn't want to be like those straight people. American heterosexuality is an incredible disaster. Everybody admits it. We were smart enough not to be like that, but we didn't know what else to be like. It was a matter of constant self-invention, and it happened very quickly. Also, there were far fewer of us. We were probably about two thousand people. Many of us were actively engaged in professions which then affected the rest of the world within six months.

We were just trying to figure out what to do next in every single aspect of our lives. It was unprecedented. You couldn't go back to Ancient Greece or sixteenth-century England. It was a brand new culture. By God, we made some bad errors of taste, but it was very much experimental. A lot of it worked since, number one, it spread to the rest of the world fairly intact, and number two, it hasn't changed substantially since 1975.

RC   The influence of gay men in determining taste for the mainstream hasn't really changed subsequently, has it?

FP   No. But it was never so subversive or instant as then, because it also coincided with the new burst of magazines that developed in the seventies, and color television. A variety of things happened simultaneously that allowed it to be as instant. If I write about it being a peak, it quite literally was. Also, I want to suggest it can come back again.

RC Some say we're still in a highly liberated sexual culture, and that in recent times, gay culture has become even more confidently sexual despite the epidemic. Many people still have a lot of sex. Are you sure we've retreated from the seventies?

FP I used to come to Los Angeles a lot doing film work in the late seventies and early eighties. At an outdoor place called "Vaseline Alley" people would be having sex day, noon, and night. They were having sex in broad daylight in Fire Island and the Village. I used to have sex at night in the middle of the street. It *is* very different. I don't know if that world could have lasted.

RC Others say the moment passed naturally; that sexual liberation was part of a series of different fashions and wouldn't have lasted anyway.

FP It didn't pass naturally. I remember the moment we realized we could trace the sexual connections between all our sick friends. Immediately we said: "This disease is sexually related." It instituted a fear I don't think has gone away yet—a deep, distressing fear, which goes beyond the reality of the situation, unfortunately. It's very easy not to get AIDS these days, yet the fear surrounding it in the gay community operates on many different levels.

RC You spoke of Balzac's stress on writing about the culture one inhabits. A contrast occurs to me here between your career and Andrew Holleran's. There's a sense of progression from his *Dancer from the Dance* to *The Beauty of Men* which relates to his getting older, but also to changes in culture. In your case, *A House on the Ocean* appeared only recently, long after the world it describes has passed. What would you reply to the critic who said: "Stop writing about what's over. Write about what's happening *now*"?

FP   A few people said that. I'm allowing *A House on the Ocean* to appear now because I want to encourage young people not to be fearful or apologetic; to go out and reconstruct gay society so there's a less fearful way to live.

RC   To some extent the book is historical, though. Couldn't it do just the opposite, by suggesting a golden era that cannot be recovered?

FP   No. The only reason you mention a golden era is to get it back. I was persuaded by younger friends to put out that book. I brought up these same questions, and a few reviewers have gone after me specifically about that. But most have gone after me because I've refused to rewrite history in the light of AIDS. I've refused to say this was immoral or wrong. I won't tailor the truth to current realities, which may change next year. I'm unreconstructed in that respect.

RC   You're suggesting there's a cultural need now to say that sexual hedonism was bad. Isn't it as acceptable not to comment, to present it neutrally? Anthony Haden-Guest's book about Studio 54, *The Last Party*, doesn't have to say the seventies were bad; in fact, he celebrates them, but with a certain distance.

FP   Except he never understood what was going on. Look, homophobia isn't dead—certainly not in the media. It exists on a widespread level. It's just a little more hidden now. I'm a great enemy of homophobes because from the very beginning I came right out. I may have been the first publicly gay author in the world. I've never given straight people two minutes' attention. I pretend they don't exist and they don't like it. They choose various ways of going after me which I don't care about. I do care about younger gay men and women who've chosen this prevailing fear; who go after people of their generation. They're trying to set up a new form of Puritanism. One thing I liked about people in the seventies was we were never sure what was going on. Nobody ever made judgments. You'd say: "That's what's happening now; that's your thing." I see people making judgments all around us now.

RC   I wanted to ask about the experience of writing not merely about a different time, but a different place: the Pines and New York. You're far away now, living in L.A.

FP   And I'm writing about L.A., too—in *The Book of Lies*.

RC   Still, in the seventies, New York and San Francisco were seen as the two great centers of gay subcultural life. Do you have any time for some people's concerns that works such as yours reflect a narrow metropolitanism; that they don't reflect the realities of typical American gay lives beyond these urban centers?

FP   I heard that for years. I always said: "Write your own books." A lot of people did, and we got a much broader picture of gay life. I was fortunate because from 1979 I was traveling around different cities in the States and was able to see different gay lives. Consequently, it was a very specific strategy of mine with *Like People in History* and *The Book of Lies* to make sure national and even international aspects of gay life were written about. In *Like People in History*, you see gay life in San Francisco, in L.A., in different times and places. The same thing happens in *The Book of Lies*, though there's a natural cultural bias on my part towards places I spent most of my time in during this formative period.

RC   Were these metropolitan subcultures ever very different? Gay urban subcultures can appear monolithic.

FP   I've never seen anything monolithic about gay culture. Even in New York, because of my friends and the people I danced and had sex with, I was aware of a very large Latino, Cuban, and Puerto Rican culture that abutted ours. The two came together at sex clubs, dance clubs, and parties. A growing black gay culture pushed in very fast and affected a lot of what we were doing. I was aware of a poor working-class scene, and a very wealthy scene—the uptown, snotty art crowd. It was *so* diverse. One nice thing about being gay then, as now, is you could float among these groups. All you needed was interest and whatever abilities were required.

RC   The subculture was and surely is discriminating on some basis— looks, for instance.

FP   It wasn't all looks. Looks got you in the door. They didn't keep you at the party.

I said to somebody of my generation the other day: "Remember the worst insult you could give somebody—the one you could ruin their lives with? " 'Bad sex.' " He said: "Yes, you could destroy somebody by saying: 'He's cute, but bad sex.' "

Dancing was a very large subculture. If you were into dancing and knowledgeable about music, that got you in. If you used drugs a lot, that got you around. There were some very attractive, able people who should've been part of these private membership clubs. They tried to get in and couldn't: they were bad at sex, bad dressers, and couldn't dance. The club owners were smart enough to pick up on who belonged and who didn't.

RC   Isn't this concerning though? It's a ruthless, unsparing culture that thinks of someone largely in terms of how good they are in bed, particularly in addition to the social stresses of accepting yourself as gay.

FP   But that was the party aspect of it. Do you really expect something less superficial? On the other hand, I gave poetry readings at all the big dance clubs in New York. Doesn't that seem totally out of context? And a nightclub like Flamingo was essentially an art club. Every weekend it was a completely different art show. One time we went there and it was a Versailles garden. Amazing. It wasn't as shallow a scene as people pretend it was.

RC I can see that in a way you're simply capturing the spirit of that scene and documenting it. Still, in not condemning it, a key principle for you, aren't you in danger of surrendering a necessary objectivity? Must one be either participant and supporter of the sexual subculture or a critical outsider like Larry Kramer?

FP You couldn't live in that culture and give an objective report. Nothing about it was objective or measured. Edmund White attempted that in *States of Desire* and didn't do a bad job, but even he admitted he'd failed.

There was a belief at that time in the counterculture in being nonjudgmental about a whole variety of things, people, and activities; in effect you achieved a wider objectivity. You presented the material as clearly and multifacetedly as you could and let other people judge its value. I've always written with that in view. Maybe that's something I learned in the sixties—how to distrust people's judgments and values.

RC I noticed how much discontent you expressed at the gay media in the seventies diaries published in *The Violet Quill Reader*. The debates seem the same now as then: Larry Kramer's views on sex; the question of positive images in culture. Should we be worried at the fixity of our preoccupations? After all, many things have changed since then.

FP First I have to backtrack a little. Though it's very difficult to see now, especially for those of us right in the middle of it, AIDS didn't have to happen. It wasn't our destiny. AIDS represents a very large but temporary blip on the screen of gay culture. I was intimately involved at all levels of it—a former housemate of mine was the first person on the East Coast to get it. Still I have to say that to a large extent AIDS is irrelevant to what else is going on. It's taken an enormous amount of energy and time out of the gay movement, gay literature, and culture. Now I wish people would put it in its place. It's time to move on to something else. We have to go on—not by pretending AIDS didn't happen, but by giving it its place, which in the end is going to be much smaller than anybody now has a clue. The whole AIDS crisis forced us to grow up a little faster than we otherwise had to. It also destroyed a lot of our most talented people. That's its legacy. But in terms of the way we look at the past and the future, if we're only influenced by AIDS, I think it's really putting us in deep trouble. AIDS is a disease that happened to come around and strike a lot of people. That's all the credit I'll give it.

RC   I'm interested in the long-established politicians/artists divide. In *A House on the Ocean*, you specifically document ways in which the Fire Island set were politically engaged. That seems to contradict *Dancer from the Dance*, whose introductory letters suggested two clear worlds—the politically engaged and the hedonistic.

FP   *Dancer from the Dance* was written around 1976. I don't think the merger had happened by then. Even though Randy Shilts, in the very distorted and skewed *And the Band Played On*, quoting virtually nobody but Larry Kramer, said the gay community responded to AIDS much too late, I'll go out on a limb and say that if AIDS had happened to any other group of people anywhere, it would've taken another ten years for anything to have been done. We reacted with astonishing rapidity and large amounts of attention, money, and time, on a level I can't believe, looking back. I'm just amazed a bunch of supposedly sex-crazed, drugged-out queens did all that so quickly.

RC   Allan Gurganus has spoken of several books he hasn't written because of his caretaking role. Does that strike a chord?

FP   Sure. Caretaking and organizing; being in intensive care rooms; washing sick people down. We never lost sight of living at the same time, despite it all. I want that on the record.

On the question of things changing yet remaining the same: a lot of that's true. A lot of basic issues to queer life remain unsolved. They're never going to be solved. In terms of culture, gay life is a very large, middle-class bar culture. It's uninterested in the arts. We've forced the arts down their throats, but they'd rather see Mr. Leatherman Contest than read Edmund White's new novel.

RC   Hasn't that got worse? Twenty years ago, surely, one went to literature looking for resonant voices, fellow travelers. People don't have to do that now.

FP   It's the same. People still want to read about their lives, which is what gay literature offers queer people. I'm pleased and surprised that when Edmund or I make public appearances, most people in the room aren't fifty-six-year-old queens. They're in their twenties and thirties, which means we're continuing to speak to people about their lives. We're not historical anomalies.

There used to be a whole bunch of gay readers who've vanished though. A lot died of old age or alcoholism long before AIDS came along: the cultured, single gentlemen of Anglo-American society. To me they were dinosaurs. I was outrageously open and they hated me. They tried to get me in bed, but hated me.

RC   In the seventies diaries you mention a seminar on the gay novel in which, to your surprise, John Rechy's name didn't come up.

FP   To this day I don't get that. Rechy's written several of the most important gay books that affected people then. If you read *Numbers* now, you're surprised how subversive it is. He's turned away from the gay aspect now and does other stuff in his writing. That makes sense. But I don't know if he's really any longer aware how much some of us appreciate him. He provided a moment of liberation with *City of Night*. When I read that in 1963, it almost sent me back into the closet. It presented such a frighteningly real look at what gay life could be. I said: "I don't want any part of this." Then I realized it was just one look. But *City of Night* was strangely liberating too. It cut away a lot of romantic crap we were getting then from other quarters.

RC   Rechy was also astonishingly explicit. I wanted to raise the question of art and the erotic or pornographic. I'm always surprised by the extent to which American gay authors with literary reputations are prepared to write expressly erotic or pornographic stories.

FP   But why? Sometimes our difference lies only in the sex we have, and if we don't write about it, who will? John Updike? Ian McEwan? Spare me! *Slashed to Ribbons* was burned on the docks of Liverpool and London because of one particular "pornographic" story. In *Like People in History* I wanted to write more sex, but couldn't get around to it. There was too much other stuff to cover. I told this to my English editor, who said: "Maybe you can get some of it in your new book." I said: "OK, I'll work on getting some hot sex scenes in." As it was in *The Book of Lies*, I got in two, tops.

RC   When you said you never got around to it, I thought of the moment in *A House on the Ocean* where you talk of the writer's single-mindedness in leaving a nightclub when a good idea strikes, or abandoning sex midflow if you're inspired. You write: "I'm no longer sure it was worth it."

FP   Well, I'm not. A couple of those parties got very interesting; I had to hear about them from others. That's the great dichotomy between living your life and living your art. You decide at the oddest times to give up your life.

RC I don't think anybody would say you had withdrawn from life.

FP I had a moment where a boyfriend said: "It's me or the novel." I said: "Forget it. Don't even joke about that." I've had these movie scene moments in my life. Another was when a Hollywood producer actually handed me a cigar. I turned and said: "I hope everybody's catching this."

RC I wanted to ask about film. Long ago you almost saw a film made of *The Lure*.

FP It was never even close until recently.

RC What's your response now?

FP In an interview years ago I said if a lesbian film producer and a gay film director wanted it, I'd do it. That's pretty much what we have. A company's been formed with a gay screenwriter, a gay director, and a lesbian producer. By the time they asked me for the rights, they'd story-boarded it already. Their respect for the book goes way beyond mine. I'd rewrite it totally.

    Eyes, which isn't gay, is still too subversive to be made into a movie. It got as close as Frank Perry—who did *Mommie Dearest*—and I writing a final screenplay. Then he made another film and his company went down the tubes. *Eyes* has been under option for nineteen years. Finally I took it off the market. Recently, a group in New York City were interested in doing a stageplay. I've given my consent and signed an option contract. If it succeeds on Broadway, I think it'll go straight to film.

RC What hold does film have on you?

FP It doesn't particularly. I was out here in 1977 doing screenplays for Universal. Before that I was doing something with *Eyes*. When that was put on hold, they kept me here and had me do various things with other movies. But the pay was too high; the life, too fabulous. I knew I'd never get any novels written if I'd remained.

RC   The prospect of tackling gay themes in film must have felt slim then. The developments in fiction in the late seventies weren't matched in film for many years.

FP   The sad part about that was being out here. I met a lot of really smart, interesting gay people in film. None of them would take a chance on anything. Many specifically held back gay projects. It was that level of hypocrisy and closetedness that sent me spinning back to the East Coast.

RC   Finally you seem to have settled on writing prose, having written in so many genres.

FP   Yes. I could give you a couple of glib reasons like: "That's where I make the most amount of money." One good reason, however, is that I keep finding things to write about and problems to be solved. I keep on writing books nobody's written before. Take *The Book of Lies*. It's the most literary gay novel I've ever read. I kept asking: "Why isn't there anything like this: pink and postmodern?" I wanted it to be a literary mystery story and fun.

   The Book of Lies probably has the most unreliable narrator ever— apart from the governess in James's *Turn of the Screw*. I'm a firm believer in making readers do extra work. With *Like People in History*, obviously I wanted everybody to suffer the way I'd suffered. They did, I'm happy to report. When people said: "I was in tears all day," I'd say: "Now I'm happy." With *The Book of Lies*, ideally at the end I want people to say: "I think I misread this entire book" and to have to read it again.

RC   Could you say something about writing practice? Do you write directly onto machine?

FP   *Ambidextrous* may have been the last book I wrote by hand. I always hated typewriters, which gave me a great deal of trouble. After the first computers came out in 1983, and as soon as I could afford to, I got one with a pretty good writing system on it.

RC   Some suspect they cripple one's potential for revision.

FP   I do much more revising now than I ever did on those damn type-writers. I guess I was lucky. Computers came to me when I'd already been writing pretty solidly for about ten years. I knew what I was doing.

RC   You mentioned things you'd change in *The Lure*. Do you ever want to return to a finished project?

FP   Only the film version of it. This came up when Frank Perry asked me to write a screenplay from *Eyes*. I said: "This means I'm going to have the read this book. I don't want to." The book was maybe a decade old at that point. I put it off forever. Finally I read it, and had no prob-lem with it. It read, as a lot of these things do, as having been written by someone else.

One thing about writing the memoirs, as you pointed out, is there's a twenty-year gap between the events and when I write them. That's on purpose. The person who experienced those things wasn't me. In some cases, the experiences have changed me incredibly from who that person was when I was twelve or twenty-one or thirty-three. That person is so different to who I am now that I have trouble identifying with him. Recently, I went through some things I hadn't looked at in ten years. One was a series of photographs of me from 1977—probably at the height of whatever looks I had. It was at a high point in my career, too—just before the publication of *The Lure*. A photo was taken for the back cover of *The*

Mesmerist by David Duncan, at that point a famous New York celebrity dance photographer. He took some book jacket shots and afterwards, as I was changing, came into the room and locked the door as I was pulling up my jeans, still wearing no shirt. He started taking more photos of me. As it was the seventies, I got into it, saying: "Take your dirty photos!" They weren't dirty exactly, but they did reflect his view of photography as erotic art. They were mostly of me buttoning myself up. But he took what turned out in retrospect to be two of the best, most accurate photos of me. I looked at them recently and remembered the session with vivid detail. I just don't know who the hell that guy is in those photos! I can see aspects of my personality and character there, but I'll never have the ease, confidence, or savoir faire that man had because of my subsequent experiences. So this gap does change things.

RC Is this gap paradoxically what allows you to write memoirs in the first person? You know it's still a fictional "I."

FP It isn't if you can recapture it. If you selected one paragraph from each of the memoirs, you'd have three different voices. Really I'm trying to be as accurate to who that particular person is as I can be. But, yes, without the gap you wouldn't have a take on what the specific "I" is.

RC Do you ever work on more than one project?

FP Yes. I work at a lot of different things at different paces. Big projects I'll generally try to cope with at one time—except for *Like People in History*, which I sat on for a year. I was really afraid to write the last sections. That was artistic cowardice. They were extremely difficult to write without self-pity or sentimental falseness. Yet I had to get my heart into them. I didn't know how to do that to begin with. I had to let it sit there and stew.

I wrote the scenes of Matt in the hospital with tears streaming down my face. It was very hard—and they weren't particularly true to what my experience had been. It was just that I was remembering the gestalt of the whole thing. I knew I had to be in a position of extreme grief to do it right. But who wants to be in that state, day after day, week after week, to write something?

RC   Do you edit a lot?

FP   No, I'm very lazy. I'll put off writing something for a week, until I feel it's really ready to be written. With a book like *Like People in History*—around five hundred pages—I'd say there's maybe fifty pages I rewrote a dozen times each. The rest was pretty fast.

RC   Can you work all day?

FP   No. I work two or three hours in the morning, tops. Toward the end of a project, when I can't shake it off, I may do some more work later in the day, or work four hours. Then my mind turns to jelly. I have a very short attention span. I'm really scatterbrained.

RC   Is it important to be surprised by what you are writing? Or do you sketch everything out in advance?

FP   I recently found some sketches I did for *The Book of Lies* in an old journal. I can't even figure out what they mean anymore—a year after writing the book. Before *Ambidextrous*, I used to plot out everything on a large scale. I had long notes on the character's fortunes. Actually, I recommend that to somebody writing that type of novel who's unsure where they're going. With *Late in the Season*, a smaller book at around fifty thousand words, I sketched it out, but it was devised in such a way I didn't have to do too much sketching. With *Ambidextrous* I had no idea where I was going. I knew I wanted to tell these particular stories that had happened to me and people around me. I threw it up in the air and let it come down where it was going to. I was pretty surprised when that worked in the first part. I tried it again with the second part—that worked. Again with the third. At that point I suddenly had more trust in whatever this combination of conscious and unconscious things is that makes me a writer.

Nowadays I have a lot of general ideas. I'll make notes beforehand on what I'd like in this book. Then I'll conveniently forget them all and start writing. But the notes are necessary in the early stages. Then I'll write the damn thing, reminding myself of certain things in my daily journals: "Better include this; don't forget that." At some point I'll go into a panic and return to one of these completely baffling sketches. They appear to satisfy me at the time. To a normal human being, they look like so much fol-de-rol.

RC   Do you have plans for the journals to be published?

FP   Well, David Bergman has approached me. One of his graduate students was getting his postgraduate degree in literary autobiography. David sent him to look at the journals. The guy said: "Are there more of these?" There are tons more! So this young man approached me directly about doing a volume when I was on book tour. I said: "I haven't read these things, essentially, since I wrote them. For the *Reader*, it was David [Bergman]'s selection. But if you want to go to the Beinecke [Library at Yale] and read what's there, I'll give you safe passage."

Everybody tells me this stuff has some value. It may well have some historical value. So, maybe in time a book of selected journals—up to 1990—will come out.

RC   We've spent a lot of time reviewing your career since the seventies. I wanted you to name some works of gay fiction that have given you pleasure.

FP   *Dancer from the Dance*, definitely. I read a lot of Edmund White which I like a lot. The book I go back to again and again is *States of*

Desire. I also like his short stories in *Skinned Alive*, which got extremely short shrift here. To my mind they're still the best book of fiction he's done. *Eighty-Sixed* by David Feinberg I read every once in a while and adore. It's perfect of its kind.

RC   Which authors would you actively seek out?

FP   Samuel Delany; Harlan Greene. I love Bernard Cooper's books. *Truth Serum* was just tremendous. The way he evoked Los Angeles was perfect.

Of the younger writers, I liked Scott Heim's *Mysterious Skin* and Patrick Moore's *Iowa*. There's *The Captain's Fire* by J. S. Marcus, about a bisexual in Berlin. And Kevin Killian. I'd like to read more stuff by Kevin Esser, who writes about man-boy love—unfortunately not very often these days. I love Michel Tournier. *Gemini* is a strange, wonderful book.

Then we go back to probably the one gay writer who's been consistently overlooked in this country. He wrote one of my "desert island" books: J. R. Ackerley's *Hindoo Holiday*. From beginning to end, it's completely delightful. It's about the gayest book I've ever read. It assumes everybody in the world's going to be homosexual, unless you say otherwise. Then you get a book like *My Father and Myself*, which is so strange, and that really funny book about his dog, *We Think the World of You*. But *Hindoo Holiday* stands by itself.

RC   On that note, thanks very much for your time.

SEVEN
ALLAN GURGANUS

Allan Gurganus is best known for his fictionalization of the consequences of the American Civil War, *Oldest Living Confederate Widow Tells All*, and for his second novel concerning the impact of AIDS upon 1980s New York, *Plays Well with Others*. Born in North Carolina in 1947, at twelve Gurganus gave a one-man show of his oil paintings. On graduating from high school in 1965, he attended the Philadelphia Academy of Fine Arts. In 1966 Gurganus joined the Navy and, while on ship, started writing. He came out at twenty-one, and moved to New York to attend Sarah Lawrence College. In 1972 Gurganus won a scholarship to the Iowa Writers' Workshop, where he was tutored and befriended by the novelist John Cheever. In 1974 Cheever successfully submitted Gurganus's "Minor Heroism" to the *New Yorker*. Gurganus taught briefly at Stanford and Duke universities before returning to New York to teach part-time at Sarah Lawrence College.

In 1981 Gurganus began writing his first novel, the comic epic about the history of the South, *Oldest Living Confederate Widow Tells All* (New York: Knopf, 1989). Gurganus's short stories, meanwhile, had appeared in the *New Yorker*, *Harper's*, *Granta*, and anthologies such as Edmund White, ed., *Faber Book of Gay Short Fiction* (London: Faber and Faber, 1991). They were later collected in *White People* (New York: Knopf, 1991). *Plays Well with Others* (New York: Knopf, 1997), Gurganus's most recent novel, is set in New York in the period before and during the devastation caused by AIDS. His story "Preservation News" featured in a special issue of *Preservation* magazine (September 1997) and was reprinted in Brian Bouldrey, ed., *Best American Gay Fiction 3* (Boston: Little, Brown, 1998).

Gurganus is currently working on a collection of novellas, "Recent American Saints," and a third novel, "The Erotic History of a Southern Baptist Church." His home is in North Carolina, where this interview took place on Tuesday, November 11, 1997.

RC   Several reviews of *Plays Well with Others* mentioned similarities to *Oldest Living Confederate Widow Tells All*. Could you comment on the relationship between them, and on whether questions of narrative and form in your work preoccupy you consciously or more intuitively?

AG   *Widow* and *Plays Well* have lots in common. They're both first-person narratives told by funny people in the aftermath of a traumatic, historically notable circumstance: the Civil War and the pandemic. They're both suffused with the seasick psychology of surviving. They're both offered in the voices of people who are mythomaniacs when it comes to others—the great ones they're explaining and salvaging for us. The hosts become mythic by creating far more mythic and adored others.

In *Widow* we have nineteenth-century lore, and in *Plays Well* the recent past. Lucy Marsden, the narrator of *Widow*, has her own stories—including domestic violence against her by a Civil War veteran, and all his stories about the War itself, which irremediably deformed him when he was a child. She also offers the tales told her by her best friend, Castelia Marsden, former slave of her husband and his family. Lucy becomes a Homeric repository for other people's tales. In some ways her truest voice is manifest when she's imitating others. My intention for that book was to create a person who spoke every language available to a human being who'd lived in the hundred years she'd survived. We all speak many languages a day: one to the delivery boy, one to our beloved,

one to our grandparents, one to our mother, one to the neighbors, one to
the telephone operator and the cabdriver. I wanted Lucy to have all
those voices available. I wanted a kind of Livia Plurabelle, comprehen-
sive psychic voice.[1]

Hartley Mims, jr. in *Plays Well* is a beginning writer in search of a
subject. He goes to New York partly because he has to get out of a small
town because he's gay and can't abide living there. He leaves partly to
avoid being monitored and checked, and partly because of his ambition
to create something beautiful. There's also his larger fantasy: to create
an address book that's a masterpiece. He wants friends even more alive,
ambitious, and gifted than he. He's a collector of experiences and people. His tale, because it covers a shorter period—fifteen years, as
opposed to *Widow*'s one hundred—is a slightly more linear narrative. I
back into the story the way I think one does in memory. One holds onto
singular images, then shifts from past to present. But I wanted the story
of Hartley's quest, his Dick Whittington arrival in New York, to have a
kind of mythic fairy-tale innocence and energy. I wanted the prose of
the novel to darken and simplify as the book rolled on. So the opening of
the book—"Before"—is very F. A. O. Schwartz: toylike, self-consciously playful, and irresponsible; heady and game; young and sometimes coy. It was heaven to write. Having lived in New York from 1979
to 1995 myself and having survived many of the things Hartley did, I
found my memory took a long time to "o'erleap the wall" of HIV; to get
back to the "garden," the beautiful innocence of the period. For me the
greatest pleasure in writing the book was reestablishing as a beachhead
that moment of early promise: the club scene; the wide-open casting-call
for good-looking, intelligent, and immensely ambitious kids. Four thousand land every day in New York, even as we speak.

In terms of narrative strategy, I think all the best things in painting
or writing come from a plan and then some unconscious inner prompt-

---

1. Anna Livia Plurabelle is a character in James Joyce's *Finnegan's Wake* (1939).

ing. If you're lucky, you're smart enough to back off then and become nanny for your own baby, saying: "Don't go near the pond, darling. You've been there before. You almost drowned yesterday, remember?" I try to keep my intuitive animal free to make mistakes and slaughter what it will. Then, once its deed is done, I go in and clean up intellectually.

I think one reason my work's been so widely received is precisely because it's so emotional that it so unapologetically glories in narrative qua narrative. One favorite fact about the notion of narrative is that it's from the Greek *gnaurus*, meaning "to know." My great faith is that narrative knows more than I do. If I trust it, setting it in motion, it exerts its own laws and rules and will lead me to places I couldn't have got to if I'd sat down the way some people do and blocked out the book in outline. For me, that'd be the equivalent of some soothsayer coming in the front door, saying: "Allan, you'll die on January 23rd, 2003, and nothing you can do will change that." To know the end at the beginning would argue against bothering to get there. I want to be startled, to make a discovery in the course of the narration as the characters do. I didn't know in *Plays Well*, literally, who was going to live and who would die. I was as surprised as the characters!

RC What is known at the outset? Do you have any sense of the shape of a narrative?

AG I'm always being outwitted. When I started *Widow* I thought it was a thirty-page story. Boy, was I wrong! Similarly, I've had stories that seemed to suggest novella length that I've then cut down to three pages. "It Had Wings" in *White People* was originally twenty-two pages; it's now three-and-a-half. I wish I could do more of that. The discipline of condensation is an immensely instructive way of learning about what you do and don't need. The French have shown us you can get a field of flowers into a bottle of perfume. That's the goal. One jeopardy of writing on computer—I see this in student work that comes to me—is that it all *looks* great. Therefore everything stays. Those of us who grew up with the arduous task of typing learned to condense for various reasons. One was that we couldn't bear to retype a redundant page, so we found ways around it.

Sometimes the work begins with a single sentence. "Blessed Assurance" in *White People*—one of the six best things I've written—began with the sentences: "I sold funeral insurance to North Carolina black people. I myself am not black." I started with an occupation I had heard three facts about from a young friend of my brother. He sold insurance for six weeks, then became so guilt-stricken he fled the occupation.

With *Widow*, I carried around the ambition to write about the South and the War for years. Every Southerner does. It's information you get almost daily—about the War. All that is still an astonishing reality here. It was only when I saw the phrase in the *New York Times* in the late seventies—"Oldest Living Confederate Widow"—and after reading a little article about how many widows were still on the payroll in Mississippi, that I suddenly had her voice—or it had me.

There's no way to predict. The only way to do it is to stand six days a week in proximity to the material. I have a friend who's a concert pianist who writes letters at the piano. He says proximity to the instrument approximates keyboard practice itself. When I go on tour for books, there's a kind of joy attached to visiting bookstores all over the States, Canada, and England. But there's also a tremendous mourning because I can't work. I've set up a system whereby I have printed-up material. I fax back changes to my assistant who types it in. It's not insanely productive, but I love working on airplanes. I can't stand flying and need something to look at other than clouds. I need to keep that constant umbilical connection to the work—frequently, to five or six things at once. I love having many things going. It's like having six boyfriends. When one spurns you, the other will come through the door looking better than ever, holding a bouquet.

RC Do you ever need imaginative recharging?

AG   Maybe the period promoting a book provides that. I can't work. I feel resigned to that fact, but I'm doing something else directly connected to the work. I'm preaching from it, reading it aloud, being John the Baptist in the wilderness crying: "The Redeemer's here. He just costs twenty-five dollars a copy!" I find it hard to take more than one day off a week. Even when I'm on vacation, I'm reading and working all the time, for the simple reason that I love to do it. I feel, after thirty years of writing, divinely equipped to do what I'm doing.

I started out as a painter, but as soon as I wrote my first page of fiction, it was: "*Here* we are. I'm not imitating anybody. This is a voice. I know how to do this." It's like oxygen. Who'd stop breathing for a week because they'd been breathing forty-five years? Writing sustains me. Apart from publication, if I were told tomorrow that nothing I write will ever be published or read again, my schedule wouldn't change much. I've been very lucky because *Widow* was on the bestseller list and was published in eight or nine languages, totally unexpectedly. It broke every rule, being too long and having an endless title when everything was titled *Don't* or *Think*. I feel very blessed. The nest egg from that finally released me briefly to write full time, at the ripened age of forty-two. Now I am still trying to write for a living. I know I can earn a living in many ways—and did, for the forty-two years before *Widow* appeared, mostly as a teacher.

RC   You spoke about the license you give your imaginative sense, then to this cautionary, editing sense. Does this suggest the literal processes of vision and revision?

AG   I think there's a constant cool and melt, like moving the hot liquid work from one vessel to another in the air, cooling with each pass and transfer. Imagining the starting text is the part I love most, but I love revision too. Auden said to be a writer you have to be a little in love with the drudgery of the profession. For me there's this great, initial flooding out, where I'm typing ninety-five words a minute and still not moving as fast as my mind. I don't care whether I hit the "t" or "j" as long as there's some semblance of the word so I can go back and correct it. You're literally blind—you don't even see the screen or keyboard. You sit there in this kind of trance, taking dictation or describing an interior landscape or this room where something dreadful and marvelous is happening. Then you put it aside and let it cool. You print it out; you hope to surprise yourself. You write over that in longhand, then type in those changes, then do the same again—until it's impossible to remember any revision. It becomes living pitch; serum; plasma. The circulation has to work. It has to have living access to the main artery, then the subordinate tributaries. The smallest toe has to be warm as the providing heart. That's when you know it's done—when it's hot all over as a feverish baby.

RC   Are there ideas you run with for a while that you then decide not to execute?

AG   I never give anything up forever. I keep drafts of stories that've been going for years. I think there's a reason they compel me to continue them. Finally, each of us only has about three stories. There are only about six in the whole world: "Man Leaves Town," "Man Arrives in Town." I have stories I've been working on for fifteen years. There's something wrong with the middle, or I don't know how to end it yet. I have a talent for beginnings, in life and art. Sustaining's another question, and getting the hell out intact is something else altogether. But there's a reversal that has to happen. You can wait a long time for it.

I have a story in progress called " A Stolen Bible Is a Noticed Bible," about a child whose father puts Gideon Bibles in rural motels in the fifties—as mine did. The father's extremely ugly but immensely charming, with a beautiful speaking voice. He sells sundries—bow ties that light up like Christmas trees; geegaws and gimcracks—at little rural stores all over the South. For years I'd take this story out every six months, saying: "Fabulous, fabulous. What? No, no." I'd add something else, then put it back. Last year I invented a traffic accident while the son and father were out. This amazing thing happened—like a thunderclap. At the moment the child looked at his father just before they crashed, he realized his father's secret: this beloved guy was black. That explained why his mother'd been unfaithful, was embarrassed by him, and why the father never spoke of his ancestry. It explained a little photograph of a black woman the son had found in the back of his father's wallet.

I'd been carrying this story around for fifteen years, and I had to experience the revelation in the same time frame as the character. I had to remain almost slavishly loyal to the story. I think loyalty's one of my great merits as a person. I've lost friends to death, but have a hard time giving up friends; saying to somebody who's behaved hideously: "Honey, I can't let you do this to me over and over again; you're out of here." It's very painful. But long-range good faith is a huge merit in fiction. All it takes is three-and-a-half stellar pages to make you immortal. I want to be loyal to those pages and keep them up-to-date with my own evolution as a citizen, lover, son, brother, neighbor. That's really what you're doing: keeping the stories abreast of your own discoveries.

RC   You speak easily of people and writing in similar terms. It made me think of the moment in *Plays Well* where Hartley does a double take on seeing his first story in print. The real Hartley feels distant from the implied author of the piece. Did that experience hold true for you? Has it been important to your writing to be surprised by the self you later perceive in it?

AG   My goal as an artist and my goal as a person are surprisingly synchronous. That means I'm lucky. My goal is to become, through lived work and and work lovingly undertaken, a more complete person. There's that wonderful quote about most of the mischief in the world coming from the inability of a man to sit alone in a chair. Since earliest childhood I've been lucky in having this immense capacity to amuse myself. My father, a very withheld and difficult if ethical man, rarely told us anything about ourselves as children. He wasn't a person who lived in any moment but the present. Buddhists would tell us he'd achieved something extraordinary. But I think for a novelist, that's tragedy. Even so, my father told me near the end of his life that, as a baby, I could be left with a pot and a spoon in the corner of a room for hours. They'd hear me inventing voices and moving things around. I think I've made a merit of that weirdness. That's what writers do: push round the pots and spoons and make them the Peloponnesian Wars, the pandemic in New York, or the American Civil War.

My work's very consistent. My first story "Minor Heroism," which opens *White People*, was written when I was twenty-six. I'm still happy to call it my own. I was very lucky in that all the work I did as a painter made me very aware of the holiness and beauty of surface. That's also something I think has been consistently true in my work. I've always cared immensely about the shape of the sentences, the coloration of the prose, its rhythms.

There's also an ethical strain in my work from the start. I don't think of myself as writing entertainments merely, though I'd like to think I'm often entertaining. But it's like your parents slipping your vitamins or cold medicine into your favorite fruit juice or beloved custard dessert. I've a method in my madness, and I'd like to think it would be possible for a reader to finish one of my books and say: "What an immensely satisfying meal that was," without feeling they'd been slipped a vitamin Mickey, ethically speaking.

I have an immense sense of mission politically. *Widow*, from the very beginning, was about the death of the patriarchy and the necessity of killing the unreasoning and brutal warrior-father. Similarly, it predicted and urged the ascendancy of the overlooked feminine principle— the generative half, as opposed to the destructive part. Lucy Marsden is so named because I wanted a word combining both war and its opposition: "Mars," the god of war; "den," a sanctuary. "Lucia" is, of course, light. I think the whole book's in the battle between one vision and the other. The same scheme is more overtly true in *Plays Well*. There it is about a straight, a bisexual, and a gay character falling in and out of love with each other in every possible permutation. It also involves trying to achieve a destiny apart from the contempt, bias, and difficulty this culture visits on anybody other than the heterosexual with three children in the suburbs. I think the book's ending as it does in "Paradise" is an essential aspect. Crucially, it's a paradise in which each of us ascends to the highest order of angels only if somebody recognizes our genitals and our hands. That recognition indicates we have, genuinely, in the course of our assigned years made ourselves known, in the biblical sense and every other, to other humans. That insistence on one's sexual substance and on sexuality's radical, central place in our lives in this self-loathing, self-punishing culture—is just part of the undercurrent and message of the book.

RC   The moral element of fiction is not something every writer would stress. Do you think of it as a rare preoccupation?

AG   I'm the great-great-grandson of ministers on both sides. I have preaching beating in every corpuscle. I get up and preach to the mirror, dogs, cats, and birds if nobody else is around. I've made my living as a teacher until recently. I'm the eldest of four children, and this caregiving, marshall-at-arms overseeing was forced on me. I don't think one chooses one's preoccupations; they're genetically encoded and come to you with the circumstances of your birth. But, given that, I welcome my obsession with "How to Live Morally." I welcome the music of all sermons. I think it makes my work more interesting.

My early grounding was in the Bible. I had a lay minister father who read the Bible aloud before every meal. I went to church, Sunday school, and every goddamn Bible meeting. I put up with having the King James Bible drilled into me whether I liked it or not. Weirdly enough, I must have mostly liked it. It happens to be a work of consummate human genius. It's full of wishes and laws; full of color and the assumption that human life, if told properly in all its mundane details, can amount to amazing universal meaning. The parable of the lost coin; that of the seeds that fall onto hard ground and fertile: what could be more basic? Yet as we sit here, it's part of our amazing joint culture. So the religious fundamentals, drilled into me early on, clearly fell on fertile ground. I've adapted them by virtue of being gay, by despising so much of what was thrust upon me. I've subverted the folktales and their implicit morals for my own odd ends.

My goal by the end of my life is to have written three or five parables and fables that will be useful to people. In some of the same ways the Bible has been useful; in showing common people struggling to maintain their own decency and an accountability to their best selves and loved ones.

RC   Have you observed, even inadvertently, the same preoccupation with the fable—or parable-like—in other writers?

AG   I'm never ashamed of influences. I've been very lucky in having brilliant teachers. My reading influences come from the great nineteenth-century novelists. Henry James was my first god—then Balzac, Proust, Tolstoy, Dickens, George Eliot, Virginia Woolf, and Isaac Babel. Preeminently, though, Chekhov and Shakespeare are the great ones for me. The goal, in terms of who's greatest—a stupid but sometimes instructive exercise—is who understands most deeply the most kinds of people in the world? We're living in an age where the goal is toward blandification; elimination of differences. There are no fourth-generation Pittsburgh steelworkers today who have immense necks because their great-grandfathers did; who sit round all day talking about the foundry and sparks, and how many gross of rods or sheets they put out the week before. The dignity of manual work; the pride in craft—even the craft of writing—seems in fast retreat. Everybody wants to live in Beverly Hills in a state of celebrity for something they haven't really done yet. Everybody expects a certain amount of praise, press coverage, creature comfort.

I marvel at the age of Shakespeare and even of Chekhov. Then it was possible to write, in one story, of a princess and her gatekeeper— and with equal compassion. Shakespeare understands Lady Macbeth as a childless, immensely intelligent, and ambitious person who has fifty IQ points on all the men in the play. She's a woman who has nothing to do but push her passive, milky husband into a course of action that turns out—precisely because of her own bottled ambition—disastrously for everybody. In the same play, the gatekeeper's doing his job. He has his favorites, knows who's coming to him and who's not. He has his own dignity, power, and career. The world is reimagined, top to bottom—an astonishing achievement.

I'd like to think at the end of my career I will have understood more kinds of people than just me and my kind. I see narrative as a license and imperative for doing that. One reason I'm interested in writing about gay, straight, and bisexual people, about foot-fetishists and nuns, is that I want to do one of each. My writer's pantheon is filled with people who've tried to treat as many people as possible with justice. Shakespeare was the son of a moderately successful glove-maker; Chekhov was the grandson of a serf literally owned by aristocrats. Put them alongside Dickens, the son of favored house servants in the great homes, and Proust, an aristocrat with a Jew for a mother, who was able to wander into the great salons without ever fully being part of them. I feel that I, as a middle-class person with access to upper-class circles and as a gay person who can pass in straight society but chooses not to, have all the hobbles necessary for complete freedom.

It's a wonderful paradox that there's never been a great novel written by a king or president. It's always those of us that have been wounded early, who've been held back or embarrassed. And we wind up singing the praises of whatever milieu we aspire to enter. John Cheever believed fervently in the Brooks Brothers, Yale, Saint Mark's, and Andover possibilities precisely because he was thrown out of school for smoking at sixteen and never spent a day in college. He always lived a marginal, hand-to-mouth existence by his wits. So his honorary degrees from both Yale and Harvard meant the world to him. We're created by what we criticize.

RC Some people think human character is inevitably shaped by changes in material circumstances—for example, technology. Are you offering a counterstatement to that, according to which character or humanity may exist as archetypes?

AG Well, "archetype" makes me nervous. There's always somebody who'll say: "You're type twenty-seven A, with a little variation in the lower register." I think the same principles apply for me that applied for Dante or Horace. That's why I can still read them with such pleasure. What's interesting: to investigate the immense ancient mystery of human character as it's brought to bear on present reality. The oldest living Confederate widow was interesting because she wasn't telling the old war story in 1910; she was telling it in 1975. She just happened to have had half a century of hard looking. She hadn't previously been asked to unpack her perfected stories. It's a question of when you choose to tell a story and how the historical circumstances of the time affect that classical conception of what people will and won't do.

I've found frequently the best readers of my work in progress aren't fellow writers. Instead, they're friends who work day jobs. They say: "I loved it until he left his wife for three days without telling her. This guy wouldn't have done that. He would've left a note or something on the answering machine. He wouldn't just have taken off four days before their fiftieth anniversary. Or if he did take off, you left out something." That's fascinating criticism; really something I can work with, as opposed to: "In terms of the book's overall structure, the symbolic substructure pertains, etc." I'd much rather have "would or wouldn't have done that." It implies consideration of the donnée. It implies I've created a person with wants, needs, possibilities, limitations, grouchinesses, biases. I am therefore wonderfully limited by the very things I've created, in the way a poet's limited by the metric stanzas he's undertaken to honor. I've given up my freedom by committing to these precepts; I'm damn well duty-bound to honor them. Of course, if you get three or four characters going who are running on very different clocks and at very different concepts of justice, entitlement, cruelty, or humor, then, by God, you've got a novel—or the energetic bassline of one.

I want to give every person who walks through this door and every person who enters any of my fiction a fair shake. It thrills me when the electricians who renovated this old house meet me in the post office and I know the names of all their kids: who's graduated, who's having trouble, whose mother has Alzheimer's. I'm lucky in many ways. One is that I'm profoundly interested in others. The paradox is there are many writers who aren't. I have an immense sense of the possibilities of community, and I celebrate that. I try to hold back from being like a bad Frank Capra ending, in which the town meeting starts singing "God Bless America." Those small-town crowd scenes in *It's a Wonderful Life*, where Jimmy Stewart says: "We may not be fancy, but by God when George's barn burned, we all pitched in, didn't we, George?"—I secretly love all that. It still cracks me up.

I'm really an old thirties Commie under this glittering, lacquered exterior. [*Laughs*] I believe and know from my own life that to be a part of a tribe is the partial antidote to this hideous end of the century. It's not a thirties works project administration post-office mural to think people can genuinely pitch in and help with the harvest. I've seen what a group of three people can do for each other. It's titanic. It's the thing one can celebrate endlessly without running out of material. It's what I have instead of religion: some weird faith in the common weal; in the promise of differing similarities between people. A perpetual motion machine. That's what literature depends upon. If my emotions were murky and mysterious to the reader, I wouldn't have three people reading me. But if I can open up all the weird particularities of my own volatile, sometimes insanely crazed and paranoid emotional life, and invite people in and orient them with a map so they always know where they stand . . .

I'm very conscious of not wanting unintentionally to disorient the reader. Sometimes I disorient him or her on purpose, but I never plan to do it accidentally. Once trust is established, you can take your reader anywhere. Then I think you can tackle him or her anywhere. You're really inviting the reader not into an entertainment but into some huge investigation as to how I, as a survivor of HIV, this miraculous, Jonah-like figure belched up on the beach, this "I-alone-who-lived-to-tell-the-tale" solitary man out of an immense generation, survived. I feel profoundly privileged and compelled to tell the truth. The more inconvenient the truth, the more guile I need to get people to stay and listen. So I feel wired and blessed—and, almost daily, if not always hourly, amazed to be alive.

RC Compared to the donnée of the oldest Confederate widow, the material for *Plays Well* came to you a fundamentally different way. To what extent did the idea for that book, given the language you've just used to describe the real experiences from which it broadly grew, present itself to you in terms of an obligation, or—as you've talked in political terms—something with political urgency?

AG I think every writer worth reading is chosen by some sponsoring subject. He then wisely defends it, saves it, and champions it. Millions of people just went down to a disease—and are going down as we speak! More specifically, thirty or forty adorable friends and lovers—cranky, gorgeous people, gifted beyond reason, died in my company. What to *make* of this?

If they'd all been drowned in one flood, one could blame an army corps of engineers, maybe, or some tasteless act of God. But this story reads like science fiction. It's a Gothic tale. Cruel, unreasoning, and heartless government agents turned their backs when the wrong kind of people were getting sick. They clapped their hands, saying: "We couldn't have set it better ourselves. Let's slash another forty million dollars and see how many go down to it next year," without understanding it would soon come for their own children and wives. You put this fragile, hopeful community in the middle of this horrific, creeping malady which has no name and whose source is totally unknown, and I think a tennis racket could write a novel about it! As a subject, it has absolutely everything; it's irresistible. And it's impossibly hard. I knew my treatment would have to be essentially comic.

It was possible for me to write about it now after sixteen years because of recent medical advances. If the treatment of HIV had stayed the same, I probably wouldn't be here, but I also wouldn't be able to write about it. What interests me is that history moves so quickly we can already look back to the early days with a different emphasis. In those days, to find you had a spot on your arm was to know you had six weeks, tops. There was nothing to do but go home, get under the quilts, write your will, and shiver to death. You were going to drop seventy pounds in a matter of weeks and die of malnutrition because the virus was feeding on you. Now, when I see friends who are positive going to the gym and looking like Godzilla they're so pumped, gorgeous, and buffed, it's possible to look back on our old spindly ones with an amazed horror, respect, and sadness for all they missed medically, and all they missed in terms of the promise of their lives ahead.

It's only possible for me now because I really genuinely believed this fall—1997—we'd have some kind of breakthrough. I had this psychic flash that this was going to be *the* fall. Of course, I've felt that every season for sixteen years—it's truly pitiful. But I genuinely believed it. One reason I worked so hard to finish the book was because I had this superstitious feeling that if I could do that, I'd help make it possible. It's all magic; it doesn't make any sense. Magic makes perfect sense; that's why it transcends logic, substituting rituals for reason.

RC   There's clear risk involved, notwithstanding your sense of certainty, in the book containing a narrative perspective so closely bound up with a particular contingency.

AG   There is. But that becomes an interesting part of the period, too. In fact, the lack of a breakthrough, so anticipated by us all, makes me love the book not less but more. It gives the book a kind of validity it wouldn't have had, had I been completely correct about my wishes. But writing about our looking after each other after a period of such heedless, outward, selfish, happy, frisky experimentation involved almost reliving it. *Plays Well* isn't about my friends who died—I mean not about literal friends. I don't really work that way. I wouldn't have spent seven years in the voice of a ninety-nine-year-old woman if I were an autobiographical writer.

Part of the joy of *Plays Well* was writing in the voice of somebody contemporary, smart, and allusive, as gay people tend to be: full of names. To use Peter Pears, Donna Summer, J. S. Bach, Maria Callas, and Gustav Mahler in one paragraph, after you've lived seven years in the voice of a woman a hundred years old, with a fifth-grade education from 1888, was a little bit of OK. It was, like, multiple orgasms in thirty seconds! But I invented characters who weren't only composites of the people I've known. Angie "Alabama" Burns is an amalgam of twenty career women in the arts I know and respect the hell out of, precisely for all they gave up to build their work, promote and protect it. She's also this wish for a woman friend I'd most like to have had; the one that's the funniest, smartest, most talented, most wild, and most loyal. One joy of being a writer is that you get to be a professional wisher. You get to make your wishes come true on the page every day. A lot of energy in *Plays Well* arrives from my wish for some intact community that will survive even AIDS.

RC   You spoke about the proliferation of books about AIDS; within *Plays Well*, Hartley refers to what other writers would do with the topic. To what extent were you writing *Plays Well* as a response to earlier novels?

AG   I "read at" a lot of the other books, but haven't really read them. I found most too disappointing to finish. This is partly a result of where they fell in the history of the pandemic. When you're in a burning building, you can't be expected to have perfect form as you jump from a fourth-floor window. You get out whatever way you can. I think my book benefits from the hindsight of sixteen years—which is really like a century, since it's hard to remember when the world was without HIV. It's necessary that we remember then. That means we can also imagine a world without it up ahead. But I'd open a book and the gay character in a third-person narration is at a clinic, gets called in and told on page one he's HIV-positive, so automatically we have sympathy for the character since that shouldn't happen to the worst pit bull in the world. But the character is being defined solely on the basis of his medical tragedy.

It seemed to me all along what was needed was a "Before" to the "After." And a "Before" that wasn't an apology. I've nothing to apologize for, living in New York from 1979 to 1995. I'm not going to state the number of people I slept with because I've never been good at math, and I've seen others crucified for giving the exact score. But it was a party of such dimensions and innocence—really a long bash not seen since the twenties in New York. *The Great Gatsby* was very consciously in mind when I wrote *Plays Well*. My book is an homage to that great novel concerning one party's beginning, ending, and failure—and an economy's beginning, ending, and failure. I draw definite parallels between the boom and the bust of prosperity in the city and our personal tragedy coming home to roost. I also wanted to write a comic novel. What's original about *Plays Well* is that it's primarily about three funny people in trouble.

When I was growing up, I was always the class clown. Then I realized I should be the class brain to protect myself. The class clown can sit on stage and go into arterial bleeding in front of the entire school. Everybody will laugh because he's the class clown; everything he does and says is funny, including dying in plain view. I got a brainstorm: I could be the Class Egghead *and* the Class Clown. That combo gave more choices, and I'm still working the contradictions. The same's true in the fiction. I'd *rather* be funny; I'd prefer to be smart concurrently. I'd rather have a good time—on the page and off. I'd like to just turn off this tape recorder now and tell you forty filthy jokes, with all the sound effects.

I think this perspective's doubly necessary when you're dealing with a subject as inherently horrific as HIV: not only HIV, but the hatred toward those of us that dealt with it in whatever ways we did; those of us who are gay and automatically considered suspect, as in: "Don't touch my child—you're gay. You'll breathe on her; she'll die in fifteen minutes." The equation between inversion and death has always been there. It's just so heightened under these circumstances. The only way to look at this eclipse is through the smoked glass of comedy and farce— because it was a farce. If one form is suitable for the way we live now, it's farce. Intelligent people love farce. Those who sneer at it are middle-brow, middle-class duds. They don't understand we all live life at a gal-lop. It's in one door and out the other. We've nothing but the instanta-neousness of our instincts and desires, and we've no time to hide those properly. There's a tremendous kind of release in farce. Joe Orton lived and died as pure farce.

So writing a comic novel about a tragedy of this proportion is my contribution. *Plays Well* is probably going to be creamed. I've been very lucky in terms of the critical response to my work. It's so carefully and lovingly crafted even the biggest boor knows he can't go after me on that front. But the hatred for gay people and for The Other in this culture is still so profound. I've been very lucky because in the first book I lined myself up—without quite meaning to, exactly—with all those people who're obsessed with the Civil War. That's about two million readers. I got credit from them. Even though I was out of the closet in *People* mag-azine, flaming all over the place, those first readers only wanted to talk about Gettysburg. Lucy seemed to them this immensely admirable per-son I'd somehow annexed. The idea that I could actually imagine her being raped on her honeymoon because somebody sorta raped me is something nobody wanted to talk about or imagine. They preferred to say: "How did you get into her head—or pants?" "Well, girlfriend, let me tell you. I once had a lumberjack after my young ass."

I'm now coming up against the grisly reality of being a gay man who's identified himself in and out of the book: on every page, an impenitent, shameless personality. They call it promiscuous now; then we called it popular. I walked into an interview for *Plays Well* and the first question from one influential straight reporter was: "I see you're one of those who thinks only gay people are creative, right?" This—from a novel in which almost every creative straight or gay person in the novel dies. This is the question he throws in my face!

RC The unambiguously gay figure is the one who doesn't make it creatively in the time frame of the book.

AG Exactly. It's like Toni Morrison bopped in to do an interview and somebody asked: "All you black people can sing, dance, and play basketball, and that's it, right?" I have to steel myself, but no matter what happens with *Plays Well*, I know it's on record, and I'm immensely proud of it. I think it'll eventually be one of the three or four texts that will be read about AIDS.

RC I was thinking of the bravura of the opening scene, in which Hartley spills thirty dildoes which bounce around a subway car. Presumably, the chance of shocking the readership *Plays Well* will inherit from *Widow* occurred to you.

AG It's essential to me. I want *Plays Well* to be totally acceptable, honest, and believable to my gay and straight brothers and sisters everywhere, and especially those who lived through all this in New York. I want them to say: "I was at that party; in that hospital; at that steam bath with him—he got it all right." I also want to reach a sixty-year-old, registered Democrat; head of the League of Women Voters in Molene, Illinois, who listens to National Public Radio and doesn't really know any gay people, because Dwayne who cuts her hair alternate Thursdays only talks about what he saw on television, in the movies, and who his favorite film stars are. He never confesses anything to her, though she tells him most everything. And Dwayne disappears three times a year, goes to Chicago, and comes back with a black eye, but looking very happy.

I want to reach those people who'll buy the book because my name's on it. This is my first novel since *Widow*. They'll have this moment of: "Uh oh—I just spent twenty-five dollars on a book full of queers!" By the time they think that, I hope they'll be implicated, interested—ready to sponsor these three main characters, who are calculatedly irresistible. That's part of my narrative strategy: to show that the circumstances are repellent, not the people, and to show that corruption involves the virus, not the sexuality that preceded it.

I want *Plays Well* to be the long-awaited chimera of the crossover novel, in which I'm speaking not only to the converted and preaching to the choir, but explaining gay culture and its recent, unheralded heroism to strangers. Everybody knows about the tragedy. You don't have to be too smart to figure out that a thirty-year-old man that winds up weighing sixty-two pounds and babbling, after being the most promising and beautiful of his generation, is tragic. But there's much more to the story than that. It's also about the survivor, the caregiver, and that community of caregiving that stepped in when the government completely betrayed and abandoned us. A crucial national document promises a government that'll defend its citizens' "health, education, and welfare." The heroism of self-help involved people who said: "I've got a Xerox machine"; or, "I have a friend who's a druggist"; or, "My brother-in-law's a doctor at Johns Hopkins"; or, "I've fifteen hundred dollars I can spend on printing up posters to put on telephone poles." Call me a Frank Capra freak, but this really *is* community at work. When George's barn burns, its rebuilding by the volunteer troop is acknowledged to be admirable. It seems the heroism of what we did and are doing has been completely and utterly ignored by a media that's more interested in Kim Basinger's waistline. It's obscene—that a movement as immense and imagined, as powerful and incredibly effective as ours has not been lionized.

RC   Even by itself?

AG   Yes. It's especially hard for us to give ourselves any credit in a world that's forever telling us we're malformed and lack gene X, Y, or Z; that we're reprobates; that we've got to keep it in our pants twenty-four hours a day; that we're good only to the extent that we abstain; that we're living on borrowed time and are damned lucky to be able to pay taxes. Fuck that. I'm *so* over shame. It's taken me so much inhaled, then pole-vaulted shame to get to the point where I can say that.

RC   Thinking of heroism, I wanted to suggest a possible tension or difficulty in execution in *Plays Well*. On the one hand, you want to focus upon heroism in a community. On the other, writers preoccupied with moral analysis surely need a range of moral responses to determine and clarify goodness, or even a polarity.

AG   *Plays Well* isn't just about these manic, attractive kids in New York. It's really about their relationship to the former generation. One movement of the book is the conversion of the parents of these kids from Republican contempt and distance to being active participants in the lives and then the deaths of their own children; of being pulled, if only by default and against their will at first, into the very community their kids have made as a kind of substitute family, as a source for the warmth they're not getting from their parents, preachers, and consumer culture.

Opposition comes not only from within the families but, interestingly, from one of the members of the group to others. Anybody who's ever done caretaking knows the favorite victim of the beloved, dying object is whoever gets closest. I've included a scene in which Robert, dying, accuses Hartley, his primary caregiver, of being a failure as an artist. He's withering and condescending about Hartley's future, with an emphasis on how much time he'll have to get it right finally. This is based on more than one such event in my life, in which the very person you're giving up everything to protect attempts with his last energy to annihilate you and your sense of self-worth. That's about the discipline it takes to reply: "I'll have to consider that; thank you for telling me." You want to say, as I wanted to under similar circumstances: "Do you think having toxins in your brain might be having an impact on how you're judging this? Is this really the best you can do for me after we've slept together for years, and after I'm spending twenty-four hours a day of my life trying to help you die with dignity? Can't you salvage a little dignity for me?" You don't say it. You swallow it, because you know that if you confronted him with what he'd done, he'd spend the last days of his life feeling terrible. You can't allow that. That's part of what care-giving is—giving over your own dignity if that's what's required to make someone comfortable.

I've tried to honor not only those interior difficulties and the exhaustion of Hartley as he shuttles with pills in every pocket from patient to patient, but also the intruding political reality. One great joy was quoting William S. Buckley in his own words from 1986. He says everybody who's HIV-positive should be interned in camps and tattooed on their wrist and ass; every person applying for a marriage license in America should be tested for HIV. If they fail, they can only marry if each agrees to be sterilized. You don't have to go to Germany in the thir-ties to find villains of immense scope. Buckley was happily at a keyboard instead of pulling the switch, but we all know what he'd have done. For me, to know there are now a hundred thousand copies of my book with his name, date, and exact words is worth the price of admission. I felt I'd vindicated thousands and thousands of deaths because thousands of American newspapers printed that.

There's a tendency to think of the whole period as soap opera. Imagine you're thirty years old and thirty of your best friends catch this unnamed disease and die. It *is* soap opera; it's beyond soap opera, it's horror film. Trying to write about it in a way that'll make it seem normative seems completely bogus. I didn't want to write a middle-of-the-road, middle-class novel. I wanted to write a comic aria about this immense, sickening loss. It's easy to do 20/20 hindsight and ask: "If Reagan had spent three hundred million dollars on the first two cases, what would've happened?" Instead they let the Pandora's box open. They actively spewed it. I want those names named. On record forever.

It's also easy to say: "Nothing could have stopped this disease" since nothing was *done* to stop it. But I don't want to write a screed or tract. I'm a painter, not a poster-maker. I don't work only in primary colors; I want to work in nuance. Posters are rendered to be glimpsed at as you rush along a cold street. Paintings can be considered indoors where it's heated and comfortable; second and third layers of meaning can evolve in time. That's the goal for *Plays Well* and the work to come.

RC Understandably, comedy has been used rarely in fiction concerning AIDS. Were you apprehensive about deploying it?

AG Well, yeah, but the period 1980 to 1995 remembers like one immense party—like the bash in *The Exterminating Angel*. What starts as a beautiful, sophisticated dinner party soon has people shitting in Ming vases because they can't leave. That's what Manhattan felt like: "The Masque of the Red Death." This costumed, uninvited visitor comes and kills significant numbers of partygoers. Since parties are joyful occasions and every host loves to hear laughter in the house, I think it's totally consistent to take a running start from comedy and see how far you can get. I'd love to read Joe Orton on HIV. The great poets that'll rise out of this will be people who have the nerve not to be pious, not to deal in merest predigested platitudes.

My particular truth comes when people laugh at themselves. The laughter in the book isn't laughter at the expense of anybody—including the parents. They're treated with amusement and yet what I hope is a profound compassion that's earned in the course of the book, precisely via them tending to the young and ill. There's a scene which for me is the emotional center of *Plays Well*. Hartley's in Florida visiting his parents. He hears his father breathing in an adjacent lounge chair. Hartley hears death coming. He's become such a medical expert he knows his father's going to die soon, because he's heard this sound so often in boys thirty-two-years old. There's an element of what Bergson defines comedy as: the mechanical grafted onto the natural. Nothing could possibly be more mechanical than these wind-up toys at the beginning of their revolution stopping, midstride. Farce, not tragedy, is the art form of our age.

There was something very mechanical about this whole "Studio 54" period. Even the spot on the arm is almost a rust spot; the body as non-functioning machine. The only way I know to get to the truth of this experience is to replicate our laughter in the face of it. The laughter starts in the book indolent and selfish. Disco culture was hardly about the milk of human kindness. It was all glitter, mirror balls, and appearance; heightening shoes, big hair, velvet and lace. It was very Regency dandified; very impenitently self-interested. But when that laughter begins to be tested by this terrible crisis and can hold, it becomes heroic and magnificent. Those high-drag mask funerals, in which all the drag queens put on their splendor and remember the dead, trying to look as gorgeous as possible for what little's left—I think they're as brave, operatic, dignified, and powerful as anything I've ever attended. We yucked it up because that was our habit—and because nobody's better at humor than oppressed minorities. Jewish shtick's the invention of people who can't leave a neighborhood, so have to defend themselves the only way they can—by saying: "You think you know about the limitations of the Jewish character? Let me tell you how limited we are." So: "You think I'm a silly queen? You have no fucking idea, honey. I go to bed dressed as Ida Lupino every night. I wake up like Bette Davis coughing at the end of *Of Human Bondage* and by 1 P.M., after caffeine enough, I'm wired and hard and painted as Joan Crawford." This is the revenge of overstatement.

It's this camp bravery—*genuine* bravery—and courageous laughter. I remember writing eulogies. In some ways *Plays Well* came out of writing twenty-two eulogies. Your lover or friend says six days before he dies: "I have one request." He takes a deep breath, then: "I want you to talk about me." You don't say: "Look, I have a deadline. I'm extremely busy, very popular, and professional; this is going to impede. I don't want to go to another little town upstate and pretend not to know how you died." You say: "I can't think of anything that'd give me more pleasure. I'm going to tell all the truth on you, girlfriend. You'd better watch out because if you ask me to do that, I'm going to dish you." Then they laugh—the *best* laugh. I've been a professional speaker most of my life, since I was the Preacher Emcee of the Second Grade Thanksgiving Pageant at Fannie S. Gorham Elementary. I love to make people laugh. To stand up and read my work, or tell a joke and hear twenty-five hundred people literally fall off their chairs—that's a huge joy. It's releasing people into themselves, knowing they'll go home, feeling this diaphragm loosening—a comfortableness you've facilitated. If that happens over and over, you've done something immense.

But the best laughs I've ever gotten have been at funerals. You stand up over the ashes or body of somebody who was thirty-five-years old and pure promise; everybody's favorite—but with outrageous, opinionated limitations and flaws. You release people to an accurate memory of the dead person by saying: "Hiram had many beautiful qualities. Financial generosity wasn't among them. I've never seen anybody stiff more waiters . . . " The release and gratitude funeral-goers feel on hearing an actual person discussed . . . And how do we know who we are? Through our flaws as well as our merits. Our flaws in some ways are more idiosyncratically endearing and unique than our "Brave, Clean, Reverent" merits.

RC   You mentioned three or four works about AIDS that might be remembered. Do you have other candidates in mind?

AG   It's hard in hindsight to say which narratives will last, partly because I haven't read them all, nor do I want to. I'm in this weird position of asking that people read mine, yet also understanding the aversion many people have to reading everything on the subject of HIV.

RC   What of Edmund White's *The Farewell Symphony*?

AG   I love him both as a person and a writer. I'm just beginning to see how much ground he's broken for us. He's our Robinson Crusoe. I have tremendous respect for Edmund, not only as a writer but as an early mentor and sponsor for lots of people. He was a Fairy Godmother to my work ten years before I ever met him. The London *Times* asked him for the best fiction of the year, and he chose "Blessed Assurance." He has insane generosity to other people—a quality I'd like to emulate.

RC   *The Farewell Symphony* tells a similar story to *Plays Well*, if in a very different style.

AG   Yes. I don't think of Edmund as a comic writer. I think he's an elegist, and one of immense and wry, knowing elegance. He's got an amazing touch; he can transform any experience. He also recalls all brand names, which petulia a boy of 1975 would wear. He's a born taleteller and a natural historian. His record will be invaluable.

RC   Could you update the tradition of fabular writing you described earlier? All of your models were historic, and not American. I had Hawthorne in mind.

AG   I love Hawthorne.

RC   Flannery O'Connor?

AG   Yes. She was profoundly original. I admire, in this tradition, William Maxwell and Eudora Welty's stories. Also the novella of Carson McCullers's *The Ballad of the Sad Cafe*, her single flawless work.

RC   And John Cheever.

AG   Yes, Cheever's a fabulist. He grew up on Bullfinch's mythology.
And Stanley Elkin and Grace Paley, two other teachers of mine. They
all tell heightened, impossible events as if these were natural occurrences
and in prose of stained-glass artifice and purity. They're not realists;
they're musical fabulists. They all have an immense sense of texture, of
improbability and condensation, a quality fables must have. In Cheever's
case, one subject he excelled in at school before he was expelled was
mythology. The Greek myths figure in absolutely everything Cheever
writes: from the names of characters—everybody's Diana or Leander—
to errant characters being torn apart by dogs. You might be looking at
Titian's paintings, but Cheever intelligently set his in the 1950s upper-
middle-class suburbs, all rendered in his own inimitable, Flaubert-like
prose rhythms.

RC   Both he and Flannery O'Connor conveyed an intuitive grasp of
how to use materials as tools for a story, and where to leave them. An
O'Connor landscape has a van, a gun, and people.

AG   That's good. You read like an American, pal. I think one characteristic of fable is that it often works better in the short run than the long.
I've never felt Flannery O'Connor's "novels" were the equal of her best
stories. She was a story writer; so was Cheever. The novels are strung-
together stories written by the same characters. Melville's tales are
equally dazzling. "Bartleby the Scrivener" is, for me, as great or greater
than *Moby Dick*. It's my nominee, long before Joyce, for the first modern short story. All the perversities and negations and executions of the
twentieth century lurk in that one tale's stubborn refrain: "I would prefer *not* to."

RC   What of the Southern Gothic tradition and homosexuality, as in
Carson McCullers and Truman Capote?

AG McCullers and Capote were in some ways very coy about sex. They were both gay—and busy little bees in the honeycomb of our lush sexual network. Yet they were of that unlucky generation still forced to make a sissyboy into a woman on the page. *Other Voices, Other Rooms* gets close to candor then veers into fandance. McCullers found it easier to write of the deaf, the dwarfed—as a metaphor for the queer. Tennessee Williams shared this with them—though, unlike them, he was a great genius, the one true genius of the period. Finally, I feel both Capote and McCullers are somewhat dishonest and therefore decidedly minor artists—as opposed to Williams, whose light gets more brilliant every day.

RC Do you revere his stories?

AG I think they're unbelievably irritating and incandescently instinctive. There are brilliant beginnings; then you see that he drank the sixth drink. Suddenly everything fell apart. But there are inventions and psychic twists in them that are inimitable. They're ferocious, honest, and hungry. He's as much a poet as Dickinson. I think Williams's *Collected Stories* is an invaluable book—terribly underestimated.

In terms of the sexual permission the South gives us, Faulkner's all the permission anybody needed. No American has written about sexuality with the authority, reckless honesty, and sexiness of "Manse Bill." A lot of people write about sex and it's just not sexy. But the sexual game in *Light in August* is very homoerotic, if only because it's so phallocentric. Joe Christmas pursues Joanna Burden, his white sponsor-mother and girlfriend. She hides at night in her plantation property. He comes and seeks and finds her and fucks her where she's lurking bare-assed under shrubs. *Light in August* winds up as insanely erotic—full of S&M, full of that push-and-pull; that "I'm on top; you aren't" that's a quality of all sexuality—straight, gay, cross-eyed. There's somebody who's a boss—if only for a second—and somebody who's taking care of the boss. I think Faulkner, with his tremendous sense of social and spiritual hierarchy, played that hand-held pipe-organ better than anybody. He's the American Genius of the dying century.

RC   People invariably speak of James Joyce or D. H. Lawrence as the sexual writers of the interwar period.

AG   There are moments in Lawrence. In one story, a miner comes home completely covered in coal dust. There's a three-page description of him washing coal dust off until he becomes this amazing, stark white, beautiful figure—fantastically erotic. But Faulkner's characters aren't just erotic when they're taking a bath. Every financial decision, every marketplace bargaining winds up having sexual domination behind it. The Snopses want to fuck the aristocrats, debase them and shit on them. It's coprophilic. That's part of Faulkner's insane energy. I don't think Faulkner ever actually tried gay sex. But maybe he didn't need to. Any man who can make himself the Poet Laureate of Bestiality can find no problem with a little cocksucking.

It's sad because when Faulkner was about forty-five, he'd already done the great work. Essentially, the alcoholism, which involved lethal doses, could only do tremendous damage. I've never felt in any other writer except Poe the presence of a controlled substance as a facilitator instead of a limitation. When I was eighteen or nineteen, I had a fast car and I'd drive drunk. I'm not bragging, but some of my happiest memories would be to go on a snaking country road in this fast car, and just go at 125 miles an hour around blind curves, with that typical eighteen-year-old heedlessness. Anybody could be in the way. Usually they weren't, because after nine o'clock everybody North Carolinian was in bed. Reading some Faulkner, that's the image I have: this careening, drunken, erectile imagination looking for something to fuck; hunting something to plug; this rapacious, outward-oriented breeding, fertile vision, speeding, scanning.

You feel the alcohol for a while washing Faulkner into places he wouldn't have gotten to ordinarily. But he's the titanic imagination.

What passes now for Southern literature is often the equivalent of coun-try-cutesy. At shopping malls across America there are these little ging-ham bonnets that show little farmgirls herding geese in a row. It's all very gemütlich and fantasized, and has absolutely nothing to do with liv-ing in the country, which is all about animal husbandry, mucking out horseshit, getting blisters, and having your crops wash away. There's a lot of middle-class falsification in Southern letters now.

I love funny and hate "cute." I love beauty and hate "pretty." I want beautiful or ugly. "Cute" is deadly and dishonest. Nothing dates faster. A lot of nice people are writing this. They publish a book a year, which you can't do if you're a serious writer. My theory is it's like having a baby every nine months. You can do three or four, but by the eighteenth, they're idiots, and you're often the last to know. You've got to save it up.

RC   Could you mention some gay writer whose work has impressed?

AG   I love Forster, the best Alfred Chester stories, pages of Jane Bowles, Whitman. Some of the early Albee one-acts like *Zoo Story* blew my fuses when I was an erectile fifteen-year-old. In terms of other gay texts that have stirred me, I think in terms also of images, so Aubrey Beardsley. As a kid, I somehow got my hands on a book of Beardsley drawings which still excite me: the ornamentation; the curdled fantasies, phallic worship, militant, self-justifying decoration; that influence of fin-de-siècle license I still find a model for these nineties. It's a paradox that every century has a life cycle. The forties and fifties are about war and prosperity; the sixties, revolution; the nineties are about mysticism, looking for alterna-tive ways to live, numerology, and visitations from other planets. All this angel stuff now is totally consistent with *Peter Pan*.

Oscar Wilde's a god and a lodestone of mine. He's futuristic, the way all pure intelligence is. It's almost a scientific, mathematic intelli-gence he had: the syllogisms, epigraphs; his clean ability to cleave the world into a single sentence that says all people are either this or that. The magic of *The Importance of Being Earnest* is a prophecy of semiology, of gay politics in a straight world, of living an encoded, Bunbury, erotic life. For me it's one of the great seminal works. I read Wilde yearly with tremendous relish and profound affection. He was, tragically, one of the kindest men. I think he's one of the least likely people to have been a good person. And yet he was. We extend privileges to brilliance that aren't held out to ordinary folks. But the thing one loves about Wilde is that he was both the most brilliant man in the nineteenth century—verbally, conversationally—and the most generous. The tragedy of his life was his eagerness to please others. But, like most of us, he had terrible taste in boyfriends. Wilde was sacrificed by his own ungainly kindness and an overliteral Christ-likeness beloved of all the masochists.

I feel my own tombstone will say: "No good deed went unpunished." I try every day to do something for others. It frequently boomerangs in hilarious, amazing ways. But I don't have any choice. I've decided that's my fate. I try to put as much kindness into the books as possible without sogging or warping them a bit. But Wilde is that paradox: the coolest genius and the biggest heart. That's what I'd wish for all artists, myself most especially.

Constantine Cavafy is the first great gay artist I encountered. When I was a kid, I had a Geiger-counter sensation when I drifted near anything with gay content. In public libraries I could almost walk blind and feel the heat coming out of the back of a book. I didn't care if it was a medical text; I'd find the hot spots. I found Cavafy early on, and knew from the beginning he was a genius. His combination of high and low Greek on a line-by-line basis is a metaphor for what I try to do in my fiction: absolute artificiality alongside complete, inevitable naturalness; comic exuberance set beside an acknowledgment of the pain, difficulty, and annihilation that's our lot—and the option of moving from one to the other with a syllable's notice, so the reader's emotional registration does what mine does, which is to go crazy all over the place every second of my life.

RC   Was Auden an influence?

AG   Auden I loved for what truth I found in "Musée des Beaux Arts" and all those things you're led to in school. You actually think: "This one's really great; it's not just they're saying it is." For the way he lived his life as an artist, Auden was tremendously influential. He went to bed at the same time every night; he wrote the same number of hours. He played Wagner before bedtime. That reified schedule is almost like the metric form itself—a way of remaining disciplined in the world; giving your life a shape that's ordinarily offered by a wife and child and those exterior props people depend on.

Also Isherwood, especially those early entertainments like *Prater Violet*. I'm less interested in the later confessional things, though I think *A Single Man* was tremendously important because the sexuality of the narrator was a given and wasn't apologized for. Anything from those so-called classics that are essentially apologies I'm not interested in, except for how they reflect their peculiar historical moment. I'm not into begging for anybody's forgiveness. I've tried to live my life honorably and I have no regrets, except for the loss of friends whose exits I haven't been able to control.

I'd say early Evelyn Waugh, too. Waugh's the gayest writer in the world, especially in *Decline and Fall* and *Vile Bodies*. This is an influence so apparent you don't even see it, but the organization of *Plays Well*— where the grown man returns to the scene of the crime—derives very much from *Brideshead Revisited*. But, pound for pound, Waugh's comedy, brilliance, and merciless humor is still devastatingly fresh and instructive.

I mentioned *Peter Pan*, so J. M. Barrie. He's obviously a gay writer writer and energetically a pedophile. Lewis Carroll's an immense influence too. For me, *Alice in Wonderland* is one of the twenty books I'd take out of the civilization in order to found a new one. It's a masterpiece; an unending source of joy and inspiration—and perhaps the single greatest act of sublimation I know.

RC   You mentioned the urgency you felt in writing *Plays Well*. You have references to other projects everywhere—from years ago, a novel, "The

Erotic History of a Southern Baptist Church," is mentioned. There's the story "The Practical Heart," part of a longer project. Why did *Plays Well* supersede these projects, and what now becomes of them?

AG   I was working on a collection of novellas including "Preservation News," "The Practical Heart," "He's One Too" and a work called "The Mortician Confesses." That book will soon appear as a short novel collection. It's about how virtue gets people into the worst kind of trouble. A continuing fascination of mine is how to make a good person dramatically interesting. One reason I have the audience I do is because most people, I think, would at least prefer to be good. It's terribly inconvenient to do that constantly, so they stop several times a day. But they think of themselves as good. If I had to describe myself, this has always been my particular cross to bear: some people would prefer to be brilliant; some, to be beautiful, powerful, alluring, or destructive. I'd like to be good. I guess it was drummed into me early. I've made the best of a bad situation; this yen for Virtue. Somebody's got to do it!

As for the other novels, "The Erotic History of a Southern Baptist Church" is the second in a trilogy that started with *Widow*. I have this great, overarching vision of how characters from that book walk into this one. Two hundred pages of it are written. What happens often, as with *Widow*, which took seven years, is that I'll be working on one thing when something else commandeers and drafts me. You have to be crazy not to follow. My plan for "The Erotic History" is to pivot on the confusion between ecstatic religious experiences and ecstatic erotic experiences—they're notoriously commingled, interchangeable. I'd like to write the history of the U.S. from the point of view of a single rural Baptist church in North Carolina from 1875 to 1975. It ends as a bankrupt television ministry. It grows from an early, hallowed, gladelike place in nature to being mired and extinct in technology.

It's a work which may take many years, but it'll be a lot of fun. I have to do it now while I still remember what the erotic is. This is one thing that happens. When I was twenty-four, if I didn't have sex with myself or others four times a day, I felt I had the flu or something. Now I'm fifty, I can actually go for a whole day without plugging the wall. That's been very time-saving and welcome, in a way. But if sexuality's your subject, you don't have to be out all night chasing people. But you do have to be able to summon up those feelings for every single character. It's not that it's melting. I'm still virile and itchy, but the long view is setting in.

There are lots of other uncollected stories waiting for a place. But I frequently find that what I think are stories wind up part of a larger piece. With *Plays Well*, "Thirty Dildoes" came first. I suddenly realized: "Here is a man with a mission." It predicted the book and called it forth. So, rather than just publish the stories in a collection of disparate entities, I hold onto them until I see they're part of a larger pattern. Sometimes they arrive as mother's triplets—trilogies, where I find meanings and connections between the three infant parts. It's a crowded nursery, but I like to keep busy.

RC   On that note, thanks very much for your time.

ETHAN MORDDEN

Ethan Mordden is best known to gay readers for four volumes comprising the "Buddies" series of gay stories set in Manhattan, as well as for an epic account of postwar gay life in America, *How Long Has This Been Going On?* He is also the author of around twenty works of nonfiction on musicals, opera, theater, and classical music. Born in Pennsylvania and raised there—and in Venice, Italy, and Long Island—Mordden took a degree in history at the University of Pennsylvania before moving to New York. His publishing career began in 1976 with a study of the Broadway musical.

Mordden's fiction first appeared as a regular autobiographical column—"Is There a Book in This?"—in the pioneering gay literary magazine *Christopher Street*. *I've a Feeling We're Not in Kansas Anymore: Tales from Gay Manhattan* (New York: St. Martin's, 1985), the first collection of these pieces, was followed by the equally successful *Buddies* (New York: St. Martin's, 1986) and *Everybody Loves You* (New York: St. Martin's, 1988).

Mordden turned to other projects in the nine years before volume four of the "Buddies" series appeared—*Some Men Are Lookers* (New York: St. Martin's, 1997). His first novel, *One Last Waltz* (New York: St. Martin's, 1986), concerned a family of Irish-American immigrants. Under the pseudonym "M. J. Verlaine," Mordden published a collection of short pieces about heterosexual life in Manhattan, *A Bad Man Is Easy to Find* (New York: St. Martin's, 1991). He has written two further novels: the epic account of gay liberation and its aftermath, *How Long Has*

This Been Going On? (New York: Villard, 1995); and a novel about gay identity, the love of opera, the cult of the diva, and much else, *The Venice Adriana* (New York: St. Martin's, 1998).

Mordden also edited *Waves: An Anthology of New Gay Fiction* (New York: Vintage, 1994). He is currently working on a novel set in Nazi Germany and a fifth volume of the "Buddies" series, which may consist of nonfictional essays. He lives in an apartment in midtown Manhattan, where this interview took place on Monday, November 3, 1997.

RC   How did the short stories on gay life in New York come about?

EM   It was a big accident. I wasn't publishing fiction. Then I met with Chuck Ortleb and Tom Steele from *Christopher Street* and the *New York Native*. I was to write an arts review column, "Cultural Advantages." Over drinks, I started telling stories about my family, which isn't just dysfunctional, but eccentric and colorfully picturesque. They were laughing and Chuck said: "You should write these down. I'll publish them."

So I started another column: "Is There a Book in This?" It began as sheer journalism about my family. Then I did a piece on getting thrown out of parties. At that time I'd get into fights with people and throw drinks in their faces. Then I was running out of things that would work. I thought: "I can use something that happened, but not be entirely honest. I'll telescope, leave some people out, sweeten this, embellish that." So the column, from being true life, turned into fiction based on true life. It was about gay life in New York because I came here right after college, and almost all the people I knew were gay New Yorkers. I was quite young and still very much on the scene—nights at the Eagle; a summer weekend in the Pines. That's where a lot of this stuff occurred.

So we move from an eccentric family to eccentric friends who get into interesting scrapes. My best friend did nothing all day but cruise. He had to have sex at least once a day or he'd completely go to pieces. He'd go after anyone he was attracted to without wondering if he was gay or straight. He eventually realized a photograph of himself at full mast was very handy to pull out if someone was hard to land. The guy was legendary on the circuit for being heavy hung.

You can imagine the trouble this guy gets into. Finally he runs across someone really cute but vulnerable. Somehow he touches this guy's heart and finds himself in a relationship that's sexual and emotional. The kid's childlike and infantile—and also six feet tall. He's also the most boring person ever.

RC   This is the model for Virgil?

EM   Yes. He'd clean house wearing nothing but underpants. He'd watch cartoon shows with the concentration of a physicist. That was his charm. Try having a conversation with him! So all these exciting things were going on. You're surrounded by a culture still making itself. What more would you want for a series of stories than that? It certainly wouldn't have been as interesting if it had been a small town in Pennsylvania, where I come from. I just made use of what was there.

RC   The stories have developed in certain ways. Your alter ego Bud emerges as the series continues.

EM   Yes. He was never meant to be a character—only the narrator. I'm a very private person. Also, I've noticed some gay readers become very uncomfortable with first-person narratives that roam into sex; books where the guy says: "I went into the bar and took home the cutest boy." You turn to the dust-jacket and don't buy it. I remember this extremely good-looking guy called Glenn Person. The build was slim and chiseled. He was the biggest hung white guy in New York—and famous for it. Glenn wrote a piece for *Christopher Street* about being the most gorgeous-looking man alive. To this day, that story makes people explode like Mount Etna with anger. I thought: "I'll leave myself out. I'll be circus ringmaster."

In the middle of *Everybody Loves You*, Cosgrove came out of nowhere. He's the only character I wholly invented. Maybe I thought we needed some enriching, or I suddenly realized Virgil wasn't going to hang around forever without his own acolyte. He was tiring of being one himself—though ultimately what tore his relationship with Dennis Savage apart was the insistence he get a day job. In the stories, Bud's a Spoiled Rich Kid, wealthy enough to support two people. But Dennis Savage's just a schoolteacher. That's different from my friend Bob Trent, whom Dennis Savage was modeled on. Another Spoiled Rich Kid.

Virgil wanted to be kept; to do what Cosgrove does—simply the chores—and otherwise have time to roam around. I didn't realize when I got to the end of "The Woggle," the last story in *Everybody Loves You*, that when I came back, I had loose ends to tie up. Cosgrove had to have somewhere to go. There are some awkward last pages in that book where Bud ceased to be ringmaster and became a character. I thought I'd better end the series right there. I wrote "this is the utmost of my report" and fully intended it. I'd nothing more to say, and plenty else to write about. Then someone said: "There's one story you never got to—Virgil confronting AIDS." It'd be interesting to see this little tyke—a self-styled, manipulative tyke, in the long run—deal with the dramatic feelings everybody had about AIDS.

RC   You're talking of the fictional Virgil now?

EM   Yes. I get very critical of how he behaves in volume five, which I'm working on now. The real Virgil's in Alaska, beyond our reach.

I enjoy writing these stories. The characters are so familiar to me. They're like wind-up toys. They go their own way, but I'm in charge. I thought I'd write the Virgil-AIDS tale for a lark. That became "Exorcis," the first story in *Some Men Are Lookers*. Somehow that led to another. Every now and then, over several years, I wrote a story for relaxation. Then, when I was editing *Waves*, I was giving $400 to every author out of my advance. I thought I'd put a nice long story in myself and save $1,200. So I wrote "The Hunt for Red October." Then I thought: "Fuck it, I've gone this far." My St. Martin's editor Keith Kahla liked the stories; it seemed sensible to put them together, then fill out the collection: *Some Men Are Lookers*.

Ultimately, I was driven to write about all this because I felt there was something very spectacular about a culture based on man-to-man sex. It produced an extraordinary number of very deep and important man-to-man friendships—and where else but New York? There's so much street traffic here, whereas everything's in cars everywhere else in America. It was a unique time; something historical was happening. I wanted to get down the day-to-day living of some basically ordinary guys—

I didn't want a bunch of Titans. I wanted regular people and some Titans. Then they could look at this world of Titans and figure it out. Andrew Holleran's *Dancer from the Dance* does that too. It's narrated by someone we know nothing about—the letter writer. I was impelled by a love of the characters and storytelling. I had this advantage: I could never have run a story cycle if I were straight. What would I have been writing about? Or if I'd been gay in the 1940s. What would I have said? It'd be the same if I started out now. It's too various; there's no uniform anymore. A lot of the stories depended on there being certain places one went to find the stories: bars, dance halls, even the baths. It's all gone; replaced by the Internet. Back then, you had only to show up along the circuit, and one friend would lead to another, and soon you were watching all these odd happenings. The eroto-romantic meeting of two lookers knee-deep in surf at the beach, touching each other and hungering and falling in love as they stood there, oblivious of a few of us staring at them. This world of ours. *Ours!*

But others would sneak in. I slightly knew—but mainly knew of—a construction worker named Bert something, rumored to have a wife and kids somewhere but, because construction moves you around, a regular visitor in Stonewall. Bert was a steamfitter or whatever, so he had the extremely heavy upper torso that early Stonewall taste doted on. He wasn't exactly handsome, but in those days that didn't matter if one had the rest of it—physique, authority, power. Bert didn't talk much. Was he a towering hunk or just vacuous? But he did have an enormous dick, really long and thick, with a pointed end. A snake. When he stripped for sex, his partner jumped out the window. So Bert developed this soothing Daddy rap to mesmerize them with some sort of mean-streets poetry. But in so doing this Titan who was supposed to be nothing more than your hot date accidentally fused the physical with the emotional. He became ultimate not just in looks but in meaning. So of course all of his partners fell in love with him.

It was a neat tale to know of, especially when Bert tried shacking up with some kid and came home the first day to find his boyfriend cooking dinner naked in an apron. "Hello, honey." *This* is Stonewall? There are different versions of what happened next. But, anyway, look how different it is today. Who knows a construction worker, not to mention this mother of all daddies? A whole way of life is gone. Our democracy's gone, along with our mythology. All the rules have changed. There used to be two ages in gay—young and invisible. Now there's totally twenty-two, twenty-eight and looking, thirty-four and cashed-in, forty-something but holding it together, and so on.

So today they write about other things. One reason why men become "gay novelists" is that they want to be perceived in a certain way. One thing that's not prestigious for some reason is to have an all-male, all-gay cast. Maybe ghetto life's so real they don't want it. But that's what Edmund White and Eric[1] and Larry Kramer were first writing about—the subculture. Our founding generation

---

1. Eric: Here and throughout the interview Mordden refers to "Andrew Holleran" by his given name.

writers chose to write about what was around them. Now it's just the opposite—writing about how artistic you want to appear to be. The notion of novels like *Dancer from the Dance* or *Faggots*: there are no straights in them! We've gotten away from that—I don't think to our profit. A lot of times books are written because the authors have figured out a way of being perceived of as "Important"—a crummy reason to write a novel. The idea of making your characters bisexuals and straights because otherwise the straight world isn't going to like it is extremely dreary.

RC   Do you think it's untrue to life?

EM   Not necessarily, but I find a lot of fanciness about it. My term for the bisexuals I've known is "60/40's." They tend to be working-class men from a very narrow background, like Bert. The notion of a gay life, of coming out or admitting they're attracted to men, is absolutely unthinkable. However, only 60 percent of their sexuality needs women. Forty percent wants men. The 60 percent enables them to have sex with women, be happily married, have a family, even cheat on their wives with other women. But there's always that 40 percent, lurking and beckoning. In books I don't see "60/40's." I see fraudulent icons created by gay writers who want a larger audience than "gay." They want the approval of straights. It's not something I respect.

RC   Some novelists say writing only about being gay would be limiting.

EM   That's amazing. Can you imagine a black writer saying that about an all-black-characters novel? It's homophobic, stupid, self-hating. I've a feeling I know who those people are. Looking at them, I'm not surprised. It's a very common source of homophobia now which didn't exist before Stonewall: "This system's made so people like me can't get into it; we can't have success in it." I don't mean literary success. I mean social or romantic success.

I can see straights saying it too, because they take themselves for granted. They think there's something wrong with something that doesn't have a lot of straights in it. They wouldn't dare say this about black or Jewish writers. The fact they can say it about us shows how vastly casual homophobia is. If you said: "That's so homophobic; you're a fucking bigot!," they'd say: "It"s not bigotry; it's literary judgment." They don't see us having a culture; being different from them as blacks or Jewish people are. I think we're *more* different.

I'm not saying these writers are disloyal to gay culture. They make their own choices. I just can't fathom why they'd want the approval of straights. I never did. I never even thought there was anything wrong in being gay. Hearing about all these teenage gay suicides today makes me so disgusted. You're going to give up the only life you'll ever have because Mommy doesn't love you? Who says the cunt has any love to give in the first place? It's like wanting the approval of your parents if you want to be a cop and they want you to be a doctor. I'd say: "What the fuck gives you the right to an opinion? You want a doctor in the family? Go to med school! I'm interested in self-fulfillment. That's why I was put on earth." "No, we nurtured you." "No. You fucked and I came out. That's all it is."

RC   Being published in *Christopher Street* meant you could presume your readers were largely gay. Did that affect the stories?

EM   This is a cliché, but probably true: you write for yourself. If you see yourself as really smart, really educated, know a lot—you write for that guy.

RC   I'm interested in the series' trajectory. You started recording actual events, then invented certain elements—even whole characters, in Cosgrove's case. After that, your alter ego Bud emerges as a character and you kill the series. Why?

EM It became too dangerous for me—not because I decided to give myself a cute boyfriend. I couldn't end the series sending Cosgrove onto the street. What I thought happens is, out of sympathy, Bud takes Cosgrove in, with the idea that the kid will soon get a job, build up a little bank account and move out. It never occurred to me that *Some Men Are Lookers* was going to have this symmetry, whereby both Dennis and Bud now have their live-ins who were comrades-in-arms. Plus, we have Uncle Carlo, thereby creating a perfect gay, nonbiological family. We're all runaways.

RC This produces the most integrated volume.

EM Yes. Now there's a really stable family structure. Carlo's the only real-life model I didn't do anything with: no embellishments or modifications. In *I've a Feeling*, I utterly failed to catch him, because he was so implausible. I figured if I put him on page as he is in life, no one would buy it. I kept trying to middle-class him in various ways, so failed to do him justice. After that, I realized you have to let him be as eccentric as he really is. He *does* talk funny; he *is* huge; he *does* make his own rules; he *has* a thuggish side.

RC You must have become more familiar with his role as the series continued.

EM I did. *I've a Feeling*, after all, wasn't written as a book. Those were separate stories which I filled out with others. That was also true of *Buddies*. *Everybody Loves You* was the first book conceived as such, though a few stories had been published before. *Some Men Are Lookers* was all written fresh—though, again, not as a book. The idea was that I was creating, finally, an ideal situation for gay people, where the older guys, having enjoyed all the choices of being a gay man in your twenties in New York after Stonewall, can settle down in a stable environment which is kept enlivened by the almost surreal exploits of the two kids. I cover that by being such a naturalistic narrator that you're fooled. Bud narrates as though everything he's talking about is the most plausible everyday stuff.

So there are two fathers and two sons. You've got surprising dangers—and a federal marshal. No bad guy can get through with Carlo around. Ultimately, what was reached was something a lot of people would like, and some have in Stonewall: the stable environment your biological family never was; somewhere you get accepted for what you are without qualification. There's nothing but support, and the hope that no great crisis hits, like AIDS. And it didn't. Though I've lost two principals, neither died that way. I promised myself when I realized this was a series that I'd never kill off a lead, no matter what happened in life.

RC   Why?

EM   Imagine if E. F. Benson had suddenly killed off Miss Mapp. You'd feel jarred. You hate her, but she has to live on so you *can* hate her. And, though I'm certainly aware of the impact of it, I only really had one relatively close friend who died of AIDS. I knew *of* tons of people. But AIDS didn't strike home in any important way to me. That's reflected in the series.

The worst thing I did was virtually putting Virgil out of the family. He has no one to protect him, cosset him, and put up with his antics. But he made his own choices. He's now living with this hot "60/40," who's totally devoted to Virgil. But he's not going to be happy. It's the kind of devotion where, if Virgil tries to leave, he'll kill him. In real life, Virgil has a boyfriend more or less like himself. He's approaching thirty-five, but still looks like a sixteen-year-old—not through a gym. He's just genetically marvelous; very youthful.

RC   I wanted to ask about the eternal youthfulness of Virgil and Cosgrove. Doesn't realism concern you? Are you interested in them maturing as characters? They're in their thirties now.

EM Cosgrove developed extraordinarily in *Some Men Are Lookers*, though not in terms of maturity. He's compelled by two things: first, a need for security; a roof over his head. Second, he needs love. Virgil supplied that; I supplied the roof. We had this great deal—except it makes for a very odd relationship between Bud and Cosgrove because they're not precisely "lovers," a term I hate. I like "live-in," which is completely neutral; "boyfriend" I love. That's very rich. It suits everything from musical comedy to film noir. "Lovers" suggests Feydeau or Somerset Maugham.

The problem is that Cosgrove has to remain under Virgil's strict regime as an acolyte. Virgil's very manipulative, and strict with Cosgrove whenever he strikes out on his own. Cosgrove's very asocialized too. We don't know about his background, but he makes weird choices and can never figure out why people are appalled. Bud finds it all very funny—as Bob Trent always did. He loved the bizarre.

RC In the model for Virgil?

EM No, in Cosgrove.

RC In what you'd invented, then?

EM Yes. Bob didn't like how Dennis Savage reacted in the stories. He thought he'd been made crabby, when in fact he was very funny and charming. Eric used to say Bob and I had this running comedy act which was very excluding of others. You know how best friends develop certain tag lines and shoot them at each other. So Dennis Savage and Bud have a completely different sense of humor from the other two. My sense of humor only comes out of Bud's mouth. Everyone else's is his own, though I created them. And it's only funny because of who they are. If you take a line out of Cosgrove's mouth and put it in another character's, it isn't funny anymore. Like *Friends*; it's character-based.

RC   Could you comment still further on how the relationship between the stories and real life changed? It's now a very peculiar setup: Virgil's based on a real person; Cosgrove's invented; two characters' real-life models are dead; Bud is based on you.

EM   I think this is connected to writing a series well. Once you know these people *that* well, they take on a life of their own as literary characters. These people are so vivid that once I have a premise for a story, *they* write it.

RC   There are moments where Bud starts discussing the processes of fictionalization with Dennis Savage. Bud's justifying the fiction to the friend who appears in it, which is deeply odd.

EM   I know. Bob and I used to meet regularly every Friday. He'd see his shrink, then we'd go to lunch, come back here and, every time I had another ten or fifteen pages of a story, Bob would sit where you are and I'd give him them. He liked to perform, so he'd read the stories aloud, acting all the parts. Every time he came on a line of Dennis Savage's that he'd in fact uttered in real life, Bob would stop, with this mock despair because I was taking something else from him. I'd say: "What do you care? You're not using it." Or he didn't like it if Cosgrove got given some line. Bob would say: "Does that *have* to be in there?" So he was reacting to it as if it were real. There was a touch of paranoia in Bob. He had this theory that I was using the stories to demote or belittle him. I said: "No, this is what the characters *do*." You just know that with Cosgrove and him, it's ontological. It's why they're on earth: to destroy each other.

RC   What do you mean exactly? Bob could only "know" that on the same level as any fiction reader—the only level on which Cosgrove exists.

EM   You have to remember Bob and I had palled around since we were eight. Bob knew me well enough to know what I'd want in my story and what I couldn't use. In that sense the series was real even when I was inventing it. Bob knew it was real in my head.

RC Do you miss him not being here to read them?

EM I miss him, period.

RC Was he the only one of the "real" characters to read the stories?

EM Carlo never read anything. He thought it was great I was making a living as a writer though. The real Virgil read one volume, for certain.

RC Has writing always come easily?

EM I have extremely good work habits and an effective imagination. I think writer's block is a euphemism for someone having written himself into a corner because he started out with not enough material in the first place. A real writer never gets blocked.

RC Are there experiences you find more difficult to describe in fiction than others—sex, for instance?

EM Not as long as someone else is having it. There's a certain amount of graphic sex in all my fiction, because it's a unique opportunity for character revelation. One of the reasons so many men have as much sex as they can—that is, with as many partners as is, to them, reasonable— is that sex is the most honest thing in their lives. It's pleasure, it's con-nection, it's an experience of the divine. But it's also information. Sometimes, when a guest is over, I'll play Anyone You Want. I show him three photos of naked porn models and ask him to choose the one he prefers. Some love to and some refuse—what will it reveal about them?

There's a lot of sex in Stonewall, so there's a lot of it in my work— for instance, in volume five, how some men regard bareback sex not as reckless but as a definition of their masculinity. The joke used to be: "Real men don't eat quiche." Now it's: "Real men don't use condoms." Remember how Diane Keaton laughed at William Atherton when he tried to sneak one on in *Looking for Mr. Goodbar*?

RC   You've used the phrase "in Stonewall" a lot, and have called "Stonewall" a state of mind. For some, the sense of cultural cohesion it implies is a fantasy. For you, presumably, it's a reality.

EM   Yes. The original title of *How Long?* was *Stonewall*. It begins before the riots, but the idea is that modern gay culture as a concept and the people it has in it: *that's* Stonewall. To me, it's the sexiest, richest, most imagination-teasing word.

RC   But to insist on the phrase "in Stonewall" suggests something more tangible than others feel it to be.

EM   Well, they're wrong. The straights and the homophobic gays are wrong. There *is* a unique life. It's anything you want to make it. It's an ethnicity. "Stonewall," to me, is like saying "the Italian tradition" or "the Irish tradition." It conjures up all sorts of associations: a certain politics, a certain religion, a way of looking at the family; music, theater, secrets.

RC   For some, AIDS ruined the potential of gay liberation captured in "Stonewall." Carlo describes this danger at the end of *Buddies*. He talks about leaving town because it's all over.

EM   Yes. I went against what really happened there. Carlo *did* leave town—back to South Dakota—and didn't come back. But the books needed him to.

RC   What if somebody said your fiction lies: AIDS *has* wrought these changes; people *have* died, sobered up, left town?

EM There's a moment in *How Long?* that has been vastly misunderstood. We're told in a very dramatic way that one of the major characters has the symptoms. Later, when he dies, it's only mentioned in passing. So people said: "Wait a minute. I didn't get the preparation." But that's what was going on then. People weren't going to memorial services anymore. They'd become exhausted. They wanted to say: "I have to tell you something. Davey died; let's get on with our lives." I was trying to reflect that in the narration: the idea that this is so painful that it has turned into whispered headlines. We can't bear the stories anymore. We hear the news and run.

RC You've written other, more clearly invented fiction. Didn't AIDS appeal as a topic for these?

EM No. I guess this has to do with promising myself I'd never kill off a lead character. I always want the series, even now that it's ending, to have the same excitement and hope.

I was an absolute frequenter of the Eagle when I first started going to bars. I was there every night—not because I was taking all these people home. I just loved the excitement of being there and thinking: "How do I know something really special isn't going to walk in and change my life— or at least my night? *That* excitement, the feeling that there's always something wonderful coming around the corner, is what I wanted in the series from beginning to end. That's what was so exciting about gay life. It's got so much wonderful performance and transformation in it, which the straight world doesn't have. Straights keep getting married. I don't know why.

RC Some gay men want to marry.

EM A couple of radical gays do. No one I know has any intention of that. The frantic terror with which these straight males deal with the notion of gay marriage must mean they're all closeted gays. Otherwise what are they afraid of? I really believe the leading homophobes are

60/40's—if not mad, screaming, closeted queens. The problem is, homophobia's been with us so long and is so widespread that everyone accepts it. But I think caring what someone else does for sex is like caring what vegetables someone eats. There must be something deeply sick and stupid in you.

RC   What's so different about the emotional investment some gays want to put into marriage and the satisfaction your characters derive from family? There's a similar stability.

EM   Yes, but it's created and shaped by ourselves and our needs, not according to what society demands.

RC   Do you feel the idea of family encompasses a sense of volition, whereas marriage can't?

EM   There are good marriages. But marriage is essentially a placating of the furies of the religions of Church and State. If they didn't create it and demand it of us, very few people would marry. Certainly straight men wouldn't marry until they were forty. There's just too much dating open to you.

There's no biological family like the one in my series, which involves a lot of freedom. My characters don't rip each other to shreds all the time the way people in families do; where everybody lets everything out, then expects everyone to recover immediately. I'll say one thing for my parents. My mother's a dreadful nag and my father a loony idiot, but they didn't believe in unloading everything all the time. Our family had a lot of secrets, which a family should have. There was a movie in the fifties called *I Want to Live!* Susan Hayward played a woman accused of murder. She was being strapped into the electric chair in the poster, screaming: "I want to live!" I remember as a little boy thinking of my mother strapped into an electric chair, screaming: "I want to nag!" You don't have any equivalent for that in this liberated family of mine. They joke; they don't nag.

RC   Things went wrong with Virgil.

EM   No one's perfect. Virgil turned out a flawed, somewhat selfish person. But even he never broke the rules of conduct.

RC   If you couldn't kill Virgil off, were you tempted to send him elsewhere?

EM   Virgil's going to fade out in the fifth book, though never entirely. He brings this very odd 60/40 into our midst. We get a chance to see what a "Real Man" who wants to fuck a kid is like. He reminds me of my brother Jim. Jim lived to date and dated to live. That was all he was interested in—making out with women. He could never understand why they had to be taken to dinner to be fucked.

In the series, this guy takes polaroids of girls. On the back he writes down their measurements. He loves making a big sensual thing out of using his tape measure. He has a beer that goes slowly flat of an evening, as he lies in bed going over these polaroids. At the same time, Virgil deliberately teases him. He'll come down the hall to stare into Virgil's room. Virgil pretends to be asleep. But the covers are all the way down. This guy has so bought into a culture of lies, he doesn't know *what* he is. There's this old joke: "In Soviet Russia, everything that isn't forbidden is permitted. In Communist China, everything that isn't permitted is forbidden." In my series—in Stonewall, in gay life as I see it—everything is permitted.

RC   You mentioned *Dancer from the Dance* earlier. I'd like to introduce Andrew Holleran's career for contrast. *The Beauty of Men* concerns the dissatisfactions of aging. By contrast, your series retains harmony between generations. For many, gay culture does discriminate strongly on grounds of age, as *The Beauty of Men* suggests. Your stories suggest otherwise.

EM   That may have something to do with the fact that Eric left New York a long time ago. Even when I first knew him, he was at his parents' house every Christmas and New Year's. He claimed to be completely defeated by those holidays and parties. Each year the vacation got longer and longer. Eric was coming back in April or June. Finally he wasn't coming back. He was living down there. Now, that happened a long time ago, and Eric didn't have to reach a certain age to do it. It may be that he has a completely different mentality, even though we were founding members of Stonewall in real life. Something went wrong for Eric, I guess, long before he was Lark, the figure in *The Beauty of Men*. He could've written that novel fifteen years ago. It would've been the same, though Eric certainly wouldn't have been remotely old enough to talk about age that way.

RC You're suggesting he pulled out of gay subculture before he needed to. His novel suggests the subculture is made only for a certain age range and type of person.

EM The fact is, Eric pulled out of this liberated, make-it-what-you-will, protean culture, to go to the closest thing he could find to pre-Stonewall culture: basically, queens looking for trade, as he describes it in *The Beauty of Men*. It's like: "I saw a house painter; he's so beautiful; I want him."

RC A lot of people tire of the subculture. The development of family in your stories offers a kind of retreat from it.

EM It does. Part of the thrill of that family was having everything going on in this building. You didn't have to go scrounging around. In fact, at one point Dennis Savage complains: "I can't go out by myself. I've forgotten where everything is." What he means is, everything's gone—at least, *his* everything. The culture changes, but also your own needs change. I think people have to make a lot of accommodations. If you asked me what the moral of this series was, I'd say: "Nobody gets everything he wants, and you have to pay a price for everything you get." It means you make certain compromises. It doesn't mean you can't have a good life; it means the number of joys is finite.

I picked five people. You might say they lead charmed lives. I'd say: "Not charmed, though they *are* under my protection. I'll guarantee none of them dies while we look on, and though one selfishly wrote himself out of the series, still the family will survive." When Virgil moved out, Cosgrove felt he wouldn't get a decent meal. So it's a rule every Thursday that Virgil comes to dinner here. That's how Virgil remains in the series.

RC   "Here"?

EM   At my apartment—in the stories. It used to throw people when I'd say Cosgrove is such-and-such, and it wasn't in the stories. But I'd figured it out. I don't have to publish something for it to be real.

RC   You said you invented Cosgrove to find a way to keep Virgil around; actually, Virgil cuts free.

EM   In the long run. The fact is, if Cosgrove hadn't come in, maybe Virgil wouldn't have been so offended at having to maintain a day job. But I think he regards that the same way I did with my parents' ceaseless determination that I get a summer job every year when I came home from college. I explained: "You're paying all this money to send me to an Ivy League school so I can become a member of the leadership class. Since the only summer jobs available are pumping gas and bagging groceries, these seem like two mutually exclusive projects. This is my summer vacation; why can't I enjoy it? All right, you're not going to give me an allowance. Fine. I'll function without one. I can sell things if I need money." The truth was that my mother, that enraged control freak, wanted her house free of other people in the summer. The younger ones would be shipped off to camp; the two older ones had left the family. I was the remaining problem. I knew this was a completely bankrupt, typically parental thing, whereby they say: "It's for your own good—to learn the value of money," or something.

They're not directly analogous experiences, because that was hypocrisy, whereas Dennis Savage was being reasonable when he said: "On my salary I can't afford to support two people." Still, Virgil saw it as a scam.

RC   The slippage between the series and your own experiences is remarkable. You move between the two with such ease.

EM   I think all writers do. Maybe I have this irresponsible view that anything that happened is fair game. Eric used to warn people: "Be careful—everything he hears goes right into the typewriter." But if you don't use what really happened, then it's *nothing* but invented.

That may prove a great weakness in volume five. Maybe the verisimilitude will fall out of it. It may disappoint a lot of people too. Instead of stories, these are essays on gay life, using my characters as illustrations and eventually developing a throughline. It's to make it more interesting for me, instead of spinning yarns again. When you're up to volume five, you need something to change the texture.

It's like what E. F. Benson did after the first *Lucia* book. He looked at what he had, saw he was going to continue with it—Lucia was so wonderful. But her husband was a lump. He killed him off between books. He also realized the gang he'd created in Riseholm weren't eccentric enough. There should've been a lesbian. So he moved the whole thing to another town, taking Georgie with him. He realized, too, the one thing the other book hadn't had was a pathetic, would-be Lucia: Miss Mapp—forever foiled, and increasingly crude in her attempts to seize Lucia's crown. It's obvious, but brilliant. He says: "I can't use what I have. I have the lead, this crazy gay friend, and an idea. I'm going to move them." After that he didn't vary it. You either like them or you don't. If you like them, you'll always want more. But I can't write like that. At a certain point it's got to have a new angle for me to stay interested.

RC   Is Benson an influence on your writing?

EM   I don't think so. Actually, I got to his books long after I started the series. I greatly admire many writers: Balzac, Dickens, Tolstoy, Dostoyevsky, Austen. It's a very classic canon I adhere to.

RC   They're all great storytellers; yarn-tellers.

EM   Isn't every long-established classic, except Sterne's *Tristram Shandy*, a yarn?

RC   Not since modernism, I'd say.

EM   That's too recent. We don't know how those books will fall out. But the nineteenth-century titles are secure, though in their day they were much disputed. They're linear narratives, stuffed with action. I say you can't *have* fiction without a story. Story contains everything. You have to have good characters; once you have those, they do the story for you.

RC   Is story mostly what you look for in fiction?

EM   Well, I enjoyed *Tristram Shandy*, though there's no story in it. But I'd never consider writing fiction that wasn't all story. Ultimately, a story shows us how real people react. I think that's everything. That's how we understand humankind and what life is—through different characters interacting.

RC   Which other contemporary gay writers capture elements of this storytelling tradition?

EM   You know, no one jumps out. I hate to say this, but I could more easily tell you who I think is terrible; who has nothing to say; who's fallen into stylistic quirks that are meant to be regarded as contemporary, hip, and true, but there's really no content there.

RC   What about Alan Hollinghurst? He talks of having nineteenth-century models for plot and character.

EM   *The Swimming-Pool Library* is an ideal example of a novel where story creates everything. It's extremely rich for that reason. He's got characters, and a very subtle interaction among them that at first isn't apparent and after a while becomes quite shocking. He's got two different generations, and the interaction that we understand is *not* occurring between them is also eventually deeply shocking. It's a brilliant book for that reason; without the story, there'd be nothing there.

I liked that book very much, but I liked the author also while I was reading it. He was good company. I think you feel that about Michael Cunningham, too, from his books.

RC   In the introduction to *Waves*, you take a swipe at some of the writers associated with the early flowering of "liberated" gay fiction in the late 1970s. Andrew Holleran's *Dancer from the Dance* you forgive the most.

EM   It's the least irritating of the three: that, Edmund White's *Nocturnes for the King of Naples*, and Larry Kramer's *Faggots*. Whether I like it or not, I think *Dancer*'s definitely established as a book that will be read. *Faggots* is very controversial. A lot of people say it's not well-written. A lot don't like what it represents—Kramer's moral tone. I think it's the lowest piece of shit and its author a jackass. I remember when he said every gay should boycott *Philadelphia* because it didn't show the two guys kissing. It was an incredible breakthrough for Hollywood finally to deal not only with gay life but with AIDS—and for Tom Hanks to put his imprimatur on it. I felt what Kramer was saying was: "I'm so furious that they didn't ask me to write it that everyone should join me in a worthless act of personal vendetta."

RC   This is only one way of reading a work: to get a sense of the author through it.

EM   Dan Menaker, an editor I've worked with, says he feels that's part of bad writing—not merely how you put words together, but the personality that comes through is part of your talent. If you're a red-hot enraged queen, you'd better cool down while composing.

RC   Your own relationship to your narrators is complex. In the stories, the Bud figure lives in this very apartment; we "know" it's you. *The Venice Adriana* has an invented first-person narrator, Mark Trigger. In *How Long?* you're the author of an omniscient narration. The "M. J. Verlaine" stories appeared pseudonymously in *A Bad Man Is Easy to Find*.

EM   Well, I'm not writing the same book every time. My narrative style is deceptive, because the strong sense of humor and enveloping plot material leads some readers to expect popcorn fiction—just jokes and fun. They get bewildered at the lack of guidance about the character relationships. But I find all that authorial "telling" clumsy and cheap. If one presents the story properly, one needn't tell. The intelligent reader has to investigate the action, analyze for himself why the characters behave as they do, what they're not saying, when they're mistaken. So I prefer first-person narration, because readers can't expect omniscience from someone who's himself part of the story.

RC   What led you to write *How Long Has This Been Going On?*

EM   I got the idea for that a long time ago. I thought of every possible version for four years: "Where does it start? Where does it end? Is it co-ed?" I also wondered: "Shouldn't it be narrated by this guy that knows everybody? He's virtually the protagonist. He'll be there at the beginning and still there at the end?" I thought: "No, it can't be in the first person. What do you do with the sex scenes?" Furthermore, no one knows *everybody*. Imagine two lesbians having sex, and this guy narrating it in the first person. That's ridiculous.

So the whole thing slowly developed. After four years I knew the best thing was to move in these heavy chunks of narrative: L.A.; Stonewall had to be in the middle; New York would be the one place we'd return to—for the Parade, so I could get as many of the principals who haven't been violently killed off as possible in together. I'd end with the narrator revealing he *is* The Kid. He takes this poor, younger version of himself home, and tells him the story of the novel.

I got into terrific trouble with it at Random House. It was the worst time of my life. Bob Trent killed himself right in the middle of it all. Ultimately, Random House suggested changes I didn't want to make. I remember Bob Gottlieb saying:[2] "You have a choice. You can refuse to make the changes. Say: 'Go ahead and publish it, because you bought it.' Or you can make the changes—or pretend to make them; that is, make *some* changes, but nothing definitive." That appealed to my sense of mischief, so that's what I tried to do. It didn't fool them, and we reached the lawyer stage before they capitulated.

RC   What made you decide on the epic scale of *How Long?*

EM   I thought if you start before Stonewall, you can show the seeds of that politically, but also the development of an ethnicity—gay culture. You can show, for instance, how when you start everyone works for straights. Over the book, people develop new professions, in which they don't have to work for straights. A guy who's a cop at first becomes a bartender, then a maker of porn.

---

2. Robert Gottlieb was a former head of Alfred A. Knopf and editor-in-chief of the *New Yorker* and was Mordden's editor in both capacities.

RC   Was the scale daunting?

EM   No. The difference was that what I usually write—short stories—if properly outlined, can be done in a couple of days or weeks. Then you know what you have. This time I spent the entire year and a half writing it not knowing how I was going to come out of it.

RC   You didn't know the shape of the book?

EM   Not until I'd finished it. I didn't know if certain sections worked. Frankly, a lot of people who claim to be readers of mine have mixed feelings about *How Long?* Bob read the whole thing out loud, then said: "I don't know. It's been so long, over the course of a year and a half." Normally he'd have read the book in a week.

By then I knew what I had. When I got the letter from the editor at Random House about the changes, I knew they were wrong. They were the worst possible things. He didn't like the idea of older/younger sexual liaisons. He said when he came out, everyone was twenty-two and having sex with each other. That's *his* book. He wanted the entire "Twin Cities" section removed. But each section supplied a number of other pieces of information that, gathered together, tell us how gay culture evolved. You can't take out the middle. Everything before it leads up to it; everything after it develops from it. But I made lots of cuts to pretend I was going along with them. The book, long as it is, is shorter than what I handed in.

RC   Is there anything in some readers' reservations over the idea of epic narrative? Everything's tightly stitched together and consequential. In reality, when the sexual liberation of the seventies is followed by AIDS, nobody knew what was going on. How do you stitch *that* sense into a book with such narrative coherence?

EM   That's a built-in paradox of any epic novel, unless things aren't tied up and it's all a big sprawl. The problem for some was it takes a lot of intelligence to get through a book of that size and keep everything in mind. A lot of readers might be happy, eager readers, but not necessarily smart. They wouldn't notice, for instance, the word "home" appearing through the book, but especially in the last hundred pages. It gets very laden with meaning. "Home" is the last word in the novel. Did they notice the terrible storm at the parade? Did people realize the way those two men were talking about the rain, that it's AIDS? A conventional novel always gives the reader what he expects. This was an unconventional novel in a conventional form. A lot of people didn't get that.

There's that strange end of the "Twin Cities" section, which builds up to the reconciliation of Luke and Tom, something we've presumably been looking forward to for the last four hundred pages. The mundane writer *has* to give you their encounter in full. It's the traditional *scène à faire*. But I had already, in various ways, sorted out what was likely to happen. There was no reason to write that scene, so I cut out at the moment they met. It's much more dramatic that way, especially as Walt caps the entire section by referring back to something extremely key that occurred nine years before. Such procedure defies generic demands, of course—but I wasn't working within genre; I was subverting it. I think some people kept getting annoyed at the book they had expected me to write rather than the one I wrote.

RC Several gay novels of similar epic scope appeared the same year.

EM Yes. My book and Felice Picano's *Like People in History* were twinned a lot. One idiot reviewer said: "In neither book do you ever see anybody at work; it's like we're all rich people and have no day jobs." Well, I can't speak for Felice. But I troubled to show people at work constantly. There's the cop. Chris, the one straight lead, is always involved in the theater world. Lois is a *tavernière*, then runs her antiques store. The idea was to show how the main way people have created gay culture is by pulling away from jobs where they work for straights, and creating these other things. If this guy is *that* stupid he didn't see it . . .

The book got the worst reviews of all my novels, but outsold the others by far. Reviews are irrelevant, anyway. They're too often by dummies, or they're about the reviewer, not the book.

RC   The novel we haven't touched on is *One Last Waltz*. What was the genesis of that?

EM   *One Last Waltz* is the only thing I've written I didn't outline. It must be autobiographical, I guess. It doesn't seem so, though my brother did try to drown me when I was a kid. I wrote it in five weeks. It's not gay. I honestly don't know where it came from. I was sitting in this very chair and suddenly realized I had a whole novel in my head. If you'd said "page two hundred and thirty-eight," I swear I could've told you what was on it. I opened up a fresh notebook, thinking: "Let's put this to the test. Yes—I've got a novel in me." Out it came.

I knew it was two different stories that were the same: one taking place then, one now; they were going to interconnect. I thought: "I'd better do some research. I don't know anything about Ireland." The folklore's just out of my head. Like this whole idea that, at a time of so much immigration from Ireland to America, a lot of times the guys already had a sweetheart who'd say: "You will come back?" They'd say yes, knowing they never would, because no one before ever had. There was this belief that if you sewed into the lining of his coat some of your pubic hair, that would put a hold on him. That's how you know how smart the woman is in the novel. She says: "I'll mend your coat." But you know what she's looking for. She finds these hairs, takes them out, and says: "He's mine." I don't know where I got that from.

RC   Why did you put that book out under your own name, and the M. J. Verlaine project pseudonymously?

EM   I didn't think *One Last Waltz* would be bizarrely different from what I'd been doing. It had one major gay character. Also, at that time I didn't think of myself as having to be limited to writing about gay life in a ghettoized way.

RC   You say: "at that time." What about now?

EM   I seem to be more in it now. After all, four of my books have all-gay casts. Then again, *The Venice Adriana* is about Maria Callas. The narrator isn't me. He's a young American gay guy in 1961; not entirely out. He goes to Venice to ghost her autobiography. Not that this really happened, of course—this is untold tales of Callas. It's like a gay "coming out" novel. Also, it's about Maria Callas. Thirdly, it's a debate on free will, using Dante and Byron as foils. Dante says every-body has free will, but as he saw the world, no one does. Byron's hero never makes a choice. Everything's done to him, yet he enjoys total freedom.

RC   One awkward comment here: since you describe a world in the sto-ries which is integrally and comprehensively gay, maybe you get the readership you deserve.

EM   Or you could argue that it gives you a head start in getting a reader-ship in the first place. A gay novel is its own marketing hook. It's unfor-tunate that when you veer away from what you're known for, whole crowds won't follow you. I'm thinking of John le Carré's *The Naive and Sentimental Lover*, which broke out of his line of spy novels, so it's the one no one reads. Of course, it's homoerotic as well. What I'm known for is what I call "the gadget"—the *Buddies* stories—because the whole cycle is misperceived by many to be really no more than a construction of moving parts. Press the button and good-looking guys have sex and camp around. In fact, it's about how men passionately create a culture they can use, to replace the one that loathes them. And there's nothing mechanical in the treatment. On the contrary, it's unpredictably vexed by emotional overloads and constantly games with its own naturalism. Maybe that's why I wanted to call it quits after the third volume. I was tired of being misunderstood, and went on strike.

In any case, my next novel takes me far from Stonewall, to Nazi Germany. I've always been fascinated by modern German history, because it's so filled with eerie mischances that had tremendous impact. The sheer number of accidents that led Hitler to power and then saved him from fail-safe assassination schemes is unbelievable. The entire Nazi era is unbelievable in ways that most educated people don't ken even today. For example, it wasn't Rudolf Hess who flew to Scotland in 1941. Hess took off, but was intercepted and a double substituted for him. I know that sounds crazy, but everything about the Nazis was crazy. One can't view them rationally. So I have Hitler making a pact with the Devil, who's a comic figure, as in Goethe's *Faust*. Goethe's in it too. All the main characters are invented, but some figures are historical, especially Rosita Serrano, a star of late-thirties German musical films. They called her "La Chilenita." This isn't a gay novel in any real sense, but a gay writer with even a shred of decency has to include that touch of cabaret.

RC What was the genesis of the "M. J. Verlaine" stories? They read like heterosexual versions of the gay stories.

EM I honestly don't remember. I think I thought the book would be a great idea, but I'd only amassed a gay readership. I thought: "I'd better do this under a pseudonym. If I do it under my own name, I'll disappoint my own readers and won't be able to get new ones."

I always think it's attractive to put together a book of separate stories that interlock in certain ways. Unlike the regular story series, these interlock in subtle ways. Someone turns up in another story in a walk-on part, or becomes the protagonist of a later story, or vice versa. But there's no throughline.

RC   What about writing about heterosexual sex? You give the reaction of a woman to what she finds disappointing in lovemaking. Does imagining this kind of situation come as easily as anything else you write?

EM   Yes. The reason why is the same reason someone like John Preston was a terrible writer. He never looked around; never listened to anything. Imagination takes off from observation. You build up a store of observation from which you have, first of all, real-life data. You can quote people from different cultures and accents; you know how they sound. Also, with this much that's real, you have something to leap off from. If you've never heard what anyone's said, if you've never looked around an apartment, how are you going to invent anything?

RC   Is there a point where, as a writer, you stop needing to observe?

EM   Never. I'm probably a congenital voyeur. I'm always curious—not about my friends' personal lives, say, because I'm very private myself.

RC   Could one be observant by habit, while in fact already knowing enough about human nature for one's writing?

EM   How could you *ever* know enough? Each person's a new encyclopedia of stuff.

RC   But you felt the characters in the series have full autonomy now. What more would you need to observe to feed into their characters?

EM   That's true—nothing; I know them so well. But if I want to do anything else, I'd better keep my eyes and ears open—and I do.

RC   I wanted to ask you about the relationship between sexuality and cultural expression. You state in *Waves* that no gay writer was influenced by the example of Tennessee Williams. But isn't there a case for sexual sublimation leading to great literature on occasion? Williams found his great subjects—the slipperiness of the social status of women; and of Southernness in American culture; arguably, he couldn't have got to the Southernness without the women. In the end, though, how did he get to the women? There's a strong argument for saying he got there through sexual sublimation.

EM   I suppose so. But I'd emphasize your use of "slipperiness." It's a slippery sexuality his characters have. In almost every play, Williams shows these beautiful men who're supposedly straight. In real life they'd be hustling or gay.

RC   But when he moved to a more open expression of his homosexuality, Williams's plays fell apart. Maybe that was an accident.

EM   There are no second acts in American lives. Williams ran out of material. The last good play he wrote was *Vieux Carré*—a retrospective of the earlier icons. Williams says: "Now, for my last great work, I want to review the tales by which I identified the human condition."

RC   Would it be misleading to say Williams stopped sublimating his sexuality?

EM   I don't think the sublimation was ever over. Williams never wrote "out" gay plays: not *Outcry*, for instance, or the one I saw him in: *Small Craft Warnings*. They've got the same materials as before. They're no more "out." *He* was out. I think he thought: "Since I'm out when no one else is, that's enough out!" I think there was this belief on the part of many people of his generation that being out was for real life and having sex. They had this ingrown homophobia in the idea that writing plays wasn't about being out; you don't have out characters. It takes a whole other generation to see there's material in gay life and gay characters. We still have allegedly major gay figures saying you have to have straights in or it's not real! That's so strange to me. You don't *have* to have anything in particular other than imagination, observation, and a view of the world. You can have nothing but Eskimos, horse-traders, or plumbers. It depends what you do with your materials. The notion that a work's quality would inhere in its setting or selection of characters— only someone penetratingly stupid would actually believe that! Talent's necessary; vision's necessary.

RC   One author I'd like to ask more about is Edmund White. We haven't talked about the book that is key in many ways to White's reputation: *A Boy's Own Story*. It's perhaps at the forefront of a tradition of confessional or "autofictional" works—his term. The reception of that book by the wider literary establishment was important in seizing on the idea that its portrayal of adolescence allowed a universal readership access to its concerns.

EM   Yes, because you're not gay until whenever—though the character is already not only thirteen—that is to say, pubescent—in the very beginning; he's fucking a ten-year-old. So he's already a gay man as far as I'm concerned. I think they'll do anything to say a work isn't gay, or an author isn't entirely gay. They still cannot understand that we're different—and better. They know blacks are different; they *look* different. They know Jewish people are different; they got killed in their millions, right? But they don't think we're different.

I suppose some gay writers who've made the statement that gays aren't different probably think that's a badge of approval. We might have slightly different politics, or a slightly different sexuality is all. I think that's utter bullshit. If I felt that way, I could never have conceived "the knowledge," that love of movies and Broadway and camp.

RC   Fans of your books acknowledge your tapping into the urban codes they understand. *A Boy's Own Story* does something very different. It's not about urban gay experience, except very implicitly. It's about the universal gay experience of another context: the family.

EM   Yes. It's possible that growing up gay in America in relatively recent times means you're really growing up as two people. One is the person you really are; the other's the person you present.

That's why I always say gay life really is showbiz. You get to choose the person you try to play. You choose your character. Because no one else in America growing up is able to see the one me that is me—the gay me—the other is the role I play. The curtains go up; I play this thing.

That makes you unusually conscious of yourself, your reactions, and other people's. Wouldn't that indeed lead to a heavy component of confessional fiction, where gay writers come into their own because we—much more than straights—are used to noticing our surroundings from a very early age; how much we react to them; how much we're allowed to show, and how much we select not to show? Kids usually haven't learned what to select. Teenagers have such a hard time in high school. It's as with Cosgrove and his asocialized behavior: he doesn't realize everyone regards him as a little freak when he's just saying what he felt was a cute, funny thing.

Gays don't usually make that kind of mistake. We're already selecting. We've already figured out we get in trouble if we just present ourselves. Everything has to be prepared, sifted, "straight-cultured." I suppose White's confessional books reflect that. *A Boy's Own Story* would be the major such work of that kind. It had to happen. Someone had to do it. Since White was earlier established than others, he's the one who got to it first. Also, he's the one who could get away with it, because by that time he'd been somewhat anointed. I think if David Leavitt had wanted to do it, he could have—and what did he give us in *Arkansas*? A very confessional sort of book. This is the kind of thing you expect from gays, because we're aware of our surroundings in a way straights aren't.

RC *A Boy's Own Story* was taken to confirm the "anointment," as you put it. It's been an important book for many people. Was it for you?

EM I don't know. A lot of times I feel it's not important whether I like a book or not. What's important is what it represents; what it succeeds in doing. The point is, unlike *Forgetting Elena* or *Nocturnes*, this is White's classic work of fiction that has to be slotted into the publishing phenomenon that goes with *Dancer from the Dance*.

RC How, then, did you edit *Waves*? Were you looking for the story that pleases or the "great" story?

EM You pick stories you think are really good. As *Waves* shows, those can be very different. It's basically effect; the effect of a story on you when you finish it is: "I want it in my anthology, or I don't." It's visceral.

 I certainly didn't want nothing but ghetto stories. Variety's the one thing you want. An anthology is a carousel ride. You've no idea where you're getting on or off. What killed me was, if ever there were an anthologized people, it's American gays. Yet, to my knowledge, no one had ever taken advantage of editing of an anthology to write a piece on gay literature as an introduction. That's the only reason I did *Waves*. Originally, I was going to write a much longer essay for the *New Yorker*. But there was so much reading involved. I thought: "I'll never be able to get a handle on this." It's like opera: you know all of it or none of it. It's too varied; too large. So I gave up. But I thought: "If I do an anthology, I can write a little introduction."

RC How was editing others' work?

EM Some stories didn't need editing. A few needed a tiny bit—like where I felt a sentence wasn't clear enough. A few needed considerably more work. I wrote half Bob Trent's. But I thought somewhere along the way I was going to run into somebody—besides Bob—who couldn't take editing. It didn't happen! Everyone was very glad to be part of the package and very easy to work with.

RC   On that note, thanks very much for your time.

NINE
DENNIS COOPER

Dennis Cooper was first published and celebrated—by Edmund White and Felice Picano, among others—as a poet, but is best known now for a series of highly innovative works of fiction featuring adolescents, music and youth culture, and explicit sex and violence, such as *Closer*, *Frisk*, *Try*, and *Guide*. Born in 1953, Cooper grew up in California. He studied for two years at Pasadena City College and one year at Pitzer College before dropping out.

Cooper's first published poetry collection, *Terror of Earrings* (Los Angeles: Kinks Press, 1973), appeared when he was twenty. In 1976 Cooper set up *Little Caesar* magazine, founding Little Caesar Press two years later, through which he published a second poetry collection, *Tiger Beat* (Los Angeles: Little Caesar, 1978). *Antoine Monnier*, Cooper's first published prose work, appeared the same year (Los Angeles: Anon Press, 1978). He became director of programming at the art venue Beyond Baroque in Venice, California, in 1979; in the same year, his third poetry collection, *Idols* (New York: SeaHorse, 1979), was published. Three further collections followed: *The Tenderness of the Wolves* (Trumansberg, N.Y.: Crossing Press, 1981); *The Missing Men* (Santa Barbara, Calif.: Am Here Books/Immediate Editions, 1981); and *He Cried* (San Francisco: Black Star, 1985).

In 1984 Cooper published the novella *Safe* (New York: Sea-Horse, 1984). He moved first to New York, then to Amsterdam, where he wrote the first of what was to become a much acclaimed sequence of novels, *Closer* (New York: Grove Press, 1989). This was followed by *Frisk* (New York: Grove Press, 1991), *Try* (New York: Grove Press, 1994), and *Guide* (New York: Grove Press, 1997). The fifth and last volume of this loose series is *Period* (New York: Grove Press, 2000).

Other work includes 1992's publication of shorter pieces, *Wrong* (New York: Grove Press, 1992). The same year, Cooper edited *Discontents: New Queer Writers* (New York: Amethyst, 1992). In 1995 his *The Dream Police: Selected Poems, 1969–1993* (New York: Grove Press, 1995) appeared. Cooper has also coauthored two cartoon storybooks: *Jerk* (San Francisco: Artspace Books, 1993), with Nayland Blake, and *Horror Hospital: Unplugged* (New York: Juno Books, 1996), with Keith Mayerson.

Cooper is currently working on two projects: a pornographic photo-novella in collaboration with the artist Vincent Fecteau, and a nonfiction book on youth culture. He lives in Los Angeles, where this interview took place on Wednesday, November 19, 1997.

RC   In an interview you gave to Kasia Boddy, you talked readily of your sequence of novels reflecting a kind of ongoing exploration of the self.[1] You even accounted for them as reflections on your own emotional disposition. Not every writer wants to reflect on work in relation to autobiography. Do you do that easily?

DC   I can. It's important. My work's so tied into those things. It's crucial for me to do that, because the books are a cycle; there is this progress, and I need to study my own emotions formally in a certain way. I've

---

1. Kasia Boddy, "Conversation with Dennis Cooper," in *Critical Quarterly* 37.3 (Autumn 1993): 103–15.

learned how to do that. Also, I was at a really emotional point with *Try*, and I was very keyed into that for that interview.

RC   I was thinking of how you discussed your work-in-progress at that time in terms of a search for "bliss." Was *Guide* the product of that search?

DC   No. The books are rewritten and edited so heavily. That's the way I work. They have to keep up with me, so at that point, that was what I wanted to do. But it was a little utopian. It's in there, though. It's just been fractured a lot. *Guide* was changed because I tend to write about people around me. The guy who became Luke was actually someone I met. That changed the whole book.

   When I talked to Kasia Boddy, he wasn't an issue yet. So it was more about my initial idea, which was about memories of the LSD state of mind, and trying to simulate that, then study my subject matter through its scrambled, subjective scrim. I wanted to create a kind of stratosphere of searching, wandering, revved, nonjudgmental thoughts around the material, as a way of both opening it up and locating it squarely within the hermetic, somewhat psychotic context that my work requires. So *Guide* is very revealing and utterly secretive at the same time.

RC   *Guide* constituted a big break from the previous novels. I don't know if its reception in the States reflected that, or even if you felt conscious of it. In terms of narrative, there's the sustained use of a single, first-person voice. But there's also a more general coherence in *Guide*.

DC   Some critics recognized it, but most people don't really get my work. I'm categorized as a certain thing, and people react to it as though it's the same book again and again. Every time I write a book I'm really trying to kill off my interest in what I'm writing about. This time, it almost did. They're all mutations of the same book; they're intentionally that way. But *Guide* is located in my mindscape, which differentiates it from the other novels.

RC   One new aspect of *Guide* is that you loiter on abstract emotional states without translating them into a kind of sustained metaphorical language of the material body, as you did before. There's something brave about refusing to do that.

DC   Thanks. I fought with myself about that.

RC   Is it something you plan to continue? You've spoken of having a sense of the novels forming a coherent, five-book project.

DC   Well, I had that from *Try* on. They were always intended to be a series, but when I wrote *Try* I knew there were two more. I'm doing the last one now. It's called *Period*.

To me, the series can be seen as a single body being alternately tortured and repaired in a certain way, so that the form of the novels mirrors the content. *Closer* is that body. It contains everything that will appear in the succeeding four novels. It's very solid, airtight, compacted. Everything in *Closer*—the violence, love, sex, art, drugs, whatever—has the same weight and is caught up in the overall rush and chill of the style. *Frisk* is that body damaged. It's structured like a dismembered yet living body. It's still extremely organized, but it's more revealing of its internal workings—its desires, fantasies, fears, hopes, et cetera. *Try* is that body repaired, restored to life. It's an attempt to live and function normally, given the damage it's incurred. *Guide* is that body after a second dismemberment. It's laid open, and what is revealed is an elaborate, rather delusional self-justification. There's little of the body left; there's mostly just the mind overcompensating for its physical sparseness. *Period* is the final rebuilding of the body. It's essentially a skeleton, a barren structure, an attempt to create an illusion, a mystique, a sense of meaning around what is essentially a decimated work, a zombie, the walking dead.

I guess it's a strange way to think about the novels, and it's not necessary that readers think about them in those terms, but I do.

RC   When you speak of each novel being involved with killing off your interest in what's in it, is that something identifiable in retrospect?

DC   Well, it's always the same thing. With each book I have a specific approach in mind, which I hope will complete my need to express it. Each book has a different approach, so it's about that. *Closer* was so impacted and tight. The paragraphs were all hypnotically the same length. I was trying really to freeze it. Then I tried to open it up. *Guide* and *Frisk* have a lot of relationship for me, because *Frisk* was really an attempt to take responsibility for the material, and that was the riskier book at that time. *Try* was written in the middle of an emotional mess. I was trying to find love. I thought if I could find the love in it, that might do it. It didn't really work. Then *Guide* was really a serious attempt to take responsibility for the work. I tried to specify the work.

I do get sick of people misunderstanding the work. I tried really to locate my relationship to the work as honestly and complexly as I could. The last one, *Guide*, is just like giving it its due.

RC   I'm interested in each book's regard for aesthetic processes. Though you speak of *Frisk* in terms of taking responsibility for the material, at the same time, of all the books, it's *Frisk* which most forthrightly frames the material within a neat aesthetic. It's not exactly a "how-to-read-this" framework, but it is more heavily preoccupied with aesthetic framing— in the opening and closing scenes with the photographs, especially— than *Try* is, for instance. But, then, perhaps that isn't so far from the word you used: "responsibility."

DC   There has to be a balance in it for me. What you're saying is true, because the form of *Frisk* was about just setting up that whole duality of the order of the world versus the disorder of the brain, and somehow making them work together. In *Guide* that's true too in a different way. *Try* was written out of a sense of my life as completely chaotic. The reason that book's the most straightforward is just because I needed something formally straightforward, and that's about as conventional as I could ever get.

RC   Is it to do with closeness to the material? You've spoken about how you wrote *Try* while a friend was detoxing.

DC   Yes. The books are all for somebody—a specific person. With *Try*, I was having a very intense relationship with a heroin addict. It wasn't a sexual relationship, but it was very intense. It played on all my worst "caretaker" nightmare roles. So that was just me trying to understand that. Ziggy in it is partially me, but also another boy I used to know.

RC   That leads to the placing of your fictional self, "Dennis," in the novels. In *Guide* there's a striking moment where this past, fictional self intrudes: the "Luke" character is discussing early works by "Dennis." Does this placing of "real" figures in the fiction—albeit projected and imagined—cause problems, either within or beyond the texts?

DC   Sure. They're completely intermixed to me when I'm doing the first couple of years of work on them. The last year is usually all refinement. At that point it's done. But, for instance, the person "Luke" is in my life: by the time the book was finished, my relationship with him was completely different than it was in the book, but I couldn't incorporate that. So at a certain point I cut off and it becomes totally aesthetic. But for the first couple of years the two are intermixed, and that organizes the book.

RC   I'm interested in the extent to which the conception of each book is clear at the outset. Are some things already "organized"? Is there an aim to be executed?

DC   Yes, but it changes. There's a start, then it changes. Writing's very difficult for me. I'm not a born writer, despite what William Burroughs said. It's very difficult. I have to write an enormous amount of material and experiment in different things just to get anywhere in the beginning. There's usually an initial idea. When I was talking in that interview, that's when I was beginning with *Guide*. I was thinking about LSD. That part of that book is true: I took an enormous amount of LSD when I was younger. I took it every day for a month. I was remembering what that felt like; to be that high all the time, and how amazing it was.

I wanted to write about that, and also about kiddie porn. I lived in Amsterdam for a couple of years, and there was a lot of it there. I was just astonished by it. I've always written about it to some degree, but I really wanted to write about it in a way that was acceptable. There are silly things, too: I had a crush on the bass player of Blur, so I wanted to write about that. I'd written an article for *Spin* that ended up being rewritten and worked into the novel. I'd been thinking about the kids that featured in that and their stories. Then I just work it all through. The formal approach takes a lot for me to get to.

RC   Do you write quickly in the first instance? Is there a kind of outpouring of raw material?

DC   Sometimes; sometimes not. I'll try different things out. I was trying to get at the LSD thing. That was the initial thing. I was having a really hard time with it; reading every novel I could find, every book about LSD: Tom Wolfe, Tom McGuane, Ishmael Reed, Irvine Welsh: everyone who'd written about drugs. I couldn't get it. Then someone said: "You should read Ivy Compton-Burnett." I loved it. It drove me crazy. It was just the opposite. So I thought: "I can write about LSD like Ivy Compton-Burnett would." That really started it. At the very beginning of the book, there's a little bit—almost too much—of Ivy Compton-Burnett. I was so influenced by her work at that point: that really cold, hard style. I can only read four or five of her novels till I get sick of them. But they are brilliant. So something funny like that will kick it in for me.

RC　Do you find it easy not to be affected by the style of the other things you are reading?

DC　Yes. I've got such a specific style. I don't even worry about it. It's been really hard for me to find a style. I only did with *Closer*, really. I trust it, and it's immutable. I'm not worried about that. Sometimes I'll sit down and try to figure out how somebody wrote, like Ivy Compton-Burnett, but as soon as I do, it's my own. I'll do a little bit in her voice, then it immediately becomes my own. It's too ingrained in me how to write.

RC　That immunity many writers would strive for.

DC　Well, I really believe in style. I'm very interested in what formal things can do, so it's not that hard for me. For better or worse, I have a very distinctive voice, and I can always write what I want to write the way I want to write it. I always study things. Popular music influences me a lot. I'm always trying to transfer ideas from music or bands I like. I try somehow to take their ideas and make them into prose. With writers, too: different books from different writers really help me write. And film.

RC　It's rarer to use pop music this way, I think.

DC　I guess so. A lot of people write about music, but I'm not sure they let it influence the way they write. I don't just pop the names in because I think kids will like the books. I really like that stuff. Usually when I write about a band, it's because I've really been studying their style and trying to do something with it.

RC I was trying to think of other writers doing that. Hanif Kureishi said punk moved him to write.

DC Yes. I can feel that in his work. There must be others. Bret Easton Ellis's work is influenced by pop music. I trust his interest in it. I know he's obsessed with it. You can see that in the work. He's not just name-dropping.

RC One reason for mentioning Hanif Kureishi was because he suggested writing came from a desire to put himself on stage in some way which couldn't be carried through in music.

DC I had bands for a while, but it didn't work. I wrote before I listened to music, though.

RC Was writing an immediate and necessary outlet when you were young?

DC Yes. I drew a lot of pictures, though, too. When I was in high school, I was more known as an artist. But I was writing as well, from when I was really young. I became really serious about writing when I was around fifteen. Then I just dedicated myself to it. It's weird, because I'm not a natural writer. Or maybe it's that I want to write complex things and it's very hard to do. Maybe if I relax a little, I could write very easily. But I can't do that. I write journalism, which I find relatively easy, but I don't think I'm very good at it. I'm lucky to get the gigs because it's not very good journalism.

RC You say writing's very hard. Could the difficulty be part of its attraction?

DC It's got to be. I love the amount of effort it takes to do what I want to do.

RC   Would you be suspicious if things came easily?

DC   Yes. Occasionally I'll write something easy, and it doesn't interest me at all. I've published some things that were fairly easy. When people like them, it bothers the shit out of me. One reason I quit writing poetry is because it just wasn't hard enough.

RC   You've spoken of your attention to form and care for language. Do you have a sense of frustration at the way your books are often considered less in terms of form, and more with what is considered extreme subject matter?

DC   Yes. It really bothers me. I don't know what to do about it. I don't take it personally. I think it's a cultural deal. People don't really write books like the ones I grew up reading and the kinds of things I like. People don't like films like that anymore, either. Godard's films open and play for three days here. Nobody sees them. I have an audience, so some people are interested. But it does amaze me that people don't want that kind of experience from writing anymore. I'm not saying my work doesn't have problems, or that it's the ultimate in anything. But it can be very frustrating.

RC   When you mention the writing you used to enjoy reading, who are you thinking of?

DC   I'm a big Francophile, so: Bataille, Blanchot, Genet, Rimbaud, Baudelaire, Lautréamont; the *nouveau roman*. Nobody gives a shit about that stuff anymore.

RC   Aren't you essentially describing America's cultural self-centeredness? You live in L.A., after all—a kind of focus for American-centered culture.

DC   Do you think it's different in Europe?

RC   To a point.

DC   I remember in Amsterdam it was different. Céline was really famous there and influenced a lot of their major writers. You don't see that here.
   David Foster Wallace is brilliant, and there are occasionally people who are really great who get successful here, but otherwise it can be frustrating.

RC   It isn't every writer who is so subject to content-led critiques of his or her work, however. I want to press you on that.

DC   I float two different ways in my work. But the content's so glaring that some people can only see the glare, no matter how subtly I try to undercut that stuff; to subvert it.
   I just realize there's nothing really you can do. I thought *Guide* would change things, and it did to some degree. But people cannot deal with the subject matter. On the other hand, the form's so complex. There's so much stuff going on in the language and style that people who might look for a visceral kick don't get it; there's too much interference. My work isn't Poppy Z. Brite. Then, being gay, there are so many gay people who just hate me, and think I'm horrible and awful.

RC   We hear less of that in Britain.

DC   The response to my work in England has been really great, comparatively. I've been really happy being published over there. And in some other European countries, too, the response has been much better. Here I still get these unbelievable reviews that are like: "This guy should be shot!" It blows my mind.

RC   There's a relatively new, bourgeois construct of "gay identity" found in, say, the *Advocate*, which seems very keen to protect itself from fictional worlds such as yours. Could the problem simply be this: many gay readers still need some sort of authentication of their lives in the literature they read, in order to feel comfortable with being gay? I can see you don't offer that to them.

DC   No. But, then, there are a lot of gay people who really like my work because they feel really alienated from all of that. Gay identity doesn't interest me. I don't buy it, personally. OK—it's great: it's a natural thing to have happened; there are so many happy people now in this neighborhood—West Hollywood—compared to what happened before. That's what's most important. But even since I've been writing, there's been this major shift. When I was first published, if you were gay and smart, you read literature. It was part of the thing. Now that's not true at all. Gay men don't need to read literature anymore. There's so much stuff available to look at, read, or see. There's queer cinema, gay art, this or that. So literature has suffered because of that. It's not like when I was a kid, where you read William Burroughs because there wasn't much else to read.

It's really interesting to do readings in A Different Light [gay bookstore chain]. On each book tour, it's a different crowd. Literature doesn't mean that much to the gay community now. But what do you do, because if I was somebody who just wanted to have a nice place, be in love, and have money, it would be great, wouldn't it? It *is* great, but it has nothing to do with me. I've never been involved in gay culture, really.

RC   But you're right that in the past, the act of exploring—or even sublimating—your sexual identity in the literature you read was an important aspect of gay culture. Nowadays gay culture is largely about sex and sexual expression, and if its literature fails to reflect the appropriate sense of euphoria or arrival, it's critiqued.

DC I suppose so. It's amazing how quickly that's changed. It wasn't that long ago that, with authors like David Leavitt and Edmund White, people read them and cared about them. It's not true anymore.

RC Implicitly, we're considering notions of readership and audience at this point. Do you have a conception of your readership that impacts on your work? Does the question of who reads you concern you at all?

DC Not in the writing of the books.

RC At some level, perhaps subconscious, though, surely it has to matter?

DC Yes, but it doesn't affect the way I write. Not with this work, anyway. When I finish the fifth book, I'm leaving myself open to any possibilities, so we'll see then. But it hasn't here—though to some degree, even though it wasn't the main impulse, with *Try* I was trying to show that in some way I wasn't a monster. With *Guide*, I was trying to show that my thinking about the stuff in it was very complex—partly because I thought people were seeing me as someone who jacked off to snuff videos. But it hasn't affected the way I write. I want my work to be very pure. It comes from a very pure space.

RC Perhaps the perpetual reduction of your work to its subject matter has hardened you. It must be shocking, though, to find, when you write about child porn and snuff videos, say, that the horror which seems absolutely conditional to the form of your work is ignored. I'm returning to this overliteral reading of your work which remains blind to that.

DC Yes. I don't know how to explain it really. My brain's configured differently to some people's, I guess, because I don't understand it when people don't understand that it's important to think about these things.

RC   When did the structure of the whole series occur to you?

DC   I knew the series would be a limited number, but I didn't know how many until with *Try*, when I knew I was in the middle. I knew if I could write *Guide* the way I wanted to, I'd only have one more approach I wanted to take.

After *Period* I want to take a break from writing fiction for a while, and clear my head and all that. I do have some unfinished short fiction and experiments that I'll probably polish up to tide me over. Basically, I need to decide whether I want to keep writing novels. I've always felt more like someone who was using "the novel" to meet my ends, rather than a novelist, and I'm not sure whether fiction will accommodate whatever I decide to do next. I'm kind of in a strange place. I'm really proud of my work, but, at the same time, I feel like I've failed myself, and I'm not sure why. I remember a few years ago a friend chiding me for still loving Rimbaud's work. His idea was that one outgrew Rimbaud and his ridiculous ambitions. But I still feel connected to Rimbaud's idea of writing transcending writing's fundaments and accessing the sublime, whatever that means. I haven't done that, of course, but I've tried very hard, and I'd still want to try. I just need to stop for a while and decide how I might go about that, and decide whether I have the ability to do that, or whether I'm just not well-equipped enough for the task. Anyway, in the meantime I'm going to write a nonfiction book—some sort of meditation on youth culture. I feel like that would be an interesting challenge, considering my inabilities as a journalist. So that's my next project.

RC   Can you say something about *Period*'s relationship to the earlier novels?

DC   *Period* reinvolves George Miles, who was the main character in *Closer*, who figures in *Guide*, and who is kind of implicitly behind all the novels' young male characters, not to mention the subject of a number of my short fiction pieces and poems. There was a real George Miles. He was my most important and influential friend from high school onwards. He was a few years younger than me, and very sweet and brilliant, but he had a severe chemical imbalance, so he was all over the place; really chaotic and unpredictable. Our relationship was intense and unforgettable, and if I have a muse, it's him. Anyway, I lost contact with him when I moved to Amsterdam in the mid-eighties, and had been trying to track him down with no luck for ten years when, at just about the time *Guide* was published, I found out he'd killed himself in 1987 while I was living in Europe.

It's strange, because I'd always intended for George to be the main character in the last novel, but *Period* has become for me a way to process his death, which was really, really devastating, but also abstract, having happened so long ago, and complicated by the fact that I'd believed he was alive all these years. In a way, I wrote the novels for him, and assumed that somehow, somewhere he was reading them, and knew how important he was to me.

I'd like to write a nonfiction book about him someday, but *Period* isn't it. It's a distillation of the ways the real George affected the work, and a kind of playing out of what his death does to all the fantasies and art and characters and ideas he inspired. It's a hard book to describe, but essentially it's a kind of tomb in the form of a magic trick that makes George Miles—and, by proxy, the work—disappear.

RC   Do you think of yourself mining a very individual literary seam? Are there "fellow travellers"?

DC   There are people in the visual arts—not even necessarily people I know, though I do know a lot of visual artists and I am influenced by conceptual art.

I feel a kinship with some writers. Among my gay peers, there's Kevin Killian, Bob Glück, Bruce Benderson, Matthew Stadler, Gary Indiana, and a few others. A number of younger, emerging writers excite me. But the huge majority of so-called gay literature is incredibly provincial these days, or, when it's "reaching out," it's so middlebrow—intellectually soft and barely artistic, except in the most bourgeois way. It's become this modest, inbred little genre whose arbiters and publishers discourage radical writing and seem to look only for possible "crossover" books, still using the tired David Leavitt model—goody goody, nicey nice, feel-our-gayness fiction. I certainly feel alienated within that. I think I'm basically on my own. Supposedly, I've influenced a number of younger writers, but I don't see that so much.

RC   It must be odd hearing or reading people suggest that there is a group of writers influenced by you. Scott Heim's name comes up often.

DC   Yes. I don't think that's so true. I think maybe I influenced him the way William Burroughs influenced me. Burroughs's work didn't influence me at all. His example influenced me. Likewise, I have a mainstream publisher; I'm publishing very difficult work. That may give other writers strength.

People always mention Scott Heim. I've known Scott a long time. He sent me his work when he was really young and living in Kansas. I encouraged him, critiqued his work; read *Mysterious Skin*. I gave him a lot of support and he admired me, but that's basically it. If there's an influence there, I don't think it's interesting. People do that to him a lot. They say: "He's Dennis Cooper, but . . . " Then it's either: (1) " . . . better because he's more accessible"; or, (2) " . . . worse, because he's not as complicated." It's really unfair to him. I didn't like it when people did it to me when I was younger either. I remember some review in the *Advocate* saying my work was just like me jacking off with a copy of Genet's *Funeral Rites* in my lap!

I get letters all the time from younger writers, sending me stories, or wanting my opinion or help. I try to do as much as I can. But I think my work's too specific to influence anyone. If there's a younger writer who writes about a boy being abused by a man, immediately they "are" me, which is just ridiculous. As if we all don't have these thoughts.

RC With Scott Heim, in terms of the way he structures a sentence, one could make a loose case for a comparison to you—in *Mysterious Skin* anyway, if not in *In Awe*.

DC I know what you mean. But maybe some of that's coincidental. When I was working on *Closer*, all my friends suddenly said: "This guy Bret Easton Ellis has totally ripped you off. Don't read this book; it'll make you so upset." So I didn't. But as soon as I finished *Closer*, I read *Less Than Zero*. I was amazed by the parallels, it's true. Then for years people were saying he ripped me off. But of course Bret didn't read me until later. We just completely arrived at the same place. And I think in sentence structure there's even something between his work and mine, but that's totally because we both grew up in L.A. and both like bands. Even in *Mysterious Skin*, though, it's Scott's own work. I never would have written that book.

RC There's this precise, symbol-laden lyricism in your writing style. Since what's coming across is that you read widely and meticulously, are there writers working in very different styles that engage you, notwithstanding the difference in their aesthetic? What about writers within the bejeweled, elaborate tradition of gay literature that came out of Proust?

DC Well, like you said, I read a lot, I guess. Flaubert himself is amazing, sure, especially *Sentimental Education*. I do like the bejeweled, though I like it better in poetry than in fiction—the Symbolist poets, Ashbery, things like that. Sade of course was massively influential on me. André Gide's *The Counterfeiters* was a watershed in my early twenties. I'm very fond of metafiction—William Gaddis, John Barth, Thomas Pynchon and, more recently, David Foster Wallace, Kathy Acker, Curtis White, and other post-metafiction writers. Minimalism interested me for a while, though not hugely, unless J. D. Salinger counts. I love him, of course. And I was influenced in some deep way by writers in German like Thomas Mann, Max Frisch, and Thomas Bernhard, all of whom I was very into at one time.

It's interesting to read something where I feel the prose has a relationship to mine, like Ivy Compton-Burnett. I immediately recognized it in the work. There are other writers like that, like Jean Rhys. But I never read Proust. I've been avoiding him like the plague. I'm afraid to read it.

When I was first writing prose, I was really amazed by Edmund White's *Nocturnes for the King of Naples*, which is nothing like my work. It was so Flaubertian. But I really responded to what he was trying to do in that work, and I really wanted to meet him. I wasn't the only one who was really empowered by that book. I was looking at what there was of gay novels at that point, and it really stood out. I wasn't interested in *Dancer from the Dance* or *Faggots*. I couldn't relate at all to that scene. But Edmund White was a real writer, who liked French writers. I remember he had a big fan base of younger writers then—at least among people I knew, around the time of that book and *Forgetting Elena* earlier.

RC   There's a small group of readers of his work that's most interested in those early works, and *Caracole* too. I know at the time of *Caracole*, Edmund had a very clear idea of himself moving between two very different styles of writing: between Nabokov and Isherwood, or between the mannered and the spare. The "Isherwood" strain struck a chord with an audience, though: *A Boy's Own Story*, *The Beautiful Room Is Empty*. *Caracole* didn't.

DC   Absolutely. *Caracole* was interesting in that sense, because it did seem like its failure was the end of a certain phase of Edmund's work. I don't think it's his best book, but I admire his intentions in it very much—in getting away from gay material. I remember going to a reading of his when he read from that before it came out. People were just pissed off that it wasn't gay. It was the end of something for him, because it was a disaster, I guess.

RC I think in future it will become clearer that he has reincorporated some of the formal ambition of *Forgetting Elena*, *Nocturnes*, and *Caracole* in the use of language in works taken to be of the "Isherwood" school. *The Farewell Symphony* in particular has many passages which hint at the elaborateness of the earlier works.

DC I like that in his works. I thought there were really beautiful sections in *A Boy's Own Story*, though, too. Several chapters in that I think are really pristine. Maybe him collaring AIDS really changed his outlook on things in a lot of ways.

RC Do you mean he felt pulled towards a more realist prose style in response to AIDS?

DC I'd assumed it was a question of time. An enormous amount of effort and time must have gone into *Nocturnes*. Maybe he doesn't feel he has the time. Now it's different, because he's doing so well. But maybe there was a certain urgency to make him speed up at one point.

RC In contrast to Edmund White, somebody like Ivy Compton-Burnett's novels shared a startling formal coherence, both within and between them. Thematically, too, they were similar. I wondered whether the sense of there being an integrity, a purity to one's whole output appealed to you in the way you thought of the five-novel sequence.

DC Very much. Artists I really revere have that. My favorite artist is Robert Bresson. There's no purer body of work than his. That's my favorite kind of work. It becomes almost religious when it's that pure. It gives the work a kind of charisma.

RC   In prose, one could say it of Genet's fiction, too.

DC   Yes, though *Prisoner of Love* was very different. Otherwise he's a good example of that.

RC   In your case, as you said, a certain purity and consistency of form in your published work has emerged rather effortlessly, it seems. Is there work hidden under the bed which you consider unsuccessful, for stylistic or other reasons?

DC   The style fluctuates a lot in fact, so there are a lot of experiments I've done which have gone pretty far. I'll usually end up publishing them, though. *Wrong* is a collection of things that didn't work, or that I intended to make into something but didn't get beyond that little thing. I try and try to be different, but I always end up fussing with it until it's like *that*; until it's like my writing again. My range is very small—on purpose.

RC   The status of aesthetics and the figure of the writer as aesthete are both central to your work. I don't mean they're presented uncritically— quite the reverse. Often there's a lacerating critique of aesthetic self-regard and the figure of the "uninvolved" aesthete. Is this a deliberate counterstatement or reproach on your part to the pristine quality of your prose?

DC   I know what you mean. One thing I don't like about a lot of work— even Genet, for instance—is the ego. I don't like the work to have an ego. Also, I do think that everything one says or writes is a lie. That's always there for me. Those two things are always playing with each other.

It's not something I calculate. I'm always questioning everything because it always seems false. So I'm this total aesthete, but really distrustful of the florid. That's why it takes so long to get things visible and omnipresent at the same time. That's Bresson, too.

RC In the fiction, the aesthete is at times described as someone who sees people as types. I was thinking of that as a criticism—not of aesthetics per se, but of its potentially abusive deployment of the variety of humanity to its own indifferent ends.

DC Yes, that's totally true. But that comes partially from the point of guilt.

RC In *Try*, you relate debates concerning art and aesthetics specifically to human relations. The figure of Roger is described in terms of how he behaves with others. The position of an artist as somebody involved in a process of distancing, formalizing, framing human experience: isn't the suggested immunity of that being progressively questioned as the books go on? Take *Frisk*: I'd say the forthright pronunciation of fixing, formalizing, framing in that book, so much a part of its structure, has melted subsequently.

DC It did in *Guide*, yes. I'm working on a book now that's restoring that. But I think there's going to be an enormous tension between where I am now and where I was with *Closer*. In terms of the narrative, *Guide* sets up this opposition, with these two artist characters who are basically doing what the book does, but visually. You hit me in a funny place, because I'm actually dedicated to returning to that sort of thing for the last one. But since I see the books as a cycle, I want it to be implicit in the last book that there's a failure to do what it intends to do.

RC I want to ask about the direct engagement with AIDS in *Guide*, which is also new. Did writing about AIDS lead to the kind of formal dissonance or difference that characterizes *Guide*?

DC Well, it's meaningful within the work that there's this piece of journalism within the novel, although I do elaborate amounts of things to justify its inclusion.

RC   People always used to ask where AIDS was in your work. Now, for better or worse, there's a Dennis Cooper novel featuring AIDS centrally, yet it appears in a slightly tangential place within the book. Does the piece's status as journalism within the fiction constitute an important formal statement, then?

DC   Yes. I wanted to negate the rest of the book in a funny way. It negates the aesthetics of the books. It's funny how people responded to that. There are people who say: "Finally, in this one section, Dennis Cooper has written something good." I just got some personal experience. I wrote this article; I knew these kids; I really liked them; they died. I was attracted to them. It was just strange.

RC   There is a whole series of debates and assumptions concerning AIDS and literature which writers shouldn't and probably can't get involved in; questions of appropriateness and responsibility, for example.

DC   That's crap, all that. AIDS is in all of the books. Here I wanted to try to frame it in the work. I've always been interested in the purity of the body. There's all these things going on in *Guide*—about fairy tales versus child pornography, and the question of whether they are the same thing.

RC   Your works have always been heavily marked by a sense of mortality. But for those for whom writing about AIDS is an overriding duty for the writer, that's not enough.

DC   For me it's hard to separate that part out. It's all connected to the different things I was working with in the whole novel. In *Guide* those characters just parallel Chris. I'm just setting up contrasts. There's a critique of gay culture and AIDS hospices and people who work in that, but that's probably just me being a jerk about gay culture, which I like to do sometimes.

RC   There are lots of moments in all your books where this rather precious, content-led reading of gay literature in terms of positive imaging seems deliberately sent up.

DC   A little bit, just for jokes. In *Try*, everybody was on my ass about the gay father thing and adopting children and all that. I think it's funny. I don't usually try to push buttons. It's usually not what I'm thinking about. But occasionally I'm aware that I can push a button, then complicate it with lots of references to other things going on in the books that anchor the joke.

RC   In the interview with Kasia Boddy, you spoke of being preoccupied with the nature of adulthood. Would it be fair to trace that preoccupation by way of artistic developments in your work? Do you see it in there?

DC   Sure. That's true. I'm not eighteen anymore, and it makes a difference. I wanted to try to inhabit the adult characters more and make them less one-dimensional   I guess because I am one, even though I don't relate to adulthood very much, or my idea of it. It doesn't interest me. My interests are in the new, which is different to a lot of people.

I feel like I have to be more responsible in my life now because I am an adult. When I was younger I did a lot of things. Now, when younger people come to me and want support, I see a difference in the way I think about it. I feel much more like I understand what they want; more than I used to, though I've been older than some of the people I've been involved with for a long time. Now I have more of a sense of what they want, just because I'm older. I try to be what they need, rather than fulfilling my own interests. I think that's in the work, too, to some degree. I feel it, and since the books come from wherever I am psychically, that ends up in the work too.

RC   There's a paradox in the idea of acquiring a greater understanding of youth as you get older and further from it.

DC   Yes. I used to just feel that whatever age I was, it didn't matter: I was just one of them, or their buddy. With *Try*, I clearly wasn't the same age as the person who was strung out on heroin. It really taught me a lot about that. But before it would just be like: "Let's explore this together and we'll both learn."

I never leaned on older people when I was younger. I didn't trust older people at all. But I understand that people need people to lean on, and to be consistent in all these different things. That's something new to me. I get a lot of weird offers. I surprise myself how responsible I've become in relation to those things.

RC   I wanted to ask about the importance of power relations and role-play in your works. Your early fiction appeared at a time where, to an extent, "good"—or balanced—gay relationships are starting to flourish elsewhere. Relationships in your novels, however, seem heavily determined by power and status—though there's a slight move away from that in the recent books. There seems to be a developing awareness of greater choices in the role-play—even, sometimes, a sense of the redundancy of the idea of roles.

DC   That's true. It's because I'm inhabiting a larger range of characters, so to speak. The characters are just configurations of the prose. But in the earlier books, my sympathies were totally with the younger characters. It's like the younger characters were real and the older characters were my fantasies. That's changing. As much as there are characters in the books, they're both equally fantasy and reality now. That's a difference. Consequently, they're more complex, because I'm giving them more room.

RC   I was thinking especially about the absence of reciprocity in sexual power relations.

DC   That still exists in the newer ones.

RC I suppose so. One could infer that the very idea of reciprocal sexual relations was either a lie or a wrong goal.

DC Or both, yes.

RC The word *love* floats around in your work now, which seems to require reciprocity.

DC I think that's totally aesthetic. The books are omniscient. They divide their consciousness between different characters. It's partially just that.

I have this mistrust of fiction: I have this specific and weird mind, and to put that reciprocal thing in there—I just don't buy it. It's too much of a lie for me to try to represent because I can't imagine what a reciprocal thing would be. That may just be personal because I'm a weird, self-absorbed person.

RC There's also an aesthetic consideration: if reciprocity is somehow to mean a settled power dynamic in a relationship, that might be uninteresting.

DC It is uninteresting to me, and I have a real resistance to it. I find there's a laxness that sets into a work when that happens. Also, I do put specifications on myself. I'm not sure I could exceed them if I wanted to. To me, all that's broken down in *Guide* because of the acid. On acid I did believe I could understand everything. Using the acid was a device to bring that in and negate it at the same time.

A lot of it's just my own experience. I'm distrustful of reciprocal love, sexually. I've always been interested in the idea of separation more than the closeness. A lot of my experiences have been with prostitutes. I was very interested in that kind of sex. I read books, and my first boyfriend was a prostitute, and so were his friends. My whole relationship with sex was determined by all that.

He was my first boyfriend. I wasn't paying him, but prostitution was his world and I was in it. You could see in *Guide* this whole thing: that real love isn't sexual. I don't believe that. I'd never say that. But in the work it's true, and I say in *Guide* that I can't write about my boyfriends because the experience of love was too confusing or self-incriminating.

In some ways for me all this might be too personal, but the greatest loves I've had were with people I haven't had a real sexual relationship with: because of the course I was set on, and because I have such an interest in what sex is and isn't, and with the aesthetics of the body and the internal organs—all these different things.

RC   In *Guide*, you engage with these debates intellectually. Specifically, you introduce Platonic ideals within the book as a kind of counterpoint to sexual relations. In that respect, I felt *Guide* engaged with preoccupations that were current a hundred years ago, and not seen much recently: the kind of morality/aesthetics debate of Wilde's *The Picture of Dorian Gray*, for instance.

DC   I'd never thought of it that way.

RC   Wilde spoke of his book in two incompatible ways: on the one hand, he claimed the irrelevance of moral approaches to art; on the other, he insisted on them, defending *Dorian Gray* against some reviewers by claiming it was too moral a work. *Guide*, ultimately, can be read both as aesthetically indulgent and incredibly moral. I introduce this because the word *ethics* itself features prominently in *Guide*.

DC   That's always been there. I just found a way to articulate it with *Guide*. Ethics has been the center of all the books from the beginning. I guess the subtlety of my approach or my burying of those issues was misunderstood. People think people who are moral or ethical don't entertain the ideas of the things they find horrifying. That's the difference: I want to understand their power, so I give things that power. Otherwise there's no point to it.

RC I want to discuss the importance of geography to your writing. What's the relationship between your prose and Los Angeles, where you live and write?

DC It's certainly part of it. But part of it's totally instinctual. I grew up here and understand the rhythms and spaces here. In order to have the purity I want for my work, I needed not to have to think about those things, by staying here. Certainly the writing's determined by that. I think of people who grow up in L.A. as a little less well-educated; more spacy and less articulate. I really love that about it. I myself am very inarticulate, I think. I have a hard time describing things. It's very bad when I try to speak. I think that's an L.A. thing.

RC A sense of intellectually unmapped space could be a great context for a writer.

DC Absolutely. It's such a mysterious place. It's incredibly organized, but you have to decode it to get there. I grew up here and understand the organization of L.A.; how formally precise it is. Other people don't see it that way. You think you're part of some secret club when you grow up here. I think I use that in the work, too. The work's broken. Things mirror each other from odd spaces. There are rhymes and echoes in the prose that are strange dislocations from each other. There's a way in which that's the physical map of L.A. There's so much secrecy and mystery here. You can write about L.A. and not describe it. It's no surprise it was the capital of serial murders. You can dump people anywhere here. It's full of all these weird, fantastic negative spaces.

RC I was thinking of geographical diffuseness. One reading of L.A. sees it as a place where received social structures are at their loosest and least defining—compared, say, to New York. The idea of the novel as a document of social manners wouldn't have much to feed on here.

DC   Except Bret Easton Ellis's work's all about that. That's what's so brilliant about it; he actually did that.

There's no social life here. That's one thing I like. You see who you want to see when you want to see them, one on one. I don't like the whole New York scene of seeing people in groups and crowds. Here you make specific plans to see people. You can go to clubs and bars and art openings if you want. The younger ones do have crowds and go to this or that place, though, like rave warehouse parties.

RC   But for those of us used to living in a more socialized world day to day, this feels the closest Western culture comes to privatized experience: homes are private spaces; and everyone drives to and from them.

DC   It's funny, though. We're in West Hollywood now—the closest L.A. comes to that socialized world. There's a whole ghetto here. People never leave West Hollywood. You feel really foreign here, because it's "The Hood." This is an attempt to build that kind of culture here. I suppose it's very successful.

RC   Do you feel ranged in by it?

DC   I suppose I do, though where I live is also like that, but not specifically gay. Los Feliz has become the hippest area in L.A. since I moved there. It's a hipster type area, not like Melrose. It's a lot more underground. I like that a lot—not that I hang out at the cafés. But I've always had a hard time with wholly gay situations. I have a nervous breakdown just walking down the Castro. It makes me so nervous. All that sexual energy—it's just freaky.

RC   Is it something to do with the sense of being the observed, rather than the observer? One way of thinking about the distinct roles in your books is to distinguish between the artist-observers and the people they observe.

DC That may be very true.

RC To enter the ghetto, to cruise and be cruised: you surrender the certainty of inhabiting one role.

DC In this ghetto at least, yes. My friends and I—here and in New York—all went out to hustler bars—not because we wanted to buy hustlers, necessarily, but because everything was so clear: the observers and the observed. It made me feel very relaxed; comfortable; invisible. It was the hip thing for years—and probably still is. The hipsters go to hustler bars.

RC For many gay men who like ghetto life, "liberation" is specifically concerned with this blurring of boundaries on many levels—ultimately, including sex itself. There's this ambiguity or doubleness in the reciprocity: you might be fucker or fucked, as well as, in social situations, being both watcher and watched. For some that's really liberating.

DC Yes. Can I ask a question about that? Have you found there's this general sense of alienation within that culture among the writers you've talked to?

RC Of course—if only because the priorities of creative writers and those of the gay subcultural ghetto now seem sharply antithetical.

DC That's interesting. I'd have guessed that.

RC It's not always expressed at every level. Your detachment from that culture feels rather more complete. Other writers might engage with subcultural life, then present that world alternating with another one; one characterized by writerly detachment. Some books are even structured around this idea of engagement and retreat.

DC Andrew Holleran's.

RC   Yes. *Nights in Aruba* is a case in point.

DC   He's interesting in that sense. He seems an awfully strange, isolated person, yet he wrote so well about Fire Island and all that stuff. He was totally interested in it. I think Scott Heim moves in that world. Edmund White used to, very comfortably, when I first knew him, but then he was with hustlers all the time too.

RC   I want to ask something more about place. I was thinking of your use of the Netherlands in *Frisk*. It reminded me of Poe's imaginary landscape. There's little of America in what Poe wrote, which has always rather concerned people. I wondered if the idea of a non-American or less American imaginary environment appealed to you.

DC   Yes. I really was thinking of Poe with that Holland section. That windmill section *is* Poe, that's absolutely true. Back in those days, I had to go there to get it out of me. I'm a strange person—an American who's only influenced by European things.

RC   The height of alienation, surely, is to be a Europhile writer living in L.A.

DC   It is. I have a lot of friends like that too. Part of what makes my work so peculiar is that it's so exclusively influenced by European—especially French—writing and film.

RC   At the same time, we're describing a cultural affiliation more than anything else. It's not the same as Edmund White's move to Paris. Yours is a literary engagement only.

DC   Yes. I felt extremely uncomfortable when I lived in Europe for those two-and-a-half years. I was living in Holland, a very strange country. I was never more miserable. Maybe it's just because I can't divide Europe up too much, but there's some kind of relationship between Holland and England: a certain repression. The Dutch are so repressed, and such a mess.

RC   That's not the first impression most people would have of the Dutch.

DC   That's what's so strange about that place. They are really weird people. That's part of why I attacked them in *Frisk* in a way. I was so frustrated with them. Everything's acceptable there, and they hate every minute of it. They're tolerant, but so angry.

RC   I agree that it's a culture with both libertarian and conservative impulses in play and in strong tension. Some Dutch people told me a more family-centered, conservative culture you couldn't imagine.

DC   It's true. It's really difficult for their artists. They hate their own artists to become ambitious. Every time an artist of theirs would become a world artist, he was reviled. Yet if anything avant-garde came to Holland, they'd just go crazy for it—not so much with writers, but then the writers are always conservative there. Even the most interesting Dutch writers are pretty conservative—at least the ones I was able to read.

RC   It's like England, you suggested.

DC   I don't mean that in a bad way. In some ways it isn't. I haven't been to England very much. I read the *N.M.E.* and *Melody Maker* [British music weeklies] and get a lot of my sense of it from that, which isn't fair.

RC   You read about the nonconformist, youthful England, then—only part of the story.

DC   But you have that great eccentricity. You have these English eccentrics; these mutants. I've never seen that anywhere else. That's so interesting.

RC   It's like the debate about who invented punk: New York or London. The English don't care, because we know all the interesting figures in punk were on our side, whether or not we invented it, because of their eccentricity. But perhaps I'm on dangerous territory here!

DC   How English of you to say that! [*Laughs*] All the English punk was very style-oriented but then so was New York. There's this whole idea of America being authentic and England being all style. It's to some degree true. We all look to English bands because their style's so brilliant. There couldn't be a band like the Pet Shop Boys in America. But Neil Young or Nirvana could never have come out of England.

RC   We have conformist icons, too—like Oasis. At the same time, we throw up talent that's so different, perhaps without even recognizing it—Blur, for that matter. We don't usually recognize the difference. What people take to their hearts is immediate conformity or ersatz rebellion.

DC   That's true. Is that true in literature, too? The Scots are throwing a wrench into that, right? I really like them.

RC   As soon as they do, they get packaged. The acceptably rebellious ones are sold—and ruined.

DC   See what's happened to Irvine Welsh. He's become this pop cultural figure. It's very sad because he's a brilliant writer. Initially I was fascinated. His work had more in common with people like Alexander Trocchi.

RC   Think of the idea that Martin Amis was a voice for disaffection, though—or Will Self! That's astonishing.

DC   Will Self is published by my publisher. He hates me; I don't like him either. It's interesting to see the phenomenon of "Will Self" though. He seems like an elegant writer to some degree. He's funny; the work's comic social satire. But it's presented as though it's a daring, scary nightmare, which is ridiculous. So what if he gets caught shooting up on the prime minister's plane. Heroin's a very reactionary, boring drug. Anyone truly daring would never have milked it for publicity.

RC We're great at ersatz rebellion.

DC Then, inadvertently, something like the Sex Pistols comes along. Regardless of their intentions, they changed my life. There was something in those songs. You heard the world opening and splitting. Now you realize it was Malcolm McLaren's calculation. At the time, here in little old L.A., we couldn't believe what we were hearing. It was like hearing "I Want to Hold Your Hand."

RC The cleverness of McLaren was not the organizational ability but that he concealed his processes somewhat. No one realized it was all a game.

DC Then he went on to Bow Wow Wow. That's where he showed his cards—and, for a brief period, that was brilliant, the way it self-critiqued.

RC Who do you listen to now?

DC I have my faves like Guided by Voices, Pavement, Sebadoh. There's stuff I'm getting an aesthetic hit off at the moment, but which I may or may not find interesting in six months, like Placebo, Cat Power, Radiohead, Stereolab. I like some electronic stuff, like Aphex Twin, Autechre, Luke Vibert, Orbital. Lately, I've been liking the Manic Street Preachers, which is strange for me, because they're kind of trad rock. I like that they're almost American sounding, but there's still that feeling that it's all style.

RC They're Welsh, which begs a question. Going back to punk, the most esoteric and interesting bands were all from the regions. The most bizarre takes on punk were the Undertones from Northern Ireland, the Buzzcocks from Manchester, the Skids from Scotland.

DC   I really liked the Associates. They must have been from some strange place.

RC   Yes, Dundee [in Scotland]. Billy Mackenzie lived with his mother.

DC   Ian Curtis of Joy Division was obviously a big influence on me. And Nick Drake, another oddball. And Spiritualized.

RC   You made that notorious reference to a member of Ride in *Try*.

DC   I almost got into really big trouble for that. I just thought he was cute.

RC   You did it again, including Alex James from Blur in *Guide*.

DC   Yes. One reason I did it, apart from having a crush on Alex James and being a fan of their work, was I knew they liked my work, so I figured they'd understand. When I was writing *Guide*, they'd put out *The Great Escape*. I thought it was over for them. I thought nobody would even know who they were.

RC   On that note, thanks very much for your time.

ALAN HOLLINGHURST
TEN

Alan Hollinghurst is best known for his first two novels, the widely acclaimed *The Swimming-Pool Library* and *The Folding Star*. Born in 1954, Hollinghurst studied and taught at Magdalen College, Oxford, where he wrote an unpublished M. Litt. thesis on "The Creative Uses of Homosexuality in the Novels of E. M. Forster, Ronald Firbank, and L. P. Hartley" (1980).

Hollinghurst's first publications were a poetry pamphlet, *Confidential Chats with Boys* (Oxford: Sycamore, 1982), and the story "A Thieving Boy," in *Firebird Two* (London: Penguin, 1983). *The Swimming-Pool Library* (London: Chatto and Windus, 1988) and *The Folding Star* (London: Chatto and Windus, 1994), which was shortlisted for the Booker Prize, were critically feted and sold well. His most recent novel is *The Spell* (London: Chatto and Windus, 1998).

Hollinghurst provided the introduction to a collection of Ronald Firbank's juvenilia, *The Early Firbank*, ed. Steven Moore (London/New York: Quartet, 1991), and his translation of Racine's *Baɉajet* has also been published (London: Chatto and Windus, 1991). He has written an introduction to a new edition of Ronald Firbank, *Three Novels* (London: Penguin, 2000), and lives in a flat overlooking Hampstead Heath, North London, where this interview took place on Monday, June 15, 1998.

RC *The Swimming-Pool Library* and *The Folding Star* were both written in the first person; *The Spell* in the third person. Could you comment on the shift?

AH   I wish I could remember more about quite what I thought and felt when I started *The Swimming-Pool Library*, which, after all, came out over ten years ago. There was never any question but that it would be written in the first person. There was with *The Folding Star*, though. I remember trying to recast an early part of it into the third person just to see if it could be done. It seemed rather forced. As it went on, it became increasingly clear the book had to be inside the mind and preoccupations of its narrator, and that a lot of its point was derived from that. But I often felt terribly constrained by the first person. I longed to be able to leap back in time, go somewhere else, or have access to material which the law of writing in the first person prevented. I think I got fed up with the technical clumsiness of the ways one can introduce other people's experience. Both the first two books have these rather self-obsessed narrators on whom other people's lives rather unwelcomely impinge. There's the way they slightly resent having to find out about all this other stuff. The ways you can present that other stuff are either by having someone read something or simply having someone tell it to them. Both, I think, are artistically rather crude and unsatisfactory.

There are all sorts of reasons for writing in the first person, however. They're partly aesthetic, partly technical—and partly something else; to do with the lack of moral heavy-handedness that comes from writing in the first person, because everything's floating and unknown. Everything's responded to very subjectively. There's an especially interesting engagement, I always think, between the reader and narrator. It's like getting to know someone in real life, forming a view, and changing your mind about him or her. It's interestingly unstable.

I actually found it very hard starting to write in the third person. I imagined it was the easy, old-fashioned way to write. But in the event I didn't just write *The Spell* from one omniscient point of view. I suppose one model for what I did was Henry James's *The Awkward Age*: the idea that each chapter would be seen from the viewpoint of a different character in a changing pattern; that these different viewpoints would illuminate a rather amorphous subject, but there wouldn't be one controlling point of view. Each position would be ironized by the ones that flanked it. That came to necessitate a sort of stylistic change in my writing too. Whereas, particularly in *The Folding Star*, I was just luxuriating in the consciousness of one person, I found myself in *The Spell* writing in a much more spare, detached way. The whole thing turned out to be a process of exclusion and elimination.

I had a feeling with the first two books that they were all I knew about their subjects; that they were the whole thing. People would say: "What *did* happen to Will?" I'd say quite honestly: "I've no idea." With *The Spell*, though, I actually know quite a lot about all the characters which didn't get into the book. The whole thing was more a process of refinement. It felt very different. I think it was a bigger challenge in a way.

RC   Nevertheless, did the experience of writing *The Spell* resemble that of writing the others? You've spoken of writing slowly but without substantial revision.

AH   Yes. With this book, though, there were notes and sketches I'd accumulated and episodes I'd envisaged which in the end weren't there. Indeed, if I'd told the story of each of the four protagonists, it would have been a huge book. I always wanted it to be a smaller, lighter, more transparent book.

RC   Do you start writing a book with some sense of its size?

AH   Yes. It's quite exact actually. *The Swimming-Pool Library* I actually wrote in a desk diary. It was a leap year, so it had three hundred and sixty-six pages of manuscript. I had twelve chapters, each of which ended at the end of the month. So that book had a finite length before I even started writing. *The Folding Star* came out within about five thousand words of the length I'd projected for it. *The Spell* turned out a little longer than I'd originally thought.

RC You've said you leave some details of plot open when you start writing. But this early sense of what a book's like must condition what follows to an extent.

AH I like to have some pretty clear sense of the main movement of the action. There isn't really plot as such in *The Spell*. There's a story, but not really plot, in the sense of some machinery going on, forcing coincidences on the characters. I wanted the form of the book to grow much more naturally out of the material; for it just to be a study of people and their relations to each other.

I have an idea of a book, an apprehension of the sort of color, tone, texture, and mood of it. Then there's quite a lot of working out what's going to happen. Things are discovered en route. I think it would be very boring to do it any other way. That's why I could never write a detective story, where one would have to have the whole thing clear in advance, then just sort of fill it in. I like the actual writing to be a process of discovery. Certainly questions, like who would carry a particular bit of the narrative in *The Spell*, were often undecided. The decision to do the breakup scene between Alex and Danny from the point of view of Danny, for example, suddenly came to seem a brilliant idea.

RC That's interesting. *The Spell* felt very much like a dance to me; as such, its steps felt reassuringly plotted—as if one were looking at something very assured and ordered.

AH I think when things are going well, that just happens. Things come together and the pattern emerges in some way: so, *The Spell* has sixteen chapters; there are four characters, and so on. It was part of the plan of the book, I suppose, that it starts off looking as if it's about Robin and his predicaments, but turns out to be about other people and their predicaments as well. His is the first voice to go out of the composition. The book starts like a rondo, with Robin as the first subject. Its structure is sort of "A-B-A-C-A"; then Robin's displaced.

I thought originally *The Spell* was going to be quite a strict rondo. I remember saying to someone: "I'm not quite sure. What do you think—could I vary it? We don't want reviewers referring to "this ruined rondo of a novel." But I always did have some vaguely musical analogy in my mind for its structure.

RC   Each of your books features some concern with aesthetics and the formal laws guiding creativity in one context or another. In *The Spell*, the context is architecture. Is the presentation of artists structuring their works significant within your novels?

AH   It must be. I'm not quite sure how I'd define it though. All my books have quite a lot about buildings. This happens to be a preoccupation of mine. I love inventing buildings and describing them. I'm interested in the atmosphere of buildings. People probably often wonder why the hell I have got an enormous description of a building at a certain point, but I'm afraid they just have to put up with it. In *The Spell*, Robin's an architect, and, particularly as a student, is someone who's had a more analytical interest in architecture. But I suppose that doesn't emerge as a major preoccupation. It's more just something that's his work, and there's a certain amount in the book about work as a refuge or compensation when your life's going wrong.

   The Folding Star obviously offers much more detailed comment on a particular artist and how he worked.

RC   Yes. That brings us to the very neat parallel in that book: the project of piecing together and reading the artist Orst's triptych and the tripartite structure of the novel itself. Presumably that came to you early on.

AH   I think *The Folding Star* was always going to be in three parts. I gradually found myself bringing in other triplets—sometimes rather capriciously: everything started to come in threes. The truth is I've always been involved in and lived a lot imaginatively in arts of different kinds. They seem to me something continuous with and deeply mixed up with the rest of life, so I've always given them quite a significant role in my stories.

RC   I want to pursue narrative and point of view in the first two novels. You talked about the urge to go to a different time and place, and the problems that created structurally. I was thinking of how literally you sanctioned the inclusion of Charles's writing in *The Swimming-Pool Library* by the explicit account of Will excavating his papers. One contrast that occurred was with Nabokov's *Lolita*. At the start, Nabokov offers a proclamatory note justifying why Humbert Humbert's story's being told. Yet, though you ground Charles's text explicitly in realist criteria, in neither *The Swimming-Pool Library* nor *The Folding Star* is there any real justification for the world of the books; for the nature of their language, for example.

AH   No, that's true. I suppose Nabokov is linking his book to quite an old tradition of presenting the whole thing as a kind of case history. In a way he's parodying the way a lot of scandalous or sexually scurrilous literature—one thinks especially of those early novels about homosexuality or drugs—is presented in the format of shocking exposés one would read with supposed sociological intent. In my books, it's true that neither narrator gives an occasion or reason for speaking.

RC   The nearest you've come, I think, is in the short story "A Thieving Boy." The narrator at one point mentions something happening which "necessitate[d] writing down."[1]

AH   Yes. I thought about this a good deal with *The Swimming-Pool Library*. It was really also to do with the AIDS epidemic blowing up

---

1. Hollinghurst, "A Thieving Boy,' in *Firebird Two*, 95–109 (quotation from 108).

while I was writing it, and wondering to what degree I should reposition the book and demonstrate within it that this crisis was going on in the world which the novel depicted. I decided not to at all, but to leave the story placed historically where it was, in 1983. Various ideas went through my head, though——having the whole thing written by Will when he was very ill, or his friend getting it off his hard disk after he'd died. They all seemed horribly corny and contrived. I think for aesthetic reasons as much as anything else I decided not to pursue them.

It wasn't a question which bothered me when I was actually writing either book. I relied on some primitive assurance that here was someone telling a story, and here in due course would be someone reading it. And I don't honestly think I can quite imagine what the future life was in which Edward would have written *The Folding Star*.

RC   There's enough to suggest Edward's innate interest in both language and analyzing one's own experiences for it to be plausible that he might write. There's that playful other reference in *The Folding Star* to a much more self-conscious method of narration, too: Proust's. It's in the image of your character Marcel, sick and in bed.

AH   You're right that there are all sorts of literary jokes in that book.

RC   In *The Spell*, you have new subject matter: drugtaking and its consequences. Do you think there's a relationship between that and the move to the third person? Could it be that writing in that mode facilitated writing about that particular topic?

AH   That's interesting. I think of *The Spell* as much more personal than the other novels, despite its being written in the third person. Perhaps my writing it in the third person indicates a recognition at an unconscious level that it was somehow closer to me than the other books have been.

RC   By using the word "personal," you leave yourself open to some rather obvious questioning about the relationship between *The Spell* and your own experiences of drugs.

AH   I think in my life, I've tended to have periods of very intense experience of some kind, after which I've withdrawn and written a book which in some way draws on them. I came to live in London in 1981 and started having a fuller and more enjoyable life by far than I'd ever done in Oxford. Part of *The Swimming-Pool Library* was to do with the excitement of being in London and about that change in my life. *The Folding Star* was partly about all sorts of unhappy things that had happened to me: people dying; my father dying.

Also, there's a way in which your own books, as you think of them and remember them, keep slowly and subtly changing as time goes past. I haven't read *The Swimming-Pool Library* for a very long time, and a lot of it I know I don't remember particularly well. *The Folding Star* was published on my fortieth birthday. I'd been rather dreading my forties. But almost at once they turned out to be innovatory and exciting. I have the sense that I've lived my life in rather a peculiar order. I had my thirties in my twenties and now I'm having my twenties in my forties. With *The Spell* I wanted to write a book about change. *The Folding Star* is so fatalistic, I think. I wanted to write a book about the changes one can embrace which enhance one's life—and the other big, slow changes one has to come to terms with as one becomes older. I wanted to write about having fun too.

RC   It's interesting to think of *The Spell* as a kind of reproach to *The Folding Star*. I hadn't thought of the word "fatalist" in connection with *The Folding Star*, but there's certainly an inexorability about it.

AH   There certainly is. With *The Spell* I wanted to write more about pleasure. I know that the idea of pleasure itself has become a slightly charged thing—for instance, with the antigay movement and the perception that pleasure's the only thing certain gay people want to have. I hoped to take a fairly ironic position on pleasure; one that shows it's good to have fun, but that it isn't the only thing. *The Spell* is different in all sorts of ways from my own experience, but Alex's experience of being rejuvenated by having an affair with someone much younger and by taking lots of drugs does draw very directly on it.

RC   If we consider Alex's experiences next to those of Edward in *The Folding Star*, though, their fates aren't so different. You give Alex a new lover at the end of *The Spell*, but only after he's been jilted for the second time—and rather inexorably so.

AH   *The Spell* always had to have a happy ending. That was very important. I could feel some perverse tug of my pen bringing it towards last-minute disaster after all, but I fought it off.

RC   The second rejection of Alex feels totally true, however.

AH   Yes. Anybody else could see it coming a mile off, of course—which I hope is very like life.

RC   I'm interested in the idea of *The Spell* doing something explicitly which your other two do implicitly: namely, coming up with ways of characterizing people and their sexual behavior that's distinct from the more rigid, preconceived forms of sexual identity. You deploy that idea of "givers" and "takers" in relationships, for example.

AH   The "givers and takers" thing is expounded as Alex's own little system. Are you saying there are tacit or inherent ways of classifying people present in the books?

RC   Yes. That may be Alex's system, but it is one which, as he articulates it, Danny recognizes and acts on in a way which suggests it might be true more generally. It's also a theory which pertains to each of the developments in all three books in a way, if only insofar as the law of "givers and takers" becomes another way of talking about the centrality of power to relationships.

AH   I suspect the power thing was very much bolder in the first two books: in *The Folding Star*, there's the fact of Edward's being enslaved to Luc, but professionally having power over him. In *The Swimming-Pool Library* there's Will's rather seigneurial relations with others.

   When you fall in love, you do give somebody else a sort of power over you. The social codification of it is vaguer in *The Spell*, I think: only Robin has that sense of social superiority and tends to think of himself as rather grand. Justin is a sort of passive-aggressive character.

RC   Part of the comedy in *The Folding Star* lies in the extent to which Edward moves ever further into abuses of power—again, rather like Humbert Humbert in *Lolita*—and finds himself trying to justify becoming involved in a dominating and abusive power relationship. I couldn't help thinking of that when I read that you'd aspired to teach, both at school and university.

AH   Yes. It's probably a good job I got out into the world of journalism when I did.

RC   But does that necessarily involve less abusive power relations?

AH   Well, if there is abuse, it works in a different way.

RC   An analysis of power dynamics within human relationships does seem central to your work.

AH   It seems so. I don't think I'm very conscious or schematic about it. It's just inevitably there. In *The Swimming-Pool Library*, the class thing

was obviously played on much more strongly. *The Folding Star* tries to
escape from all that—partly by taking the action to another country. It's
far more a book about bourgeois life.

RC   To me *The Folding Star* is the stronger, because it disavows some of
the easier privileges of power Will has in *The Swimming-Pool Library*:
youth, beauty, class. Will's social advantages seem to stack matters so
heavily in his favor. With Edward in *The Folding Star*, tutorial domination's about all he has over Luc. Consequently, the power dynamic's
more interesting.

AH   Edward's circumstances are almost deliberate inversions of Will's
situation in *The Swimming-Pool Library*. I'm conscious that I was playing
around with archetypal things in those situations and, as it were, denying
Edward so much Will took for granted. One book's a sort of comedy of
sexual success; the other, a comedy of sexual frustration. I think *The
Folding Star* is sexier in a way; it's more permeated with the unattain-
able. By contrast, Edmund White said he thought *The Spell* very
utopian, which I hadn't thought of myself.

RC   There's quite an easy interaction between generations of gay men in
The Spell. That might appear rather utopian.

AH   Perhaps *The Spell* was always supposed to have some of the elements of Shakespearean romantic comedy. In it, there'd be an older
man, but essentially people would be young, attractive, and getting in a
muddle. The characters might be too generously touched with glamour,
but I don't think they're impossibly so. Part of the joke of *The Swimming-Pool Library* was, as you say, that Will's given the maximum opportunity to do what he wants. He's spoiled.

RC   Paradoxically, that opportunity doesn't bring rewards: the book, as
you suggest, is finally less sexy—even, I'd say, less romantic than *The*

Folding Star. Edward anticipates fulfillment in this one, longed-for encounter, whereas Will's sense of confidence in himself is tied to a sense of disappointment in others—or a sense of not being satisfied by others.

AH   Yes. Danny in *The Spell* has some of those characteristics, except he's much more hard up and much less sophisticated. But he has low expectations of others and is obviously frightened of anything bigger and deeper.

RC   Both Danny and Justin seem to be missing a whole register of responses to the world that Alex retains—or acquires. Bob, the drugs dealer, remembers Alex as the one who falls in love with people—which suggests that's exceptional in metropolitan gay subculture.

AH   I suppose something is being hinted at, which may be true to a greater or lesser extent. I think it's likely that if, from when they're very young, people live in a metropolitan gay subculture, they'll be like this. I know so many people like that—people who become heart-hardened when very young. They live in the gay world almost as though no other world existed. That fascinates me, because it's so much the opposite of myself. That conversation between Bob and Alex is not unlike conversations I've had with friends who say they've never been in love, whereas I feel I've more or less spent my entire life in love. That sort of polarity is one I wanted to touch on. Whether it's strictly a generational thing I don't know, but I suppose it's more and more likely to happen if people live in this particular metropolitan gay culture there is now.

RC   You use the polarity between types of people for dramatic ends. There are people who seem hardened in that way; then there are others, who are acted upon. Presumably, it wouldn't be interesting to explore the psychology of the hardened people. You don't suggest they have deep levels of generosity buried underneath. These people are only interesting insofar as they become tools for the development of the others.

AH You may be right. Justin and Danny are the two characters who only have three chapters each in the book; the other two characters have five chapters each. Perhaps one reason is that they don't have the richness of inner life the other two have; they're there as agents of the confusion and misfortune of others. But I wouldn't want to be too categorical about that. There are just people who are much more susceptible in all sorts of ways than others, and who have a much greater awareness of the complexity of everything going on around them.

RC Peter Brooks, in his book *Reading for the Plot*, talks of Balzac's characters as "desiring machines" whose urges motor the plot forward.[2] Though you've rather disclaimed plot in terms of your own creative priorities, I wondered what your response would be to the idea that—certainly in *The Folding Star* and, in a way, in *The Swimming-Pool Library* too—sexual pursuit and desires more generally constitute the chief engines of plot.

AH I quite agree with that; these are appetites of one kind or another. It's the same with *The Spell*: quite what "the spell" is remains elusive, but clearly falling in love is part of the desire to be taken over by something that transforms your life and makes it more beautiful. It may be a temporary thing or an illusion. It may just be a trick. But I think desires, appetites, and their innate tendency towards addiction, towards obsession, towards a need which becomes a habit, is what *The Spell* is about.

In my first two books I did feel it made for a sort of tension, which I tried to rationalize as between one sort of narrative, in which nothing in

---

2. Peter Brooks, *Reading for the Plot: Design and Intention in Narrative* (Oxford: Oxford University Press, 1984), 39–40.

particular happens except for people hanging around and waiting for something to happen to fulfill their desires, and some other, more abstract notion of plot.

RC   This deployment of desires to further plot doesn't strike me as especially English. I can think of more books in French that work that way—particularly in gay fiction. Jean Genet's do, explicitly. There's Renaud Camus's *Tricks*, where gay desire motors plot in a fairly transparent way. But these books don't necessarily distinguish themselves from a mainstream literary tradition.

AH   Well, Genet's so alternative in most respects. One feels even his writing about sex is really about something else.

RC   I was thinking of a tradition of using sexuality in narrative going back at least as far as de Sade.

AH   That's right. It's perverse, isn't it? It deliberately comes from another angle. I suppose I recognize something of that deliberateness in what I was doing when I was starting out, except that I was simply coming from an angle that was, broadly speaking, my own, so it seemed natural to me. It just seemed a way of getting at the truth.

RC   There were one or two hostile responses to *The Folding Star*'s libidinity. The objection has been that the book shares the morally dubious territory of *Lolita* in its apparently cavalier narration of an abusive power relationship—one which leads to sex between two people of very different ages, notwithstanding the fact that you make Luc seventeen.

AH   Yes. It hadn't crossed my mind that the relationship was abusive until the book came out in America—which shows my general moral turpitude, I suppose. The question did come up quite a bit there, in a way that here in Britain it didn't.

RC   The status of seventeen-year-olds may become one of the defining moral questions of the age.

AH   There's a particular local reference to Britain's age-of-consent debates there. But I had checked and knew that the age of consent in Belgium was sixteen anyway!

RC   I want to move from the harnessing of sexual desire to propel plot forward to a much more prevalent tradition, thinking of English gay authors, particularly. This is to do with neutralizing desire; deadening or preventing it before it starts. In *The Spell*, there's a brief reference to Robin as somebody capable of compulsive behavior who, because of that, turns off the tap completely. Nowadays in gay literature there generally aren't these wounded or flawed characters at the margins of books; people who've devoted themselves to their club-footedness, or to artistic sublimations of sexual desire.

AH   Bringing to the center people who could acknowledge and fulfill themselves, however compromised or satirized it may be, was certainly part of my conscious intention in *The Swimming-Pool Library*. The idea was not to write about people in some way disadvantaged and sitting in the margins but up there—out there, in your face. So one doesn't associate those characters with habits of mind and repressive social patterns one wants to discard. But I think I've always had characters who can't quite make it into this world of hedonistic fulfillment. Will's friend the doctor in *The Swimming-Pool Library* very much sublimates his feelings into his work. Hugh in *The Spell* is similar.

RC   These are very real figures in the gay world: people who dedicate themselves to watching or staying on the margins.

AH   Yes. I don't think that is necessarily just a gay thing. I think it's like that in life generally.

RC   Within fiction, such figures can also act as a useful brake.

AH   That's true. Certainly as I was writing those first two books in the first person, it was very important to have some sort of foil; something to contextualize and ironize; to provide a dissident voice to the self-adoration or self-absorption of the narrator.

RC   This contextualization also relates to the importance of etiquette and manners in your work: the Jane Austen-like scope of it, as it has been called.

AH   Well, all sorts of people are saying *The Spell* is very Austenesque. It had never struck me. Carmen Callil came up with a brilliantly detailed analogy of how *The Spell* is like *Emma* or *Sense and Sensibility*. When characters go to the club, it's like going to London or Bath; both books play with the ambiguous merits of village society, and so on. At some level, although the whole procedure of my book is so different, it does, I suppose, refer to that tradition. I think *The Folding Star* is much more self-conscious in terms of literary analogues and prototypes—in the deliberate play with *Lolita* and Thomas Mann's *Death in Venice*. *The Spell*, apart from the odd joke about Thomas Hardy, I didn't really think of as having those kinds of affiliations, but perhaps it does.

RC   The heavy element of literary referentiality in *The Folding Star* might lead it to be read in the light of other books. An author surrenders his book ultimately, of course, but even so, does this concern you?

AH   You mean: "Not as good as . . . " [*Laughs*] I think of the book as being itself; not in sum like any other book. But I couldn't help but draw on those things with *The Folding Star*. It's just the way my mind works. It could be read and enjoyed, I hope, by somebody who hadn't read *Lolita* or *Death in Venice*, or the other obscure books I fed into it.

RC I wasn't aware until recently that you'd taken Orst's life from a Belgian symbolist novel.

AH Yes—*Bruges la Morte* by Georges Rodenbach. No Belgian reader I spoke to had ever heard of it, of course.

RC I wanted to draw on the M.Litt. thesis you wrote at Oxford on the importance of homosexuality to the writings of E. M. Forster, L. P. Hartley, and Ronald Firbank. I was surprised to find just how much that work fed directly into *The Swimming-Pool Library*.

AH *The Swimming-Pool Library* grew in part out of that thesis: the idea of juxtaposing what couldn't be said with something that could now be said loud and clear; the contrast between concealment and display.

RC One or two other novels have been attracted by the same topic—and the same counterpoint of older and younger gay experiences and sensibilities: Mark Merlis's *American Studies*, for instance.

AH Yes, that was very good; an amazing first novel—so controlled; and terribly depressing.

RC You both used the 1950s to reflect some highly significant social shift. The great critical response to *The Swimming-Pool Library* reflected in part, I think, a sense that it answered an unresolved question concerning the British gay literary canon: namely, what is the relationship between gayness as a matter of content and gayness such as it might be traced as literary style. In the thesis, you argue for a clear division. For instance, you say Christopher Isherwood's *A Single Man* is "not distinctively homosexual, for it relies on a new moral climate free from discrimination against homosexuality."[3] Literary critics have recently taken

3. Hollinghurst, "The Creative Uses of Homosexuality in the Novels of E. M. Forster, Ronald Firbank, and L. P. Hartley," 10.

such matters up; clearly, when you were working on the thesis in the late 1970s, you were working in a much sparer context.

AH   That's true. I don't want to exaggerate, but actually no one had written much about these things then, about a lot of things which soon became fairly current or commonplace, even. I had an excitement of discovery about it then which I can't quite recapture.

RC   Gay writers, of course, don't only draw on other gay literary influences.

AH   Quite. Other literary precedents we've been talking about suggest that, in formal or stylistic terms, what you use, however consciously or unconsciously, does not necessarily arise from the gay tradition. There are writers I find imaginatively useful like Nabokov, one of the most heterosexual writers ever.

RC   Presumably you have to suppress some of the inquiring instincts that went into the thesis in writing fiction yourself: concerning questions relating to audience, historical context, and so on. A writer probably shouldn't think about these in relation to his own work.

AH   I'm not aware of them really. It would be absurdly self-conscious to be thinking about your audience all the time. One of the most beautiful and enjoyable things about writing novels, I think, is going into an inner space and doing this private thing. I try to shut everything out.

I suppose there are writers who do sit there thinking about their audience and their place in the canon, which would be a kind of inhibition. But I've never felt a conflict between being a critic of any kind—which I hardly am at all now—and my own work. The nice thing about being a critic or reviewer is reading something and finding out about it. I've never been at all theoretical, in my cast of mind. What I enjoy in other writers is partly the question any practitioner has: "How does he do that?"; matters of atmosphere, sensibility; things you might get not from novelists at all, but from poets. All the time I was writing *The Folding Star*, I wasn't reading fiction. I was reading Milton or Gerard Manley Hopkins. I feel my imagination's much more saturated with poetry than with fiction.

RC   The idea you just described of entering a fiction-friendly state sounded rather dreamlike and uncensored.

AH   Yes, it is one which is free of censorship, I suppose. It's a field of play. One's not overlooked. I loved that feeling when writing *The Swimming-Pool Library*: that nobody had seen a word of it; nobody knew about it, or had any particular expectation of it. It just seemed to evolve quite easily according to the terms I'd established.

RC   Is it easy to stay free of such senses of expectation as more books come out?

AH   I think you never recapture the innocence of the first exercise of your power. After that, the pleasure is always more fleeting or occluded.

The short middle-section of *The Folding Star* I wrote in a very exhilarated state, though. I did what I still do to some extent, but then I had a part-time job as well, so it seemed more dramatic: just taking four weeks off; literally unplugging the telephone and not seeing anybody; getting totally immersed in writing, and having the lovely feeling of being able to think about the work deeply and continuously.

I've found each book in general harder to write than the last, which must be something to do with increased self-consciousness. It has partly to do, perhaps, with a dread of repeating oneself. It's frustrating to think: "Actually, I've described this perfectly well in my first book," but having to find some other, perhaps less satisfactory way of describing it—simply because one mustn't repeat oneself. Or, of course, you forget. You come up with some wonderful phrase; it turns out you've used exactly the same phrase in your previous book. Nicholson Baker wrote in *U and I* rather cleverly about not wanting to repeat yourself and the almost absurd procedures of variation you introduce—which is probably just personal vanity actually. Nobody else would notice it, and it would hardly matter if they did.

RC   Some writers become more and more aware of peculiarities of vocabulary.

AH   Yes. It's very striking reading something through in proof, I always find. You're often suddenly aware of whole patterns of word usage. Quite unsurprisingly, they can be Freudianly revealing ones. I hadn't realized the extent to which *The Spell* is permeated by oscillations between the words "doubt" and "reassurance" which run the whole way through it. I knew that this was an idea in the book—of people longing to be reassured that everything was all right. But I hadn't realized quite how thorough my subconscious had been about the whole thing.

RC   That could be an alternative title: *Doubt and Reassurance*.

AH   [*Laughs*] That would get them in!

RC   When do titles come to you?

AH   With *The Spell*, I had the title before I began—with a slightly uneasy feeling that there must already be a famous book called *The Spell*. There doesn't seem to be. It sounded right. Then someone said: "There's Hermann Broch's *Die Beʒauberung*." That probably won't worry too many readers, though I don't yet know what the German translation of my title will be.

RC   Have the previous novel titles been translated literally? That would be difficult, I should think.

AH   Well, both my previous titles are absolutely impossible to translate. *The Folding Star* tended to be called *The Evening Star*, or some poetic term for it. That's fine, except when you get to the passage where the narrator muses on the sense of the word "folding." You can't do it. With *The Swimming-Pool Library*, because you can't use nouns as adjectives in other languages—certainly not Latinate languages—you have to introduce some other grammatical relation. So it's called *The Library of the Swimming-Pool*, which of course isn't quite the point. *The Spell* shouldn't be so difficult, although it won't carry the other resonances of the word: "a spell of time," as it were.

RC   Do you pursue your works in translation?

AH   Only *The Swimming-Pool Library* has been translated into French. I read that in manuscript. It had been abominably translated. I was glad I'd read it, and I made hundreds of corrections, but I couldn't bring myself to read the final version. I've read the Italian translations of my first two books in proof and been able to pick up some misunderstandings. My Italian's really not very good, but when you wrote the book yourself, you know at least what's supposed to be going on. I encourage translators to ask me if they don't understand something, but often they don't. If it comes out in Japanese, I've got no way of knowing.

RC   Were you involved in the proposed television adaptation of *The Swimming-Pool Library*?

AH   The BBC sat on it for ages, then decided not to do it. Kevin Elyot wrote an excellent screenplay, originally in three parts. Then he was asked to recast it into two; then they still didn't do it. I read it at each stage and made one or two tiny suggestions, but thought he'd done it brilliantly. So I was involved, and knew the putative producer. The option lapsed three years ago. Channel Four looked at it, but they were doing another series of Armistead Maupin's *Tales of the City* and said they couldn't have two gay-themed things in the same year.

RC   It would have been daring for television.

AH   I guess. It was my first experience of this whole process which so many people go through: the tension and disappointment of trying to get any film project off the ground. I've lost interest in it, I'm afraid, though of course I'd be very happy if someone decent wanted to do it.

RC   *The Spell* would seem the easiest book to do as film. The first-person narration of the first two books needs fundamental restructuring for film narrative.

AH   Yes. It had absolutely never crossed my mind, but several of *The Spell*'s early readers said it would make a good film. I can imagine it being done, I suppose, by someone with a very distinct style. But, again, so much of the narrative procedure of the book would go by the board.

RC   Did your interest in the proposed adaptation of *The Swimming-Pool Library* reflect artistic engagement in the other medium, or financial interest?

AH   Well, with *The Swimming-Pool Library*, I wouldn't have made much money. I was attracted after a while by the idea of its being transformed into another medium, and having it watched by thousands of people simultaneously.

RC   But the key matter would be that it was in a version you respected?

AH   Yes, though who knows how it would have changed when it was actually being filmed. I've rejected various requests from people who obviously sounded hopeless or whose approach I didn't like very much.

RC *The Folding Star* is too dangerous for film, I guess.

AH If you had a director who was a real artist and could thoroughly reimagine the whole thing in expressive cinematic terms, it could be rather good—though as you say, very bold. I wouldn't fancy having to raise the money.

RC It's clear that various forms of artistry interest you from the novels; film doesn't seem among them.

AH No. I go to the pictures from time to time, but it's not a big preoccupation for me.

RC Is that because with film the unit of meaning's predominantly visual, and your interest is with the linguistic?

AH Well, I think of myself as quite a visual writer; quite a descriptive writer. When I do go to the cinema, though, it's rarely enough for me to be completely dazzled and overwhelmed by the miracle of the medium itself—the beam of light. It's fantastic. I have, of course, been very moved by films. I probably go more often than I do to the theater. My experience of theater here tends to be rather disappointing, but that's partly just laziness, I think.

RC You wrote for the theater, translating Racine's *Bajazet*. Would you do it again?

AH Well, I loved doing it. There was something fascinating about the moment when suddenly a group of serious professional people got together to learn the words I'd written by heart. I got very absorbed in that. It's a bit like going into your own space to write a book—going to a freezing cold rehearsal room in Islington every day, and all these people are there, doing this mysterious thing, then going back out into the world where no one knows what they've been doing, which is storming up and down, delivering great tirades. That was rather amazing. The atmosphere clung to me for a bit, but it was a long time ago. I wouldn't mind doing another. I have a vague ambition to translate Corneille's last play, but I'd only do it if somebody wanted to put it on.

RC   Your comments remind me of Henry James's disappointment in the theater. He understood the potency of a live audience reacting immediately to one's work, as opposed to the less direct relationship to one's fiction readers.

AH   Yes. He was stagestruck, one could say. James lived life in so many degrees of reserve that there'd have been something peculiarly exciting to him about the idea of a live audience and that immediate contact. Obviously, he felt his recurrent, persistent failures very keenly. I've never myself thought of writing a play.

RC   Do you think constructing dramatically is something you don't do?

AH   I take so much pleasure in describing things. Of course I like writing conversations, and I don't really think of them as separate categories. I like to think I can do everything I try. But I do like describing buildings, for example, so I think if I did write a play, I'd have to have these intolerable stage directions describing everything in enormous detail—like George Bernard Shaw's.

These things happen to me. I don't go out and look for them. So far a play has never suggested itself.

RC   You've spoken of how, having started writing poetry, the impulse simply left you.

AH   Yes. It just stopped, or I stored up the energies and kinds of observations I was making at the time and put them into the fiction instead.

RC When you get the impulse to write about something, is there always also the sense that this is the idea for a novel, rather than for anything else?

AH Yes.

RC If it weren't, would you avoid pursuing it?

AH No. I'd happily write a short story if something came along with the "short story" light flashing. It's just never happened. My whole procedure seems to be one in which things are allowed to resonate in quite large structures. It must be terribly hard writing short stories.

I just start with little ideas—a picture of a room in my head, and the people who might be in it. I have odd moments of porousness when everything I see seems somehow usable or suggestive, and others when I'm quite closed to such possibilities. I find that at this current time— approaching having a book out—I'm absolutely closed. The idea of writing anything is utterly remote at the moment. There are other times when I'm highly suggestible. And usually, when I do start getting ideas, they are so disparate that they could only be accommodated in something reasonably capacious.

RC Is part of the pleasure of writing, then, the intellectual one in linking together disparate things?

AH Yes; to juxtapose. The only story I ever wrote, "A Thieving Boy," did just come to me suddenly like that. I saw it whole and wrote it extremely quickly. There wasn't that process of the discovery and articulation of something, which is what really interests me about writing novels.

RC "A Thieving Boy," early as it was, suggested to me that you'd discovered a very distinct writing style fully formed.

AH   I haven't read it for such a long time that I can't remember it very well. It has the technical trick of being written in the first-person plural, so you don't actually know whether it's the husband or wife writing it. But I can't remember how successful it was now.

RC   It has the technical assurance of your later work. You've previously mentioned there being several unfinished novels before *The Swimming-Pool Library*—presumably they fall between that and the story.

AH   Yes. I abandoned several novels earlier on.

RC   What caused the shift from writing unfinished novels to *The Swimming-Pool Library*, do you think?

AH   Partly it was just growing up and my rate of change slowing down. It takes such a long time to write a novel. When you're young, you grow out of things before you've got very far with them. You can immediately see what's wrong with something. Partly it was because I used to read things to friends and spoil what is for me some essential magic of privacy. I'd told the story already, so why bother to go on and write the book? I'd given it away in some sense— killed it somehow. So I learned not to do that. Partly too I think it was simply the weakness of the material itself.

RC   Others might be describing the same thing when they talk of learning their craft, but they don't often describe that in terms of this personal development.

AH   I don't think I did learn a craft really—not in any deliberate way.

RC   Don't you think of the earlier novels as exercises in craft-learning?

AH   Not really. The earlier ones, which I wrote in my late schooldays, were very free-form. I tried writing an explicitly gay novel when I was a graduate. Again, it was a novel glamorized by London. A bit later on, I started more seriously writing a rather Jamesian novel, set in Venice and about a teenage boy who has an affair with his father's mistress. I think parts were quite well written, but there actually just wasn't enough to it. That Jamesian or Proustian disguise of trying to write about an affair with a middle-aged woman was kind of beyond me, I think. Perhaps I could do it now, I don't know—but I certainly couldn't do it then. So I abandoned that. Then *The Swimming-Pool Library* slowly took shape.

RC   Were these stories that reached you from others or that you'd invented?

AH   I invented them, I think.

RC   Then you came across certain elements that you were going to piece together into *The Swimming-Pool Library*. Given that you've already said certain key elements of a book's plot remain unknown to you, was the successful completion of a project also about learning to resist the impulse to complete a story first in your head before bringing it to the point of articulation?

AH   Yes. There may be some not fully conscious wariness of that; of having to leave it to some extent unknown. There are two things here: there's giving away the story, and giving away the novel. The former is some quite primitive thing which must be to do, I think, with what must be a stronger narrative impulse in me than I recognize. The other thing is being in a position as I start a book of not exactly knowing what's going to happen in the later parts, or what twists it might take en route to an end I may see fairly clearly. For example, I wrote the last paragraph of *The Spell* first. I knew it was going to end on the clifftop. But there were all sorts of twists before the characters got there that I hadn't fully envisaged.

RC   Was this a new strategy—to start at the end?

AH   It wasn't really a strategy; just how it happened. Usually the clear moments I've had have been where something has crystallized to do with the early stages of the story. Unusually, in this case, I saw an image with which I wanted to end the book.

RC   You've said the sex scene between Edward and Luc in *The Folding Star* was only clear to you just prior to writing it. I was interested in the open-endedness of the final image of the book—the picture of the missing Luc. Did that come to you similarly late?

AH   Yes. I was about to do a huge contrapuntal, thirty-page resumé of all the novel's motifs, but I thought: "Fuck it, I'll write this one paragraph instead." That seemed to be it, which was a great relief—for me and everybody else. It's enigmatic and involves a sort of double take. You have to read the paragraph twice to see what's going on in it. A lot of people don't realize what's going on: that Edward is looking at a photograph of Luc. People have given me extraordinary interpretations of it: that he's looking through the window of a ferry, for instance.

RC   Both *The Folding Star* and *The Spell* end in a rather open-ended way.

AH   They all do, I think.

RC   But, though in *The Swimming-Pool Library* one feels one's been given everything that's important to the story—the story of Charles's life is complete, that is—there is that gesture of Will's, his refusal to write the life. Surely that offers a thematic ambiguity: the suggested connections between him and Charles aren't forced into some easy move to closure.

AH In both *The Swimming-Pool Library* and *The Folding Star* there's a lot of plot business just before the end. Then they have a sort of coda leaving everything in suspense or solution.

RC Is that something you realized only in retrospect?

AH No. I knew what I was doing.

RC You spoke of reading poetry during the writing of *The Folding Star*. Do you consciously avoid reading novels when writing?

AH Yes. In general I don't like reading other fiction while I'm writing fiction, so I go back to old favorites.

RC You said you read Milton, whose voice is very strong. Some writers complain of the dangers of being taken over by another voice.

AH I know. I actually read James's *The Wings of the Dove* in the middle of writing *The Folding Star*, which slightly goes against what I was saying and was potentially suicidal in that sense. I think I got away with it. In the particular case of Milton, it involved *Comus* especially—and the very end of *Paradise Lost*. I was reading him more for the imagery of the woods and lawns, which is reused in the common in *The Folding Star*. I love writing about trees.

RC So is it simply pleasure that takes you back to poetry?

AH I'm not sure. Poetry often moves me very intensely. I suddenly feel I must read it—as I did yesterday. I thought: "I must read W. B. Yeats's 'The Municipal Gallery Re-visited.' " I took it down and felt completely overcome. I love that compact effect of a poem. You can read it very quickly, which of course you can't do with fiction. It's something to do with the consolation of rhythms you know unfolding, too; rhythms you're familiar with. It's like listening to great music. You know what to expect and still you keep hearing it afresh.

RC   Rhythm and poise are equally central, presumably, when you write prose.

AH   I think rhythm's important. I've never stood back from myself as I was doing it quite enough to know what it is I'm doing, though. Sometimes my rhythms are too euphonious.

RC   The slow, measured method of composition you've described makes it sound as if the musicality of the prose concerns you constantly. There isn't that vast unburdening of a first draft some writers mention.

AH   I can't analyze it terribly clearly, but I know I've never done that torrential thing. I write other things like that—I write long letters torrentially, and with an odd lack of style. Well, I suppose they do have a style of their own. But I recognize that as quite distinct from the way I'd write fiction.

RC   You spoke of having no sense currently of what the next novel might be. Is there a big gap between works where you don't know what will occur?

AH   I may have misled you slightly. What I find tends to happen each time is that when I'm writing the last bit of a book, suddenly I'm full of ideas for another one—which is very nice, of course. I've made a lot of notes and thought about it a lot, but for the last two or three months I haven't, really, and I won't come back to it until *The Spell* has been published. I'm not nearly ready to start writing yet. I'm going to Houston, Texas, for the fall semester this year to teach creative writing, so I think I won't write anything until I come back. The invitation to do that just came completely out of the blue, and, in the way some things are offered to you that you'd never yourself have thought of doing, I just said: "Yes, all right."

RC Does the proposed break from fiction not concern you? Perhaps you've never had the worry that your talent might dry up.

AH I haven't. I've always had an underlying confidence that things would happen in due course. There are times when I find it difficult to write, but I've never really had the experience of writer's block.

RC The idea of being bombarded with ideas for the new book as the previous one closes is familiar to many writers, I think. One theory I've heard is that it's a prompt from the subconscious to encourage the completion of what's at hand without too much further delay.

AH I recognize that event—the feeling that of course you're aware of what's wrong with this book, and if you took another year you could make it a much better one, but actually you've just got to let it go. The mingled relief and dissatisfaction in that moment is rather hard to describe. There's this sudden presence of other ideas: perhaps it is the subconscious trying to get you to force the book closed. It could be the opposite, though—the subconscious saying: "You've got all these other ideas—why don't you put these in the book as well?" But you defy it, saying: "No, this is the end."

RC Is there a lot of material from the notetaking you don't finally use?

AH I think part of the point of the long gap that's happening now is that these ideas have the chance to settle. You go back to them and think: "That's not much of an idea after all." But there will be things there that will go into it.

RC   You sound quite confident about things having to reach a point of maturation—which rather begs a question concerning the teaching of creative writing. That involves, by definition, writing to order.

AH   Yes. It's not that I don't believe skills can't be honed by exercise, because they obviously can. But I think it's so much more difficult in prose writing anyway. If you can get everybody writing sestinas, that's different.

RC   In America it's often a criticism to say a novel feels as if it has come out of a creative writing program. Just as honing is useful, there's a danger of overstating the importance of technical lessons.

AH   Of course there is, yes. I'm really very skeptical about the whole thing. One has to have something to say.

RC   In the introduction to *The Early Firbank*, you wrote of the world of his novels constituting a kind of child's exposure to the world of adult conventions.[4] I couldn't help connecting that to the introduction of Roops, Will's nephew in *The Swimming-Pool Library*. Roops has this morality-free understanding of homosexuality—a nice way of indicating the importance of changes in gay life in the last decades: that a child might have an unprejudiced view of homosexuality.

AH   That was his function in that book. It informed or is in some way parallel to a kind of innocence in Will's own attitude. That whole idea of being like a child—I still recurrently feel like a child. I'm quite surprised to find how incredibly old I am. That's certainly a motif in *The Spell*, too: the idea of having a guide or mentor; the person who helps you to be yourself or change yourself, or shows you things you didn't know.

---

4. Hollinghurst, "Introduction" to Ronald Firbank, *The Early Firbank*, ed. Steven Moore, vii–xi (x).

There's quite a lot of imagery in *The Spell* to do with that. And it's also partly to do with another twist in *The Spell*: the treatment of the relationship between son and father. That's obviously another buried preoccupation of all the novels, I think: that, generally, there are sorts of substitute relationships. In *The Swimming-Pool Library*, Will's parents we never even see. But he has a representative figure—his grandfather—from an older generation.

RC   There are ways in which what seem like vertical relationships get played out horizontally in all your novels. Such themes might have preoccupied some writers in terms of the exploration of psychology. Your treatment, however, involves a sort of aloof dramatization of possible ways of behaving. This distinction between the dramatic or social and the psychological is rather crude, I admit, but it does work as a basic differentiation; a way of distinguishing the work of many gay writers, for instance, from the heavily psychologizing novel tradition of, say, D. H. Lawrence.

AH   Yes, especially because they want to escape that sort of psychiatric pigeon-holing.

RC   This school of fiction occurs subsequent to the impact of Freud, whose work was key to certain modernist writers but not others. I think you're right in saying gay writers are invariably reluctant overtly to psychologize because of the history of gay men being read psychologically to their detriment.

AH   Yes. This returns us to the idea of the novel as motored by impulse and desire. I always loved the idea of just describing people's behavior: that this is what this person did on this occasion, and not really saying any more about it.

RC   I think it's no accident that somebody like Lawrence—despite his psychosexual preoccupations—isn't interesting to most gay novelists.

AH Firbank was the least psychological writer there ever was, and his allegiance is more to late seventeenth- and eighteenth-century ideas of character, which don't have any psychological dimension at all. I suppose his approach comes out of a comedy of types and humours, ultimately: the feeling that people just *are* their impulses and caprices; they don't have any inside to them. That can be very funny and sort of true. It was certainly one of my ideas in *The Spell*: ruling passions; the idea that everybody goes through their lives with particular fantasies, dreams, and beliefs which could never stand the test of reality but which nonetheless dominate them.

RC Perhaps concomitant to this, and something to do with the open-endedness we talked of earlier, is the fact that the obvious novelistic reward of self-knowledge isn't given to your characters.

AH That's right. Whilst the reader's given the opportunity to learn something, Will, one feels, won't be changed by this experience.

RC The concluding gesture of *The Swimming-Pool Library* remains the possession of the reader. Will articulates what the conclusion of the tale is, but doesn't himself give it due importance.

AH No.

RC You've spoken of your lack of religious beliefs. At the same time, your books have a keen interest in morals. Presumably you simply don't look to the Church for guidance in that area.

AH I honestly don't, which I think comes partly out of having had a very intensely religious adolescence, followed by a total revulsion from religion. I've retained a fairly steely distance from the whole thing. To me it's an irrelevance—which isn't of course to trivialize the whole nightmarish chaos that religions bring about in life. I'm simply not preoccupied with theological questions, I don't think—which one could be, as an atheist.

RC   What of the fiction writer's choice between describing a world that's predominantly material or one which suggests that consciousness has—like it or not—spiritual undertones?

AH   I don't think my books are wholly material. I'm not saying I don't have a spiritual sense. But it isn't a religious sense, although I am very susceptible to aestheticized kinds of religious emotion—in buildings, music, and poetry. I find Hopkins's religious sonnets wonderfully moving and convincing, for instance, even though I don't believe.

RC   The power of the aesthetic seems a suitable theme on which to close. Thanks very much for your time.

ELEVEN
DAVID LEAVITT

David Leavitt is best known to gay readers for a range of fiction on gay themes, especially *The Lost Language of Cranes*, *Equal Affections*, *Arkansas*, and *The Page Turner*. These have been celebrated by many gay and nongay writers, including Edmund White. Unusually, Leavitt's first published work, *Family Dancing*, was a collection of stories, featuring both gay and nongay characters. Born in Pittsburgh in 1961, he grew up in Palo Alto, California, then studied for a degree in English at Yale University. Before graduating in 1983, Leavitt saw his first published story—"Territory"—appear in the *New Yorker*.

His first collection, *Family Dancing* (New York: Knopf, 1984), was published the next year to much acclaim and was nominated for both the National Critics Book Award and the PEN-Faulkner Award. This was followed by two novels—*The Lost Language of Cranes* (New York: Knopf, 1986) and *Equal Affections* (New York: Weidenfeld and Nicholson, 1989)—and a second collection of stories, *A Place I've Never Been* (New York: Viking, 1990). In 1992 *The Lost Language of Cranes* was made into a film, relocated in London, for the BBC.

In 1989, Leavitt was awarded a John Simon Guggenheim Foundation fellowship and became writer-in-residence at the Institute of Catalan Letters, Barcelona. He moved back to New York for a while, but eventually settled in Northern Italy with his partner and sometime collaborator Mark Mitchell. Their coedited *Penguin Book of Gay Short Stories* (New York: Viking,

1994) was followed by Mitchell's own *Penguin Book of International Gay Writing* (New York: Viking, 1995), which featured an introduction by Leavitt. Next they coauthored *Italian Pleasures* (San Francisco: Chronicle Books, 1996) and coedited *Pages Passed from Hand to Hand: The Hidden Tradition of Homosexual Literature in English from 1748 to 1914* (Boston/New York: Houghton Mifflin, 1997).

Leavitt's fiction career continued with the troubled reception of 1993's *While England Sleeps*, a historical novel on gay themes set during the Spanish Civil War (new edition: Boston/New York: Houghton Mifflin, 1995). This was the subject of a lawsuit in Britain by the writer Stephen Spender, alleging plagiarism, which was finally settled out of court. *While England Sleeps* was withdrawn, reappearing two years later after Leavitt made changes to the text. It was shortlisted for the Los Angeles Times Fiction Prize. Next came *Arkansas* (Boston/New York: Houghton Mifflin, 1997), a collection of three novellas—"The Term-Paper Artist," "The Wooden Anniversary," and "Saturn Street." Leavitt's next novel, *The Page Turner* (Boston/New York: Houghton Mifflin, 1997), is set in the world of classical music. Leavitt has since completed a new novel, *Martin Baumann* (Boston/New York: Houghton Mifflin, 2000). Though Leavitt still lives in Italy, this interview took place in London on Monday, March 23, 1998.

RC I want to start by asking about the subject of AIDS. You've written about it in several short stories or novellas: "Gravity," "A Place I've Never Been," and "AYOR" in *A Place I've Never Been*; "Saturn Street" in *Arkansas*. Others, though, have tried to write about the subject on a larger canvas—within a somewhat epic novelistic account of gay life often. Were you tempted to write something on that scale?

DL   No. I'm not, generally speaking, a big reader of epics. I very much like trilogies and tetralogies. I'm envious of Edmund White having had such a representative life. That allowed him to write a series of three novels that were both intensely personal or autobiographical and also historical. My life's been so unrepresentative I can't imagine how doing a similarly immediate project to Edmund's would represent the last couple of decades. In relation to AIDS, the novel's gotten a lot of crap. It's basically been agreed that the novel's the least successful form in dealing with AIDS.

RC   Many people are suspicious of invention around the topic, and prefer memoirs. Paul Monette's *Borrowed Time* was a big seller.

DL   Yes. I'm not a big admirer of that book, personally. I reviewed his *Becoming a Man* for the London *Sunday Times* and was the only person who said anything negative. It's the sort of book you don't dare speak against. My feeling is that fiction comes out of really weird, quasi-unconscious parts of the psyche. There's always a mixture of conscious and unconscious attraction to certain stories. You almost need to write the story in order to figure out the explanation for its interest. This is something I take for granted, but I find nonwriters don't understand it. I don't think any serious writer could sit down and write a good piece of fiction for ideological or propagandistic purposes. That's why in the AIDS context I often harp on about Christopher Coe's novel, *Such Times*. A lot of people hated that book. To me it's extremely strange, but that's all to its credit. *Such Times* is a response to the AIDS epidemic from the perspective of someone really bizarre. Christopher was a complete lunatic. Yet it has the integrity of representing his viewpoint with such clarity, elegance, and intelligence that I find it immensely rewarding and entertaining.

RC   To me, Coe misunderstood the key elements of the tragedy of AIDS by wrapping it in material concerns. There are so many references to designer clothes that no longer fit, for example.

DL   Well, I wasn't great friends with him, but the fact that I knew Christopher will affect my reading here. *Such Times* is a very autobiographical book. Christopher did have a much older lover who was in a relationship; he was very rich; he did become sick and lose everything. He went from being immensely rich to being tragically poor, living in terrible squalor. Knowing that, and having visited him at his apartment, where he almost didn't have money to eat . . .

RC   But that squalor isn't in that book.

DL   No, but it was in his life. I'm committing the aesthetic sin of reading the book in the context of having known him. *Such Times* is almost an elegy for an extremely glamorous but unhappy life. Christopher was an alcoholic and drug addict who had a rough time. But he always loved luxury—with a connoisseur's passion almost. That was the life he shared with Hans.

 Your objections I understand totally. What I'd finally say about *Such Times*, though, is that for me it's clearly a piece of serious literature— written by someone who's a writer first, and a writer with AIDS second. That was something I harped on about at the Key West Literary Seminar on AIDS and Literature: I consider myself a writer first, and a gay writer second. If I had AIDS, I'd still consider myself a writer first. The world wouldn't, but I would, and that's the point of view I'd write from. I write for posterity. I think it's a crock—the idea of people not writing for posterity but for other people in the same situation at this time. No real writer would ever think that, no matter how desperate the situation.

RC   Gore Vidal once wrote that in the past he'd had a peculiar nineteenth-century sense of writing for posterity. I thought: "What's peculiar or nineteenth-century about that?"

DL   Yes. Edmund White annoyed me a little in his lecture at that seminar. I don't think a good aesthetic argument means anything personal; in fact, it's a healthy thing. I don't think Edmund believed many of the things he said there. It isn't borne out by his work. Edmund's clearly writing to place himself in the pantheon. He was thrilled to be inducted into the American Academy. He's very much writing with a sense of himself as a great writer who'll be remembered.

I know this will sound harsh, but in the context of AIDS literature, everyone in the world thinks their story's interesting. AIDS has made writers out of many people who wouldn't have been writers otherwise, or it's given mediocre writers a sense of being better than they actually are. Some will survive; it's a crapshoot which ones. I think the one we're all agreed on is Allen Barnett's *The Body and Its Dangers*. Carole Maso, Peter Cameron, and I were the judges of the PEN-Hemingway Award the year we gave the prize to Bernard Cooper for *Maps to Anywhere* and the citation to Allen Barnett. It was a terrible struggle deciding which to give the prize to. Nowadays I regret we didn't do it the other way around. We simply felt some of the stories in *The Body and Its Dangers* weren't as strong as others, whereas *Maps to Anywhere* was pretty much consistently very strong. We were judging in a very cold, aesthetic way. But "The *Times* As It Knows Us" remains in my mind the greatest piece of fiction written about the AIDS epidemic, without question: not because of its political content; not because of what it's about, but because it's so well written, so smart. That, to me, is what makes anything last: the integrity of the prose. I do believe in the distinction between writers who're under the gun—who're dying—and those in a more contemplative position, as I am. But "The *Times* As It Knows Us" distinguishes itself from, say, Paul Monette. It stands out far above such works. It doesn't mean these books haven't had immense value in their moment. The one book on AIDS that's going to last, though, is *The Body and Its Dangers*—and, I think, *Such Times* too. Little else, unfortunately. But we'll wait and see.

RC Has anything with humor impressed you? John Weir's *The Irreversible Decline of Eddie Socket*, for instance?

DL *Eddie Socket* is a good book. I regret he didn't write anything else yet. John Weir's a good writer who has been very unpleasant to me, consistently, so it's hard to stay objective. By comparison, Andrew Holleran was a saint to me at the Key West Literary Seminar. That made me feel very ashamed for what I'd written about *Dancer from the Dance*.[1] He was so above silly attacks that I felt chastened to some degree.

RC I think you were wrong about that book.

DL I may be. It was what I felt at that time. Unfortunately, we have to stick by our opinions, but I'm always willing to change my mind. I certainly admired him immensely there. Holleran's a wonderful writer. I probably overstated this in my "Introduction," but the flaw in his work is that he's too distracted by beauty. An obsession with male beauty intrudes in *Dancer from the Dance* in a way. As I said, whereas we can afford to be distracted by beauty, literature cannot.

RC That's a less worrying "mistake," though, than the suggestion that there's a flaw in a writer's style. Are you saying beauty's simply too dominant as an element of the story?

DL Yes. Edmund White's always felt I was too harsh on Holleran. He said: "That's Andrew. He's obsessed with beautiful boys," and dismissed it. My response was: "I'm obsessed with beautiful boys, but I think it'd be a mistake to allow that to control my writing."

RC To return to the subject of AIDS, are there other works of fiction that will last?

---

1. See Leavitt's "Introduction" to David Leavitt and Mark Mitchell, eds., *Penguin Book of Gay Short Stories*, xv–xxviii, xvi–xx.

DL I think Edmund's stories are very good.

RC Have you read Adam Mars-Jones's stories from *The Darker Proof*?

DL Yes. He's someone else who's been really nasty to me in the press almost consistently. I was such an admirer of his *Lantern Lecture* that I wrote him a fan letter. When *Family Dancing* was published in the U.K., he came to the party. I don't understand why he's taken every opportunity to attack me that he can. Among English writers, the one I admire most is Alan Hollinghurst, a terrific writer. He hasn't dealt with AIDS that much. Yet, according to Larry Kramer, Hollinghurst must be a piece of shit because he writes about sex. But Hollinghurst writes so brilliantly, obsessively, and neurotically about sex. I find it horrifying but also gripping.

Sex scenes succeed when they're not only about sex; when they're about psychology. That goes without saying in Hollinghurst's work. I hope it's true in my novellas and novels. I don't see the point writing sex scenes otherwise. Sex isn't of inherent literary interest unless it provides a way of revealing something not only about people but about the way they interact. What better measure of an intimate relationship than the way people interact sexually? When I wrote "Saturn Street"—in certain ways a very autobiographical story, even though "Phil" doesn't exist—I was trying to describe a very low period in my life when I'd slipped into a terrible situation. The epigram "failure is forming habits" applied.

RC The accounts of telephone sex lines rang very true.

DL I've a friend in London who calls English phone lines all the time. He tells me these hysterical stories. But that became to some degree my life. It was a very demeaning moment. When I read part of "Saturn Street" out at the Key West Literary Seminar, it infuriated me that Larry Kramer said it was in poor taste. I was trying to describe that sense of horniness as a form of depression, which is the context out of which the whole novella evolves. But it's very particular to the age of AIDS too, because it's also about what happens when the libido continues to make demands, but the soul's incapable of actual intimacy—particularly after a lover's died; in this case, committed suicide. I played with that later on, when the narrator Jerry gives Phil the impression his lover died of AIDS even though he didn't.

RC   The positioning of Jerry as sexually needy, compared to Phil, who is HIV-positive, finding relative satisfaction felt totally persuasive. I felt you were undermining traditional AIDS pieties there. Stories often resonate that way when they eschew assumed values.

DL   That's absolutely true. John Hersey's story about AIDS—"Get Up, Sweet Slug-a-bed"—also does that. In "Saturn Street," though, the other thing I'd emphasize is that Jerry isn't HIV-negative. He's refused to be tested and very well might be HIV-positive.

RC   Yes. I've made the same assumption he makes: that, in not testing, he can position himself comfortably among the HIV-negative.

DL   Exactly. I didn't want Jerry to say: "Of course, my sexual history is such that I knew there was a 99.9% chance I was HIV-negative." I wanted it to be very uncertain. He's been in a long relationship, but it's not clear it was monogamous. He needs to think of himself as HIV-negative in order to survive, and he'd rather not know. Phil's the same way: that's what links them in a strange way.

RC   Years ago you said on the BBC's *Late Show* that you felt attracted to AIDS as a theme but hadn't written about it. You've subsequently written a number of stories about it. Do you feel you've mined the seam now?

DL   Bear in mind that when I wrote "Saturn Street," I didn't set out to write a story about AIDS, but about Project Angel Food. I was most interested in the experience of volunteering to do something very important in the context of what I considered an extremely disreputable group. That remains part of the story. However, Phil took it over. He wasn't at all meant to be the center of the story when I started writing. In that weird way characters do in fiction, he asserted himself. I'd invented someone I'd never met that I could easily have fallen in love with. There was someone like Phil when I was delivering, who I only talked to for ten minutes. But he stayed in my consciousness.

So often fiction for me is a "what if" proposition, concerning things that didn't happen . . . but what if they did? I wrote *Lost Language of Cranes* along these lines: "What if my father were gay?" He isn't, but what if he were? What if I'd fallen in love with someone to whom I was delivering meals? How would I have responded? In "Saturn Street" I'm not Jerry, exactly, but he's like me. Frankly, I find strictly autobiographical writing less interesting than writing that's speculative. "The Term-Paper Artist" too is certainly speculative.

RC   You allowed yourself a swipe at mainstream American culture in the figure of "Dr. Delia" in "Saturn Street."

DL   Well, Dr. Laura Schlessinger, who's the model for that character, seems pretty ripe for parody at this point. She's such a public figure.

RC   But you're also parodying the indulgence of those who listen to her.

DL   Yes. Curiously, my agent's one objection to "Saturn Street" was that he thought I was too hard on Hollywood. He thought the whole sequence where the actress comes to deliver meals and everyone bends over backwards for her photo opportunity was too much. But that really happened, exactly the way I described it. Reality is often unconvincing in fiction. I decided to take the risk there because I felt quite condemning of a certain self-serving element in AIDS volunteerism.

RC   It also seemed to be about American positivity: the indiscriminate hugging and so on.

DL   That's completely valid. Like most Americans, however, I have a love-hate relationship with all that. In a certain sense, I despise it, and that's why I live abroad. In another, I'm deeply attracted to it. Whenever I'm in Los Angeles—and I'm there on average two months a year because my family lives there—I listen to Dr. Laura religiously. I'm almost addicted to it. Addiction itself is an American phenomenon.

RC   I want to move on to ask you about E. M. Forster. He seems to be creeping more and more centrally into your work—even as a character in "The Term-Paper Artist." He's referred to in all three *Arkansas* novellas—and in *The Page Turner*. For many gay men, Oscar Wilde's legacy as a gay writer is a more prominent one. Comparing the two seemed very suggestive in relation to your work, especially in the light of the comment of the narrator of "The Wooden Anniversary": " 'Wilde is like Freud. Everyone thinks that just because he said something, it's automatically true.' "[2]

DL   Wilde's someone I love. He and Forster have a really peculiar relationship. Forster almost never talks about Wilde; he makes perhaps two references to Wilde in all his writings. Mark and I are both convinced this is intentional; that there's an avoidance of Wilde. The one thing Mark came up with is a funny phrase in *A Room with a View*. Someone talks about having a "mauvais quart d'heure," which is also in Wilde.

---

2. Leavitt, "The Wooden Anniversary," *in Arkansas*, 75–132 (quotation from 109).

This can't be proved, but it suggested to me that Forster was very famil-iar with Wilde's work.

Wilde certainly had a much more interesting life than Forster. Both, for me, are sources of immense wisdom and importance. Henry James is the writer who's really problematic for me and who I"d put in opposition to both of them. I have an extremely complex love-hate relationship with James. He was horrible to Wilde—probably out of jealousy, because of the failure of his own play. Forster, of course, had an extremely ambivalent relationship toward James in *Aspects of the Novel*. I was talking to someone recently who felt I'd really been influenced by James. I said: "If it's true, it's against my will." I'll always admire James, but never love or even like him.

RC   In *Pages Passed from Hand to Hand*, you placed Forster in a summa-tive position—as the last featured author before gay literature goes aboveground, as it were. But the legacy after Forster isn't straightfor-ward, is it? Among others, Wilde, James, Forster, and Proust all exercise clear influence on gay writers. How do you compare the inheritance of each of these, specifically in the context of gay writing?

DL   My feeling is that if you go beyond Forster, James, and Wilde and into the rest of the twentieth century, there's suddenly an enormous amount of gay writing. But the more there is, the less of it exists that's serious. It's infinitesimal. If you look at a serious writer like Edmund White, you see all three of the English writers in his work—then, obviously, Proust above all. But there's certainly a Jamesian obsession with detail, and a certain Wildean irony, and I think there's also some Forster in his work. I think for any serious writer of the twentieth century—gay or not—those three writers are of immense importance. The other two I'd add would be Virginia Woolf and, curiously enough, Ford Madox Ford.

RC   I was interested that you used him in *The Page Turner*.

DL   *The Good Soldier*'s my favorite novel, period. It's magnificent. What makes it perhaps of particular interest to a gay writer is that it's about sexual obsession, a recurrent theme in gay literature. Something I've often noticed is that the vast majority of really great male writers—gay or straight—share a certain sexual obsessiveness; whether it's Ford Madox Ford, with all his ex-wives, or Oscar Wilde and Bosie. Forster's appeared in a very suppressed, undirected way because his mother was always in the way. But I think he had great longings in his life that were never fully expressed.

Influences are rarely obvious. That's becoming clearer and clearer to me. A lot of times I've felt when people have asked me about them and I've mentioned Alice Munro or Grace Paley among more contemporary writers, there's a sense of great disappointment—certainly among stupid gay journalists. They ask: "What about gay influences?"—as if by necessity my literary influences have to have been gay. To me that's completely irrelevant.

I have an idea about this which I had hoped a visit I made to Paris this last weekend would address. I was supposed to be in a debate—a very French thing. But the guy who ran it not only gave me the wrong time for the debate. He gave me the wrong subject. He said it was on the question "Is There Such a Thing as Gay Literature?" But I was supposed to be on a panel for: "Is There Such a Thing as a Homosexual Hero?" That's one of these French subjects about which I have nothing to say, so I pretended to be sick. I couldn't take part. It was going to be me and three French lesbians. I knew they'd all have long speeches prepared. I had prepared too—but for the wrong subject. Anyway, what I was going to say about the matter of whether gay literature exists was that I think it's the wrong question. To me the important question is: "Is there such a thing as a gay reader?" That's infinitely more relevant. Whether one thinks of oneself as a gay writer is beside the point. What's important is that whether there are people who seek out books with gay content. Obviously there are. As long as there are gay readers, there will be a tradition—one of reading, not writing. And it's a fascinating thing

to trace—especially before gay literature reemerges from the underground—the extent to which this readership defined a tradition. But you
don't tend to see what a lot of more simple-minded critics want, which is
a sort of chain of influence, of the sort Harold Bloom mapped in relation to poets.

If you look at things like niche marketing, the way people market
gay books: that's based on the knowledge on the part of publishers that
there's a set readership. The problem emerges when that readership is
appealed to with such intensity that other readers are shut out. But that's
a very contemporary problem.

RC   It ties in with Reed Woodhouse's designation of you as an "assim-
ilative" gay writer—in other words, appealing to a mainstream readership.[3] I wondered how you felt about that description.

DL   It doesn't bother me at all. A feminist writer called Susan Brown-
miller, who wrote a famous book about rape, *Against Our Will*, said
something very smart to me: "Feminists are my constituency, but they're
not my readership." It made a lot of sense. It suggested that in a political
sense she felt an alliance with this group, but it wasn't exclusive. That's
how I feel. Gay people are my constituency and form a part of my readership, but they're not who I write for. I don't think any serious writer
writes for a particular readership. The readership will sometimes define
the writer's role. But it seems backward to look at this question purely in
terms of the writer.

RC   Have you ever written with the reader's perspective in mind—in
other words, chosen to write something because you felt it was something you would like to have been able to read?

---

3. Reed Woodhouse, originally in an article, "Five Houses of Gay Fiction," for the *Harvard Gay and
Lesbian Review;* subsequently in his *Unlimited Embrace: A Canon of Gay Fiction, 1945–1995*
(Amherst, Mass.: University of Massachusetts Press, 1998), 139–55.

DL   That was certainly true of *The Lost Language of Cranes*. That book I wrote simply because it was a book that hadn't existed when I was a teenager, so in a sense I was writing as a reader; I was writing the book I wanted to read. But that was probably the only instance where I wrote from the point of view of a reader. The only other way I've done something similar is that sometimes I imitate. I don't mean *While England Sleeps* and the Stephen Spender controversy. That wasn't imitation at all. But all writers imitate. If I read something I admire, I'll often end up trying to imitate it, though usually it eventually won't resemble what I started imitating at all.

RC   Edmund White has spoken of having an ideal reader in mind. Has that never been necessary to you?

DL   Not really. I understand what Edmund's saying. He's imagining a pure reader—someone who brings nothing to the book except appetite. But I don't need to think of that consciously.

RC   Appetite—but also literariness. Many writers want an understanding of the circumstances of gay life, plus literariness.

DL   Or literariness, and "gay" second. I think most serious writers find it very tiresome to be pigeonholed. I hate to use that word because it's such a cliché. Still, it is tiresome to have constantly to deal with the expectation that, because you're an openly gay writer, you're also, as it were, a professional homosexual who can be expected to give a disquisition at the drop of a hat on any political topic relating to homosexuality. This happens to me all the time. I'll be on a radio show and will suddenly be asked to comment on gay marriage or something. I do the best I can. But I'm not an opinion machine. Something else I think is problematic is the fact that you're expected constantly to stay on good terms with the gay community in America. This can result in being put in some really low-level situations which other writers would not find themselves in or tolerate.

I had to cancel my American book tour for *The Page Turner* because we were moving house. But one reading I was supposed to give was at a gay bookshop in Atlanta. I've no idea if this is a serious bookshop, but the publicist from Houghton Mifflin called me up and said: "We've had a change of schedule. They said if you read on Thursday, no one will go because it's gay bingo night." I thought: "It's hard to imagine Julian Barnes, Jeanette Winterson, or Susan Sontag being told that." Likewise it's hard to imagine any of those people tolerating having to give a reading in front of a huge display of porn videos, which I've done on hundreds of occasions—most recently in Paris at Les Mots à la Bouche. The situations you find yourself in are so undignified, yet you're expected to tolerate them because this is the "community." I don't mean to say I've anything against degeneracy at all. I'm a great fan of it. But when I'm doing a literary reading, I'd like to do it in a dignified setting.

RC   A lot of esteemed American gay writers are quite happily associated with erotic writing and porn. Many seem happy to feature in anthologies of it.

DL   I'm not. I doubt Edmund is. I think he doesn't have as complicated or tormented a relationship with the so-called gay community as I do. I find the normality and social acceptance of porn in American gay circles a little weird. First, it makes porn much less exciting. Second, it institutionalizes a very questionable industry. If you look at a lot of porn videos, these kids are victims of exploitation. They're all on drugs— tons of drugs are available on those sets. They're dying of drug overdoses every second—like Joey Stefano. Yet the head of a big porn video company's treated almost like Harvey Milk in San Francisco. He's on every board; he's the constant guest at various dinners for AIDS foundations. He's an eminently respectable citizen. I've got to say I find that really disturbing. I'm always happy to do readings at gay bookshops, but I prefer those that have a somewhat more serious aspect.

RC Some of the shops that are more about books, and have diversified less into porn, are closing.

DL Yes—because porn's their bread and butter; what they make their money on. I don't even mind that, necessarily. But when I read at A Different Light in Los Angeles, a store I like, they don't put me in front of a cock! At Glad Day in Boston, I was reading with Falcon videos right behind me. It was the weirdest thing.

RC It's an interesting example of the late twentieth-century novelist being surrounded by visual culture.

DL Exactly. I'm not a prude at all. You can tell from my writing. However, I require a certain amount of seriousness. I consider writing a deeply serious business. In the context of my work, I feel I never take myself seriously enough. The last line of the very long novel I'm now writing is going to be: "And I went off to try to learn to be serious." My main complaint about most gay writers today is that very few are serious.

RC By "serious," do you mean single-minded?

DL I mean taking literature as an historically serious matter.

RC What would they do to demonstrate that?

DL Well, to give an example, if you look back in time, it's much clearer that Oscar Wilde was a serious writer and Ouida wasn't.[4] I don't know if you've ever had the "joy" of reading Ouida's *Friendship*. I read it when I

---

4. Ouida (1839–1908) was the pseudonym of Marie Louise de la Ramée, a Romantic novelist of Anglo-French origin.

was obsessed with the English community in Florence. But she's not a serious writer. She was writing to sell, not to change the world or be part of literary history. Wilde was—that's obvious.

RC   Yet Wilde's veneer of profound unseriousness has had its legacy in gay culture. Many writers mask a real dedication under a superficial flippancy.

DL   Yes. When I say this, I don't mean to be humorless. A lot of the work in *Pages Passed from Hand to Hand* I wouldn't call deeply serious. But it's work of deep historical interest. Unserious work can be interesting in terms of learning about history. But it's not interesting in terms of changing your life, the way I believe great literature can be. Moving into the present, this is all much less clear. But if you read a writer like Allen Barnett, it seems obvious he's a serious writer; likewise, Allan Gurganus and Edmund White, though he's a very unusual case. There's a certain glibness that finds its way into Edmund's work at points. It seems so shockingly different from what came five pages before.

RC   When you speak of literature as potentially life-changing, it occurred to me that, at its narrowest, the popular idea that gay literature might act as a tool for affirming one's sexual identity is not about changing lives at all. If "affirmation" is what's needed, that invariably means something highly conservative.

DL   Yes. It's like Roland Barthes's distinction between "plaisir" and "jouissance"—pleasure and bliss. Pleasure is what confirms everything you already believe; bliss is what cuts right to the quick.

RC   I want to ask a little more about your public profile. Some of your views, as expressed in the press and in the "Introduction" to the *Penguin Book of Gay Short Stories*, have been controversial. Even so, other writers, on occasion, have unleashed some surprisingly strong negative comments on you, as you've already mentioned. Do you think in part this has to do with your crossover success?

DL   It has to do, I think, with a certain envy, based on the fact that I've had a degree of crossover success that's somewhat rare. The only other gay writers I can think of offhand who've achieved the same degree of crossover success would be Edmund, Allan Gurganus, Alan Hollinghurst, and Jeanette Winterson. Even Andrew Holleran's read primarily by a gay audience. Three people have been consistently vicious to me: in the States, Ethan Mordden and Felice Picano whom I've never met, and in England, Adam Mars-Jones. With Felice, it seemed clearly a generational thing. He wrote somewhere that I wrote as if I didn't have a penis. Mark said if I ever met him I should say: "Mine's bigger than yours!" Adam's attacks on me have amazed me, because I respect him so much, and have always been nice to him. On the other hand, Alan Hollinghurst has been very nice. He reviewed *Equal Affections*, which he didn't like, but wrote a very intelligent negative review. That never bothers me. It was a review I learned something from. Then I met him; he's been extremely friendly to me. I think Hollinghurst's a serious person who understands as I do that there's no reason why people can't disagree and still respect each other. I don't mind being criticized at all; I mind being attacked. There's a clear difference.

RC   I think the range of attacks on you is interesting. Felice Picano speaks of you as a neutered writer; on the other hand, *While England Sleeps* saw you accused of being unduly pornographic.

DL   I just ignore this. All this kind of criticism seems irrelevant because it's not coming from anyone serious. To use an Italian expression, it is on a very low level. It's criticism that doesn't derive from serious thought about a work. It's derived from a political position; from a desire to have one's own voice heard. Every writer who's ever lived has to deal with this—particularly in the cesspool of gay politics.

RC   What leads you towards being sexually explicit at a particular point in a novel?

DL   I've always followed the edict of Flannery O'Connor there. Her feeling about writing about sex was: "Do it if it's necessary." There are situations where sex is an important aspect of human experience and becomes relevant. For example, in *While England Sleeps* I was writing about an intense love affair between two young men. Sex is going to be a part of that. I was always trying to use sex as a way of depicting the evolution and eventual falling apart of a relationship. Pornography's much more about the marketplace; about selling sex. There's nothing wrong with that. I like pornography. But I don't consider what I write pornography, because I write about sex as a way of pursuing a literary agenda. Given that the relationship in *While England Sleeps* is deeply sexual, it seemed to me eminently obvious that was the way to do it.

I have sexual obsessions. I'm aware of that. It's something I've criticized both Andrew Holleran and Robert Ferro for in their work. But I have the same thing: my little, extra-literary obsessions that work their way into my work. Mark's always saying: "Goddammit, you have such a fetish about boxer shorts. If I read one more scene with someone in boxer shorts, panting!" He's right, so I'm trying to control that. It just happens. But by and large the instances where I allow an extra-literary concern or obsession to find its way into my work are rare. I'm proud of the fact people have generally really admired my sex scenes. They say they feel real. Gordon Lish once said that the mistake everyone makes in writing about sex lies in thinking the sexy thing is the black silk stocking; what's really sexy is the dirty white sock.

RC   Is sex a subject you find more difficult to write about than any other?

DL   Not for me. I know writers for whom dialogue's a nightmare. Dialogue too is very easy for me. But descriptive writing's the hardest—particularly descriptions of nature and landscape. I don't have that natural knack for it that Forster had. Whenever I describe landscape, I find I always slow down. It becomes a bit labored. Also, descriptions of people's physical appearance often aren't easy. They can be—Eric in "The Term-Paper Artist" was very easy to describe because I imagined him so fully— the thick, stupid lips and so on. In my early work—the stories in the *New Yorker*—my editor would say: "You forgot to say what she looks like."

RC   In terms of characterization, do you feel there's an inappropriate pressure on gay writers to prioritize the sexual; to insist on the centrality of sex, sexuality, and sexual expression to character?

DL   Yes, but once again that's subject matter. Subject matter, I think, ultimately is the least important aspect of literature. I find criticism centered on subject matter often seems to miss the point. Also, I think some of my books have been very focused on sexual identity as a subject: *Lost Language of Cranes* preeminently, and some stories. Others haven't. *The Page Turner*'s a love story in which the protagonists are gay, but I don't see sexual identity as particularly relevant to that novel, with the exception of the scene where the mother meets Kennington.

RC   In the preface to *While England Sleeps*, you wrote of your aim of producing a post-Stonewall account of an earlier period; implicitly, one which can be more overtly interested in questions of sexual identity than books written in the thirties. *The Page Turner* though, one can think of in a contrasting way. I compared it to the Victorian erotic novel *Teleny*; it seemed like a version of that, with the explicit sex taken out. Both works feature the representation of sexuality through music, for instance: there's that obsessive passage in *Teleny* relating to watching a pianist touch his keyboard.

DL   In terms of *The Page Turner*, my own jury's still out. I don't know whether it's a good book. I've very mixed feelings about it. I read it over recently and really enjoyed it. I thought it was a readable, pleasurable book. But I don't think I'll ever think of it as one of my most important. It was a very tormented book to write, but if I compare it to the book I'm writing now, I think that book's a thousand times better. *The Page Turner*'s a small, quiet novel. I think it's quite successful in those terms. But I don't see it as a work of great importance. It was a transitional novel—something I had to do to get on to what I'm writing now. It's called *Martin Baumann*, which is the name of the hero.

RC You've dashed my hopes by not having had *Teleny* in mind when writing *The Page Turner*.

DL Well, I very much could have, subconsciously. I was writing that book all during the period Mark and I were doing *Pages Passed from Hand to Hand*. *Teleny* was very much on our minds. Mark wrote the introduction to it in the book. He was fascinated by the way *Teleny* literalized that old cliché of "musical" meaning "gay." He's just finishing a book on virtuosity, in which there's a long analysis of *Teleny* as an example of the virtuoso as *sexual* virtuoso, one of various ideas about piano virtuoso Mark wants to write about. I find *Teleny* fascinating.

RC You've always displayed a keen interest in unearthing the architecture of past gay lives, *While England Sleeps* being perhaps the most distinct example. With *The Page Turner*, I felt that, in writing about the present, you'd chosen a slightly unusual context—the rarified, conservative, slightly anachronistic world of classical music. There's only music and maybe the world of antiques that still offer this particular, highly aestheticized and still sublimated or indirect homosexuality.

DL Yes. What fascinated me about it was the exploitative edge. This happens in the world of literature too, but much more on the surface; much more blatant. The blatancy's one thing that freaks me out.

You're right; antique hunting is the other world—and interior design, where there's this old-fashioned idea of taking a younger man under your wing. Of course it's not Kennington, finally, but Mansourian who does that in *The Page Turner*. It's this idea of a network; of passing boys back and forth. That I think is very true. What I think makes the novel have more than that is the fact that Paul is so arrogant and idealistic. He's not one of the cynical young men who's perfectly willing to do this. He just finds himself in the situation where, suddenly, instead of what he expected—this romantic idea of a great love—he finds himself propositioned by an older man in exchange for tickets to the Berlin Philharmonic.

RC   I want to ask you about working method. You revealed that you already had the last line of the novel-in-progress established. Could you talk a little about the importance of knowing that to your sense of the book's structure as a whole?

DL   My friend Amy Hempel always begins with the last line. She says it gives her something to work toward. Almost always I begin with the last line too, but not always.

RC   Is it a confidence trick; something that allows you latitude in the middle section while affording some sense of security about the novel as a whole?

DL   Yes. The last line of *The Page Turner* was sort of its beginning, too: "as if a moment could be lived so hard it bruised." Exactly what that moment would be wasn't clear to me. Initially, *The Page Turner* was set at the end of the nineteenth century. It was going to be about a young man on a Grand Tour's painting of the Tuscan sky in this purple color "as if a moment could be lived so hard it bruised." It went through all these incarnations before it finally occurred to me that that was the ending. I desperately wanted the book to have a happy ending, but I realized there wasn't one for Paul and Kennington, so I gave it to two minor characters, Bobby and Teddy, whom I adore.

Likewise with some of my stories I've begun with the last line; "A Place I've Never Been," for example. With the three *Arkansas* novellas I didn't. In fact, the last line of "Saturn Street"—probably my favorite ending among anything I've ever written—came about miraculously: " 'Anywhere's always been my favorite place.' "

The novel I'm writing now is very autobiographical. It clearly had to end with the narrator at a low ebb, realizing he's gone completely in the wrong direction and that he has no choice but to try to start again; probably to leave America. The novel begins in 1980 and ends on New Year's Eve 1990. It's clear that the last line will be: "And then I went off to try to learn how to be serious." The character has just been told by his teacher that his great mistake as a writer has been that he's never been adequately serious. That's why his career, which began at a high ebb, has sort of fallen apart. Mine hasn't, but in the novel it has. I'm not writing about what happened with *While England Sleeps*, but psychologically that's the moment where the book's going to end.

RC   What do you have other than the last line? This book may be differently structured if it's closely autobiographical.

DL   Sometimes I have a very clear arc; others not. It's always different. I usually begin with the donnée; what James called "the air-blown grain": some little nugget of story. With *The Page Turner* it was this idea of a mother, her son, and a man, and the idea that the mother mistakes the man's intentions and thinks they're for her, not her son. It was originally called *Citizen of the World* and set in the English community in Florence around the turn of the century. The Kennington figure was a kind of exile from a British sex scandal. But I never got anywhere with that. I wrote eighty pages that are going to be part of my archive at Yale.

Then there was the second donnée, which came from going to a lot of concerts with Mark and seeing a page turner, a young woman in an Angora sweater with big tits, page-turning for some very heterosexual pianist. Every time she reached over to turn the page, these tits were in his face. I thought: "God, that must be very distracting." She was very sexy and clearly dressed to allure. You don't wear a sweater cut down to here, then lean over, which you have to do . . . I thought: "This is such a potentially erotic situation—a page turner and a pianist."

RC   That's the erotic angle. There's also an analogy in the literary world: the idea of the literary "page turner"—the editor or proof editor of others' work; once again, someone at a very frustrating remove from creativity.

DL   I see the closest literary analogy as the Bread Loaf Writers Conference. It's this horrible, big, money-making conference which takes place every summer in Vermont. Amy Hempel calls it "Club Bread." They've an extremely complex system whereby you go on all these different levels. It's an amazing meritocracy. At the very top are the really famous writers who're treated like gods, like E. L. Doctorow. There are two other levels for writers there to teach. They eat in different dining rooms. For the students who apply, on the lowest level you pay; on the next, you have to work as a waiter. You're still a student, but you don't have to pay. The next level has the full scholarships: they don't have to pay or work as waiters. Can you imagine being an aspiring writer, and working as a waiter, bringing food to E. L. Doctorow? It's horrifying! A lot of these male writers go there because they know they can get laid. Pretty girls who're aspiring writers say: "Oh Mr. Whatever—I admire your work so much." "Why don't you meet me for a drink after?" So this is very similar to *The Page Turner*, except that Kennington's a decent guy. He's not out to exploit Paul.

RC   He's tricked into behavior which suggests a greater cynicism than he has.

DL   He's not cynical. He's still longing for that early love he never had because he got hooked up so early on with a much older man. That was the other thing I wanted to explore. I've always been fascinated by age-divergent relationships. I've never been in one, but I've always had a little bit of a "daddy" complex. I've always had fantasies about one. In me as a young man, there was this great divergence between my sexual fantasies and my romantic ones. My romantic fantasies were always about finding a peer; my sexual fantasies were always about finding a dominating older man. Because I was eighteen, by "older" I meant a thirty-year-old!

RC   Haven't you used a similar disparity in *Equal Affections*? A character talks about the recurring problem of wanting someone to strip off but not respecting him.

DL   I think that disparity's very common. It makes sense to me. The person about whom you have the most intense fantasies isn't necessarily the person with whom you want to spend your life, because in choosing a partner you're choosing somebody you're with all the time. That's very different than sex. Sex is part of it, but I think most people—heterosexuals as well—don't end up marrying the people to whom they're most intensely attracted—almost without exception.

RC   A similar divergence is the source for the many narratives about adultery you've written.

DL   Exactly. I've gone through so many ideas about this whole question in my own life: the fact that it seems so normal in gay relationships to be open and have sex outside the relationship. I've ended up being extremely conservative and monogamous because in my case I don't think a relationship could withstand the pressure of too much extracurricular activity.

RC   I was thinking of "Houses," where Ted tells Paul: "You can't love two people." Paul tells himself: "It's possible in the heart but not in the world." That's a comment born of ethical concerns. Do you think of yourself as a writer who is interested in ethics?

DL   I certainly believe I am. The thing I'm struck by is that without exception, almost all the male writers I know are just such out-of-control whores—gay and straight! The straight ones I know get away from their wives and just instantly want to get laid. With the gay writers, it's much more overt. I do think there's this obsessive-compulsive element to most gay men's pursuit of sex. Edmund has written brilliantly about how the great preoccupation in the seventies was the feeling that everyone else was getting more sex.

RC   There's a searing honesty to his writing on sex, which falls short of disavowal. Nevertheless in reading it, you can only see things going horrifically wrong.

DL   I think that's a very smart strategy on his part.

RC   The reader is left to do the work of judgment.

DL   Yes. It also allows him to write about it with immense humor, which is what makes *The Farewell Symphony*, for all its flaws, immensely readable. The flaws, I think, have to do with the moments it ceases being a novel and becomes a not-very-interesting autobiography. He should have left some stuff out.

But sex is ultimately so much about obsession. Obsession's what makes sex interesting. It's also what makes life fatiguing. As my therapist once put it, at a certain point—when you can give up your fantasies and give up being obsessive about sex—suddenly there's so much more time for other things. Also, life's suddenly so much more peaceful.

RC   Heterosexuals are conditioned to accept this state by their mid-twenties.

DL   Yes . . . though most male writers I know are just shameless. They
get away from their wives for three seconds and they're looking for
nookie. I was just at the Harbourfront Conference in Toronto with Colm
Tóibín, who's openly gay, but it's only one of many issues for him. We
were probably the two most virginal people at that entire conference. It
was so funny: here were these two gay men not doing anything. All the
straight guys there were desperately looking for sex.

RC   A leap now: when do you write best?

DL   It always changes. I never write longhand. I always write on computer, which I find an immensely helpful tool. It means I can experiment;
I can play around. I can look at sentences five different ways and decide
which is best. I think it's essential, though, to read material over in hard
copy, because it looks totally different on the page than on the screen. I
can't explain why, but a sentence that looks good on the screen can read
horribly on paper. I've talked to other writers about this and they all
agree.

RC   Can't the neatness of the printout also pose a danger—it looks
great; why change it?

DL   No, because I mark it up. It doesn't look professional once you start
going through it. You see how bad certain sentences are.

RC   How many drafts do you go through typically?

DL   Thousands. There's a constant process of printing out, reading
over, marking up, then going back to the computer. I generate huge
amounts of paper. I have to print out all the time. I'm also constantly
saving older versions of things, so I'll have all these files: "MB" is for
Martin Baumann, so: "MB 1"; "MB 1—old version"; "MB 1—older version." I want to save them in case I want to go back to something. I

always have a file called "Bits and Pieces." That's where I put things I cut out that I might want to use later, though I almost never do.

I've never written in longhand. I think and type faster than I write, so it's much more sensible.

RC   When do you work?

DL   These days, in the mornings. Other times, in the afternoons, but never at night. I don't write well at night. I'm an "early to bed, early to rise" person. Mark and I are usually in bed by ten and up by seven. I need a lot of sleep. I like to sleep nine or ten hours' sleep per night if I can. Now we're in the country, there's not really anything to do at night, so we read, play with the dog, talk. I think once I'm settled in the country, I want to be on a schedule where I write early in the morning; where I get going at eight and work until noon, maybe. I don't assign myself a schedule because I know there are going to be days when I write more and days when I write less.

RC   Your new rural setting makes me think of the preface to *Pages Passed from Hand to Hand*. There's a slightly nervous concession in it to the importance of the urban among gay men. At the same time, there's the peculiar recognition that you've recently moved from the city to the country. There's a sense of personal reclamation suggested in that.

DL   Very much so. We became obsessed with the "greenwood." It's such a recurrent theme in gay literature before 1914; in fact it's *the* theme.

RC   The pastoral context was the only one in which gay desires could be played out, historically.

DL   Yes. It was very much after 1914 that you start to see this reversal; where the city is the place where the young gay man finds freedom. The ultimate example of that, I think, is *The Seraglio* by James Merrill—and, of course, Willa Cather. Forster's comment in the "Terminal Note" to *Maurice* was that he felt he was writing about an age in which it was still possible to disappear. But he felt at the time of writing the note it no longer was. I don't think it's possible to disappear, but I'm a great believer myself in the advantages of rural life. I've lived in cities, but I've never really felt like an urban person; that it was my context. It's curious. There's a real phenomenon of writers who can afford it moving out of the city now: Allan Gurganus; Jeanette Winterson, who's off in the boondocks somewhere. Now she says she's just bought a house in London. But having a house in London and a house in the country does-n't make sense to me. I don't want to go back and forth at this point. I don't want a split life. I like visiting cities, but what makes the visits possible is the knowledge that I still have my house awaiting me.

RC   To return to the idea of the donnée or inspiration for your work: you write stories, novellas, and novels. Is it easy to see whether you're being given one as opposed to another?

DL   Usually. The only exception was "The Wooden Anniversary." It began a novel and became a novella. The donnée there was the cooking school, and the battle over the Italian between Nathan and Celia.

RC   So the scale of a work's invariably clear to you?

DL   Yes. I knew *Martin Baumann* was going to be a very long novel.

RC   Are you moving consistently towards greater length?

DL   Not necessarily. I've written another short story, which hasn't been published yet. I intend to write more stories. I have ideas for them, and a contract to write another book of them. Whether my novels will grow longer, I don't know. For me the more relevant question's that of mov-ing toward my own life as a source for the fiction. I wrote *While Eng-*

land Sleeps because I felt I'd exhausted my own experience as a place to go in looking for stories. I've written so much that derives obliquely from my own experience that I wanted to go into something completely unrelated. But *While England Sleeps*, curiously enough, ended up from a psychological standpoint being very autobiographical. At that point all my best writer friends were feeling the same thing: the need to get away from their own experience. Now I feel quite the opposite; I feel the need to delve back into it. Aspects of my life that I never thought worthy of writing about I suddenly see as eminently worthy. I used to have a great fear of the literary novel, for instance—the book set in the world of writers. There was a great prejudice against it that Cynthia Ozick articulated in a story called "Levitation." The couple in it talk about the "forbidden thing," which is to write about writers—more specifically, to write about writers in New York, which she calls the "forbidden city." It suddenly occurred to me that, just as sex seemed valid a subject for fiction, why not write about the literary world, so long as you write about it somewhat from a point of view away from it. Anything that's too much "insider" alienates readers. You have to assume the position of someone exploring the world as if he weren't part of it.

RC   That must be the invented or fantastic part.

DL   It's a very fantastical novel. It's also historical. It's set specifically in the New York literary world of the early eighties, which is history to me. It describes the literary "brat pack," so called, in very fantastical terms. I'm going to have these two opposing gay "mentor" writers, who couldn't be more different, fighting for the soul of the writer. The writer is trying to decide between, on the one hand, the "good man"; on the other, the "good artist."

RC   It's a pull between the politician and the aesthete, then.

DL   Exactly. One mentor is a literary man; the other is not an aesthete or a great writer.

RC   There's a paradox to this: in this interview, you have positioned yourself clearly within the aesthetic camp; for the novel you presumably have to see the virtues of the other camp.

DL   Absolutely.

RC   Thanks very much for your time.

TWELVE
PATRICK GALE

The prolific British novelist Patrick Gale is known for a large number of commercially successful and critically praised novels, many of which feature a mixed group of characters in terms of gender, sexuality, and age. Armistead Maupin has long been a vocal admirer and supporter of Gale's works. Born in 1962 on the Isle of Wight, Gale went to Winchester College and Oxford University, after which he moved to London and immediately began a fiction-writing career.

Gale's first two novels were *The Aerodynamics of Pork* (London: Abacus, 1986) and *Ease* (London: Abacus, 1986), published simultaneously. *Kansas in August* (London: Century, 1987), *Facing the Tank* (London: Hutchinson, 1988), *Little Bits of Baby* (London: Chatto and Windus, 1989), and *The Cat Sanctuary* (London: Chatto and Windus, 1990)—which featured only women characters—all followed. In several works, Gale has stuck to the fictional milieu of "Barrowcester," a provincial English town based on his experience of Winchester.

The novella "Caesar's Wife" appeared in the coauthored volume *Secret Lives: Three Novellas* (with Tom Wakefield and Francis King; London: Constable, 1991). In 1995, Gale's most ambitious novel, the epic *The Facts of Life* (London: Flamingo, 1995), was published. This featured the lives of three generations of characters from a single family and sought to draw analogies between the experience of tuberculosis sufferers early in the century and gay men with AIDS in the 1980s.

Next came the collection *Dangerous Pleasures: A Decade of Stories* (London: Flamingo, 1996) and, most recently, the novel *Tree Surgery for Beginners* (London: Flamingo, 1998), loosely inspired by Shakespeare's *Winter's Tale*. Gale completed an unfinished novel by his friend Tom Wakefield, *The Scarlet Boy* (London: Serpent's Tail, 1998) with an "Afterword" by Gale. He has recently published a short biography of *Armistead Maupin* (London: Overlook Press, 1999) as well as another novel, *Rough Music* (London: Flamingo, 2000). He lives on a farm in Cornwall, though this interview took place on Tuesday, August 18, 1998, in Holland Park, London.

RC   In *The Cat Sanctuary* there's an account of the novelist Judith's creative process. How does your experience compare?

PG   Judith has a pretty idealized view of the writer's life. We have in common the setting though, and Judith plays around with real events and people, often unconsciously—something I certainly do. The trick she plays of changing genders—which you first see in the story "Dressing Up in Voices," then again in *The Cat Sanctuary*—is something I've always done. I'm nervous if I'm consciously putting a real person in, so I change the gender, partly to protect a person's identity. Also, suddenly it can throw an interesting light on a situation. [*Laughs*] It means you end up with an awful lot of butch women and fey men though.

RC   Judith's unable to stop one character going a particular way. Are your own plots subject to a similar loss of authorial control?

PG   I always start a novel with a tiny idea. With *Kansas in August* I had this image of a young man finding an abandoned baby. With *The Cat Sanctuary* the idea was the husband being blown up. It was nothing to do with the "all-female book" then, though I knew I wanted to write one. I play around with one idea for ages. Then I try to plot out a book's entire arc. That usually starts in my head. I do an awful lot of work while walking the dog. I go for long walks and find it quite liberating to have no pen or paper in sight.

RC   Is it important not to write things down?

PG   Yes. It keeps it fresh and fluid. I feel if an idea works, I'll remember it. If it doesn't, it wasn't worth remembering. I don't get paranoid about things slipping through the net. Then I try to get a narrative arc down on the page in quite a lot of detail—even chapter by chapter. Especially with a complex plot I find that helps. But I never stick to it. Always, two-thirds of the way in, the characters snowball. They acquire characteristics, an inner logic. Funnily enough, I don't panic. That's the moment I know the book's starting to work: when it takes on a life of its own and rebels against the plot I'm setting for it.

   I'm currently having a terrible time with the work-in-progress, *Rough Music*. It's a double story, rather like *The Facts of Life*. Rather than telling first one story, then the other, I'm trying to tell the two simultaneously. It's a bit like an old J. B. Priestley time play, swinging between the present and the 1960s. The same group of characters does similar things in the two periods. I'm starting to worry I've made it too complex for me to relax enough to let it take on its own life.

RC   What is "rough music"?

PG   It's peasant folklore. Most people know it best from *The Mayor of Casterbridge*. The locals turn up with puppets and make a lot of noise outside the window. Rough music exists in some form in every culture. It's a way a community can express disapproval—usually for a sexual misdemeanour; something which isn't governed by law but personal morality. If, for instance, a wealthy older man married a woman the community deemed far too young, they could turn the rough music on. They'd bang pots and pans outside his window.

There are all sorts of terms for it. I particularly like *Rough Music* because within my plot it has multiple meanings. The heroine in the 1960s is introduced to soul music by her brother-in-law—the lover she commits adultery with. The music's part of his seduction of her. She has a very pure musical mind and hasn't been exposed to that stuff. When suddenly he plays her Aretha Franklin, it's very rough and mind-blowing. Also, in the modern section, there's a character from *The Aerodynamics of Pork*, Roly. He's now making sound sculptures out of bits of old driftwood and stone. They make a noise when the wind touches them.

RC Beyond not writing things down at an early stage, isn't it important not to talk about work-in-progress? You're talking about *Rough Music*.

PG I don't talk until I'm very secure in what a book's going to be. Then it becomes my nemesis. I can't escape it; nothing's going to stop it; no amount of talking makes it go away. Actually the talking can help. Sometimes in talking it through I suddenly realize what the book's really going to be about. It might begin being about one thing and become something quite other.

RC Do you abandon projects?

PG Yes, but never fiction. The novels have all come to fruition sooner or later—though sometimes not in the form I thought. There's an original film project I'm working on now which I was going to write as a novel.

RC In 1991, when *Secret Lives* came out with "Caesar's Wife" in it, your biography mentioned two screenplays.

PG   Yes. All these screenplays are kicking around. If they don't appear, it's usually because the production companies that commissioned them ran out of money or met a dead end. Some just take a very long time. *Little Bits of Baby* I adapted as a miniseries for the BBC. It's one of their many dead scripts, sitting in a file somewhere. I find that enormously frustrating, though I imagine if I wait long enough, the rights will revert to me. I still think it's viable. *Kansas in August*, optioned three times, is now finally happening. It was meant to go into production this month. Now it'll be summer 1999, I hope. It's funded with lottery money, having begun as a BBC project, then a Really Useful Group project. There've been three different scripts—originally by me, now coscripted.

RC   What about the gay television sitcom?

PG   That's very sad. It was going to be by me, Kevin Elyot, and a straight writer. Funnily enough, it was the straight writer's idea. We wanted to write a sitcom that was entirely gay, though not all the characters were gay. My idea was that all the straight characters, sooner or later, would be proved to have had some kind of gay experience or temptation. It was a fantasy sitcom, to that extent. Every bit part, like a policeman in the first episode, would turn out, by coincidence, to be somebody's lover. So there was no such thing as a bit part. From the actors' point of view, it would've been a lot of fun. Once the viewers realized this was the format, they'd have great fun waiting to see when somebody was going to turn up in the central position.

You just have to let the thing go. Legally we've no control; it belongs to the BBC. Channel Four have their own Manchester-based gay series coming along, *Queer as Folk*. Cynically, I imagine if the Channel Four one was a huge success, the BBC might suddenly remember they have a perfectly good gay series in their files and will dust it down again. The sad thing is I don't think I'd necessarily want to write it now. I feel so sour about the whole thing.

RC   You always bring your novels to fruition, yet several collaborative projects haven't seen the light of day. Why persist?

PG   Crude economics. When I write a novel, I know it'll be published in two years. With the film projects, I've no idea. The difference is, the advance I get for a novel is a fraction of the money I'll make from a film—even one that never gets made. In an ideal world, I'd like to alternate: do a novel one year; a film script the next.

Writing novels is very lonely. You're entirely self-reliant. I find it enormously exciting to get out there and start collaborating. The *Kansas in August* script has been so much fun. Working with a cowriter on the final version helped enormously. Ian Sellar and I enjoyed working together so much we're now both working on an original idea of mine. I'm learning a lot from Ian about filmmaking. He's also a director; he made *Venus Peter*. I'm also learning from Angela Pope, who made *Hollow Reed* and is now the director of our project. It's terribly good for me to learn because I'm a lazy writer.

There's a syndrome you can get in movies where big money is involved, however. They end up written by committee. You start with a wonderful original project, written by two writers at most. Then the financiers and producers have ideas. Everybody gets his oar in. You end up with a project so far removed from the original it doesn't really hang together. It's amazing how often when you see a film you can see somewhere in there the ghost of the original script. Then you see these layers of other people's ideas stuck on. Part of the problem's economics. There's so much money hanging on a film now people can't bear to leave it alone. The great era of movie-making was when films could be made very cheaply. They were all made in-house with a repertory company, including writers who slaved away producing scripts that weren't fiddled round with. They were more like playscripts—and it showed in the finished project.

RC   So, considering the money, does the potential frustration at seeing a film project remain unrealized not matter?

PG With *Kansas in August* I've reached the point where I'm almost prepared to wash my hands. It's gone through so many drafts it's a long
way from my original idea. I feel a grudging affection, but it's become a
Frankenstein's monster now; not really my baby. I never thought I'd
reach this point, but now I could say: "Do it on ice! Do it with rock
music! Just do it and pay for my new kitchen!"

RC Some novelists are conscious of working in a less prominent
medium compared to film.

PG People are pointlessly gloomy about that. They keep saying the novel's
dead. It clearly isn't. It's thriving. What you have to accept is that it reaches
a small audience compared to television. That's one thing I'm learning,
working for television and film. It puts my other work in perspective and
reminds me that most people haven't heard of me and never will, which is
salutary. I've a very Protestant streak in that way. I feel it's good to be taken
down several pegs regularly; to go into meetings with film financiers, to
whom the idea of me being a novelist cuts no mustard at all.

RC The Protestant streak seems manifest in your productivity.

PG I churn them out! I still feel guilty about being only a novelist, not a
priest or doctor; something useful.

RC Why "priest"?

PG I had a very religious upbringing. My parents clearly hoped I'd be a
priest. They sent me to a Church of England choir school. I appeared
fairly pious as a child and have a love affair with High Anglican church
culture which I'll never really get out of my system. I love the architecture, the music, the King James Bible. I have a major problem with religion, that's the trouble—though it's a minor stumbling block, judging
by some priests I know.

There's a priestly tradition in the family. My grandfather and great-grandfather on my father's side were both priests. With my father, I think it's highly likely he'd have been one, had he not married and been diverted. He became a prison governor—a kind of priest. You're looking after lost souls on a daily basis. There was a terrific sense of duty they instilled in us all. My brother's a doctor and my sister an epidemiologist. They're both involved in changing or saving lives.

It took me a long time to gain any self-respect as a writer; to think it could be worthwhile. So it matters enormously when I get letters. For some reason—I think because of the things I write about—I get a lot of letters. At the risk of sounding like Patience Strong [popular British author of sentimental verse], it's awfully nice to have people write to you, saying "your book changed my life," or "it cheered me up when my lover had died." Then I can see writing does matter; it does reach out to people.

RC   Did you imagine doing anything else? I read about you descending on Notting Hill from university and apparently just starting writing.

PG   I was incredibly lucky. I got a bedsit in this house in Notting Hill run by a mad old French woman. When she discovered I wanted to be a writer, she refused to cash my rent checks. She put them in a drawer, saying: "I'll cash them when you get your first advance." Of course when I did, it disappeared into this black hole of unpaid rent. But that was wonderful. And I was incredibly lucky getting published so quickly. My first and second novels were published the same day. It caused a ripple and got them widely reviewed. By the time I'd finished *Ease*, I'd found a publisher for the first, *The Aerodynamics of Pork*, who wanted the second as well. Just as the deal was going through, they—Abacus—were bought by Penguin, who wanted to clear the decks of old projects. It worked very well. *Ease* went into hardback and was published as if it were my first; *The Aerodynamics of Pork* appeared alongside it in paperback.

Ease was actually written a year after *The Aerodynamics of Pork*. Looking back, I regard both, and *Kansas in August*, as juvenile scribbles. I've an affection for them, but they're very underwritten and under-edited. They'd probably be twice the length if I wrote them today. I think of *Facing the Tank* as my first mature work. I hesitate to say "mature" as I was only twenty-four when I wrote it, but it's the first novel I don't feel embarrassed by. The other three I'd dearly love to rewrite. They wouldn't change greatly, but I'd take more time over them. They feel so thin, as if I'm skating over the surface of the characters. I find it hard to see how I could've written the characters so thinly, compared to the way I write now.

RC   Were you rushing?

PG   No. It's youth. Those books have a youthful vigor to them I can't imagine getting back now. The other joke is that those three books were written on an electronic typewriter—one of those dinosaurs that came and went in the early eighties. It wasn't quite a word processor. It had a finite memory you couldn't expand. Basically, when the memory came to an end and was full, I'd think: "That"s the end of the chapter." So they had terribly short chapters. From *Facing the Tank* onwards, I got into the habit of writing my first drafts in longhand. As a result, the books became much longer and fuller.

RC   Your midperiod works *Facing the Tank* and *Little Bits of Baby* still feel pithy and concise, as if you've relaxed your prose style subsequently.

PG   Yes. In some ways I miss that concision and want it back. I got terribly baggy with *The Facts of Life*. Part of it was the way I planned my books then. Each chapter was like a short story, with beginning, middle, and end. Sometimes I think I should go back to that. I've taken to writing books more like films. They're far more fluid. But I do enjoy a novel where you think: "I"ll read one more chapter before bedtime," and it's very satisfying because it packs the punch of a short story.

RC   Who does this?

PG   Barbara Trapido. She and Carol Shields are wonderfully deft writers. They have humane understanding in their books, yet they hide their technique. They make it look the easiest, lightest thing in the world. Yet each chapter's carefully structured and packs an emotional punch. The cumulative effect is enormously satisfying. Barbara Trapido in some ways is like a female Armistead Maupin. She enjoys weaving together characters who didn't think they were going to meet. Also, the latest Alison Lurie I enjoyed enormously—*The Last Resort*. Again it plays that game.

RC   Alison Lurie has some stylistic affinity with you.

PG   I was reading her a lot when I began writing, along with early Iris Murdoch, who I absolutely love: *A Severed Head* or *The Bell*.

RC   *The Bell* in particular might be an example of the High Anglican tradition you describe emerging in English fiction.

PG   That tradition comes out in many ways. One important one is morality. I think my books are very moral. They play wicked games with immorality and amorality, but they're actually quite old-fashioned, in terms of judgments passed on characters and punishment meted out. Take the hero of the modern section of *The Facts of Life*, Jamie. Obviously, AIDS isn't a punishment, but there's an element in which Jamie is made to suffer, one way or another, for being so superficial when the book begins. There's a process by which we see his character deepening in the course of his illness.

The Anglican tradition also comes out in my interest in the idea of "community." I'm fascinated by closed, monastic communities and whatever the female version is: "convent communities." I've got these two imagined religious communities on little islands which I refer to occasionally in the novels. Also, in *The Cat Sanctuary*, I posit this all-female world.

I was educated at Winchester——a very strange experience; quite unreal. I was living in these ancient buildings of unparalleled beauty, surrounded by gardens, water meadows, rolling green hills, lovely trees, and beautiful music. Winchester is in large part my model for the imagined cathedral city of Barrowcester. I have a love-hate relationship with it. My parents still live there, so I go back regularly. It's so beautiful; so comfortable. It offers you the luxury of thinking you can just sit back and spend your days reading or in quiet study.

Winchester's also something I've fought against. I was very tempted by the academic life. I was offered a place to do research at Oxford, which I found so appealing. I think part of me's very frightened by the outside world; dealing with people. I'm very shy. I find it very hard going to parties. I'd like to withdraw from the world. I suppose I ended up doing that by moving to Cornwall, where I have a very simple life most of the time.

RC   Many of your characters retire, one way or another.

PG   They do withdraw from the world. Maybe one day I'll end up doing it myself. I'll just stop writing and become a farmer.

RC   Iris Murdoch's novels have this very mixed tapestry of gay and straight characters, worldly and unworldly, moral and immoral. In that sense they're rather like Angus Wilson's.

PG   Yes, but Iris Murdoch's far more comforting. She's a more generous writer than Angus Wilson. I enjoyed his books a lot, but there's something profoundly uncomfortable about them. Like her, though, he's very moral. Anglicanism does come out in that way. Unlike her, he doesn't offer playful solutions. What I find intoxicating in her fiction, especially her early to middle period, is this sense of the novel as a game. She's playing with these characters. Though they're real, in another sense they're not. She puts a philosophical distance on the whole thing I find intoxicating.

RC   Would you like to be compared to her?

PG   I'd be enormously flattered if somebody said I was writing in that tradition. But I think I'm probably not. I lack her detachment. I fall in love with my characters too much. I think I'm in danger sometimes of overweighting the argument in favor of the gay characters. I try to give my gay characters—therefore my gay readers—quite a hard time. I force them to spend time with straight people, for instance. One of Armistead Maupin's great achievements was to make a whole generation of gay readers fall in love with this single straight man, Brian, and understand the similarities in what he goes through, compared to a gay man. That's something I'd like to do. I find straight male characters very hard, yet I persist in trying to write them.

RC   The breadth of experience you cover is another link to writers like Iris Murdoch. Few gay novelists write about the experience of pregnancy.

PG   That's something I find quite bewildering in the way books are received: the assumption that you can only write about things you know. People keep saying: "It's so surprising to find a gay man who likes writing about women." I think: "What kind of novelist would I be if I couldn't write about people other than myself?" After all, it's nothing new. The great nineteenth-century male novelists all wrote enormously memorable female characters. The women wrote some incredible male ones. Half the fun of the form is losing yourself in these other personalities. I'm very aware that my social breadth isn't particularly wide, though. Occasionally I try to broaden it.

RC Do you mean in terms of class?

PG Yes. Class is so unavoidable in the British novel. Ultimately it comes down to mechanics. If you have characters from very different social backgrounds, it can set you plot problems. They're unlikely to be inter-acting in the way you want them to. To that extent, I don't mind being like Iris Murdoch—quite rarefied. It sets you free to write about what you want—for me, relationships. I'm not very interested in writing about politics or class. Others do it better.

RC Where do manners fit in?

PG Manners, ultimately, are to do with communication, with how much you reveal of your appetites, how much you recognize the misbehavior of others—or choose not to recognize it. To that extent it's the stuff of my novels. It sounds awfully puffbally though. "Comedy of manners" always sounds desperately light. I'd almost rather have "sex comedy" than "comedy of manners." The problem is, it has overtones of "man-nered"—the kiss of death for a novel.

But I think manners in the old-fashioned sense are fascinating. In some ways for me they have a moral implication as well, in terms of the revelation of character. My father has what I consider absolutely perfect manners. He treats everybody the same, regardless of who they are or where they come from. He's at pains to make everybody feel comfort-able. That for me is inseparable from the ethics by which he lives his life. It's very easy to think of manners as being about how you hold your knife and fork. But I think ultimately they're to do with how you treat each other. Manners in the truest sense are what make us civilized and what hold a community together.

RC You spoke of forcing your gay characters to live among heterosexu-als. That suggests contrivance or artifice in your fictional worlds. You're not interested in writing mimetic works about, say, current realities for gay men. You wouldn't write a novel set in the urban gay ghetto.

PG   No. Or if I did, it'd only be precisely for its artificial qualities, perhaps: rather like in *The Cat Sanctuary*, it's a closed community. To that extent my books are highly artificial. I'm constantly aware I'm playing a game. I perceive the plot as a kind of arena into which my characters— and readers—are forced to enter, and in which they enact various conflicts. I don't for one moment think of them as "slice of life" novels, which I don't see the point of. We've got the news for that. I want people to be able to escape, but not necessarily without being made to confront things. Sometimes you escape in order to look at your life with a cooler eye and be returned to it transformed. In an ideal way that's what a book should do.

RC   One consequence, though, might be that you're compelled to avoid ascribing obvious motives to certain characters. You've invented a series of gay protagonists, for instance, who'd never dream of moving to the city—a move which we know in reality is quite common.

PG   We know it's common, but, at the same time, the moment I left London, I realized there was an enormous gay world out there that has nothing to do with the commercial scene. There are farmers, postmistresses, and teachers all across the country who haven't set foot in a gay pub in their lives—and don't see why they should. When it comes down to motivation, I think that circles back to what I was saying earlier about having a fixed plot in place, then, part-way through, finding the book rebels against the system I've set for it. There comes a point where motivation is character. The character that's built up by chapter ten will steer someone in a certain direction.

RC   Armistead Maupin insists that the pluralist, half-gay, half-straight world of Barbary Lane is absolutely true to life. You're saying something rather different about the construction of your fictional worlds.

PG I think we probably approach things from different directions, but you end up with the same effect. He'd say he takes a reflection of the real world. I'd say my world starts out utterly artificial. The irony is that by filleting out all the stuff that doesn't interest me—what some might call realistic motivation—I often end up with a psychological or emotional truth which people recognize as a reflection of their own reality. So where I think I'm telling a fantasy, for some people it'll be exactly what they've been going through.

RC I wanted to ask about the peculiar hairpin bends of plot and the cool precision of sentences in your middle-period fiction. Was Ivy Compton-Burnett an influence?

PG Ivy Compton-Burnett I love. She's definitely an enormous influence on my earlier novels, particularly in terms of dialogue, and having passages which are nothing but dialogue; where you have to infer what's going on. Compton-Burnett is one of the great writers of dialogue.

RC Her dialogue's artificial.

PG Yes—artificial as Molière. Hers is almost like an eighteenth-century, powder-puff world. Yet what her people say is incredibly shocking sometimes. I think she's one of the great figures of sexual experimentation in English literature. In some ways, she's the first great gay novelist. Because her work is so odd, people didn't notice, I think. One novel begins with two men, one sitting in the other's lap while they're talking. You don't realize at first. I was devouring her work at the same time as early Iris Murdoch. I'm sure they both fed in as influences. I even quote from Ivy Compton-Burnett at the beginning of *The Aerodynamics of Pork*.

RC Sometimes people say she kept writing the same book.

PG I don't see what's wrong with that. People are silly about this. There are so few plots to go around. If you find a subject that interests you, you should carry on writing it. You could say her plots are all the same; then, you could say every family's the same. Even as you say it, you know it's not strictly true. The structure may be the same: a father, a mother, so many children; problems with money. But it could be interpreted many different ways.

One reason Compton-Burnett's work is so fascinating is that she's almost like a composer who decides she's only going to write string quartets. It's like a problem she's going to work and work at until she's turned the thumbscrews so tight that the problem cracks. She takes the family and goes and goes at it, goading it into weird twists and deformities until the family will never look the same again. If you read all her books in succession, you'd have a very strange view of things.

I think this assumption that we must all come up with each book very different from the one before is fed by the publishing industry. It wants its novelists to get bigger and better all the time. For me it's nonsense. If you find a writer you like, you like them because of who they are and what they write. If they keep changing from book to book, it gets enormously frustrating. You want more of the same. At least I assume people do. I think there are enough writers out there for us all to be doing very different things. If we repeat ourselves, it really doesn't matter. We won't entirely be repeating ourselves. Iris Murdoch repeated herself, but each book's slightly different.

RC One way you repeat yourself is in recycling characters.

PG Yes. I hate waste. If you've created a fictional world, it seems an unnecessary labor to create another, parallel world. Why not build on the world you've already got? I think it's rather fun for readers suddenly to recognize that somebody passing through this novel is somebody they've spent a lot of time with in a previous novel. It can evoke nostalgia in them, because they miss that character or want more of him or her, but this time 'round it's only a fleeting, bit part.

RC   *Tree Surgery for Beginners* has roots in Barrowcester, the community you use so often. It is, though, relatively footloose.

PG   Yes. That's partly to do with the form. *Tree Surgery for Beginners* is very self-consciously a fairy tale for grown-ups. Writing in that romantic tradition, I felt the hero had to go on a voyage, an adventure. Although in part I'd taken as my model the madder, late Shakespearean comedies, where the character ended up going to Bohemia or some mythical version of it, I chose America—our late twentieth-century dream factory. America's where all the legends come from nowadays, so it seemed a fitting place to send Lawrence. But it's not America; it's an entirely mythical version.

Keeping to the same town settings is a kind of shorthand. Barrowcester, for better or worse, has become a kind of all-purpose middle-class English community in which anything can happen. I think it's because I want to cut to the chase. I'm impatient with having to make up a wholly new place; I want to get on with the characters' emotional lives. *Rough Music* is again set partly in Barrowcester, though the world I'm describing is very different to the town we've seen before. It's Barrowcester prison. It's about prison life and is based on my strange childhood memories of growing up in Wandsworth Prison where my father was governor. That was my first closed community, I suppose.

RC   Hardy is perhaps the most celebrated of novelists to have created a fictionalized "map" of England.

PG   Yes. His Wessex is real, but not real. Similar is Simon Raven, whose extraordinary *Alms for Oblivion* sequence I've just discovered. Raven brings back characters repeatedly. You can watch someone who begins as someone's rather mousy wife rise to a position of monstrous importance and power. He does it so deftly. In some ways his is a far better record of early twentieth-century history than Anthony Powell's *A Dance to the Music of Time*, which is remarkably flat by comparison. Quite apart from Raven writing like an angel and Powell writing in a rather dry style, Raven's understanding of history and psychological motivation is so acute. If somebody is due for a revival, it's him. *Alms for Oblivion* covers much the same period of history as Powell but isn't hung up on trying to be an English Proust. It has a much more vigorous, Anglo-Saxon approach.

RC   Regardless of their own merits, Proust and James are ambiguous models for writers. Your books are full of people struggling with Proust.

PG   Proust was an early love of mine, as was James. They're both writers I reread religiously at regular intervals. Every time I reread them now, I'm faintly appalled at what they expected of their readers, and how much they did themselves down. Both Proust and James are terribly funny, but it's as if they couldn't bear to be thought of as only comic. So they reached for this monstrously prolix prose style that, however elegant, ultimately serves to mask the real business of the novels, which is arch, high camp basically. Time and again in James you think: "Get on with it; it's so funny when you do." But they're very bad influences in some ways. James's fiction can be a wonderful influence. Someone who took *The Spoils of Poynton* or *Turn of the Screw* as a model would be doing very well. *The Golden Bowl* or *The Ambassadors*, however, have that high seriousness creeping in, which rapidly turns into pomposity.

I think America suffers in a related way from teaching creative writing in this very homogenized way. It's like a writing factory, churning out these young writers who all write the same way. Gradually, they find their own voices—but so late. Some never find them at all; they give up or disappear. One great advantage in this country is that—the University of East Anglia aside—we tend not to teach writing as a discipline.

It's something you pick up by reading; by being immersed in lots of different voices.

RC   Is reading the only way to become a writer?

PG   I think you can't separate the two. When people say, "How do I become a writer?," I say: "Write." You just have to get up and do it and do it, but never lose touch with this amazing pool of writers around you. I know ultimately that was my way of learning: imitation, basically.

RC   What do you read when writing?

PG   I'm very nervous about other voices and plots slipping in, so when I'm on a real roll with a novel—as opposed to being in the early, chugging stages—I tend to stop reading fiction. Often I'll read related works of nonfiction. When working on *Tree Surgery for Beginners*, I read a lot of books about trees. I'm fascinated by botany and wild flowers. I also read a lot of books about the Caribbean and holistic medicine. With *The Facts of Life* I was immersed in nonfiction about the war and AIDS respite care. With the current book, which is really about my parents' marriage, I'm not sure what I'll read for research. Probably their photograph albums!

RC   Do you write first thing?

PG   Yes. The morning's definitely a writing time.

RC   You have several characters who write in bed.

PG   I wish! I used to do that until I got a dog. Now I have to get up to walk the dog. Morning's the time my brain's most awake, so I tend to get up fairly early. I try to write all morning. The afternoon's for lazier things—reading and gardening.

RC   Does your brain get too tired to go on?

PG   Yes. Some days I can tell very quickly it's not going to be a productive day. I've learned the best thing to do is something completely different; something that gives you a sense of achievement so the Protestant guilt doesn't kick in. Now I have the perfect way. My lover's a farmer in Cornwall. If I'm having a bad day, he'll give me a tractor or combine harvester to drive. I can harvest five fields of barley and end up completely exhausted. I really feel I've achieved something. I haven't done any more to the book, but I don't feel guilty. I used to find it very hard to find other things to do that didn't just leave me feeling I was frittering my day away.

RC   So you wouldn't return to the novel later on?

PG   I will if I'm ready to. But you can't force it. I can always write something. I find it very easy to write things. That's half the trouble. But if my heart isn't in it, I'll just produce a load of crap and throw it away the next day, so there's no point.

RC   Do you revise as you write a first draft?

PG   One advantage of writing in longhand rather than on the computer is that it's very easy to polish as you go to some extent. You can see your crossings out; you can reinstate passages you've cut. I try to do as little of that as I can in the first draft. I just get a version down on paper so I can stand back and see the weak points. Also, there's a kind of superstition to it. There's a relief if you can get a version down on paper. You can see the skeleton of the book, then go back and put some meat on the bones.

RC   After getting rid of the electronic typewriter, did you keep to writing in longhand?

PG   Absolutely. In the mid-eighties I got a word processor like every-body else. I very quickly learned to mistrust it. It produces a superfi-cially polished version, which looks so finished on the screen, whereas if you look at a big fat notebook full of crossings out, it stops you relaxing too much and thinking: "It's done now." It keeps the book alive for me—though it's also terrifying, because you have this physical thing you carry around which you can lose very easily. I keep it with me at all times.

RC   Have you ever lost one?

PG   No, thank God. I've lost things on the computer though—whole chapters. I do the whole first version in longhand. The second draft takes the form of me typing it into the computer, and in the process, pol-ishing and changing it. There'll usually be a third draft, and probably a fourth.

RC   For those, do you print a version out from the computer?

PG   Yes. I don't look at it for a couple of months. Then I reread it. Also, I involve my agent and editor very closely. I use their feedback. If I'm really nervous, my agent will occasionally get all the women in the agency to read it. He knows I value the input of women. He invites me in; we all sit down with a bottle of wine. Then they tell me what they think. It's quite terrifying.

RC   It sounds unusual.

PG   I think a lot of writers fib by pretending they do it all themselves. I think most writers need and use a sounding board somewhere in their life—a partner, an editor, whatever. I've nearly always had women edi-tors, though I briefly had a gay man editing me. I'm much happier with a woman editing me. I need that different gender viewpoint.

RC   It sounds rare to have such strong relations with both editor and agent, and to use these in polishing your work.

PG   Yes. My agent used to be an editor, although he's very cautious about suggesting changes. He knows I want reactions though. My editor's very bold. She'll never suggest major changes, but she'll encourage me to talk about them, often because she knows that, by being forced to justify something, I'll be led to see where the weak points are and I'll strengthen them myself. She's quite canny that way.

RC   Do you have a circle of friends reading?

PG   Funnily enough, I don't involve my friends—I think because I have such a horror of friends of mine giving me a novel to read before it's published. I involve friends sometimes for proofreading. I'm a lousy proofreader. I have some very persnickety friends who'll spot things I won't. Publishers have so little money nowadays to spend on proper proofreading. It's notoriously something that doesn't get done. Copy-editing's done on a very superficial level as well. I do a lot of reviewing and am shocked at how often a novel has been desperately under-edited, never mind under-proofread.

RC   How does reviewing fit in with the cycle of producing novels?

PG   It's always useful to have a bit of reviewing going on in the background. It gives me something to do on the bad days. If I can't do any farming or writing, I sit in an armchair all day and read somebody else's novel. Sometimes reading a book completely unrelated to your own gives you a way back into your own work. My agent hates the idea of novelists reviewing each other because often it's one of his clients savaging another. But I'm not very savage. If anything I'm a painfully generous reviewer. Literary editors get rather pissed off with me for being too kind. But I don't see the point in a bad review. If a book's bad, I often won't review it. I send it back. So many novels are fighting for so few spaces. I don't hold with the view that bad reviews make for good reading. I'd far rather turn to a books page and be told about a wonderful novel I might've missed. Also, as a novelist reviewing novels, I think you can't help but be fascinated to see what others were trying to achieve. Often, rather than pan a book out of hand, I'll try to see what a book's trying to do. An interesting failure can be a lot more stimulating than a polished success which may not have attempted anything as brave.

RC   There are clearly a lot of women writers you respect; you like women reading over your work. Do you theorize about this?

PG   As a writer I'm just far more interested writing women than writing men. I think women, like gay men, have to make themselves up as they go along to some extent, if they're not to have completely downtrodden, mundane lives. They have to assess their situation early on and take quite bold steps to make up a personality. Nobody's going to give them one—whereas heterosexual men can run on such smooth rails until relatively late in life. They tend to have their crisis in their forties, whereas women have theirs much earlier on. As a result, they're far more interesting to write about.

Women juggle their lives more. Gay men do too. They tend to have secrets. An awful lot of gay men are not out at work, and therefore have more interesting lives. They might not be nicer, happier lives, but from a writer's point of view there's a lot more potential conflict. Similarly, a woman who works will often have to be very different at home. She's called on to nurture at one time, then to be brutal at another.

I've been told by women friends that my female characters are quite monstrous; quite hard and unscrupulous. Maybe they are. Certainly I grew up with very strong female role models. I was raised largely by women. I didn't really know my father's personality until I was well into my teens. I think he wasn't very comfortable with small children. He was very loving, but I didn't have much sense of him being there until later on, whereas I was very much under the care of my grandmother, mother, and sisters. As a result, I grew up knowing a lot more about women than men. Certainly straight male culture remains largely a mystery to me. I'm learning as much as I can, and don't particularly like what I'm learning.

RC   How do you learn?

PG   Talking to people. Television. I eavesdrop a great deal. I often sit in public spaces alone and listen. I take a lot of public transport. I've discovered you learn an awful lot through the Internet. Lots of men out there pretend to be women and infiltrate women's chat rooms. I do exactly the same, but pretending to be a straight guy interested in cars. It's extraordinary. You find yourself in this stifling atmosphere with all these competitive men. They don't seem to like each other. I don't know how they survive—talking as blokes about cars, sex, whatever. Occasionally I think: "How weird—maybe all the people in this chat room are pretending, and none of us is male. We're none of us "blokes"!

RC   It sounds as if you read more women writers too.

PG   Yes. That comes down to personality. For better or worse, when you read a novel you're spending three or four hours in intimate company with that writer's personality. I find the company of women more congenial. That probably extends to my reading tastes. I'd find it hard to enjoy a Martin Amis novel. He's a wonderful writer and incredible technician. Will Self too I admire on a technical level, but I find the character—the writer's personality—so rebarbative that if it's a choice between spending time with him or Barbara Trapido, there's no contest. I want to be with somebody who's interested in other personalities, not just forcing his or her own personality onto the reader the whole time. That seems a particularly heterosexual, male way of writing. They get out there and show off, whereas for me the whole point of fiction-writing is to lose your own personality; to mask it in order to ventriloquize, basically; to take on other voices.

RC   You talk of reading as spending time in a writer's company, yet think of writing as an escape from personality.

PG   Yes. I don't kid myself that my personality's disappeared. But I'm very aware that at least in trying to make it disappear, I'm doing something very different from the writer who tries to force that personality on you. Ironically, Jeanette Winterson, I think, writes like a man. She's a very heterosexual, masculine writer. It shows in the way she's been lionized by that coterie of straight male writers. They regard her as one of the lads, and she writes just like them. It's not a style that interests me particularly.

RC   Many American writers are like this: Philip Roth, say.

PG   Saul Bellow. It doesn't get to me at all. If I wanted to have all that, I'd have become a psychotherapist and listened to it for hours on end. I'd never say they were bad books. I'd just have to say they do nothing for me. For that reason I'd refuse to review one if I was asked, because I couldn't give it a fair hearing.

RC   I want to return to *The Facts of Life*, much bulkier and stylistically different to your earlier novels. Did that come out of its subject matter?

PG   Partly. I knew it was going to be a family saga. My agent and Carmen Callil got together and decided I should do a family saga next. I thought: "Preposterous." But it took root. I originally planned a trilogy of shorter novels, each about a different generation of the same family and a different social disease. We were going to have the first book about tuberculosis, the second about the clap, the third about AIDS. As I started work on the first, though, I realized the subject matter was going to be so interlinked that I could gain far more by allowing the middle act to implode and act as cement for the first and third acts. That's what ended up happening. The unsung heroine is the woman who's treated most harshly: Miriam, the daughter of the first half and the mother in the second. She doesn't really get her say. But the subject matter was always going to make a long book. These aren't stories that can be told quickly.

RC The length of your sentence changes.

PG Yes. There's a slightly magisterial quality. I think that comes in partly unconsciously when you know you're working on a big book. The style gets big to match, whereas in *Tree Surgery for Beginners*, which I always knew was going to be mischievous, the style became lighter and more playful. Short stories are another case in point. When I work on a story—which I find far harder than a novel—I'm aware all the time that it's only going to be, say, seven pages long. As a result, the prose has to be very finely honed. There's no room for excess baggage.

RC Some writers would reject the idea that you could plan a novel in terms of themes; knowing what a book's "about." Many novelists say writing the book involves finding out what it's about.

PG Yes. For me that's quite alien—though, as I said, midway through a book, it takes on its own momentum and life. *Rough Music* I began thinking was going to be about a husband and wife's marriage. Now I see it's far more about a character who was going to be just a member of the family. Suddenly I'm aware she's the victim of the story and its prime mover. She's hijacking the book, basically, and I'm having to rethink all my plans. [*Laughs*] Another monstrous woman!

RC The subject matter of AIDS must have brought particular difficulties for *The Facts of Life*. At one point Jamie, the character suffering from AIDS, is reading novels about the syndrome, and finding them unsatisfying.

PG   Yes. *The Facts of Life* was written in a way as my response to what I saw as a failure in AIDS novels to date. They weren't speaking to me, giving me comfort. They were more like a brutal kind of journalism, if wonderfully written. The Anglican in me wanted to offer comfort, rather than just report from the battlefront. Take, for instance, Edmund White and Adam Mars-Jones's collection *The Darker Proof*. It was trailblazing when it came out. Adam's stories were breathtaking, but cold in a way. They were brutally accurate, but weren't giving the reader anything. They were just saying: "This is how it is," which is what was needed at the time. But I was writing *The Facts of Life* a good ten years on, and trying to put AIDS in perspective as the latest in a series of social diseases. Particularly the TB parallels seemed a way of doing that. Also, I wanted to put the gay character with AIDS firmly back into a family context—once again, to show perspective; to say: "He's dying from AIDS, but ultimately he's just dying." People die of all manner of things. Families have a way of coping. The structure of a family will extend around and beyond the death.

RC   People die a lot in your books.

PG   They do. I'm in love with death—always have been. I have a morbid streak.

RC   Rereading the novels together made them darker than I'd remembered.

PG   Yes. There can be an Agatha Christie feeling. You think: "Oh, which one's going to die?" You can be sure one of them will.

RC   Doesn't this tend to contradict the idea of becoming too devoted to your characters?

PG In *The Facts of Life* I found it terribly hard to kill off the mother in the first book, Sally. I was completely in love with her. That was very much a case where the plot had begun to take over. Somebody had to die. I realized I wanted it to be a book about a straight man's very slow and painful education in how to love and accept. Sally, Edward's wife, was always a loving and accepting character. Brutally getting rid of her would force him into having to be the witness, rather than her. But she was hard to kill.

I use deaths as a very formal plot device; not so much for the morbid satisfaction it gives me to kill someone off—though if it's a bad character, that is great fun. But I tend to kill off characters I love. It's more to do with the chance it gives me to have an emotional explosion following the death; the warmth that can generate. It's usually related also to my abiding fascination with the broader family, and the way in which as a structure it can absorb the impact of a death and is forced to restructure itself afterwards. *Tree Surgery for Beginners* offers a perfect example. It's about a family that's forced—first by a divorce, then by a child's death—completely to break down and rebuild itself into a bigger, stronger structure.

I think the extended family's an experience almost peculiar to gay people, precisely because so many of us are rejected by our families when we come out. So we tend to form tribes when we leave home. We don't marry and often take a long time to find a partner who fits. Along the way we form very deep friendships, and a broad, often quite complex network of ex-lovers, friends, friends' ex-lovers. Heterosexual people often miss out on this. They tend to marry quite young and put all their eggs into one basket. Then they're desperately vulnerable. Something I enjoy doing in my work—in *Tree Surgery for Beginners*, for example—is giving straight people a gay education; in other words, making them learn that you're far better off with this bigger structure than just with this immediate family, and that it's terribly hard for anyone to be a good parent. One way to make it easier is to encourage your children to elect other parents to take up the slack. Gay people do this naturally. We tend to find and elect new mothers and fathers. I know I've had several mothers—not all of them women.

RC It sounds deeply subversive.

PG Yet it isn't. It's perfectly natural. As the century draws to its close, we've a crisis in the family caused mainly by economics; by the fact both parents need to work. The family isn't there because the parents aren't there. If only we encouraged more of this trans-familial bonding early on, the way it would be naturally in an African village tribe where children freely move from one hut to another, there'd be less talk of neglected children and less conflict between parent and child in later life. One thing I've learned living in Cornwall is that this still goes on outside big cities. Where I live, basically a village, people tend to marry very young. They go back to work as soon as they've had their children because they need to economically. They use grandparents in a way we've forgotten in cities. The children get parked with grandparents from a very early age—and often also with somebody else's grandparents. You see this much tighter network as a result. Crime levels are incredibly low. That's partly to do with living in a tighter community where everyone knows everyone else. You get a little crime blip in the summer when tourists come along. They're the ones who break into houses and steal cars! But I think it's also much more to do with the sense of social cohesion you get if you throw your net a bit wider and don't just rely on your parents.

RC Part of the "liberation" in many early, self-consciously "emancipated" gay novels was the idea that you left family behind. Your novels, though, have a deliberate social heterogeneity in which family relations remain important. In part that's to do with the small community setting.

PG To some extent. Also, I write as I see. Luckily I wasn't thrown out by my parents. There's been continuity in my life. To some extent, though, I think I'm harder-nosed about this than gay writers who turn their back on the family, in that I know the family's something you cannot escape. Sooner or later you have to deal with it; a parent will get old and need looking after. For better or worse, we were all made by families.

RC Turning to the short stories in *Dangerous Pleasures*: the preface indicates that each story was written with a single reader in mind. Does that condition the story that results?

PG Yes. The great difference between my stories and novels is the stories tend to have a specific cause—a commission, or a specific person or reason for writing the thing: to cheer somebody up whose boyfriend has just dumped her, whatever. Sometimes I combine the two. I'd be asked to write a short story for a collection and I'd be thinking: "What am I going to write?" Then I think: "This might cheer so-and-so up." So I'll do it for the commission, but send it to the person that needs the story. They all have very personal elements in.

RC How do you find the right plot for the short form?

PG That's the nightmare. You need to find story matter that packs the emotional punch of a novel but doesn't just feel like a first chapter. I haven't always succeeded. In some cases I've gone back and resuscitated a character for a novel. Several characters in *Tree Surgery for Beginners* cropped up in stories. Bee and Reuben, the sister and brother on the cruise liner, were in the first story I had published, "Borneo." *The Cat Sanctuary* grew out of "Dressing Up in Voices." Six years on, I wanted to know what happened to them next. So I revisited them.

RC Why are stories so difficult?

PG They have to be so disciplined, unlike a novel. Space is so limited. The prose has to be very tight and deft. The subject matter has to be right. Quite often I'll begin one, then think: "This isn't going to work; this is too big a subject." Other times you pick something too trite. It's that balance between narrative and revelation. Most of my short stories have a revelatory moment: a breakthrough or realization, or somebody cracks and takes action. But it's a finite thing.

RC   In one daring story you omitted, "The Road to You," someone deliberately punctures a condom, potentially to expose himself to HIV-infection by his lover.[1]

PG   Yes. It was very personal. I wrote that when I'd fallen deeply in love as a present to the person I was in love with. He'd been fretting that he was so much older and more experienced than I was. I didn't include it because I felt it'd never really grown beyond its personal context. I felt it meant so much more to me than to others reading it.

RC   You choose tangential titles for both stories and novels. Few make clear statements: *Facing the Tank*, for instance.

PG   That's a playful one. You've no idea what it means until you reach that moment. I don't know where the titles come from. They just pop up.

RC   Do they come early or late? *Rough Music* is titled.

PG   Usually pretty early. The bluntest one so far has been *The Cat Sanctuary*, but even that has double meanings. It refers also to all these women you've got fighting it out.

---

1. "The Road to You" may be found in David Rees and Peter Robins, eds., *The Freezer Counter* (Exeter, Eng.: Third House, 1989), 10–14.

RC   *The Facts of Life* is nearest to a statement of intent; it announces a serious book.

PG   Yes. [*Laughs*] *How to Deliver a Child.*

RC   Was *The Facts of Life* published in America?

PG   No. All my novels were published in America up to and including *Little Bits of Baby*. Dutton was taken over by Penguin and I was spat out promptly. I didn't make enough money. I've just signed a new contract in the States for *Tree Surgery for Beginners* [New York: Faber and Faber, 1999]. They're talking of bringing out *The Cat Sanctuary* and *The Facts of Life* in years to come, depending on how *Tree Surgery for Beginners* does.

RC   It must be frustrating to disappear from a market.

PG   Yes. I was doing really well. *Little Bits of Baby* had a wonderful review in the *New York Times Book Review*, which is always the benchmark. Once you get into that, you think: "I've arrived now." So I was just relaxing about the States, thinking it was time they got me over for publicity and they never did. Very frustrating. It halved my income overnight.

RC   People ascribe notions of Englishness to your works—does that help cultivate readers abroad?

PG   I have no way of knowing. I have to accept my books are intensely English, for better or worse. My style is quite fey, and their landscapes, despite the occasional excursion to America, are very much rooted in the English countryside. Maybe that's part of the appeal. Certainly when I was being published in America, that was something they picked up on and liked. But it seems a Catch-22 situation. American publishers either say: "We love this book—it's so English," or: "We can"t publish this—it's so English."

RC I wanted to ask about chapter divisions. You've a slightly old-fashioned tendency of starting chapters at earlier points than where you'd previously arrived.

PG I didn't realize I did that until a few reviewers started getting quite bitchy, saying it irritated them intensely. I quite enjoy doing the back-tracking, in terms of filling in somebody's recent history. It's rather overloading it if you do that when you first introduce a character, so sometimes I'll defer it, get you into the action, then wallop you over the head with three solid paragraphs of backtrack.

RC You withhold information for an age at times, too—the affair between Joanna and Julian in *The Cat Sanctuary*, for instance. Presumably you plan such dramatic devices carefully.

PG Yes. It's playing with you. I think you've not just to play with the reader but play the reader as well. You know certain psychological effects can be induced if you withhold information until later, or give him or her a shock at a certain point. That's one thing I'm learning more from working on film scripts: learning to view the novel not as a linear thing but as an arc. You need pillars at certain points to hold things up; at others, you need an injection of new material. I'm learning to view the novel rather like a film in terms of rhythm. Ultimately though, you have to write a novel you'd like to read.

RC In the early novels, what you describe as injecting new material is there, perhaps in a slightly different way. You seem to offer an ever-expanding range of characters.

PG   That's true. You'll suddenly get a quite in-depth viewpoint from somebody you've never met before and never see again.

RC   It got quite dizzying at its peak—*Facing the Tank*.

PG   Yes. It's all new characters until you're about ten chapters in. Then you start going back to ones you've already met. That was self-consciously my homage to Trollope and those big Victorian cathedral novels. I wanted to have a big cast list.

RC   It's also a challenge.

PG   Yes: can you juggle all these balls at the same time? The satisfactory ending's always a challenge as well—tying the ends up. With *Tree Surgery for Beginners* I had a lot of fun with that—daring to marry everybody off. Even a man who's murdered his mistress gets married off in prison.

RC   To some extent, the play on Shakespearean plots prepares one for that.

PG   That's true. You know the territory you're in; you can therefore relax and enjoy it. Some people found that book a bit disturbing at first. People who'd never read me before thought they were in for a detective story. They were bewildered when these characters suddenly go on this Caribbean cruise and desert P. D. James territory.

RC   Have you ever wanted to write a novel in the first person? There's only your novella "Caesar's Wife" and a few stories. Otherwise you've kept to indirect, third-person discourse.

PG   I enjoyed doing the first person in "Caesar's Wife." But I couldn't help thinking that part of the irony of telling a story that way is in what you're missing out. Readers are well aware there are other sides to this story they aren't getting. Mostly I'm more comfortable giving all the different sides to a story—partly so you get a more rounded viewpoint. But it's also to do with what I was saying earlier about losing my own personality; using the characters as masks and splitting myself up in ten different directions. That feels more natural. With "Caesar's Wife," doing just this one personality felt very much like a camp turn.

RC   Your third-person narrative style is very recognizable.

PG   That's true. The thing I'd always beware of would be the "gentle reader" approach—being arch and knowing—which is quite easy with third-person narrative, especially comedy, unless you're careful. That's why I try to write from inside personalities.

RC   You mostly lean very heavily on an immediate sensibility, but not always. There's a recognizable narrator's sensibility too.

PG   Yes, I still have that. It kicks in in "backstory" passages. For instance, in *Tree Surgery for Beginners* you get quite a long passage in the beginning describing Lawrence's birth and his fascination with trees. There's a long passage about his mother's relationship with his uncle— her backstory. At those times my narrator's voice comes out. Then I try to kick back into personality-led narrative.

RC   At those points, you're also offering a generalizing narrative voice, one which offers a summary of shared understandings.

PG   Yes; "we know this is the way things are"—that sort of voice, if you can keep it quite cool and waspish as well.

RC   It sounds as if this voice might offer a sense of communal values.

PG I think it's more that the novel itself becomes a sort of community if you have these multiple voices, none of them quite arriving at the truth. The reader, one hopes, comes to a point where having all these different voices is like being in the heart of a community. He or she can see things as they are.

RC Where else do you see this "waspishness"?

PG Ronald Firbank, perhaps. His *Vainglory* was very much a starting point for *Facing the Tank*.

RC What about George Eliot? I was surprised Trollope featured earlier, not her.

PG Eliot for me feeds straight into the Iris Murdoch tradition of providing what's basically entertainment with higher philosophical concerns. When it works—*Middlemarch*—it works absolutely brilliantly. Even if it doesn't work—*Daniel Deronda*—it's fascinating to see what Eliot's trying to do. With Trollope, though, it's pure entertainment; *Facing the Tank* likewise. There's no axe to grind. I wrote that while living in France, feeling terribly homesick. It's a nostalgic romp.

RC Do you think of every book distinctly? If someone described your books in the same way, would it concern you?

PG I'd be a bit disturbed. But I'm philosophical about that, once the books have flown the nest. I do feel they're pitched at different levels. Although the plot structure may be similarly wild from book to book, the tone varies. *The Cat Sanctuary*'s essentially dark; *Facing the Tank* light. I think of them as swinging between urban and country novels, and between gay and straight novels. Each reacts against the one before. *Tree Surgery for Beginners* was distinctly light compared to *The Facts of Life*.

RC But *The Facts of Life* followed on from *The Cat Sanctuary*.

PG Yes, though there was a big gap between the two—the biggest I've had.

RC I thought that was the size of *The Facts of Life*.

PG No. A lot of time was taken up working on television series that didn't happen, like *Little Bits of Baby*.

RC Is this swinging between polarities theory after the fact?

PG No, it's conscious. I do it as much to give myself relief as the reader. I'm well aware most people don't read the books in the order they're written. It's up to them to make their own way. From my point of view, if I've been submerged in a very dark narrative world, it's sometimes a relief to stretch out into something lighter. *Rough Music*'s a hybrid. It's high comedy, but rooted in very dark, painful family stuff as well.

RC When you spoke of Eliot's moral tradition leading into Iris Murdoch, I wondered how you responded to modernism.

PG In some ways I feel modernism was a dead end. People had to try to stretch the novel as far as it could go, but what resulted was a realization that ultimately the novel form, a bit like the symphony, is essentially fairly conservative and not very flexible. It works best when you play on certain areas. I'm shameless in thinking of my books, however modern their subject matter, as very old-fashioned in structure and manner. That's as much to do with accessibility as anything else. It also cuts back to what I was saying about the male heterosexual voice drawing attention to itself. I feel for a narrative to work well the writer has to be almost invisible. Certainly any labor that's gone into the prose should be invisible. If you can see how hard the work's been, the writing's failing.

For me, what matters is the communication: getting a story and involving the reader. If the reader's noticing the nuts and bolts, you're not getting through to him or her, just drawing attention to your own cleverness.

RC   Virginia Woolf, then, fundamentally wouldn't impress.

PG   I find Woolf more of theoretical interest than anything else, precisely because she ends up showing why it doesn't work, though we all learn from her. One thing we get is the use of interior monologue to get inside a character's personality. No one would think they were doing that because of Woolf, but what she did fed into the tradition and had an effect. But other things I do are things she found anathema.

RC   The staging of moral dilemmas she always fudged.

PG   Exactly. She fudges everything. E. M. Forster's a writer I devoured as a teenager, like Conrad, and have never been able to read since. I think gay men would hate to admit him as an influence. Actually, though—the terrible *Maurice* aside—I think Forster's books are unwitting early exemplars of what the gay novel was going to do. They're quite old-fashioned in structure, but address moral dilemmas.

RC   Forster was always highly readable.

PG   Yes. The whole trouble with a novel, as opposed to music, is that it's not performed by an expert but by whoever reads it. Ultimately, it's got to be something their "instrument" can play, whereas with a string quartet, you know the players you're writing for. You know they'll be able to give it the best possible performance. Whether it's accessible is another matter. That's why I feel modernist writing is ultimately always sterile. You're expecting your reader to do things most readers can't. Joyce's *Finnegan's Wake*, amazing though it is, fills me with horror: so much labor to produce something so few people will ever be able to appreciate. It communicates so little to so few. That's a kind of artistic nightmare— especially in a writer who showed that, if he were prepared to be traditional, he could write so beautifully: in *Dubliners*, *A Portrait of the Artist as a Young Man*, and big chunks of *Ulysses*.

RC   You talked of "masculine writing" as drawing attention to itself. Arguably, though, other prose styles do that and are often taken as subversive. Baroque or mannered writing, for instance, doesn't prioritize accessibility. As soon as your own sentences move away from the cadences of everyday speech, they head towards manneredness.

PG   Absolutely. They're very high-flown. I think the distinction is between books about other people and books about the writer. Most books fall into one camp or the other. It's to do with the extension of sympathies; that Forsterian thing: "only connect." It's funny how I'm always so queasy about Forster. He's so patently a huge influence, so he's probably the last writer anyone's likely to admit as one because his influence is so strong. Forster's the perfect example of someone who absolutely writes about other people. You have very little sense of who he is in those books, though maybe he's everybody. You get an almost Buddhist sense of loss of self in search of the truth. Of course, it's all completely artificial, because he's a novelist writing that book. But in terms of the world of the book as you read it, that's what comes across, whereas with Hemingway, say, you can barely see over the big man's shoulders to the story he's ostensibly telling.

RC   There's a clear debt to both Hemingway and Fitzgerald in gay fiction.

PG   Certainly in the American tradition there is. I speak as somebody who devours a lot of American stuff. Like a lot of gay men, my first encounter with any gay writing was through American books—so much so it was quite confusing, growing up in the provinces where there was no gay world at all, and all my earliest images of it built by American fiction. It was all New York. *Dancer from the Dance* was a very early book I read; Edmund White's novels too. And awful things like Larry Kramer's *Faggots*. The strange thing about that was that it was a very black comedy but published as a lurid romp.

RC   Such books could be important in ways other than literary.

PG   Absolutely. When I read them, I switched off all critical faculties. I remember as a teenager adoring those terrible Gordon Merrick novels like *The Lord Won't Mind*. I knew they were complete trash, but they were so exciting.

RC   Among what you read, though, what did have literary appeal?

PG   I can't begin to separate them from the personal, educative role they played. The real breakthrough, of course, is when gay fiction starts to write bad gay characters; people who aren't heroes.

RC   Where do we find that?

PG   Alan Hollinghurst's *The Swimming-Pool Library* and *The Folding Star* are real breakthrough novels in that sense. They both have obsessive, rather unlikable men as their voice; men who're also dominant sexually, which is rare. I feel the last ten years have been a breakthrough period for gay publishing, to the point where it's redundant. Mainstream publishers have realized that literature by out gay men doesn't have to be ghettoized. There's a whole group of us floating off in slightly different directions. I wonder whether in ten years there'll actually be an identifiable genre at all, or whether people will think this was a funny little period the novel went through.

RC For publishers, "gay" has been a useful marketing niche; a way of reaching more people. Yet many gay writers complain there's a ceiling in terms of potential markets—a pretty low one, if you're sold as a gay novelist.

PG Yes. My publishers took a long time realizing a lot of women love reading my stuff. I think I have a bigger female than gay readership nowadays—not least because I don't write many hot sex scenes. That's one of the hooks for a male audience, whereas women are very interested in character. A woman will happily read a novel about a gay relationship if it's about the relationship, rather than just about sex and cruising.

RC On that note, thanks very much for your time.

BETWEEN MEN ~ BETWEEN WOMEN
Lesbian and Gay Studies

Lillian Faderman and Larry Gross, Editors

Richard D. Mohr, *Gays/Justice: A Study of Ethics, Society, and Law*

Gary David Comstock, *Violence Against Lesbians and Gay Men*

Kath Weston, *Families We Choose: Lesbians, Gays, Kinship*

Lillian Faderman, *Odd Girls and Twilight Lovers: A History of Lesbian Life in Twentieth-Century America*

Judith Roof, *A Lure of Knowledge: Lesbian Sexuality and Theory*

John Clum, *Acting Gay: Male Homosexuality in Modern Drama*

Allen Ellenzweig, *The Homoerotic Photograph: Male Images from Durieu/Delacroix to Mapplethorpe*

Sally Munt, editor, *New Lesbian Criticism: Literary and Cultural Readings*

Timothy F. Murphy and Suzanne Poirier, editors, *Writing AIDS: Gay Literature, Language, and Analysis*

Linda D. Garnets and Douglas C. Kimmel, editors, *Psychological Perspectives on Lesbian and Gay Male Experiences*

Laura Doan, editor, *The Lesbian Postmodern*

Noreen O'Connor and Joanna Ryan, *Wild Desires and Mistaken Identities: Lesbianism and Psychoanalysis*

Alan Sinfield, *The Wilde Century: Effeminacy, Oscar Wilde, and the Queer Moment*

Claudia Card, *Lesbian Choices*

Carter Wilson, *Hidden in the Blood: A Personal Investigation of AIDS in the Yucatán*

Alan Bray, *Homosexuality in Renaissance England*

Joseph Carrier, *De Los Otros: Intimacy and Homosexuality Among Mexican Men*

Joseph Bristow, *Effeminate England: Homoerotic Writing After 1885*

Corinne E. Blackmer and Patricia Juliana Smith, editors, *En Travesti: Women, Gender Subversion, Opera*

Don Paulson with Roger Simpson, *An Evening at The Garden of Allah: A Gay Cabaret in Seattle*

Claudia Schoppmann, *Days of Masquerade: Life Stories of Lesbians During the Third Reich*

Chris Straayer, *Deviant Eyes, Deviant Bodies: Sexual Re-Orientation in Film and Video*

Edward Alwood, *Straight News: Gays, Lesbians, and the News Media*

Thomas Waugh, *Hard to Imagine: Gay Male Eroticism in Photography and Film from Their Beginnings to Stonewall*

Judith Roof, *Come As You Are: Sexuality and Narrative*

Terry Castle, *Noel Coward and Radclyffe Hall: Kindred Spirits*

Kath Weston, *Render Me, Gender Me: Lesbians Talk Sex, Class, Color, Nation, Studmuffins . . .*

Ruth Vanita, *Sappho and the Virgin Mary: Same-Sex Love and the English Literary Imagination*

renée c. hoogland, *Lesbian Configurations*

Beverly Burch, *Other Women: Lesbian Experience and Psychoanalytic Theory of Women*

Jane McIntosh Snyder, *Lesbian Desire in the Lyrics of Sappho*

Rebecca Alpert, *Like Bread on the Seder Plate: Jewish Lesbians and the Transformation of Tradition*

Emma Donoghue, editor, *Poems Between Women: Four Centuries of Love, Romantic Friendship, and Desire*

James T. Sears and Walter L. Williams, editors, *Overcoming Heterosexism and Homophobia: Strategies That Work*

Patricia Juliana Smith, *Lesbian Panic: Homoeroticism in Modern British Women's Fiction*

Dwayne C. Turner, *Risky Sex: Gay Men and HIV Prevention*

Timothy F. Murphy, *Gay Science: The Ethics of Sexual Orientation Research*

Cameron McFarlane, *The Sodomite in Fiction and Satire, 1660—1750*

Lynda Hart, *Between the Body and the Flesh: Performing Sadomasochism*

Byrne R. S. Fone, editor, *The Columbia Anthology of Gay Literature: Readings from Western Antiquity to the Present Day*

Ellen Lewin, *Recognizing Ourselves: Ceremonies of Lesbian and Gay Commitment*

Ruthann Robson, *Sappho Goes to Law School: Fragments in Lesbian Legal Theory*

Jacquelyn Zita, *Body Talk: Philosophical Reflections on Sex and Gender*

Evelyn Blackwood and Saskia Wieringa, *Female Desires: Same-Sex Relations and Transgender Practices Across Cultures*

William L. Leap, ed., *Public Sex/Gay Space*

Larry Gross and James D. Woods, eds., *The Columbia Reader on Lesbians and Gay Men in Media, Society, and Politics*

Marilee Lindemann, *Willa Cather: Queering America*

George E. Haggerty, *Men in Love: Masculinity and Sexuality in the Eighteenth Century*

Andrew Elfenbein, *Romantic Genius: The Prehistory of a Homosexual Role*

Gilbert Herdt and Bruce Koff, *Something to Tell You: The Road Families Travel When a Child Is Gay*